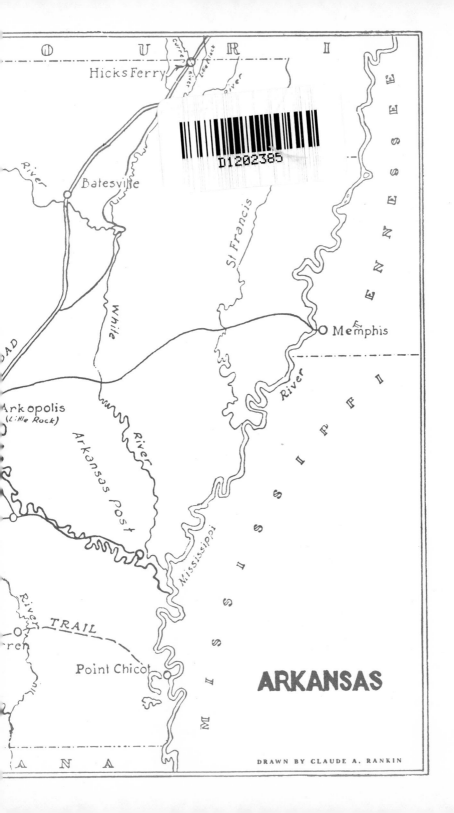

ARKANSAS

DRAWN BY CLAUDE A. RANKIN

Cornbread Aristocrat

Cornbread Aristocrat
Claud Garner

August House/Little Rock
Publishers

Copyright 1983 by the Mary Wepfer Trust.
Published 1983 by August House, Inc., 1010 West Third Street,
Little Rock, AR 72201. Printed in the United States of
America. All rights reserved. No part of this book may be
reproduced in any manner, except for brief passages quoted
for purposes of review, without the prior written consent of
the publisher.

ISBN 0-941780-16-3 Hardback Edition
ISBN 0-941780-17-1 Quality Paperback

Library of Congress Catalog Card Number 83-71547

First Edition: November, 1983

This book was published by August House, Inc.,
a nonprofit organization for the written arts in
Arkansas. No government funds have been used in
this publication. By your purchase of August House
books or memberships, you make possible the
publication of new Arkansas books and the
preservation of Arkansas's literary heritage.

The body of this book, including the endsheet maps, is a
facsimile reproduction of a 1950 hardback edition published
by Creative Age Press, New York.

Cover design for this August house edition by
Madeline Collins.

This is a work of fiction. All of the characters and events
portrayed are fictitious and any similarity between them
and real persons or events is coincidental and unintended.

Book One

The Young Gentleman from Virginia

1.

Toby Giles gave the rawhide latchstring an impatient jerk and pushed open the heavy door. The creaking hinges announced his return to the tavern, and the eight half-drunken men slouched at a table in the rear of the room looked up to see him standing in the doorway holding a jug of corn whiskey, reluctant to enter the dark, foul-smelling hostelry that stank of cheap liquor and tobacco and the damp buckskin clothing of the frontiersmen. Toby was young, the baby of the party, and he looked even younger than he was, but there was a kind of determination in his sea-pale eyes and the set of his square chin that should have forewarned any stranger who hoped to take advantage of him.

"Don't stand there fiddle-faddling. Shut that door and bring me the liquor!" It was Ira Walker, leader of the group, a powerful man with a pock-marked face and a mean, evident temper, a big man who used his size as a threat. Toby slammed the door behind him and walked into the room, swinging the heavy jug to the table.

"Stoge Rowden says if you want more liquor you're to send the money to pay for it," he announced, addressing Walker, who seized the jug without ceremony. "Guess he figures that with us moving on to Texas he won't have much chance to get his reckoning paid."

"Hell-fire!" Walker poured raw whiskey into a gourd dipper. "It'll be another two weeks 'fore the Red River falls enough so's we can get our teams across. How's Stoge reckon

3

we're gonna live that long without liquor?" The men at the table roared with laughter.

Spring floods had mired the lowlands of southwestern Arkansas Territory, rutting the roads for the heavy wagons and making travel impossible, so that for weeks the men of this Texas-bound caravan had been holed up in the log hamlet of Washington, on the frontier, drinking and fighting and lying to one another to pass the time and help forget their eagerness to be over the river and on their way to the free land and riches promised by Stephen F. Austin. One of Austin's posters was tacked to the log wall of the tavern, and Ira Walker crossed the room to read it, though all of the men had by this time memorized its contents.

"A League of Land for married men," Walker read in his foghorn voice, thickened by liquor, "and a Labor of Land for single bucks. All free." He wiped tobacco stain from his chin, using the sleeve of his buckskin jacket. "That reads all right to me." He looked challengingly around the room. Self-appointed leader of the caravan, Walker was eager to hold the group together, for the larger the number he led into Texas, the greater would be his prestige with the authorities.

"Why don't them greasers talk American?" the tavern-keeper wanted to know. "How much is them Leagues and Labors, anyway, in honest United States acres?"

"Says right here a League of Land's more than four thousand acres," Ira bellowed. "That's enough land for anybody. Even me!" He laughed loudly and walked back to the table, taking the gourd roughly from the man who held it and drinking carelessly so that the whiskey dribbled down his chin. "Reckon if I'm satisfied the rest of you ought to be!"

"Yes," said Toby, who had found a place near the window in the back of the room, "a League of Land's all well and good, but a Labor of Land's not so much. Single men only get a hundred and seventy-seven acres." Toby was the only single man in the caravan, and, of all the group, the only one who

4

didn't hunger for the wilderness and the wild life that went with it.

Walker smiled grimly. "Ought to be enough for you," he said. "Anyhow, I reckon when we get there we'll take what we want. I don't aim to let a bunch of greasers bother me."

While the others talked and drank, Toby read Austin's handbill once more. He had seen it first on the bulletin board of the side-wheel steamer that carried him down the Mississippi to Memphis. It had been posted also in Memphis, and on the White River Cutoff, and again at Arkansas Post. He stood staring at it now, the magic name TEXAS burning forth from the printed page; then he turned away in disgust, for the long overland journey through the wilderness had cooled Toby's enthusiasm.

"A single man's a fool to go down into that wild, womanless country," someone at the tables said musingly, staring at Toby. "A man ain't much good alone, to himself or anyone else."

"He can always find a light-skinned squaw," Walker grinned.

"I wouldn't want no squaw," protested Toby.

"Squaws ain't bad," insisted Ira, in a tone that indicated he knew what he was talking about. "Their blood is hot and their breasts are soft and you can't tell the difference in the dark."

"Smell kind of high, though," a man objected.

"Don't smell no worse'n you do," Ira said.

"How about one of them señoritas?" the tavernkeeper asked. "Plenty of them down Texas way."

Ira shook his head. "We'll be fightin' them greasers one of these days. What'ya think the government gave you rifles for? A fellow couldn't handy use a Mexican wife."

All the way from Memphis to Washington, Texas-bound settlers had heard the rumor that the money Congress had appropriated for the improvement of the Southwest Trail was really to be used to help finance American families headed for Mexican territory, people with enough spirit to take the land and hold it. At Arkansas Post, before he began the trek through the wilderness, Toby Giles had been given a saddle horse, a new long rifle, powder and lead, and a bedding roll. Like the others, he had signed a statement to the effect that he had worked out the value of these articles on the Southwest Trail, though in fact neither Toby nor any of the others had done a lick of work on the Trail. Congress wanted American settlers who crossed into Texas to be well armed and prepared to defend themselves.

Ira Walker pounded on the table. "Hey, Rosy!" he bellowed. "Run over to Stoge's and get us another jug. This one's dry."

Toby stiffened. His dislike for Ira Walker, growing during all the weeks on the road, suddenly distilled into active hatred and prompted him to rebellion. He knew that his fresh complexion made him look like a stripling, but he was conscious of his broad shoulders, powerful arms, and thick chest; he was tired of being the errand boy and was determined to be treated like a man.

"You want any more liquor, Ira," he said slowly, "you just trot over and get it for yourself. I'm through runnin' whiskey for the likes of you."

"Don't give me no back talk," Ira commanded. "You're gettin' too big for your breeches anyway. Now bounce over there and get me another jug of whiskey and be quick about it."

"Just hold your breath till I do," answered Toby. He spat on the floor at Ira's feet, turned quickly, and walked out of the tavern, crossing the town's single street toward Stoge Rowden's store. He had business with Stoge Rowden, but it didn't concern getting whiskey for Ira Walker and his crowd.

Stoge was in the back of the store opening cases of print goods. He looked up and smiled at Toby. "Did you tell brother Walker what I said?" he asked.

"I told him," Toby replied. "But it won't do no good. He's wantin' another jug already, but I ain't takin' it to him."

Stoge laughed. "Well, son, while you're resting, how about

giving me a hand with that barrel of salt there in the corner?"

Before Stoge could make a move to help, Toby tilted the heavy barrel and swung it into place against the wall, using his powerful, thickset body with considerable grace, wanting Stoge's approval. "Where's your hatchet?" he asked. "I'll bust the head out for you."

Stoge handed him the hatchet. "I'm obliged to you, Toby," he said. "A barrel of salt's a mite heavy for my weak back."

Toby knocked out the head of the barrel, then turned to Stoge. "Do you want me to take that stuff out of the boxes and stack it on the counter so's it'll be easier for you to check?"

"Don't mind if you do," the storekeeper said.

Toby took off his pistol and laid it on the counter, then began to stack the fresh, pleasant-smelling bolts of calico, muslin, and woolen goods, working quietly, whistling to himself, aware that Stoge was watching him, doing the work efficiently and enjoying it as he had never enjoyed hacking his way through the overland trail.

"You know, Stoge," he remarked casually, "it wouldn't take much to make me stay here and keep on doing things like this, and forget all about going to Texas."

Stoge nodded agreement. "I ain't never been able to understand why settlers pass up this country and go on to Texas. Must be wild blood in their veins, I guess." He paused reflectively. "Course, some of them's mighty anxious to put the border between them and United States law. Some of 'em's runnin' away from debt, or from women. For a lot of those fellers, I guess Texas and free land is a kind of last chance—forlorn hope, you might say. But for a young feller like you, I can't see no *sense* in Texas."

"These old sand hills look good to me," Toby said. "And I like a town, like this one. I'm sick of the wilderness. Just plain don't like it."

Stoge laughed. "Son," he said, "you ain't seen no wilderness till you cross the Red River. There's miles and miles of boggy

7

marshes and cypress swamps and canebrakes. There's quicksand suckholes that can swallow a wagon and a four-up team." Stoge paused to let his words sink in. "You think we got insects here?" he went on. "Sure, we got a few, but down there they got lice and ticks and body crabs. And leeches that'll suck the lifeblood out of a man. Lots of human vermin, too, down Texas way. Dark-skinned vermin. I don't want nothing to do with them Mexicans."

Stoge broke off as the door burst open, then slammed shut with a noise like a cannon. Ira Walker, more than half drunk, and ugly, stood with his big hands on his hips, his eyes narrowed as he bellowed at Toby. "Why in hell didn't you bring me that jug of liquor like I told you to?" he demanded. "You lookin' for trouble, you sawed-off runt?"

Toby's muscles tightened and his heart pounded as he watched Ira stretch himself to his full six feet four, then rise gently to his toes, a trick he used to take full advantage of his height. There was the metallic taste of fear in Toby's mouth and his palms began to sweat, but he stood his ground and said, "I've done my last waitin' on you, Ira Walker. Get somebody else to fetch for you."

"Why, you little whelp!" Ira's gun was out, but he hesitated when he saw Stoge reach for Toby's pistol.

"Put your gun on the counter, Ira," the storekeeper ordered. "I don't aim to have nobody shootin' up my place of business. Besides, Toby ain't armed, and I'm seeing that this is a fair fight, man to man."

Stoge didn't raise his voice, but a quiet authority in his tone and the pistol in his hand made Ira pause, then shrug his shoulders and surrender his own weapon. The big man shucked off his coat, tossed it aside, and stood spraddle-legged, ready for action. "I ain't intendin' to shoot up your place, Stoge," he said. "But I sure aim to teach this runt a lesson."

Toby sucked his breath. He was smaller than most of the frontiersmen, for the wilderness attracted big men, and his

8

stature made him the butt of their jokes, but he was strong, and compactly built. And he was fast on his feet. Before Ira could brace himself, Toby charged, ramming his head into Ira's belly and driving his fists into the bigger man's groin. He landed two hard blows before Ira sprawled backward, hit the rough log floor, and rolled away in agony, the fight gone out of him. Toby stood with his fists ready, waiting for his opponent to get to his feet, but Walker remained on the floor, grunting with pain. Stoge smiled. "Spillin' blood over a jug of whiskey would have been powerful foolish, Ira," he said. He poured six ounces of raw corn into a tin cup and knelt beside Walker, cradling the man's head in his arm. "Here, drink this. Serves you right, anyway, pickin' a fight with Toby for no good reason."

Ira drank the whiskey, then pulled himself painfully to his feet. Reluctantly he took the hand that Stoge made Toby offer him, admitting that the fight was over, and conceding defeat. But Toby knew, watching the big man stagger to the barrel for a gallon of Stoge's liquor, that Ira's handshake meant nothing. He had endangered Ira's prestige and made a mortal enemy. If he stayed with Ira's outfit, sooner or later, some night out there in the wilderness across the river, Ira would kill him. He watched Walker pick up his pistol and walk out of the store without a word, then turned to Stoge.

"Guess I'll have to join up with another outfit now," he said. "Unless I can get me a job around here."

Stoge returned to his work of pricing merchandise. "You did a pretty neat job on Ira," he commented drily.

"There are lots of jobs I could do around here," said Toby.

Stoge laughed. It was a mellow laugh, and good to hear. "By whacky," he said, "it was *worth* a gallon of whiskey to see you put him on the floor." Stoge paused, frowning. "But you hit him pretty low, Toby. I like my fights, and my business dealings, on the clean side."

"I know Ira Walker, Stoge," Toby explained. "I've seen

him fight, and never once have I seen him fight fair. I didn't want him sticking a knife in my back. His standing there, spraddle-legged that way, gave me a target I just couldn't miss, so I let him have it."

"Bet he don't do no tomcattin' for a while," Stoge chuckled.

"Feller did it to me once," Toby admitted. "I walked bow-legged for a week."

He crossed to the counter and began to help Stoge, handing bolts of goods to the storekeeper. He liked the clean, crisp feel of the cottons, the fresh new smell of the dye. He liked the orderly pace of the work, and the store, with its fine stock of supplies, gave him a feeling of security. He felt, somehow, that this was where he belonged, in this store on the frontier, helping Stoge and learning how to become a merchant. "Why don't you give me a job, Stoge?" he asked, after working a while in silence. "I could make myself mighty handy around here. You need someone to help out."

Stoge rested his elbows on the counter and smiled at Toby, looking him over. "You're right, young fellow, I *could* use somebody," he agreed. "But I gave a lad a job once and he made himself a mite too handy. Damn near stole me blind."

Toby shook his head. "Only one thing that'd make *me* steal from you, Stoge, and that'd be if you didn't pay me enough to live on."

"That's straight talk," Stoge approved. "And I like straight talk. What kind of a livin' would you be expectin'?"

"Well," said Toby, "I wouldn't be satisfied long on corn pone and sowbelly. Where I come from I was used to hominy grits and ham."

"You don't say. Just where did you come from?"

"Virginia," answered Toby, pronouncing the lovely name with a flourish and a good deal of pride. "From the Tidewater."

Stoge was impressed. "Great state, Virginia," he said. He inspected Toby shrewdly. "How old are you?"

"Twenty-four."

"You don't look it," Stoge said bluntly. "Anyway, I'd have to know more about a young buck than that he came from Virginia and was twenty-four and didn't look it before I let him sell my goods, handle my money, and sample my liquor. Who'd you work for, back in Virginia? What kind of work did you do?"

"I worked on my father's plantation, bossing slaves."

"Warn't there no opportunities in Virginia? Why'd you come out here?"

"Plenty of opportunities, but not for me," Toby explained. "In families like mine, the youngest gets the leavings. I want to be a man. I don't want to be no pine sapling in a forest of big oaks. So I struck out for myself. I made for Texas, but I like this better."

"Well, son, guts is what a man needs in this country, and I can see that's what you've got plenty of. But a fellow can't be afraid of moiling." Stoge glanced at Toby appraisingly, admiring the thick set of his shoulders and the heavy muscles in his forearms. "It's a hard country. There's lots of work."

"I'm not afraid of work," Toby said. "I'll make you a good man."

Stoge nodded. "All right, Toby," he decided. "I like you and I'm going to give you a try. Be here in the morning, good an' early. We'll see how we hit it off."

"I'll be here when the first cock crows."

They shook hands on it, and Stoge smiled as he watched Toby's broad back go through the doorway, then frowned, wondering whether he had made a mistake.

Toby walked briskly down the long street to the edge of town, then made for Ira Walker's camp, a mile away. There, twelve heavy caravan wagons were drawn up in a circle for protection against prowling Indians or bands of marauding white outlaws, and the ponderous, meditating oxen were grazing near by at their hobbles. A few of the caravan's womenfolk, in sunbonnets and calico dresses, greeted Toby and he answered them pleasantly, but he kept his plans to himself. He collected his bedding roll and rifle, saddled his horse, and mounted quickly, riding back into Washington just as darkness was falling. Walker, he knew, had by this time drunk himself into a stupor and would not learn of his desertion until morning.

The air was moist, and lowering blue-gray clouds threatened more rain. Toby stowed his rifle and bedding roll under the floor of Stoge's store, then hobbled his horse where the animal could graze. He walked up one side and down the other of the one-street town, feeling already a sense of communion with the place in which he had decided to try his fortune. There were three stores, the tavern, a courthouse, and a small church, all built solid to the ground with no air space beneath them. Toby decided to sleep under the shed of Stoge's store, and walked back there, reaching the building just as the soft spring rain began. He crawled under the floor boards, shoving his rifle and blanket roll well back, out of the wet. He used his saddle for a pillow and stretched out on the ground, the rough puncheon beams a few inches from his nose. It was a warm night, despite the rain, and pleasant there in the dark, with the dripping of the rain from the roof, the occasional mournful howling of a dog, and the casual, nocturnal noises of the town.

He was thinking of Virginia, of the lush, rich Tidewater country, and of the Maison Plantation, with its great house and commanding acres. For the Maison Plantation represented to Toby the ultimate in aristocracy and riches, and the pattern of life there was fixed as his ideal of life as it should be. Drowsing, half-asleep, with the drip-drip-drip of the rain lulling him comfortably, he cast memory pictures in the darkness—the Maison Mansion on a night when the captain was entertaining a hundred guests, the thousand wax candles glowing in their gleaming crystal sconces, the white, hand-woven linens, soft as silk, the rugs from the Orient that glowed like jewels and were as thick and soft underfoot as the groomed turf that surrounded the house. He saw the graceful men and beautiful women, whirling, bowing, saluting one another in the courtly dances of the day, disporting themselves on a ballroom floor waxed to the smoothness of glass, moving in perfect unison to the music of a slave band. And there, in the center of all that luxury, Toby saw the tall, aristocratic figure of the master of the mansion, Captain Maison himself, the perfect embodiment of all that was best in the whole line of Virginia blue blood. From the moment Toby first set eyes on the captain, clad in snowy buckskin breeches and a scarlet coat, mounted on a horse that had been groomed till it glistened like satin, its delicate, finely articulated bones somehow suggesting a beautiful woman, his imagination had been captured and his goal in life had been set. He wanted to become an aristocrat, if not from Virginia, then from somewhere else, but in any event, an aristocrat, wealthy beyond care, possessed of bearing and elegance, and showing, in his relations with others, something called *noblesse oblige*, a term that Toby was dimly aware of but could not quite have defined. Captain Maison represented to Toby, in one human being, everything that the boy admired and had never known, except as an onlooker.

For Toby was not a Tidewater aristocrat, as he had boasted to Stoge Rowden, though, indeed, he came from Virginia, from the rat-infested Norfolk water front, from the depths of squalor and poverty. His father had never owned a foot of land or a stick of furniture, let alone a slave that Toby might have bossed. Most of the money his father earned by sporadic labor alongshore was spent on cheap whiskey rather than on the family's food, so that, of Toby's childhood, what he remembered most vividly was hunger—stark, omnipresent, gnawing hunger taken for granted as a fact of life, like the menacing rats, dangerous as tigers, the merciless sun of high summer, or the knifing winds that came in from the sea during the wet, rough winter months.

13

While Toby was still too young to work he lived like an animal on the dockside, fighting with other raggedy children over scraps of food discarded by the ships. He learned before he was able to walk that you must guard your food like gold, and soon after he was able to walk he learned to fight as a dock rat fights, hitting first and hitting low, always taking foul play for granted. What he knew about rough and tumble had served him well on many occasions, but never better than this afternoon, when he put Ira Walker on Stoge's floor with one charging frontal assault.

Toby was tough, and he didn't lack courage, but there was no future for him in Virginia, nothing to which, as a dock rat and the son of a dock rat, he could logically aspire. As soon as he was old enough to make himself of the slightest use, his father had bound him to Captain Maison, to work for his keep without wages. Bound boys in Virginia were often hardly better off than slaves, but Toby was lucky, for Captain Maison was a kindly master who treated him well. During his years on the plantation he had been well fed and decently dressed, and he had gone through the fourth grade at the plantation school. Being a shrewd, knowledgeable boy and eager to better himself, he learned a lot about large-scale farming and got a taste of bossing slaves, learning how to command loyalty and obedience from his blacks without being harsh or cruel, by artfully using that intricate protocol which holds a slave society together.

But there was nothing ahead in Virginia for a bound boy from the Norfolk shanties who didn't own even the butternut coat on his back. Free land in Virginia was long since gone, and class lines in the Old Dominion were as rigid as those across the water in England, upon which they had indeed been patterned. If he had a future, Toby understood, it was somewhere in the West, far from the rich Tidewater country, in the rude new land being opened up by rough adventurers in wagon trains. It was the West, for Toby, or nothing, and he was too ambitious to be satisfied with nothing. Therefore, in the predawn damp one morning, when the first streaks of pink showed in the east, Toby saddled one of the captain's blooded horses, took what food he could carry, and said good-by to the plantation. He rode west, over the Alleghenies to Pittsburgh, where he sold the horse for sixty dollars and bought passage on the packet boat going downriver to Memphis, his only possessions, aside from the few dollars, being the clothes on his back and the captain's English saddle.

It was aboard this side-wheel steamer that he first read Austin's handbill, with its promise of adventure and free land. He saw it again in The Gut, in Memphis, where he met Ira Walker in a grogshop there, drunk and filled with extravagant phrases, eager to augment the strength of his caravan even by the addition of a raw youngster who had yet to grow a beard. But in the end it was a woman who forced Toby's decision. A sixteen-year-old prostitute in one of the brothels of The Gut, a girl with the face of a depraved French doll and the heart of a prison warder, completed Toby's introduction to sex, which had been started on the Maison Plantation by a golden-skinned girl from the slave shanties. Along with the pleasures of the bed, she showed him those of the bottle, and one cold morning he came painfully awake in a stinking alley in the depths of The Gut, broke and hungry, without a friend. He stumbled out into the sunlight and found his way to Ira Walker's caravan, which was making up that morning for the long trek to Texas, and he had been with the caravan from Memphis to Arkansas Post, and from Arkansas Post to Washington, a long, hard journey over wilderness trail.

Somewhere off in the distance an owl hooted mournfully, and Toby shivered, then smiled to himself in the darkness, snug and warm beneath Stoge's shed. He nestled his head in the leather of the saddle and chuckled to himself, remembering Walker rolling on the floor, and a few minutes later he fell asleep.

2.

With the first streak of dawn Toby rubbed his eyes and rolled out from under the shed. He crossed the street to the well in front of the tavern and drew himself a bucket of water, scrubbing himself in the watering trough. When Stoge came to open the store, he found his newly hired clerk waiting and ready for work. Toby's face shone from its scrubbing, and his short black hair was well brushed. He gave the store a thorough sweeping and dusted the counters and shelves, then borrowed a quarter from his boss and went to buy his breakfast.

Toby was proud of his new job. Stoge's store was substantial, twenty-five feet wide and one hundred feet long, built of heavy squared logs. The walls were twelve feet high and the steep roof was covered with cypress shingles. The store proper was well stocked with drugs, groceries, dry goods, shoes, and hardware, and there was a supply of rifles, powder, and lead. The fancy piece goods, drugs, and small items easily picked up by browsing Indians or gum-fingered whites were displayed on crude shelves. The counters in front of the shelves were laden with heavier merchandise.

Stoge prided himself on displaying the biggest assortment of liquors in Arkansas Territory. A sturdy rack along the rear wall of the store supported twelve barrels placed side by side. Two held native corn whiskey; one, aged mountain dew; another, raw firewater. A barrel of sweet wine and one of sour, together with a barrel of cane rum, completed his homemade stock. His shipped-in liquors included a barrel each of straight grain alcohol, white gin, Monongahela whiskey, Kentucky rye, and New Orleans brandy. He usually kept a barrel or two of reserve stock upended in the corner. A flexible tube was used to siphon the liquor into the containers.

When Toby returned from breakfast, Stoge gave him his instructions. "I don't want no one-drink-at-a-time customers in here. This being mainly a store, we don't have time to fool with idlers who want to set around all day jawin'. They take up time I haven't got to be wasted, and neither have you. It's the big sales we cater to. Sell them from a gallon to a barrel, and try for the five-gallon demijohn sales."

"That's the kind of business I like," said Toby. He had never done any selling, but he felt the instinct for it in his blood, and he decided it would be about as easy to sell a five-gallon demijohn as a gallon jug to a farmer or Texas-bound settler with a thirst.

"Another thing, Toby," Stoge went on. "This is a respectable place. We've got lady customers buyin' bolt goods and provisions, and they sure as shootin' don't want to come in here with a passel of drinkers hangin' around. Them that wants to do their drinkin' away from home can go to the tavern. There they can loaf as long as they like, while they're whittlin', chewin', spittin', and cussin'."

"I'll see none of that goes on around here," Toby promised.

"And don't be handin' out my Webster's almanacs to no strangers," Stoge cautioned. "I got them for my regular customers."

"I've been reading one myself," Toby said. He grinned. "Helps me keep up with what the weather's going to do."

"Where you plannin' on sleepin', Toby? The tavern comes pretty high for its lodgin'."

"I thought maybe I could fix a bunk in the store," Toby said. "Then I could be on hand to watch things."

Stoge nodded. "I guess you can use the back room. You'll have to clean it out, and you can bunk on that old cot." Stoge pointed to a crude cowhide cot and led the way back through

17

the store to a small storage room. "You can look after the place nights. We ain't never *had* no thievin', but that don't mean there won't be some."

Toby was pleased with the room. It meant shelter and no rent, and it indicated that Stoge was disposed to trust him, or he wouldn't have given him a key to the store and turned him loose in the place.

"I'll speak to my daughter," Stoge said. "And see if she can spare some old blankets."

"I didn't know you had a daughter, Stoge," said Toby, his curiosity aroused.

Stoge gave him a quick glance and said sharply, "Don't know's there's any reason why you should. I keep my home and my business separate." Stoge's fur seemed to rise and his tone of voice warned Toby to proceed with caution. Nevertheless, he knew that eventually he would meet Stoge's daughter, and he wondered what she was like. That she was a good woman he took for granted. On the frontier there were two kinds of women—good women, the ones men married, and whores, and Stoge's daughter would be a good woman. But Toby wondered what she looked like, how old she was, whether she was pledged to some young buck who had his eye on Stoge's profitable business.

During his first week at the store, Toby knew that Stoge was watching him closely, and he worked hard to gain his approval. Toby soon had the store looking like a different place. The shelves were scrubbed clean and the merchandise was stacked neatly on the shelves and counters. He quickly learned how to wait on trade, and the instinct for selling he had felt in himself proved to be real. He had the merchant's flair, and Stoge, pleased at the way he took to the job, gave him a free hand and made no comment.

Late one afternoon, after Stoge had gone home, Toby was cleaning out a drawer in one of the counters and came across a tin box stuck far back in a corner. He opened it and his eyes bulged; the box was filled with paper money—fives, tens, and twenties. His fingers itched to count it then and there, but he restrained himself until darkness. That night, after supper, he hung an old deerskin over the window of the room and knelt on the floor to count the money, stacking it in hundred-dollar piles, whistling as he made the total—seven hundred and fifteen dollars. It was more money than Toby had ever seen before, and a wild, momentary impulse tempted him to take it as a stake and head west. Then he thought it out. It wasn't enough. He knew Stoge might have set a trap to test him, might even be watching now, and he smiled to himself as he put the money back in the box and returned the box to the drawer. If it *was* a trap, then Stoge hadn't baited it with enough sugar. A thousand or two might have prompted him to steal, but Toby was too shrewd to become an outlaw for seven hundred dollars.

The next morning, when Stoge entered the store, Toby shoved the tin box across the counter. "I found a wad of your money," he said, "cleaning out that drawer."

Stoge opened the box and smiled. "This stuff ain't no account," he said.

"It ain't?" said Toby. "Looks good to me. What's wrong with it?"

"It's all counterfeit," Stoge explained.

"Where'd you get it?"

"Oh, it's the accumulation of years. Every now and then some sharpster slips me a bogus bill."

"I'd 'a thought you'd've got smarted up, 'fore you took this much," said Toby.

"A man don't never get smarted up, Toby," advised Stoge, "till just before he dies."

"How much did they slip you?"

"Last time I counted it there was about five hundred dollars," said Stoge. "But I've taken in more since."

Toby took a bill from the box. "Some of this stuff looks awful good," he said.

"Sure, it looks good or I wouldn't have taken it." Stoge went to his desk and got a paper-backed booklet. "Here's a little book that shows the difference between good and bad paper money," he said. "You better study it."

"I sure will," said Toby. "I don't want nobody making a fool out of me."

Stoge laughed. "Sooner or later, somebody will," he said.

Toby put the booklet in his pocket. Evenings, after work, he had plenty of time to study it, for he avoided the tavern, not wanting trouble with Ira Walker, and the tavern was Washington's only place of diversion. Sooner or later, he knew, he would have to face Walker, for the Red River was falling fast and it would soon be possible for the caravan to move. As soon as the oxen could ford the river, he knew that Ira would be on his way, for the big man was eager for Texas, impatient at being cooped up.

On a Monday morning, Ira broke camp. The long line of heavily loaded covered wagons, drawn by four-up ox teams, moved slowly up the hill. The deep sand and steep grade made the massive animals labor, and as they neared the store Toby heard the sharp crack of the bullwhips and the shouted curses of the bullpunchers urging the teams along. Above them all rose the raucous bellow of Ira Walker, who directed the caravan from horseback, shouting his instructions. He galloped up to Stoge's doorway and swung out of the saddle, stalking past Toby without a word. Toby followed him into the store, but Ira ignored him, addressing Stoge. "Got to have grub-stakes for my men," he said.

Toby stepped forward. "Count me out of your plans, Ira," he said. "I'm staying here to work for Stoge."

Ira turned, a sneer on his lips. "Damn glad to get rid of you," he said, "but I sure as hell want that horse and rifle back."

"You'll sure as hell not get them," Toby insisted. "Your name wasn't even mentioned when I signed for them."

Stoge smelled trouble. "Listen to me, Ira Walker," he said levelly, "if you and your men want grubstakes from me, you'll do as I say. I know you need food, but I've already let you have nine gallons of liquor on credit, and that's against the rules."

"You can add that four dollars and a half to my grub ticket," said Ira. "I'll sign it."

"Trail-work charges ain't supposed to cover nothing but food and supplies, Ira, and you know it." The storekeeper rested his elbows on the counter and looked at Ira, smiling a little, sure of his ground. He was the only merchant in Washington authorized to issue supplies to settlers bound for Texas, and Ira Walker would do as he said, or not get grubstakes for his men.

Ira knew better than to have a showdown with Stoge. "All right," he conceded, "let him keep the horse and the damned old musket. But I'm a'tellin' you now, keep the little skunk out of my way."

Toby took a step toward Ira. "The further I stay away from you, Walker, the better I like it," he said.

Stoge came from behind the counter and stepped between them. "You leave Ira to me, Toby," he ordered. "I'll wait on him myself. Step outside and tell the others to wait till I've finished with him, then they can come in, two at a time, and we can wait on 'em."

Ira Walker left the store with his grubstake and two jugs of corn whiskey. He signed a receipt that covered all of his indebtedness to Stoge. The others filed in, two by two, and Toby helped wait on them. No money changed hands, but each man signed a receipt for the provisions issued to him, and these receipts would later be redeemed with federal funds, appropriated by the Congress of the United States for improvement of the Southwestern Trail. In a few hours, more than four hundred dollars went to strengthen America's tightening grip on Texas, and a score of families were on their way to join Austin's pioneers. Toby listened to the spurs ring as the last two men crossed the puncheon floor, carrying their supplies. He went with them to the door and stood on the porch, watching the ox teams strain to start the heavy wagons, following the long line with his eyes until the last team was out of sight and Walker's band was gone, swallowed up by the wilderness to the west. He watched them go, and some impulse prompted him to wave farewell, but he had no regrets. He felt only relief at Walker's going, and sighed contentedly as he walked back into the store and resumed his work.

3.

Stoge was inspecting his stock of liquors, shaking each barrel and listening with an expert ear, judging the amount by the sound of the splashing fluid. The barrel of firewater was about empty.

"Mail rider just rode in from Arkansas Post," he said to Toby, "and said he passed another caravan of settlers headed this way. Eleven wagons. Toby, you better git over to my house, hitch the old gray mule to the drag sled, and fetch another barrel of corn liquor out of my cellar." It was Saturday, almost a week after Ira's outfit had departed. Toby, by now, had settled into the routine of his work, but he had yet to see Agatha, Stoge Rowden's daughter. He was excited, therefore, when Stoge called after him as he went out the door, for Stoge said, "Son, tell Agatha to give you my specs. I'll be needin' 'em to write out the charges."

At Stoge's house, Toby found Cato, one of Rowden's slave Negroes, and told him to get the barrel of whiskey up from the cellar. Then he went to the front door and knocked importantly, tipping his hat to the tall young woman who answered his summons. She was plainly but neatly clad, with none of the blatant sexuality of the girls in the Memphis Gut, yet she lacked the desiccated, worn-out look of many "good" women on the frontier. Her calico dress was starched and spotless, and her color was vibrant. She wore her heavy blue-black hair in a towering pompadour that made her look taller than he. There was about her a placid coolness, a calm self-assurance, but beneath that there was a warmth, and Toby sensed, looking into her fine, really beautiful dark eyes, an untapped reservoir of energy, a capacity for passion that had not been tested.

"I'm Agatha Rowden," she said, in a rich voice that made his spine tingle. "You must be Toby Giles, father's new hired man."

Toby felt the blood rise to his cheeks and knew that he must be scarlet, then found his tongue and said falteringly, "Your father sent me after his spectacles, Miss Rowden."

Agatha smiled. "I'll fetch them, Toby. You just wait here, please."

While she went for the glasses, he waited on the porch, feeling bewildered and uncomfortable. Ever since Stoge mentioned his daughter, Toby had been thinking of his first meeting with her, and he hadn't planned it this way at all. He had intended to impress her with his best Virginia manners, to make her aware of what a grand fellow he was, and here he stood, waiting like a schoolboy, hardly able to utter a word when Agatha returned, holding out the spectacles to him with a "Thank you, Toby," that set his ears burning, then dismissing him with a short nod and closing the door behind her.

23

Toby climbed down the porch steps, embarrassed and resentful of Agatha's use of his Christian name. He knew that quality folk in Virginia addressed only hirelings by their first names, and what Agatha had intended as an overture of friendship toward a newcomer Toby took for high-toned snobbery. But as he rode back to the store, sitting astride the barrel of whiskey behind the weary old mule, he cooled off a bit. Agatha Rowden might be a bit stringy, as women went in those days, and she might be a bit high-toned. But her father was the wealthiest storekeeper in Arkansas Territory, a man of parts, and Agatha was his only child. Some day what Stoge had would belong to her—and to the man she married. Toby laughed aloud to himself, remembering the way he had stood there staring when Agatha opened the door. By the time he pulled up the old mule in front of the store he was whistling a lively tune and his head was buzzing with ideas as he bucked the heavy barrel up the steps—ideas that concerned his future and that of Agatha Rowden, for the tall, dark-eyed girl had made an impression on Toby, stirring him up as he had never been stirred in his life before, and the fact that she was Stoge Rowden's heiress was only part of what quickened his blood when he thought of her.

4.

On Sunday mornings Stoge closed the store and went to church with his daughter. Afternoons, the back door was open, for someone was sure to want a vial of paregoric for a sick baby, or an ounce of laudanum for a colicky horse, or some quinine for a slave down with chills and fever. Almost every Sunday, too, one of the town ginheads would run out of firewater.

Toby had the day off, and spent most of it giving the town a thorough looking over. It was a growing frontier community, given added importance by the fact that it stood at the crossroads of four major wilderness trails. The oldest and most important was the Southwest Trail, leading north through the woods to Missouri and Tennessee. Another wandered south, into Louisiana and Texas. Another went east, into Mississippi. The newest was the freshly blazed wilderness track that led into Indian Territory. There were fifty families in the town itself, and on each trail there were settlers here and there. In every direction, flanking out from the town, land was being cleared for the planting of corn.

A dense pine grove invited Toby. He turned his horse and rode into the woods, enjoying the fresh, lively smell of the needles. The land sloped gently into the valley, the soil changing from sandy loam to red clay, and deeper in the wilderness to rich hammock marl. Toby knew something about farm land. He swung himself out of the saddle and dug into the rich topsoil with his knife, finding no bottom to the black, fertile earth. He played with the thick black dirt, crumbling it between his fingers. This was land upon which a man who knew his business could get rich. This was better land, once cleared and plowed, than he had ever seen in Virginia, and Toby decided, kneeling there in the wilderness, that in this place, Washington, he would make his home and his fortune; here he would settle, finished with wandering, and here he would become what he wanted most to be—an aristocrat, a man of authority, like Captain Maison. Riding back into town, daydreaming, Toby fancied himself on a horse, not the government-issued gelding he rode, but a blooded horse like Captain Maison's, with an English saddle. In the daydream he saw himself wearing white buckskin breeches like the captain's and a scarlet coat made for him by the finest tailor in Savile Row, London. He saw his house, the house he would build here in the wilderness, finer even than the Maison Mansion, and he saw his bride, Agatha Rowden, clad in a Paris-made dancing gown, swirling to the music made by slaves who were Toby's own private property.

5.

Washington was crowded with braves and their families, migratory Indians making an enforced pilgrimage from their old haunts to the strange, faraway land set apart for them in the newly established Indian Territory . . . remnants of a once great race, now a people without a country, doomed to be pressed still farther westward as the white man's insatiable hunger for land impelled him to devour a continent piecemeal . . . shambling in gait and apathetic, hopelessly filthy, submerged in despair. But they had money, pressed on them in lieu of their land, and United States certificates of indebtedness, redeemable at face value in many establishments, of which Stoge's store was one.

Standing on the front porch of the store, Toby watched the Indians plod dustily up the street. Their hopelessness and obvious air of defeat moved him to sympathy, for he had known rejection and cruelty as a child, and he understood the distrust and resentment these caused. There was in Toby, added to his shrewdness and ruthlessness, a kindliness and humanity that made for ambivalence in his character, so that while he was moved to sympathy by the sight of these homeless tribesmen, he also saw that the dollars they carried, combined with their simplicity of temperament, made them prospects for easy profits. As it does so often, in this struggle between the dollar and the generous gesture, the dollar won out.

Toby found the Indian leader, a tall, muscular brave named Running Deer who spoke English well enough to be understood. "How, how," Toby greeted him, raising a hand in friendly salute. "Many miles you travel to get to this place?"

"Many miles and many moons," answered Running Deer. "My people are tired. We rest."

"I welcome you." Toby said. "I work in this store. I like to help you. Your people need food and warm blankets for their journey."

Running Deer shook his head. "Have blankets," he said.

"But not mackinaws," Toby said. "Heap warm coats. Come. Me show you." He led the Indian into the store and spread the brilliantly colored mackinaws on the counter. "Pretty coat," he said. "Much warm. You need him where you go." With the skill of a salesman in an eastern clothing emporium, he slipped the coat on the Indian. The many pockets fascinated Running Deer, and he caressed the soft, bright wool with his hands. Then he saw a coat on the pile, made of brilliant red and green checked cloth.

"Me like that one," he said, pointing.

Toby didn't hurry his customer. He fastened the big red buttons and buckled the belt. "Running Deer make fine looking chief in that coat. Running Deer fine looking brave."

"How much money?" asked the chief.

"To Chief Running Deer, just ten dollars."

"Me take." He handed Toby a new twenty-dollar bill.

"Me change money," said Toby. He took a counterfeit ten-dollar bill from the tin box and offered it to the Indian, who looked at it blankly, then stuffed it in his pocket. For a moment

27

Toby was tempted not to go on with the fraud, for the Indian seemed so simple and childlike, but he consoled himself with the thought that Running Deer would have no use for money in the wild country that was his destination.

"Many braves need mackinaw," he said, adjusting the coat on the tribesman's shoulders. "Your people will be treated right in Stoge Rowden's store."

Running Deer nodded. "I send," he said.

Toby gave Running Deer a twist of tobacco for himself and a card of bright red buttons for his squaw. "Here favor from house to Chief Running Deer," he said, presenting the gifts with a flourish.

The next day the Indians came in twos and threes to trade with Toby, and before nightfall the tin box filled with counterfeit was half empty. The counterfeit was in the Indians' pockets and their good money was in Stoge Rowden's till. After he had cheated Running Deer, Toby fought a losing battle with his conscience; the temptation to get rid of the queer money by passing it to these simple savages was too great to be resisted.

But Stoge didn't like it. "Kinda rough on them redskins, ain't you, Toby?" he asked.

Toby looked his boss right in the eye. "I wouldn't pass that stuff to a man it would hurt," he explained, "but where them Indians are going, bad money will be just as useful as good money. There won't be no place to spend either one."

Stoge was persuaded by Toby's logic; he was glad to get rid of the bad bills. He wouldn't have passed them himself, but he was pleased that his clerk had found a way to unload them without hurting anyone. He was becoming more confident in Toby, and while he still carried the day's receipts home with him each night, his trust in the new clerk increased, and at the end of the week he gave Toby a raise in salary, saying to him, "You're doing right well, son. You've got a natural head for business. A real knack for a dollar."

6.

The Sunday after he got his raise, Toby dressed in a suit of store-bought clothes he had purchased with his first wages. He was determined to see Agatha Rowden again, even if that meant going to church. Besides, he reasoned, being seen in church might help his standing with the solid element in the community. So he slicked himself up, and when it was time, made his way into the building and took a seat in a rear pew.

He saw Stoge, in the front row, looking uncomfortable in his Sunday best, and then spied Agatha in the choir. She wore a small black-silk bonnet with white-lace trimming and tiny handmade rosebuds spaced around the edges. Her dress was gray silk, severe but becoming, and as Toby watched her, sitting erect, her fine head high, she seemed even more desirable than he had remembered. When the choir sang the first hymn, he heard Agatha's clear, sweet voice, and it thrilled him in the same way it had when she spoke to him the day he met her. He enjoyed the singing, but the long-winded prayer had him squirming on the hard pew before it was half over, and when the parson started his sermon, Toby knew that he was going to suffer.

The parson was a fire-eater with a walrus moustache, and his theme was hell. He pictured with such vivid imagery the fiery furnace reserved for sinners that Toby could all but feel the Devil prodding him with his sharp, pointed tail. When the preacher really warmed up to his subject, the air of the church seemed to be tinged with the fumes of brimstone, and the sinners who sweated in the congregation winced under the

29

clergyman's blast. He went on to list the glories awaiting those who heeded God's will, and described them in such glowing detail that Toby was half convinced the parson must have witnessed these things himself. When the long sermon finally ended, Toby heaved a sigh of relief and dropped a quarter into the collection plate, hoping that his generosity would be noticed by Agatha, or at least by Stoge Rowden. He passed out of the church with the crowd and idled on the steps until Stoge and his daughter appeared. The storekeeper seemed surprised and pleased to discover that Toby had been among the worshipers.

"Mighty glad to see you in church, son," he said heartily. "You know my daughter, Agatha."

Toby bowed in the best Virginia style, imitating the elegant gentlemen whose manners he had studied on the Maison Plantation, and when he spoke he believed that he used the courtly tones of a Tidewater cavalier. "Yes, Mr. Rowden, sir. I had the pleasure of addressing Miss Rowden when I called at your house on an errand for you concerning a pair of spectacles. How do you do, Miss Rowden?"

On this occasion it was Agatha who turned scarlet in confusion, and stammered, for the sight of Toby in his Sunday clothes instead of the buckskins he wore in the shop, and the perfect poise he displayed when he spoke, seemed hardly to fit the rough fellow she had addressed as her father's hired man. "Yes, pa, father, I mean," she faltered. "I met Mr. Giles when he came for your specs." She paused, blushing, and lowered her eyes. "Perhaps if Mr. Giles isn't otherwise engaged he will accept an invitation to dinner."

Stoge seconded the invitation. "You're welcome to eat at our table, Toby," he said. "We'll be pleasured to have you."

Toby's elation and eagerness to accept made him forget his cavalier phrases, and when he answered he relapsed into the speech that was natural to him. "I'm powerful pleased to accept the invite, if you're sure it won't put you folks out none."

He blurted out the crude phrases, ready to kick himself the moment they were uttered, but Stoge seemed not to notice the difference, though Agatha glanced quickly at him, and he thought he noticed a twinkle of amusement in her eyes.

Toby walked beside Agatha, and her closeness made him tingle with excitement. In church, while the parson was describing hell-fire, he had been able to study Agatha carefully. She was one of those women whose true beauty emerges slowly, as you observe them, rather than the flashy type with nothing under the surface. Her instinctive taste became apparent on closer observation, and her strong, well-made body had subtle, appealing curves that were missed by the first casual glance. Toby had made discreet inquiry among his few acquaintances in the town, and learned that she had been kindly though strictly reared, and that Stoge worshiped her as the greatest treasure among his possessions. With a woman like this one, Toby understood, a wharf rat from Norfolk, with nothing in his pockets, and only his word to substantiate his claim to aristocratic forebears, would have to move carefully. Stoge Rowden was bound to be particular about the man who married his daughter. Anxious to make a good impression, Toby held his tongue during the walk home, permitting Stoge to dominate the conversation. Toby had discovered that the good listener is usually applauded as a splendid conversationalist by the man who does the talking.

When they reached the big Rowden house, Agatha took the men's hats. "Make yourselves comfortable," she said, with a warm smile that made Toby glow inside. "I'll look after the dinner."

Stoge's house was one of the few in Washington with glass windows. It was forty feet square, built of huge oak logs adzed smooth on the inside. There were four rooms, and behind the house, built onto it, was a low-roofed shed room divided for cooking and eating. The furniture showed Agatha's touch; two big rockers were covered with bearskin, and a brightly colored Indian blanket on the settee offered a cheerful note. There were pictures on the walls, and everything was scrupulously neat and well kept. Toby looked approvingly around the room and admired the strength of the house. "If we ever have an Indian raid," he said, "I'll head straight for your house. I think these walls would stop any bullet."

"We had a raid once," Stoge said. "I felt safe enough against bullets, but no house is safe against Indian fire torches."

While Agatha was preparing dinner, Stoge showed Toby over the place. On the way to the big barn they passed the slave quarters. The Negroes were loafing in front of their shanties, taking the sun and enjoying their day of rest.

"How many slaves do you own?" asked Toby.

"Eleven, countin' the children," answered Stoge.

Toby wondered why, with so many slave women around, the daughter of the house was preparing the food, and the bewilderment must have shown on his face, for Stoge observed, "Agatha always cooks the Sunday meal. She's particular about the food she serves when we have company. Especially if it's the preacher."

They continued their inspection of the property, with Toby becoming more and more impressed by the quiet, unpretentious, but extremely solid evidences of Stoge's affluence, until Agatha sent a slave child to summon them to dinner. When he saw the food on the table, Toby smiled, and realized that Stoge must have repeated to his daughter Toby's remarks about the food he had been used to, back in Virginia, for Agatha had prepared a steaming dish of fluffy hominy grits, a succulent-looking ham that gave off a tantalizing aroma, and a dish of good red-bottom gravy. There were hot biscuits made with white flour, fresh churned butter, and a comb of wild honey. Agatha took off her high-bibbed apron and sat down, bowing her head while Stoge said grace, then taking up her fork as a signal for the men to begin to eat.

Table manners were one of the things Toby hadn't learned

in Virginia. He had never eaten in the Maison Mansion, nor seen the guests at the dinner table, so he lagged a little behind Stoge and his daughter, watching the way Agatha handled her knife and fork, then trying to imitate her technique, though he found it awkward, for Toby, until now, had always found that a knife served as well as a fork. In his eagerness to convince Agatha that he was really a Virginia gentleman, he talked more than he intended to, commenting effusively on the food, the china, the silver, and the table linen used in his plantation home. He described the Maison Plantation in detail, and offered a eulogy of Captain Maison, representing the rich, influential planter as his father, cringing a little with shame as he spoke, recalling for a moment his real father, rolling drunk along the Norfolk docks, clad in rags and distinguished by a matted, tobacco-stained beard. He talked horses, which he understood, and farm land, which he knew well, and while he was on these subjects he saw that Stoge was interested and impressed. But when he veered off again into a rhapsody over the elegant appointments of the big house at home, and a description of one of the costume balls, he forgot himself, being so absorbed in what he was saying, and slashed into his pie with his knife, scooping up a piece and shoving it into his mouth in his customary fashion.

Stoge watched him from across the table, and an expression of annoyance crossed the storekeeper's face. Stoge Rowden was a well-to-do man, but he was plain spoken and plain mannered. He admired neither braggarts nor liars, and after a moment, watching Toby eat with his knife, he said quietly, "Toby, you talk like an aristocrat, but you sure don't eat like one."

Agatha stiffened and her face turned scarlet. "Pa!" she remonstrated. "I've never known anyone to be so rude!"

Stoge was apologetic; never before had Agatha criticized a word he had said. "I didn't mean no harm, daughter," he said, then turned to Toby. "Sorry if I hurt your feelings, son."

Toby was mortified with shame, and by the terrible fear that he had deceived neither Stoge nor Agatha, but he managed to stammer, "That's all right, Mr. Rowden. I plumb forgot my table manners. Eating on the trail, we didn't have anything but a plate, a knife, and a spoon and I got in the habit of knifing my food."

"I didn't mean no harm, Toby."

Toby eased his knife out of his hand as carefully as if it had been a rattlesnake, then took up his fork, dabbling delicately with what was left of his pie. "Tavern eating, with fellows like Hank Tribble and Squire Tatum, don't help table manners." Toby had lost his appetite, but he was determined to cover up his mistakes. He was greatly relieved when Agatha rose, indicating that the dinner was over, and led the way into the parlor. He recovered sufficient self-confidence to say, "That was a mighty fine meal, Miss Rowden. I never ate better food." He spoke rather humbly, trying to make amends.

"You're a flatterer, Mr. Giles," Agatha replied, a little flash of amusement in her fine eyes. "I'm sure your Virginia cooks are much better."

"Virginia food may be fancier," Stoge interrupted, "but it ain't no better. Agatha's a fine cook. And a good manager." Stoge's eyes swept around the well-kept room and his face beamed with pride. Agatha blushed.

"You'll have to excuse pa, Mr. Giles," she said. "He's always bragging of his daughter."

Stoge denied this, saying, "Braggin' and statin' facts are two different things. I'm statin' facts."

A voice called from outside the house: "Hello . . . hello!" and Stoge stepped through the door to the porch. "What you needin', Scott?" they heard him ask.

"My brats are a-chillin' " the voice replied. "I need a refill of them quinine bitters."

Stoge returned to the parlor, picked up his hat, and glanced at Toby as though undecided whether to leave him with

Agatha or take him along, but he finally said, "Toby, you and daughter can visit a while. I'll go down to the store and get Scott Johnson his bitters. You come along later."

For weeks Toby had anticipated the moment he would be alone with Agatha and had planned exactly his approach, but now that the moment was here his self-confidence deserted him, and the two young people sat for several minutes in awkward silence, listening to the ticking of the wooden-worked clock and the muted conversations of the soft-voiced slaves that drifted from the shanties. It was Agatha who broke the silence.

"I hope you stay with pa," she said. "He's needed someone like you for a long time."

"I hope he lets me stay," said Toby eagerly. "I like your father, and I like the work."

"I imagine you find it lonely here, after the life you were used to back in Virginia."

Toby's poise was returning. "It has been lonely, Miss Rowden," he said, using his most elegant accent, "but this visit has brightened my stay." Toby had never been on terms of social equality with a "good woman" before; he wanted to impress Agatha with his importance and potentialities, and he was eager to display his respect for her, but he didn't know exactly how to proceed, and his words, as he spoke them, seemed stilted and insincere, though, in fact, they were honest enough.

"We have church sociables and picnics in the summer," Agatha said. "And there'll be more entertainment as the town grows."

"That sounds pleasant," said Toby. His heart pounded a little as he added, "I hope I may have the honor of escorting you to a few of those gatherings. Your father seems to approve of me, and I hope that his daughter will approve too." As he finished his speech he was blushing like a schoolgirl, but Agatha seemed pleased. Her candid gaze became demure and she twisted the lace handkerchief in her lap. "I usually like my father's friends, Mr. Giles," she said. "I admire his judgment."

There was a quality about Agatha of which Toby was becoming aware and which both attracted him and disturbed his assurance. In the tall, modest girl who sat before him he sensed a quality of real beauty, a beauty that stemmed from nobility of character, and that on closer acquaintance made her the most intensely desirable person he had ever met. He felt himself drawn to her as a person, and she stirred him as a woman, not in the way he had been aroused by the prostitutes in Memphis, but in a more powerful, compelling way, and some instinct persuaded him that here was the woman he wanted for a wife and for the mother of his children. In that moment, sitting across from Agatha in Stoge Rowden's parlor, Toby Giles ceased to be a boy and a wanderer and became a man, with a goal in life. He knew that he must move warily, and his judgment advised him that this was the time for strategic withdrawal rather than attack. He got to his feet and bowed.

"Thank you for the dinner, Miss Rowden, and for this most enjoyable visit. I must go now, but I will be honored and happy if you will permit me to call again."

Agatha rose to bid him good-by. "I'm sure pa won't have any objections, Mr. Giles," she said quietly.

Toby looked into her eyes, and could not resist a personal compliment. She had abandoned the high pompadour that made her look taller than he; her fine blue-black hair was parted in the middle and drawn severely back to a tight beehive at the nape of her neck. It was much more attractive that way, and Toby said, "I like the way you have your hair fixed today." He paused, then said, "It's beautiful."

"Thank you, Mr. Giles." She lowered her eyes at the compliment, but her face glowed with pleasure and Toby knew that he had said the right thing.

As he walked toward the store at a thoughtful pace, he could not help wondering whether she had changed her hair so that she would not look too tall for him. His spirits rose as he reviewed the visit. He knew that he had made a few blunders, but he reasoned that he couldn't have said or done anything too bad or Agatha wouldn't have consented to his calling again. He decided that the general impression he had made was good, and he was pleased with himself, quickening his pace and whistling a tune as he approached the store, then breaking off his music, remembering that it was Sunday and doubtful that Stoge would approve such levity on the Lord's day.

Stoge stood in front of the store, engaged in conversation with the preacher, and as Toby approached he saw the storekeeper hand the parson a bill that looked like a ten. He slowed his pace and watched the preacher depart, then approached Stoge.

"Thanks for asking me to dinner, Mr. Rowden," he said politely.

Stoge was watching the parson's funereal back as the man of God walked up the street, and he answered Toby without looking at him. "Glad to have you, Toby. But it was Agatha that asked you."

"You have a daughter to be proud of, Mr. Rowden," said Toby. "It was a real pleasure to visit with her."

Stoge nodded. "I was glad to see you in church, Toby," he said. "Men like you and me, bein' in business, we need a lot of preachin' to."

Toby understood that the ten dollars Stoge had given the preacher was a form of conscience money, to make up in part for the way he and Toby had cheated the migrating Indians. He was learning things about the storekeeper, getting to know him better, and he was discovering that Stoge Rowden, though a rough frontiersman in his manners and dress, was a man of honor, and one of the kindest human beings on the face of the earth.

"I reckon a lot more Gospel preachin' wouldn't hurt me," he said rather sheepishly, knowing that Stoge was thinking of the Indians too.

"Gospel preachin' never hurt nobody, Toby. A man needs a spiritual prop."

"You go on home, Mr. Rowden, and get some rest. I'll stay around and wait on anybody that needs anything."

"That's right nice of you, Toby," agreed Stoge. "I think I'll do that."

Hank Tribble, town loafer and itinerant fiddler, sat on a stump a few yards from the store, idly strumming on the strings of his instrument. After Stoge was out of earshot, Hank said to Toby, with a chuckle, "You're lightin' on a kinda high perch, ain't you, Toby?"

"That's where I aim to roost, Hank," answered Toby. He knew Tribble casually, having met him at the tavern while he was still a member of Walker's caravan, and though he liked the fiddler, he knew that a man with ambitions such as his own had little time to waste on loafers like Tribble.

"Saw you comin' out of meetin' today," said Hank.

Toby couldn't resist bragging, "Miss Agatha asked me to eat with them."

"I took a few squints at Miss Agatha myself," the fiddler said wistfully. "But she wouldn't wipe her feet on me, and I didn't reckon she would on you neither."

Toby grinned. "You can't tell about women, Hank."

"No, you can't," Tribble agreed. "I had a woman once that tolled me to church."

"Your wife?" inquired Toby.

"Yes and no," explained Hank. "I lived with her, but I didn't have no papers on her. She kept gettin' religion, so I had to quit her."

"What's wrong with gettin' religion?" Toby wanted to know, feeling a little smug because he had been to church that morning.

"Nothing wrong, as such," conceded Hank. "But my woman had a bad case. Every time a stray preacher came along, she got us both sanctified. I ain't gettin' sanctified regular for no woman."

"It might've done you good, Hank," Toby remarked.

Hank snorted. "A drink'd do me more good right now," he said. "How about one?" The fiddler glanced suggestively toward the back of the store, indicating that a dram or two would never be missed from one of the barrels. Toby was tempted for a moment, knowing that he faced a long, dull afternoon, and Hank Tribble, carrying just the right amount of liquor, was an entertaining companion. But the memory of Agatha was still too strong, and he answered the fiddler rather curtly.

"Stoge don't allow no drinking in his place, Hank. Specially on Sunday."

Hank's face was mournful as he got to his feet and tucked his fiddle under his arm, going downstreet to the tavern, needful of a drink and bent on fiddling it out of someone. Toby went into the store and stretched himself out on his cot, happy to have resisted the loafer's suggestion and warmed by the pictures of Agatha that he conjured up in his mind as he lay half drowsing on his cowhide bed, dreaming of marriage and riches and the bright day, somewhere in the future, when he would have enough money and land and slaves to count himself an aristocrat. Somehow, though, as he thought of Agatha, his mind turned back almost against his will to the savage, passionate little prostitute in Memphis who had taken his money and turned him toward Texas, and he burned with shame at his own impudence for remembering those few wild nights at the same time he was thinking of Stoge Rowden's daughter. Agatha was so infinitely more desirable. He saw that now, and he yearned for her as he rested in the back of her father's store, filled with ambitious ideas for the future, eager for the time when he would possess her.

7.

The lazy, mild days of early summer were slipping away pleasantly. Toby was stirring at dawn and busy as long as the light lasted, waiting on trade, checking stock, making certain slight improvements here and there in the daily routine of the business, happy in the knowledge that he was gaining Stoge's admiration and respect. Two weeks had passed since his dinner at the Rowdens, and in that time Toby had not laid eyes on Agatha. He knew that on Sunday the unmarried parson was going to be in town, and he went to church to get a look at him, hoping also that he might get another invitation to the Rowden table.

Through the long sermon and the singing, Toby sat impatiently, hardly hearing what the parson was saying. When the congregation rose and filed out of church, he jockeyed himself into position so that he fell in beside Stoge and his daughter. Agatha gave him a friendly smile and greeted him pleasantly, but it was the parson who got the bid to dinner. Toby stood in front of the church, watching Stoge and the parson walk away with Agatha between them, all three engaged in animated conversation. He kicked angrily at the dirt, then walked back to the store. At least if he looked after trade that afternoon, Stoge would stay home and chaperon his daughter.

Hank Tribble was squatting on the porch of the store. "I see the parson gets the eatin' bid today," he said.

Toby nodded. "I hope Agatha feeds him fish with plenty of bones and he gets one hung in his throat," he said, making no effort to conceal his anger and disappointment.

Hank laughed. "I had a Bible-banger take a woman away from me onct, Toby," he said. "You better watch out."

A settler plodded up the street, wanting a bottle of colic medicine, and Toby went into the store with him. When he came out, he saw Tribble wandering away, looking for more cheerful company, and in a fit of loneliness and frustration Toby almost called him back to suggest a hell-fire, arm-waving drunk, but he checked himself, remembering that Stoge might take his daughter for a buggy ride that afternoon and look in at the store.

But Stoge and Agatha made no appearance, though late in the day Stoge sent Cato, his head slave, over to the store for two chopping hoes. The Negro greeted Toby respectfully and Toby treated him civilly. He knew that Cato had belonged to Stoge for more than twenty years, and had moistened Stoge's land with his sweat, plowing, planting, and harvesting many crops for his master. Cato's wool was tinged with gray, but age seemed to emphasize the strength of his features; he had strength and endurance far beyond that of most white men of his age. Toby knew how to get along with Negroes, and he had an idea that Cato liked him. He decided to pump the man.

"Cato," he said, "how long have you belonged to Marse Stoge?"

Cato scratched his graying wool and flashed a smile. "A long time, Marse Toby, sho' 'nough. A long time."

"He's a fine man," Toby observed. "I hope I can please him as well as you do."

The slave was a diplomat, as were most successful Negro slaves, and he realized that he was talking with another diplomat in Toby, anticipating Toby's curiosity at once, and grinning. "Marse Toby, suh, Marse Stoge say you is the most uppinist and doinist young gemman in dis yere town. Dat's what Marse Stoge say."

Toby smiled with delight. "He does? What does Miss Agatha say?"

41

"Miss Agatha, she do her talkin' wif Linda, an' Linda do her talkin' wif me. Linda, she tell me, Miss Agatha likes you just first rate."

"How about the preacher that's out there to dinner?"

Cato laughed. "Doan' you worry none 'bout him, Marse Toby. He too well fixed with chilluns what he got fum he othah wife. Fo' of 'em. Linda, she say Miss Agatha ain' studyin' him none."

The slave was eager to make friends with Toby. He knew that one day Agatha would marry and that this young employee of Stoge's was a likely candidate, in which case Toby might well become his master. Cato made friends with all of Agatha's suitors, but he was taking special pains with this one, for his native shrewdness showed him that Toby had the best chance of all the young men who had appeared so far, and Linda, his woman, had told him she saw the signs in Miss Agatha, sure enough, and that the young white gentleman had made an impression.

Toby was buoyant after Cato left. He was certain that Agatha wouldn't marry a middle-aged widower with four children; she was the kind of woman who would want to bring her own children into the world. He went back to his work with pleasure, humming to himself as he stacked the shelves with fresh bolts of brightly printed calico.

A few days later, in the afternoon, his heart gave a leap when Agatha walked into the store. He was drawing a gallon of molasses for a customer, and in his confusion at Agatha's arrival he let the jug run over and his hands became covered with the sticky stuff. Agatha had caught him in his old buckskins, with dirty hands and his hair uncombed. He tried to make up for his appearance by displaying especial politeness, saying, "If you will be kind enough to wait for a moment, Miss Rowden, I will be pleased to take care of you."

Agatha smiled graciously. "I won't bother you, Toby. Pa can bring my things home tomorrow." She did not seem to be distressed by Toby's rough, workmanlike appearance; indeed, he was sure she cast an admiring glance at the powerful sinews of his forearm. Her hair, he noticed, was combed flat to her head, and he guessed that the pompadour would not be seen again.

"Waiting on customers is my job, Miss Rowden," he said. "Please don't deny me the pleasure of serving you."

"All right, Mr. Giles," she agreed. "I'll wait."

"We have some new bolt goods you might like to look at," Toby suggested. He hurried back to his room to wash his hands and comb his hair, returning to the store to find Agatha occupied with the new prints that had just come in from Arkansas Post.

"Now, Miss Rowden!" he exclaimed. "I'm ready to serve you." He began to fill Agatha's order, piling the things she asked for on the counter, where her market basket rested. "I'll stow these things in your basket later, Miss Rowden," he said.

She watched him gather things from the shelves and counters, impressed with his efficiency and his knowledge of the thousands of items in the stock. "Are you happy here at the store?" she asked.

"I'm snug and happy here, Miss Rowden," answered Toby, pausing before he added, "except that it gets awful lonely."

"Haven't you made any friends in town?"

"Oh, I've met Squire Tatum and a few old codgers like that," he said. Tatum was the notary and town barber; a salty old frontiersman who enjoyed his dram of corn. Agatha had heard her father say that Squire Tatum was a poor companion for Toby.

"Our preacher could introduce you to some nice young people," she suggested. "I'll speak to him about it."

"Which preacher?" Toby asked. "The one with the four children?"

Agatha blushed and lowered her eyes in confusion. "No, he's gone. Our regular preacher is back now. The next time he

43

comes to dinner, I'll ask him about having you meet some young folks."

"I'd rather be there and ask him myself," Toby said.

He had been a little too bold; Agatha caught her breath and offered Toby a cool, reserved expression. "You'd better finish my order, Mr. Giles. I'm sure you have more important things to do than talking to me."

Toby completed Agatha's order, not saying anything more, afraid that his boldness had offended her. When he had found the last item he said, "I'd be glad to carry your basket home for you, Miss Rowden."

"Oh, no, thank you, Mr. Giles. Pa wouldn't like it if you left the store."

"I'll bring it tonight after supper," he promised.

"Please don't trouble," Agatha said, moving toward the door, seeming anxious to get away. Toby followed her to the edge of the porch and watched her stride off, her head held proudly. She did not look back. Toby returned to the store, shaking his head bewilderedly. Perhaps he was going about his courting wrong, he reflected, trying to remember what the customs were among the Tidewater blue bloods, then realizing that he had never really had a chance to learn them. Perhaps the only proper place to advance his cause was in Agatha's home, where she had the protection of her own roof, of the home's sanctity. He decided to carry the basket over to Stoge's that evening, and after supper, his work done, he groomed himself with special care and took the basket under his arm. Linda, Cato's woman and the Rowdens' house servant, showed him into the parlor, where Stoge was seated enjoying an after-dinner pipe. There was no sign of Agatha, though Toby had the uncomfortable feeling that she might somehow be watching him and judging his conduct. Stoge was brisk, though not unfriendly. "What brings you here, Toby?" he asked.

"I brought Miss Agatha's basket," answered Toby, hesitating, then deciding to risk a frontal attack. "But mostly I came to ask you if I could çall on Miss Agatha," he said.

Stoge glanced quizzically at him, making a gesture with his pipe. "What does my daughter say about it?" he challenged.

"I don't think she will object, sir," answered Toby boldly. Once having admitted his purpose he felt himself on firm ground, and he was resolved to present his case forcefully. He stood courteously, waiting for his employer to speak. Stoge stared at his pipe, eyeing it with wonderment, as though he had never seen it before. Then he looked up and nodded.

"I'll think about it," he said. "I'm a little vigilant about the kind of people that come into my home."

"I'll behave right toward her," Toby said. "I admire your daughter very much."

Stoge smiled. "Maybe you haven't noticed that Agatha's got a mind of her own. I don't cross her too much."

"Oh, I would want Miss Agatha's permission," said Toby.

Stoge stood up, and Toby realized that this was not the time to carry the discussion further. "I'll see you at the store," Stoge said. "Leave the basket. I'll give it to Agatha."

Toby walked slowly back to the store, his head down, lost in thought, trying to figure out whether Stoge was just being normally cautious, or whether the storekeeper had already decided against his courting Agatha. On the frontier, where women were few, someone like Agatha—strong, intelligent, well-endowed, scrupulously trained in the household arts—was almost unique, and a father was right to be on his guard, Toby admitted to himself. Then there was the fact that Agatha eventually would inherit Stoge's considerable property. That would make Stoge doubly careful about the man who married his daughter. Toby reached the store and flung himself on his cowhide bed; more than ever he realized that his sights were set extremely high for a wharf rat from Norfolk, and he would have given a lot to know just how much he had succeeded in fooling Stoge Rowden and his daughter about his background in Virginia. His mind in ferment, he fell into a troubled sleep, awakening several times with a start, aware of a sensation akin to fear. But after a while he began to construct his fantasies again, the bright dreams of the golden future when he would lord it over thousands of acres, with scores of slaves at his command, a blooded horse between his thighs, a scarlet coat from London on his back, and Agatha, his faithful wife, waiting for him in his elegant mansion. In the dream, she was passionate and beautiful, the picture of aristocracy and breeding.

8.

For several days Stoge avoided the store, passing all of his time at the farm, leaving Toby to look after everything. During the day Toby was so busy that he found little time to brood, but the nights were filled with conjecture and suspense. Several times, in the agony of loneliness, he was tempted to walk downstreet to the tavern to seek out Hank Tribble or Squire Tatum, knowing they would be glad to join him in a drunk. But he resisted the impulse to break loose, and was glad he had when Stoge finally made his appearance.

Toby gave his report on the store and Stoge nodded absently. Then he said, with an effort to be casual, not looking at Toby, "They're having a singing practice at the church tonight, son. Agatha thought you might like to escort her to the gathering."

Toby's heart pounded like a hammer and the blood surged through his veins, but he controlled his voice as he answered, trying to match Stoge's casual tone. "I'll be glad to escort Miss Agatha. But I can't do much singing. I've got a voice like a bullfrog."

Stoge laughed. "Well, it'll save me staying up pretty late," he observed, "and she thought it would do you good to mix with the right kind of people."

When Toby arrived at the Rowden farm that evening, right after supper, his boots had been polished with bear grease, and his hair was slicked back carefully. He had doused himself with Stoge's bay rum, and his store-bought suit, after a conscientious brushing, was impeccable. He saw the approval in Stoge's eyes as he climbed the steps to the porch, and he saw admiration in Agatha's eyes, too, when she came out, wearing her black bonnet and gray silk dress, looking even more fetching than she had the first Sunday, when Toby had come to dinner.

It was dusk as they strolled toward the church. A full, favorable moon competed with the rose afterglow of the sun on the western horizon, and the dense fragrance of emerging life was in the air. It was one of those spring evenings, redolent of the rich summer to come, that made a man feel glad to be alive. Without thinking, Toby laughed, a soft, gentle laugh.

"What are you laughing at?" asked his companion.

"Because I'm happy," he answered truthfully.

Agatha's hand touched his arm as they crossed a rough spot in the roadway, and he felt the pressure of her fingers as she balanced herself. This brief physical contact excited him, and made him bold.

"Miss Rowden," he said politely, "may I call you Agatha?"

"I like Agatha better than Miss Rowden," she replied.

"And I like to be called Toby," he said. "I hate being addressed as Mr. Giles." Somehow, he no longer felt there was any hint of condescension when she used his first name.

47

"Then I shall call you Toby," Agatha said, laughing pleasantly. "And I'm glad, Toby, that you are coming to the singing. It will be a chance for you to meet some nice people."

"I'm with the nicest person in town right now," said Toby. Agatha caught her breath. "Mr. Giles—Toby—I'm not used to such bold compliments."

"You'll have to get used to them, Agatha," he announced. "I could spend the night paying you compliments." He glanced at Agatha, seeing her face bathed in moonlight, and detected the excitement which he had inspired. Agatha was shy, he knew, and inexperienced in romance. Moreover, she was a good woman, carefully reared, but Toby intuitively sensed that the things he had said made her heart beat faster and her blood run warm, and he knew from the way she smiled at him that she was not displeased by his bold approach.

At the church, Agatha joined the ladies, while Toby found a seat midway back, where he could listen to the rehearsal and watch Agatha. He found himself completely enthralled by the singing of these pioneer women, which had a quality he had never encountered in music before. The primitive, untrained voices had a plaintive sweetness that was soothing to the ear and satisfying to the heart, and though the songs were sometimes melancholy, the chorus somehow conveyed a message of exhilarating hope, a positive and lyrical expression of the aspiration that sustained the frontiersman and his family, the confidence in the future that would witness a new world rising from the wilderness. Toby found himself enraptured as he followed Agatha's tender but strong voice carrying the lead melody. A physical and spiritual expression of strength made her face radiant, and her evident happiness touched Toby's heart.

When the singing was over, Toby was introduced to a dozen ladies and their escorts, but he was still so affected by the music that he scarcely caught their names. Walking slowly home beside Agatha in the moonlight, he listened to his companion hum one of the hymns. The stars were out, and the sky seemed very close.

"I like you, Agatha," he said. "I like everything about you. The way you look, the way you sing, the way you smile, the way you hold your head in the air. I like you better than anyone I have ever met."

"Even better than the girls in Virginia?"

Toby's blush was hidden by the dim light. "Much better," he said.

Agatha laughed gently. "You are easily pleased, sir."

"Not me," Toby answered. "I'm hard to please and you suit me down to the ground."

"I like you too, Toby. Or I wouldn't have asked you to escort me tonight."

"The more I see of you," Toby said, "the more I know that I want you for my wife."

Agatha's gasp was audible. "Mr. Giles!" she exclaimed. "Now you are too bold."

Toby stopped, and they stood in the moonlight. The silver glow made Agatha's face radiant, and Toby thought that he had never seen anything more lovely. He moved toward her a little. "Your father told me this wasn't any country for a timid man, and I'm taking his advice. My intentions are honorable. I want you for my wife. And you will never be sorry," he promised. "I know that I am going to make good."

Agatha listened, excited and a little frightened by the vibrant assurance in Toby's voice, the drive and energy that came into his tone when he spoke of the future. In a moment she was in his arms and he kissed her on the mouth. For an instant she responded, then pushed him away with such firmness that Toby knew better than to try to hold her. She stepped forward and began to walk rapidly toward her house, breathing quickly, saying nothing. Toby was immediately at her side.

"I didn't mean to frighten you, Agatha," he said. "A man

49

doesn't want to hurt the woman he's going to marry. I just couldn't help myself. You looked so pretty, there in the moonlight."

"You'll have to give me time to think," she said nervously. "And I'll have to tell father."

"If you tell Stoge I kissed you," Toby said calmly, "be sure you tell him I want to marry you. I'm not ready to die yet."

They reached the house and said good night. Toby made no effort to kiss her again, and took his leave formally, in a voice loud enough for Stoge to hear, for he guessed that the storekeeper was waiting up for his daughter. Agatha hurried into the house and Toby went slowly home, walking as though he trod on the clouds, filled with a sensation of triumph, for he knew that while Agatha had pushed him away, she had not been offended by the fact that he had kissed her, and in the brief instant when their lips touched, he had been aware of the passion that lurked beneath the surface, waiting only to be quickened to life by the man she loved. That man, he was determined, would be Toby Giles, frontiersman, former Virginian, future aristocrat.

9.

Bound westward on another lap of their tortuous journey toward extinction, another caravan of Indians drifted into Washington, well supplied with government paper and good American dollars. The old chief who led them traveled with a young Negro slave. Owl Eye, the chief, was erect and proud, despite his gaunt frame and ragged clothes. He admitted to Toby that he was frightened of the wilderness to the west, which he thought of as a realm darkened by bad black spirits and haunted by ghosts, a region too far from the Land of the Rising Sun. He valued his Negro slave, Josh, for he thought the intelligent young black man might converse with the ghosts and spirits and help to appease them.

Toby made it his business to get to know Josh, to "make friends" with the Negro in that curious fashion, guided by instinct on both sides, in which a white man became the friend of a black. Josh had learned much from the Indians, but he had not succumbed to their slothful ways, being neat and clean, with the strength of an ox, moving with the silent, graceful stealth of an Indian. He hung around Stoge's store, for he admired Toby and was always willing to do odd jobs to pay for the privilege of talking with the white man.

"I don't hanker for that New Land," he observed cautiously one day. "I sho' ain't itchin' to go theah with no Indian, neither. I ruther stay here with you all."

"Looks like you got to go, Josh," Toby pointed out. "Old Owl Eye is your master. He owns you."

A sudden appeal came into the slave's voice. "Buy me, Marse Toby. Let me stay with you. I'm a good worker. You know that. Buy me."

Toby looked into the slave's eyes. He had a genuine affection for the strong, intelligent black man, and Josh had not exaggerated when he said he was a good worker. With a white man for master, Josh could be made into a useful, productive slave. But he was worth, perhaps, a thousand dollars. Toby shook his head. "I can't buy you, Josh. I haven't got the money. I just work for Stoge Rowden."

Josh didn't answer, but went on doing odd jobs. A few hours later, Toby found him in his room, cleaning his saddle and bridle.

"What are you doing with that?" Toby demanded.

Josh looked up and grinned with a flash of white teeth. "Mighty fine saddle, Marse Toby. With a little trimmin' it could be mighty flashy."

"It's flashy enough for me now," said Toby curtly.

But Josh just grinned; he understood his white men, as Toby understood his blacks. "Marse Toby, with some of them red buttons on the bridle and some of them silver doodads on the saddle, this rig sho' would catch some Indian's eye."

"That saddle's too damn good for an Indian," said Toby.

"Yes, sah!" Josh said. "And Josh is too good a nigger for any Indian."

Toby grinned, understanding what Josh had in mind. "Do you reckon old Owl Eye will like it?"

"Marse Toby," Josh said conclusively, "Marse Toby, us'n can fix up this saddle so old Owl Eye jus' *got* to have it. Ah knows him. He likes them red buttons and fancy tassels. Ah c'n make them tassels out of rope."

"You make the tassels, Josh. I got the red buttons. Hell, we got purple, blue, and yellow ones too. We'll use 'em all."

"When us gets it fixed, I'll show it off to him, slow an' easy. Then you swap with him, Marse Toby, this saddle for me."

This was a scheme Toby liked. He would acquire a Negro man slave, giving him prestige, and at the same time he would get rid of a saddle and bridle that dredged up uncomfortable Virginia memories every time he used them. "Get it fixed up, Josh," he said. "We'll see if the old bastard will trade."

A few days later Josh displayed the resplendent saddle and bridle to the old Indian. Toby broke one of Stoge's strictest rules and gave Josh a jug of firewater to use as an aid to trading. Josh understood old Owl Eye and pretended indifference when his master stared at the saddle. He gave Owl Eye a stiff drink of firewater, and left the jug where the Indian could help himself, waiting until Owl Eye was pleasantly mulled and slightly befuddled before picking up the saddle. "Gotta put Marse Toby's saddle away," Josh said.

The Indian touched the fine leather with his fingertips. "Heap pretty saddle," he grunted. "Me like. Me buy."

Josh gave Owl Eye another drink. "Marse Toby no sell," he advised. "Mebbe Marse Toby trade for me."

Toby remained at a distance while Josh fed the old man liquor. When Owl Eye seemed ready, Josh winked and Toby approached the slave and his master.

"Fine saddle," he said. "Worth much money."

"Me ride saddle once," said Owl Eye. "Me like. But me need Josh, talk to black men in New Land."

"There are no black men in New Land," said Toby. "You don't need Josh, and you do need saddle." Toby handed the chief a tin cup filled with brandy, thinking that the brandy, mixed with the white lightning Owl Eye had been drinking, would surely soften up the old man.

"Need horse for saddle," the chief haggled.

Toby agreed. "I'll trade you the bridle, saddle, and fancy blanket, and I'll throw in a good horse to boot."

Josh led out Toby's horse, placing one of Stoge's bright-colored blankets on the bay's back, then topping it with the heavy saddle, resplendent with trimming. The old Indian walked unsteadily around the animal, feeling its legs, looking for spavin, but unable to take his eyes from the gorgeous saddle on the horse's back.

"Me take," he decided, his tongue thick with liquor. "You take Josh."

Toby turned to the slave quickly. "Josh," he commanded, "run down the street to the square log hut and ask the justice of the peace to come up here."

Squire Tatum, portly and red of face, town barber and justice of the peace, drew the necessary papers. The bill of sale described Josh as having three healed gashes across the back, one hole in the left ear, one toe—the second on the right foot—missing, and listed him as thirty years of age, five feet eleven inches tall, with a very black skin. Toby held Owl

Eye's hand and helped the Indian make his mark, then the squire witnessed the signatures. It took Toby, the squire, and Josh to hoist the chief into the saddle. The Indian had just ridden away when Stoge arrived.

"You just missed seein' Toby here make a whang-dang trade," said Tatum.

"How's that?" asked Stoge.

"Just traded his horse, saddle, and bridle for Josh."

Stoge's eyes wandered over the frame of the powerful Negro, and he complimented Toby. "You've got yourself a strong, healthy slave," he said. Stoge admired men who were sharp traders; he was impressed with Toby's energy and aggressiveness, and Toby knew that Agatha would hear that night of his fortunate trade. In the few minutes since the papers had been signed, he noted already the hint of deference Squire Tatum displayed toward him as a slave-holder. He didn't want deference from Stoge, but he wanted respect, and he was sure he was on the way to getting it.

Stoge seemed to be granting his daughter more liberty since the night of the church singing, for she came into town several times a week. Stoge seemed not to object to the growing friendship between her and Toby, and as the spring passed they found more opportunities to be together, though rarely were the circumstances as fortunate for Toby as on that moonlit night when he had kissed her. Twice he tried to repeat the performance, but each time she was on guard and rebuffed him firmly. Nevertheless, he knew that she was becoming more and more fond of him, and he was content to wait, for the prize was worth it.

One day in late spring he put it flatly up to Stoge. "Mr. Rowden," he said, "I'm afraid I don't know how to go about courtin', but I'm plumb in love with Miss Agatha, and I guess she knows it. I'd like your permission to court your daughter."

There was a twinkle in Stoge's eye. "Appears to me you've

54

been courtin' her without my permission," he observed, taking out his familiar pipe. "At least you been mighty friendly."

"Maybe I have," Toby said. "I couldn't help it. I love Agatha." As Toby uttered the words, he knew in his heart that they were the truth. He was completely, overwhelmingly in love with the tall, placid, deep-eyed girl, and he realized that he would have wanted to marry her even if she had not been Stoge Rowden's only child, who stood to inherit Rowden's money.

"Sit down, Toby," Stoge said, puffing at his pipe, and pausing before he observed, "You know you ain't fittin' to be Agatha's husband."

"Maybe I ain't," Toby conceded. "But I love her just the same, and I aim to marry her, with your permission."

"Toby," Stoge said reflectively, "that girl's all I got. She means a lot to me, and I ain't aimin' to let her make a mistake in the man she chooses."

"I'd try to make her a good husband," Toby promised.

"Try hell!" Stoge exploded. "The man that marries Agatha *better* make her a good husband, or have me to talk to. And I can be mighty mean when the occasion calls for it."

"You can depend on me," Toby said.

Stoge shook his head, looking off into the distance at a smoke trail from a cabin chimney, far beyond the edge of town. "I don't know, Toby," he said finally. "I'll have to think it over."

A customer came into the store and Toby busied himself filling his order. When he finished, Stoge had gone. He wasn't worried. Stoge was not a man who made quick decisions. He would sleep on the problem and talk it over with Agatha, Toby knew, and his hopes were based on the fact that Stoge respected him. And Agatha—well, he liked to think that Agatha loved him.

That evening, just as Toby was closing the store, Squire Tatum stopped by, having passed the afternoon shooting in the brush. The justice of the peace had a dozen partridges in his bag, and invited Toby to join him for a quail supper at the tavern. The squire wore a coonskin cap at a jaunty angle; he was a good storyteller, with much of the actor in his make-up. He and Toby partook freely of Stoge's best brandy while Josh cleaned the birds, and when they departed for the tavern, Toby tucked a bottle under his arm.

"You and Agatha'r gettin' mighty chummy, ain't you?" asked the squire, when they were seated at a table in the tavern.

Toby reddened. "Agatha ain't a woman for flap-lipped tavern talk, squire. You know that."

"Don't be so touchy," the squire chuckled. "I didn't mean no offense. No reason to act like you'd swallowed a cactus."

"Miss Agatha's a fine lady," Toby declared rather pompously.

"Who in tarnation said she wasn't?" asked the squire. "I've knowed her since she was in didies."

Mention of this intimate detail caused Toby to choke on a quail bone. Squire Tatum pounded him on the back to help relieve his coughing; when the fit was over, he laughed and said, "Don't blame you for courtin' Stoge's daughter. You'll never find a finer woman than Agatha. Here, or in Virginia."

Mention of Virginia embarrassed Toby; he was not anxious to discuss his past, preferring to keep it vague and mysterious and aristocratic. The camaraderie encouraged by Stoge's brandy was gone, and when he had finished his sixth quail, Toby excused himself.

"What's your hurry, son?" asked the squire in a disappointed tone. "Night's young yet." Toby knew that the older man had looked forward to an evening's drinking and yarning; earlier, that would have appealed to him too, but now he had no stomach for it.

"Gonna get some shut-eye," Toby said. "I'm dogged out."

He left the brandy bottle on the table for Squire Tatum to

finish and went outside into the seductive early-summer night. He couldn't resist the temptation to walk by Stoge Rowden's house; the lights were still burning in the parlor and he knew that Stoge and his daughter were sitting up, Stoge with his pipe, Agatha with her sewing. It was past their customary bedtime, and Toby would have given almost anything he owned to have listened in on the conversation, for he was certain they were talking about him and his request for Agatha's hand. The cheerful glow of the lighted window made him feel lonely and forlorn in the darkness. He was tempted to be brazen and knock on the door, but his good judgment dissuaded him, for he reasoned that the hour was too late and that the whiff of brandy on his breath would not be the best recommendation for an ardent suitor to offer his prospective bride and her father.

The next day Stoge came down to the store early, but he was closemouthed and meditative, not speaking to Toby except on business matters. Late in the afternoon, Toby could restrain himself no longer, and he blurted out without prelude, "What does Miss Agatha say?"

Stoge looked at Toby with a glint in his eyes. "That's for me to know and you to find out," he said. He walked back into the store and poured himself a stiff drink of Monongahela whiskey. Never before had Toby known his employer to take a drink in the store. He knew that Stoge was under pressure, and was cautious enough not to question him further. Twice more Stoge visited the Monongahela barrel, and just before he left for home he said to Toby, "Maybe you'd better come over to the house tonight and talk to Agatha yourself."

Toby's heart leaped. He desperately wanted to ask Stoge what the verdict had been, and only great effort restrained him. "What time?" he said.

"After supper," the storekeeper answered.

As soon as Stoge was out of sight, Toby closed the store and hurried downstreet to Squire Tatum's.

"I want a shave and a haircut," he told the squire. "And put a little bay rum and bear grease on my hair, so's it'll lay flat." He examined himself in the mirror. "Better give me a shave first, though," he said, rubbing his chin.

The squire chuckled. "You're wastin' money shavin', son. That peach fuzz on your chin won't show at night."

"Don't make no difference," insisted Toby. "I want a shave and I want you to massage my upper lip. Maybe that'll help the whiskers grow."

Though Toby's fresh, rosy complexion gave him an attractive, youthful appearance, he was ashamed of it, and longed for a dark, wiry beard that would make him look older, more suited to his role of young businessman and slaveholder. He watched himself in the mirror while the squire lathered his face.

"Boy, you're really gettin' spruced," Tatum said.

"I got important business tonight," answered Toby darkly. "Got to look right."

When the squire had shaved Toby and cut his hair, he rubbed the perfumed bear grease into his scalp, then combed down Toby's cowlick. "Boy, you look slick as owl grease," he said, admiring his own handiwork. Toby regarded himself in the mirror and agreed. He went back to the store and scrubbed himself, then dressed in his Sunday clothes. Josh rubbed beef tallow into his boots and buffed them until they shone like glass. He helped Toby with his coat, then gave him a good brushing.

"Marse Toby," he said admiringly, "yo' sho' looks fit to knock 'em over."

Toby answered his slave with a grin. "I hope so, Josh. I hope so."

Stoge and Agatha waited for him in the cheerful parlor lighted softly by four large candles, Agatha sitting near a table where the favorable golden glow of a candle illuminated her face. Toby had never before noticed her long, fine lashes, but he observed them now as they were caught in the light.

She was wearing a fetching, simple dress with a touch of lace at the throat, and looked so desirable that Toby for a moment was overwhelmed and felt a lump rising in his throat as he made his greeting.

Stoge rose and offered Toby a chair, then went to the hearth and knocked out the dottle from his pipe. "It's past my bedtime," he observed. "I'll leave you young folks to visit. But don't say up too late."

After Stoge left the room, Toby fidgeted uncomfortably in his chair for a few minutes, then coughed and said awkwardly, "I guess you know I asked Stoge if I could marry you," blurting out the words in a rush, then sitting as though he had turned to stone, hardly breathing, with a prickly sensation running up and down his spine as he waited for Agatha's comment.

Agatha sat with her eyes downcast, toying with the whisp of cambric handkerchief in her lap, rolling it into a little ball, then unrolling and rolling it again. Finally, without looking up, she said, "Are you sure you wouldn't rather marry one of those Virginia belles?"

Toby crossed the room and rested on one knee beside her. "Miss Rowden—Agatha," he said soberly, "there's no one else on this earth I want to marry but you. And I knew that 'most from the first time I saw you."

The color rose to her cheeks and the sound of her breathing was audible in the quiet room. Beneath the stiff bodice of her dress, Toby saw her bosom rise and fall rapidly. He touched her hand and she jerked it away quickly, as though from a fire.

"You haven't said you would marry me," Toby said. "I wish you would. I love you, and I'll make you a good husband."

She seemed frightened, and Toby saw that her eyes were glued to the fawnskin curtain that screened off Stoge's room from the parlor. He suspected that Stoge was listening to everything being said between them, and that Agatha knew it. That would account for her reluctance to display emotion.

"I'll give you my answer in a few days, Toby," she said at last. "I must be sure."

"Don't keep me waiting," Toby pleaded. "Tell me now."

She smiled warmly, and something in her smile told him that the answer, when he got it, would be yes, though all she said was, "Not tonight, Toby. I won't be rushed." She paused, smiling at him again. "And you'd better be getting on to the store. Pa won't sleep a wink till he knows I'm in bed."

Toby got to his feet and Agatha walked with him to the porch. A full, round, pervading moon was high in the heavens, bathing the lush countryside with a rich golden glow that seemed liquid. The winelike summer air was heady, intoxicating. The young couple stood on the porch for several minutes, caught and entranced by the beauty of the night. Then Toby took Agatha in his arms and kissed her slowly, feeling her hand tighten on his shoulder as she responded to his kiss, feeling, as their lips met, an exhilaration at once noble and unbearably exciting, and in those few seconds that he held Agatha he felt, somehow, that he possessed her utterly, body and soul. He released her gently and their eyes met, understanding coming to both of them at the same instant. Then Agatha stepped back a few inches and said quietly, "Good night, Toby. Sleep well."

"Good night, Agatha." Some impulse prompted him to take her hand for a moment and kiss it quickly. Then he vaulted from the porch and walked quickly toward the town. His heart was pounding with excitement, and he was exultant over his success. He had been in Washington only five months. Not long ago he had been nothing but a bound boy in the Tidewater, a contemptible dock rat spawned on the Norfolk water front, offered a crust and a secondhand coat. Tonight he was a man of parts, with a future that shone in the distance like pure gold. He had a good job and a hundred and sixty dollars in his pocket. He owned a thousand-dollar slave. He was about to marry the daughter of the richest man in town, and in addition to the fact that she would one day make him wealthy, he was madly, tantalizingly in love with her, and she with him. There were few young men on the frontier who had reason to feel his confidence.

When he reached the store he found Josh curled up on the porch, asleep. He nudged the slave and woke him. "Take the bucket and get some fresh water, Josh," he said. "I'm thirsty."

Josh crossed to the well in front of the tavern and returned with a bucket of cool water. Toby drank, slaking his dry throat. He had been thirsty, but the real reason he woke Josh was because he had to have someone to talk with.

"Josh," he said, "I'm going to marry Mr. Rowden's daughter. So you'll have a mistress as well as a master."

The slave beamed. "Tha's fine, Marse Toby. Jus' fine. Cato, he tell me Miss Agatha, she one fine lady."

"Cato knows quality when he sees it," Toby observed. He paused, contemplating the heavy shoulder muscles of his slave. The Negro was his property, as much his chattel as the coat on his back or the dollars in his pocket. He could beat him, or sell him, or chain him like a dog. He could find a black woman and breed Josh like an animal. Yet somehow, paradoxically, Josh was his friend as well as his slave, and it seemed perfectly fitting that Josh should be the first person to know of Toby's contemplated marriage.

"Josh," Toby said ruminatively, "I've made a deal for you to work for Mr. James Beck. He's the best farmer in these parts, and I want you to keep your eyes peeled and see just how he does things. Then when I have my own place you'll know how to raise good crops."

Josh nodded. "Tha's a good idea, Marse Toby."

"James Beck is good to his slaves," Toby said. "I expect he'll be good to you, but if he isn't, you let me know and I'll bring you home."

They went through the store to Toby's room, and Josh knelt on the floor to pull off Toby's boots. "When I get married," Toby said, "you can move into Mr. Rowden's quarters. I'll keep track of the days you work for him, so when I get my own place he can pay me back with work from his slaves."

"Cato says Marse Stoge is a kind master and a knowin' man, a mighty fine farmer.

"Cato is plenty smart," agreed Toby. "You watch him and learn a lot about farming. One of these days, Josh, I'm going to be the biggest farmer in this part of the country, and I'm countin' on you to help me."

"I knows you is, Marse Toby. Me and Cato is both goin' to help you."

"Mr. James Beck is not only a good farmer. He's the best blacksmith in these parts, too. You watch him and learn how he does it, so you can sharpen my plows and tools when we get started."

"I's a man what keeps his eyes open an' his mouth shut, Marse Toby."

"Be sure you do," Toby warned. "Ain't no reason anyone should know how I got you in that trade."

When Stoge unlocked the store next morning, Toby and Josh were still asleep. Toby heard his employer moving about and leaped from his bed, giving Josh a hard poke in the ribs. "Don't you ever let me oversleep again!" he said, raising his voice so that Stoge would be sure to hear him. But when he had hurried into his clothes and gone out to greet him, Stoge had been unconcerned. "Toby, I'm going to be gone all day," he said. "Keep everything in the middle of the road." He took two lengths of plowline and left. Toby scrubbed his face and went across the street for his breakfast.

At noon Squire Tatum stopped by the store. Washington, of course, was too small to have a newspaper, but it had Squire Tatum. The justice of the peace made it his business to keep abreast of the news and to disperse it. "Well, Toby," he said cheerfully, "Are you plannin' on a weddin'?" The squire's eyes were still bloodshot and his face was puffy, indicating that he had finished the bottle of brandy Toby left on the tavern table.

"Not yet, squire," Toby said, knowing better than to give Tatum any information he didn't want spread around. "Agatha don't know for sure she wants me."

The squire laughed. "Boy," he said, "I'll never forget the night I got married. My wife's folks didn't have much of a house. Just one big room for sleepin' an' eatin' and a lean-to for cookin'. The big room had three beds, with just thin cotton curtains between 'em. Me an' my wife slept in the middle bed, an' her folks had just stuffed the tick with fresh corn shucks. I ain't never heard such noisy shucks. Every time I moved in the bed, you could hear them shucks from here to Memphis." The squire laughed long and loud at his own story, and Toby couldn't help joining him. Then the squire sobered and said, "You'll be a lucky dog if you get Agatha, Toby. There's a fine girl."

"I ain't got her yet, squire," Toby said.

But in his heart he knew that wasn't so. Late in the afternoon, Agatha came down to the store, ostensibly to do some shopping. Between them there was a tension almost unbearable to Toby, and he noticed that Agatha's hand trembled. But he said nothing until, showing her a particularly beautiful piece of satin he had held out from the new shipment, he looked into her eyes and observed, "Here's something for your wedding dress. It'll look beautiful on you."

She blushed and ran the tips of her fingers over the lustrous, rich fabric. "It is beautiful," she agreed. She paused, tapping nervously with her foot, then said, "I talked with father again this morning."

Toby made an effort to be calm. "What—what did he say?"

Agatha laughed, and suddenly the tension was broken. "He said if I was determined to marry you, we might as well get it over with."

63

Toby wanted to whoop for joy, and a huge grin lighted his face. He leaned across the counter and kissed her, then held her hand. "When will it be, honey?" he asked.

"Sunday after next?" Agatha suggested, falteringly. "You'd better see the preacher."

"I'll see him today," Toby promised.

Agatha withdrew her hand. "All right, Toby," she said. "And now I'd better get back home."

"But you haven't ordered anything," Toby protested.

She was at the door, where she turned, blushing again. "I didn't want anything, silly," she said. "Except you." Then she was gone; Toby stood stock-still, his hands resting on the counter, staring at the empty doorway. A customer came into the store, but Toby didn't hear him, and the man rapped loudly on the counter to attract attention, bellowing, "What's the matter there, Giles? You look as if you was a thousand miles away."

Toby sprang to attention, apologizing. "Sorry, mister," he explained. "I was thinkin'."

The settler guffawed. "Thinkin' about Stoge Rowden's daughter, I bet," he said, with a knowing wink. Toby looked him squarely in the eye, and the look was almost a challenge, for Toby's chin took on a stubborn line.

"That's right," he said, "I was. Miss Rowden and I aim to be married Sunday after next, so I guess I got a right to think about her."

"Waal!" The settler's jaw dropped. "Waal!" he said. "You move mighty fast, don't you, Giles?"

"Fast enough to get where I'm goin'," answered Toby curtly. "What can I do for you now?" He was glad the news was out; in an hour almost everyone in the frontier community would know that he and Agatha were pledged. The tongues would be wagging, and many a jealous young buck would insist that what made Agatha attractive to Toby was the size of her father's holdings. But Toby didn't care what they said; he noticed the increased respect showed him by the settler after the man learned the news, and he knew that by marrying Agatha he would acquire automatically a share of Stoge's prestige, which was greater than that of any other man in town.

That night he could not sleep, but tossed about on his cowhide cot, his brain feverish with excitement, and he was relieved when the first pink streaks of dawn showed in the east. He had the store swept and dusted before Stoge arrived.

"Well, Toby," his employer said. "Agatha tells me you two have decided to get hitched."

"Yes, sir," Toby said. "Sunday after next, if you don't object."

Stoge sat down on a barrelhead, caressing the bowl of his cold pipe. "When I was a young buck," he said, "if two young folks wanted to get married, they just went to their paw and maw and talked it over. If the parents didn't object, they just became man and wife. Sometimes they read a few Scriptures from the Bible, but more'n likely they just killed a hog and had a big feed, and maybe a little wine. Then the young couple went on to bed. Them kind of marriages stuck, too. Just as tight as newfangled weddings, with a preacher and all."

"Marryin's new to me," said Toby. "However way Agatha wants is all right."

"Daughter's bound and determined on a Bible-readin', prayer-preachin' church weddin'. So I reckon you better make the arrangements for the church. Sunday's a good day, and waitin' over one Sunday will give daughter a chance to make a new dress. Might be you'll want a new suit, too."

Toby nodded. The next day he took a length of Stoge's black broadcloth to the town's one pay seamstress, since Washington boasted no men's tailor, and she agreed to make him a suit, using his old one for a pattern. Agatha's wedding dress was being made from the satin Toby had selected. He and Agatha, Toby guessed, would be the best-dressed bride and groom the frontier town had ever seen.

10.

Stoge cried at the wedding. The big, strong frontiersman was overcome when Agatha and Toby walked up the aisle of the little church and stood before the minister. He had given his life to his daughter, his only child, and now he was handing her over to a young man from Virginia about whom he knew very little beyond the fact that he was ambitious, possessed a canny head for business, and was loved devotedly by his bride. There must have been a moment during the solemn ceremony, Toby knew, when Stoge's doubts rose in his throat and prompted him to cry out against the marriage that meant he would lose his child, and as he watched Stoge's eyes, damp with tears, Toby resolved to be so good a husband that Stoge would never have cause to regret the match.

The wedding itself was private, but Washington's leading citizens and their wives turned out en masse for the reception that followed. James Beck brought his fiddle-playing slave, and Cato enlivened the occasion with his banjo. Josh served the drinks and was kept at a trot, bearing a pitcher filled with Stoge's best brandy. Linda, Cato's woman, looked after the food and saw that the table was covered with an abundance of refreshments. Stoge's house was filled with people, and the sturdy rafters shook with the music and the peals of hilarious laughter generated by the brandy and the festive spirit of the day.

Toby saw that Squire Tatum was getting pretty well liquored up, and with a momentary pang he envied the justice of the peace, but he himself drank moderately and was careful of his manners and language, eager to impress both Agatha and the guests with his gentility. Even the strait-laced parson should find no fault with his conduct. He mingled with the guests, complimenting the ladies with artful reticence, assuming a manly tone of affairs with their husbands, keeping Josh on the jump with the brandy. At ten he saw Stoge yawn, and knew that his father-in-law was tired. But Stoge stuck it out until midnight, when, with more frontier candor than diplomacy, he let the company know that the party was over. When the last guest had departed, Toby and Agatha went into the kitchen to receive the blessings of the slaves, assembled there by Cato. Toby saw to it that some of the brandy was taken to the slave quarters so that the Negroes could have their own celebration; he wanted to start right with Stoge's slaves, and though he was impatient and anxious to be alone with his bride, he waited courteously until Cato had concluded his flowery speech. He and Agatha stood in the doorway, watching the slaves go back to their quarters. The bright moonlight played on her face, and Toby caught her in his arms and kissed her, then stood awkwardly for a moment, not knowing what to say. He was consumed with desire for her, yet too embarrassed to take the initiative. In the end it was Agatha who said, "I'll go to my room now, Toby. Give me a few minutes to get ready." There was a soft, purring excitement in her voice which tantalized him. His throat contracted so that he could hardly answer, and when she had gone he could not stand still, but paced up and down outside in the moonlight impatiently, ticking off the minutes, then finally turning and entering the house.

The candles in Agatha's room were covered with hand-embroidered shades, softening the light. Agatha stood beside the heavy bedstead, wearing a simple, straight nightdress; her long blue-black hair was down and fell loosely about her shoulders, destroying the almost prim effect it gave when done up, and making her look extremely feminine and soft. A rush of tenderness possessed Toby when he saw her, and he crossed the room to her slowly, taking her in his arms very gently, astonished, almost shocked, for an instant by the soft, seductive contours of her body which his hands felt beneath the thin fabric of the nightdress. Her lips were warm and moist when he kissed her, and she responded eagerly, clutching him to her breasts. All knowledge of women seemed to begin for him at this moment, with this virginal girl who was his bride, and as he caressed her, his passion rising, a wave of shame swept over him, for he remembered momentarily, then thrust from his mind, the hot, squalid room in The Gut in Memphis where he had lain with the little whore.

"Toby," Agatha said. "Look on the dresser. There's a present for you." Her voice was shy. Toby unwrapped the package he found on the dresser; it contained a hand-sewn nightshirt. He kissed Agatha, then blew out the candles and hurriedly drew off his clothes. He climbed into the bed beside her, and could not help recalling Squire Tatum's account of his wedding night on the corn-shuck mattress. The bed beneath him was stuffed with goose down, soft and silent. He turned on his side and put his arms around his wife, then his hands sought her body, reaching under her nightdress, his blood tingling with excitement as his fingertips touched her warm, naked flesh. She turned in the darkness and he realized that she was crying. "Toby, Toby," she said softly. "Be good to me, darling. Please be good to me."

She cried again, afterward, sitting up in the bed, but they were tears of gladness, tears for her maidenhood, and Toby, in the bed beside her, knew that she was happy and proud to be a woman and a wife.

The next morning, at breakfast, watching the quiet efficiency with which Linda served the fried venison, scrambled eggs, and hot bread, the assured way in which Agatha poured the coffee, the general atmosphere of snugness, Toby suddenly realized that he had never actually been a member of a family before. He remembered the shanties of his childhood, each meal a grabfest, and contrasted that wild, rough life with the serenity he felt at Stoge's table. Stoge said grace, bowing his head reverently. "Heavenly Father, we thank Thee for this food and for all Thy mercies. Forgive our sins and bless this new member of our family. We pray for Thy guidance for this young couple. Lead them into a life of peace and happiness. Amen."

Toby had heard Stoge say grace before, but this prayer touched him more than any he had ever heard; Stoge's voice was humble and appealing, endowing the simple words with solemnity. During breakfast, several times, Toby saw Stoge looking curiously at his daughter, as though he expected some miraculous change to have taken place. Indeed, the change had occurred, thought Toby, remembering the passionate consummation of their love the night before, but outwardly Agatha was the same, placid and poised, presiding over the table with habitual grace.

Linda stopped at Toby's place, her face aglow with pride. "Marse Toby," she said, "we wants you to be good to our chile." The slave woman had reared Agatha; she had five children of her own, but none was dearer to her than Stoge Rowden's daughter.

"Linda doesn't mean to be impertinent, Toby," Agatha said, when Toby hesitated after the slave's remark. "She looks upon me as her very own."

Toby grinned and nodded. "I'll be good to her, Linda. Don't you worry."

There was warmth in the old Negro woman's voice as she answered, warmth and real affection that made Toby glad in his heart. "I knows you will, Marse Toby. I jus' *knows* you will."

Walking down to the store with Stoge, greeting the settlers and townsmen on the way, Toby was aware of his new importance. He was no longer merely a hired hand at Stoge Rowden's store, a young buck in from Virginia, with wild dreams in his head, who might be off with the next caravan to Texas, leaving a girl of the town in trouble, or taking the contents of the till with him. He was now a solid citizen, a member of Stoge's household, Stoge's son-in-law, and the next thing to being the partner of the richest, most influential, and most respected man in the community. He talked farming with Stoge, who seemed surprised that his son-in-law knew so much about the land. Toby was not bluffing here. During his years on the Maison Plantation he had kept his eyes open, learning much about farming, and this knowledge served him well now, for Stoge was impressed.

During the hot, sweet days of summer that remained, Toby made himself as useful on the farm as at the store, bossing slaves and looking after the fields as though they already belonged to him. He was happy, totally happy, for the first time in his life, though he was far from satisfied. In fact, the taste of authority and security made him thirst for more, and strengthened his resolve to make himself a rich man and an aristocrat.

His life with Agatha was congenial, and their passion did not dwindle, but rather increased in intensity, becoming a familiar thing and a delight to both of them. Agatha, while she lost not a trace of her modesty, discovered in herself an enormous capacity for love. Toby at first found this surprising, for he had not dreamed that under his wife's serene exterior there coursed so much physical vitality. From a virgin girl who trembled at the touch of his hand, Agatha became a warm-blooded woman as sure of herself in matters of love as she was in everything else that concerned her.

So the summer passed, and they lay together during the

short, hot nights, the fragrance of the blooming countryside perfuming their chamber, the gentle summer breezes whispering through the shards of the growing corn, and when fall came, and harvesttime, they knew one another as man and wife, and Toby Giles, the wharf rat from Norfolk, was happy with his choice and counted himself the luckiest man in Arkansas Territory.

11.

Colonel Samuel Withers rode into town on a Friday afternoon in late September, astride a prancing thoroughbred stallion. Both horse and rider attracted notice as soon as they reached the frontier town, for the proud-headed animal looked as out of place on the sandy street as a Parisian *grande dame*, and the colonel was obviously no frontiersman, dressed as he was in British riding clothes. Behind the colonel lumbered his train of three two-wheeled oxcarts, heavily laden with books and personal belongings. The colonel looked straight ahead, giving his horse free rein, but he was not unaware of the stares he occasioned and seemed to enjoy being the center of attention. He pulled in his horse at Stoge's store and dismounted gracefully, securing his stallion at the hitching rack. Stoge followed him into the store.

"Good afternoon," announced the colonel. "Am I addressing the proprietor of this establishment?"

Stoge scratched his head. "Guess that's me," he observed. "I own the place. What c'n I do for you?"

"I'll have a gallon of your finest whiskey. Your finest, mind you."

Stoge drew a gallon of Monongahela and took a twenty-dollar bill in payment. He examined the note carefully before he gave the stranger his change, then watched the colonel take a few sprigs of mint from his pocket and proceed to mix a mint julep.

"I was fortunate enough to find this mint," the colonel said absently, preoccupied with his task, "but ice is needed for the correct tempering of whiskey. An enterprising town such as Washington should have an icehouse. Ice is a part and parcel of civilization—that is, of civilized drinking. Warm whiskey is barbarous."

The colonel seemed pleased with his own iceless concoction, however. He sipped it, looked relieved, and took a deep pull at the glass, then sighed contentedly. "I am well pleased with the appearance of your town, sir. It is larger than I expected and more prosperous, more forward looking."

"You aimin' to go into business here?" asked Stoge, trying to hide his curiosity. Strangers like the colonel were rare in Washington, where most newcomers were farmers or woodsmen, homesteaders or Texas-bound pioneers.

The colonel removed his hat with a flourish. He seemed to have brightened after the drink. "Permit me to introduce myself, sir," he said. "I am Colonel Samuel Withers, attorney at law, late of Paducah in the state of Kentucky."

Stoge offered his hand. "Glad to meet you, colonel. I'm Stoge Rowden."

"Mr. Rowden, sir!" The colonel shook hands formally. "Is the tavern across the way your best hostelry?"

"If you mean lodginghouse, yes," Stoge replied. "The meals are good too."

"I shall require a place to stay temporarily, while I await a message from the nation's capital," the colonel said.

"Goin' to hang out your shingle here?" asked Stoge.

"Ah, perhaps. Perhaps," the colonel replied. "But the prac-

72

tice of law is merely incidental to my real business here. That is another matter entirely."

Stoge was impressed and mystified. The colonel finished his drink, thanked Stoge courteously for the information, and departed. A few minutes later Squire Tatum arrived, looking for information, pointing his nose like a hunting dog as he inquired, "Who was that august personage, Stoge? Friend of yours?"

"That was Samuel Withers, *Colonel* Samuel Withers, from Paducah, Kentucky."

"Thought he might be Stephen F. Austin, on his way back to Texas," said the squire. "He's sure got a mess of law books."

"He can keep his law books," remarked Stoge. "But I sure would like to have that stallion."

That night, at supper, the topic of conversation at every table in town was Colonel Withers, who appeared early next morning dressed in a suit of silk and black velvet and repaired to the courthouse, where he directed the unloading of his law books. Toby, who had been fascinated by Stoge's description of the newcomer, approached the elegant figure boldly.

"Excuse me for bothering you, colonel, while you're getting unpacked, but I want to welcome you to our town. I'm a Virginian, but I passed through Paducah on my way west."

"I am always honored to meet a Virginian," the colonel said graciously. "What is your name, young man?"

"Tobias Giles. I married Stoge Rowden's daughter. I believe you met Stoge yesterday at the store."

"Ah, yes, Rowden," the colonel said. "He sells good whiskey." The colonel's fragrant breath indicated that he had enjoyed an eye opener of Stoge's Monongahela. But his elegant clothing and aristocratic manner impressed Toby, who sensed that in some way this stranger, with his law books and thoroughbred horse and velvet suit, would affect his own destiny. He realized that the colonel was sizing him up, and decided not to be too familiar.

"I won't keep you now, colonel," he said. "However, if

there is anything I can do for you, any way I can be of assistance, please know that I will regard it as an honor if you call upon me." Toby spoke in his best Virginia accent, and bowed slightly from the waist. The colonel nodded.

"Thank you, my boy, thank you," he said. "It is most gratifying to find a little true Virginia courtesy here in the wilderness." He paused. "Of course, the first thing I must do is to purchase a desirable tract of ground and contract with someone to erect a suitable house for my family." He cleared his throat. "I'm not a woodsman, you know."

Toby smiled. "You won't find any housebuilders here, colonel," he advised. "Every fellow builds his own."

"There must be someone who will build a house for money," the colonel said.

"Maybe so," said Toby. "Maybe so."

He took his leave, walking down the street to Squire Tatum's, knowing that the justice of the peace would be able to tell him more about the colonel's business, if properly pumped, than he ever would get from the colonel himself.

"Squire, I've just come from the courthouse," he said. "Colonel Withers is unloading his law books there, and he's taken over one of the rooms for an office."

"You don't say," observed the squire.

"If I was the law and order around here," Toby chided, "I'd durn soon find out what right this feller has in the courthouse."

"Well, son," Tatum said benevolently, "when you want to know anything, you just come see the squire. That feller Withers is the new land agent. That is, he says he is, but his papers ain't come from Washington yet."

"You mean he'll have the sale of all this government land?" Toby asked.

"Well, he has a letter from his Kentucky senator, saying that the president was goin' to appoint him. So I guess he is."

"Hmmm," Toby said, "all that government land." He passed

74

the time of day with the squire, but his mind was elsewhere. If Colonel Withers had the sale of the government land, he would be one of the most powerful men in the area, and a man for Toby to be friends with, a man who could help him. All that afternoon, waiting on trade and doing his chores around the store, he cudgeled his brains for a plan that would ingratiate him with Withers. Just before he closed up, an idea struck him and he snapped his fingers with delight.

Next morning he sought out the colonel, who was now established in a room in the courthouse lined with hundreds of yellow-backed law books. "Colonel, I've been thinking about that house you want built," he said, losing no time in getting to the point. "I think I can help you."

The colonel closed the book on his desk and looked at Toby. "How can you help me, young man?"

"Me and Stoge will build it for you, colonel," he announced boldly, though he had never in his life built so much as a rail fence. "We have some good workmen, who know how to hew logs, and I'd be glad to supervise the construction for you."

"That's mighty gracious of you, Mr. Giles," the colonel said. "Mighty gracious. We can get together on this."

"Good!" said Toby. "And when you get ready to talk business on this government land, there's some I'd like to have first shot at." He watched the colonel's face carefully, following this remark, for he thought he might have been a little too obvious. But Colonel Withers winked.

"If you help me get my house built, young man, I assure you that you can depend on first refusal of any land you want."

"Now, colonel," Toby said, "that's mighty fine of you, and I appreciate it."

"Not at all, Mr. Giles. Not at all. It's an old Kentucky custom, you know. You scratch my back, and I'll scratch yours."

"How big a house will you need?" Toby asked.

"About like the Rowden house," answered the colonel. "I

have one son and two daughters." He took a darkened tintype from his desk, carefully blowing away the film of dust that had collected on the lacquered surface, then passed it to Toby. "My family, sir," he explained, a note of genuine pride in his voice. Toby studied the picture, which showed a proud-looking mother, protectively surrounded by two attractive girls and a rather arrogant boy. In the background a white-porticoed mansion figured prominently. If that was the colonel's house, reflected Toby, then Withers must be a true aristocrat, for this house was as fine as the Maison Mansion. He handed the tintype back to the Kentuckian. "A fine family, colonel," he said. "Thank you."

"A pleasure, sir." The colonel rose and walked to the door with Toby, shaking his hand. "You build that house for me," he said, "and I'll see that you get your land. *Quid pro quo*, my boy. It's only fair."

Bursting with excitement that evening, Toby told Stoge and Agatha of his plan. Agatha's eyes gleamed as she listened to him talk, responding to the enthusiasm in his voice, but Stoge was doubtful.

"I'm all for having you get the land," Stoge said. "But housebuildin's not your line. How do you know you can do it?"

"I'm figurin' on buildin' me a house of my own pretty soon, and I might as well get some experience buildin' the colonel's," he said.

Stoge guffawed. "By cracky, that's right!" he said. "Might as well botch up his as your own."

"I don't figure on botching either of them," Toby said, looking straight at his father-in-law. There was no humor in his voice, but that grim, tough note of determination that fascinated and sometimes frightened Agatha. "I'll measure the logs in this house, your house, and have our niggers cut a set just like 'em. Then all I'll have to do is build the foundation and put the house together."

"Toby, that sounds smart!" Agatha admired. "But where will you get the timber?"

Toby smiled. "Well, since he's workin' for the government, I'm figurin' he won't mind if I cut it off government land."

Stoge shook his head. "By cracky, Toby," he said, "you're a sharp trader. Some day you'll own half of Arkansas Territory."

"What's the matter with the other half?" Toby said, laughing.

That night, after he and Agatha were in bed, Toby lay awake for hours, though his wife's peaceful breathing told him that she was asleep. This was his chance, he knew, his chance to become a landholder, his chance to take the first real step toward success. Outside, far away in the wilderness, a panther screamed, making a hideous sound, but Toby was not disturbed. He moved closer to his wife, feeling the soft, warm length of her body against his own, and put his arms around her, drawing her tightly to him. She half woke in the darkness and he kissed her, stroking her face. With her beside him he was content, without fear of the wilderness or the beasts in it, of the town or the men in it.

12.

"Damn! Hell! God! Cheat!" exclaimed the tall young Indian in broken English, continuing in his native tongue, "White man cheats Indian. This morning my brother bought same coat for ten dollars. Now white man wants fifteeen."

Josh interpreted the Indian's complaint; Toby, behind the counter, sized up the young brave, who was a member of another caravan moving through town, westward to the New Land. He could see that the Indian wanted the coat; since he sold the first mackinaw to Running Deer, the fame of the brilliantly colored garments had spread among the tribesmen until now every red man of importance felt that he must have one of Stoge Rowden's coats to protect his prestige in the New Land.

"Tell him I have just one coat left," Toby said to Josh. "I can't get any more, and if he don't want it at fifteen dollars, there will be someone else who will."

In Stoge's storeroom, packed in sturdy pine crates, was a new shipment of the colorful coats, but this was the only one on display. The Indian glanced at the shelves, then around the store, grudgingly conceding the apparent truth of Toby's statement. He took a rawhide moneybag from his belt and counted out fifteen dollars, roughly seizing the coat from Josh and walking quickly from the store, making the atmosphere bright blue with a string of artful English cuss words. Both Toby and Josh roared with laughter as soon as the door closed behind the Indian.

"Why in hell don't them Indians cuss in their own language?" Toby asked.

"The Indian languages don't have no cusswords, Marse Toby. They say they never had no need for 'em till the white mens come."

Toby was alone in the store while the Indian caravans were in town, with Josh to help him by interpreting the language, for Stoge conceded by now that his son-in-law was a master at dealing with the tribesmen and he kept to the farm when they were in town. Also, Stoge knew that Toby would use the tin box of counterfeit in making change for the Indians, and while he was delighted to get the queer stuff off his hands, he found that watching Toby pass it to the Indians troubled his conscience. Toby, of course, held back a percentage of what he made by passing the counterfeit; he found it so easy to use with the red men that he was worried when the box got low, and wished he had more of the stuff to distribute.

Some of the Indian caravans lay over in Washington for several weeks, fitting out for the journey westward. One day, after a group had been in town for a month, Josh came to Toby with a problem. The Negro stood with his hat in his hand, fumbling for words.

"Marse Toby, I'se got troubles," he said. "Powerful bad troubles, Marse Toby." The slave's eyes were downcast and he shifted nervously from one foot to the other.

"Must be woman trouble," Toby surmised, smiling at Josh.

"Yes, sah, Marse Toby. Woman troubles. Her name's Minnie. She's a Georgia nigger, an' one of them Indians here in town done bought her back in Georgia. He use her like his squaw, an' now she got two little girls, Marse Toby. But Minnie, she don' like Indians. Her Indian, he so mean, he got Minnie jus' tired of livin'."

"What do you want me to do, Josh?" Toby asked.

"Well, Marse Toby, Minnie, she doan' want to go to that New Land. She wants to stay here, Marse Toby. She want you to buy her and her children."

"Did you tell her how I bought you?" Toby said.

"Yes, sah. I tole her. She's a good worker, Marse Toby. Be a powerful help to Miss Giles."

Toby laughed. "And a good woman for you, eh, Josh?"

"Tha's right, Marse Toby. Sho' would."

Toby wanted more slaves and he knew that Josh needed a woman. He had a reserve of cash, but he wanted that as down payment on the government land he was going to get from Colonel Withers. He considered the problem for a moment, then said, "This caravan of Indians will be pulling out 'fore long. Minnie and the girls might get left behind."

79

"How you mean that, Marse Toby?" the slave asked.

"I think she can find friends on Stoge Rowden's farm," Toby explained. "They'd be willing to keep her and the children safe till the savages were too far away to make trouble."

Josh grinned his appreciation. "Thank you, Marse Toby," he said. "Minnie's going to be mighty happy. Mighty happy." He paused, then added, "Me too!"

Josh went back to his work. Toby leaned on the counter, thinking, a slight, reflective smile on his face. He had told Josh just enough; the slave would know what to do, and in a few days Toby's possessions would be augmented by the addition of a young Negro woman and two healthy children, several hundred dollars' worth of property, at a net cost to him of zero.

A few days later Colonel Withers sent for Toby. "My boy," the Kentuckian announced, "I have found a suitable tract of land. If you are agreeable, we can discuss the construction of my house." The colonel paused, sipping at the bourbon-and-water highball that seemed always on his desk. "You understand that it must be a good house, Giles. The very best that can be built under these primitive conditions."

"Of course, colonel," Toby said. "Why don't you and I look over the houses in the area? You pick out one that suits you, and I'll duplicate it for you, with improvements."

"Splendid idea!" agreed Withers. "Splendid!"

On Sunday, Toby and the colonel rode over the area, inspecting the larger houses in the community. Toby had little difficulty persuading Withers that Stoge Rowden's home was the best in town, and it was agreed that Toby would build its mate for the colonel. Over a bourbon and water in the colonel's office, tired and dusty from their ride, they discussed terms. Withers insisted on a turn-key price, a flat sum to be paid in cash when the house was completed.

"I can't give you a flat price offhand," said Toby. "I'll have to do some figurin'."

"Do your figuring, my boy, then let me know."

Toby finished his drink, savoring the sweet, winelike taste of the excellent bourbon, then shook hands with the colonel and departed. By nightfall he had counted and recorded every log needed to construct the house, taking his measurements from Stoge's house. He discovered that he would have to cut and hew one hundred and forty logs eighteen feet long, twenty logs four feet longer, and four johnny poles. Rafters he would make of straight saplings, to be had for the cutting, but he would have to have twenty squares of cypress shingles, ten glass windows, and seven doors. The shingles could be cut by Stoge's slaves, and the doors would be made from split pine, but the windows would have to be bought and fetched in from Arkansas Post or Memphis.

Toby figured for several hours, then walked downstreet to the tavern, where he found the colonel at his favorite table. "Well, my boy," the Kentuckian said, "what is your price?"

"Seven hundred and fifty dollars," answered Toby.

The colonel whistled. "Isn't that steep, Giles?"

Toby nodded. "It is, colonel, but you will have the finest house in Washington. And I don't think you'll find anyone else in town prepared to build a house with glass windows."

Withers gazed reflectively at his whiskey, then agreed. "All right, Giles. It's a deal."

They shook hands on it; Toby knew enough about Kentuckians of the colonel's variety to understand that a written contract was not required. He stood up to go, then paused, saying, "If you have no objection, colonel, I'd just as lief you didn't mention our terms to anyone in town. I'm a newcomer here, like yourself, and there might be jealousy."

"Very well, Giles," Colonel Withers agreed. "The matter will be between us."

Toby intended to create the impression in town that he was merely helping the colonel get a home ready for his family. In that way he would avoid resentment and gain a reputation for good neighborliness.

Stoge snorted when he learned the price Toby had asked. "I can't make up my mind which is the bigger durned fool," he said. "The colonel for payin' such a price, or you, Toby, for thinkin' you can build such a structure."

They were at breakfast, and Stoge emphasized his remark by slapping the table with the flat of his hand, so that coffee slopped from the cups. "Pa!" Agatha said tartly, "That's no way to talk. You ought to be pleased that Toby's going to build the colonel's house." She turned to her husband. "I have a few hundred dollars of my own, Toby," she said. "You're welcome to it, if you need cash for labor and windows. That's how much I believe in your ability to do it."

"It would help," he admitted. "Thank you." He cautioned Stoge and Agatha against mentioning the contract. "We don't want folks to think we're braggin'," he explained.

The next day he hired two of the best bullpunchers in town and yoked up two of Stoge's best teams of oxen. He took Josh and four of Stoge's slaves, armed them with axes, and led them into the near-by virgin forest—all government land, of course. In three days he had the timber cut, and the logs were snaked to the building site. The rest of the week he spent in organizing a community log-hewing and rafter-cutting party, enlisting Agatha to provide refreshments. She made gallons of crushed grape juice, and this Toby spiked with plenty of corn liquor and sweetened with sorghum syrup.

Sunday morning the settlers turned out en masse to the party, those who owned slaves bringing their Negroes to help. Before dark, every log had been hewn on three sides and stripped of bark on the fourth, and the ends had been mortised, so that each log was ready to be set in place. A towering pile of long, straight saplings, skinned and beveled for rafters, loomed against the evening sky. Toby regretted that he hadn't dragged up more logs so that the settlers could have split them and riven them for the puncheon floors. The crew of generous volunteers, inspired by Toby's concoction of grape juice and firewater, had accomplished more in a day than a paid crew would have done in a month. Toby's scheme for using free labor to build the colonel's house was working better than he had dared hope; the heavy part of the work was done, and the rest was clear sailing.

On Monday morning, Toby hired the only journeyman carpenter in town to help with the house, and within a week the walls were up, mortised and pegged, the ceiling joists had been raised, and the sapling rafters were closely covered with a watertight roof of cypress shingles. White-oak slabs for the puncheon floor were smooth-faced and stacked to dry while Toby prepared for his trip to Arkansas Post, where he hoped to obtain the glass windows he had promised the colonel.

Colonel Withers watched the raising of the house with satisfaction. Clearly, Toby was putting the best of materials into the structure, and the Negro field hands, under the carpenter's expert direction, were doing a careful job. When it was finished, the colonel realized, his house would be the most impressive in Washington.

Stoge, of course, was amazed—at the speed and efficiency with which Toby worked, and at the fact that his young son-in-law was able to build a house at all. He watched the slaves sweating at their work, chanting in unison as they swung the heavy timbers into place, and puffed at his cold pipe, ruminatively running a rough-palmed hand over the growth of beard on his chin, wondering what grandiose project Toby would tackle next.

He soon found out.

Toby persuaded Stoge to buy the pair of wide-tired Conestoga wagons that the storekeeper had been talking about for months. One of these, Toby explained, he would load with goods for the store, while the other would carry the colonel's glass windows. Thus the journey to Arkansas Post would profit both of them, Toby pointed out. Two bullpunchers were sent ahead for the wagons, while Toby took two of Stoge's best horses for himself and Josh, setting out with a thousand dollars of Stoge's money in his belt. This, plus his own accumulation of cash and the money Agatha had loaned him, gave Toby a working capital of almost two thousand dollars.

Four days later Toby and his slave rode into Arkansas Post. The two bullpunchers had found some corn and were hopelessly drunk. Toby left Josh in charge of the teams and set out to make his purchases, but he found that glass windows and Conestoga wagons were as scarce at Arkansas Post as in Washington, and for a moment he was discouraged. Then he had an idea. He stabled Stoge's horses and found quarters for Josh and the two punchers.

"Josh, I'm going to Memphis on the side-wheeler," he said. "You take care of these bullpunchers. See they don't get so drunk they won't be able to drive."

"Yes, sah, Marse Toby." The slave's wistful expression indicated his desire to accompany his master to Memphis, but Toby wanted to make the trip alone. The thought of Memphis reminded him of The Gut, the dark, close whorehouse room, and the hard-eyed little prostitute he had stayed with on his way west.

13.

The packet boat docked near dark the next evening, too late to do any business that day. Toby disembarked, excited by the smell of the water front, which reminded him of Norfolk, thrilled by the bustle and hurry of the city, the scent of affairs in this river town. He stood on the pier for several minutes, watching the river, and the laboring Negroes, singing as they swung the cargo from the holds; then he turned toward the town. His feet carried him to The Gut, and he was hardly conscious of having decided to visit the section before he discovered that he was there. Darkness had fallen. A river ruffian brushed rudely against him and cursed; Toby quickly felt in his pocket to make sure that his money was safe. An ancient ruin of a woman, her body wasted by too little food and too much liquor, put a bony hand on his arm and begged for a copper. In the squalid doorways of the hideous houses, men and women rested in drunken stupor; some of them would be dead in the morning, but most would draw themselves painfully back to consciousness, to continue the debauch, the rapid cycle of degradation that would carry them, one day, to death in an alley or in a doorway in The Gut. It was the old, old story of poverty and sin, the pathetic efforts of the poor and overworked to blur the sharp edges of an intolerable existence.

The raucous blare of a slave band burst through the swinging doors of the place Toby sought, spilling music into the street, mixed with the babble of many voices and the occasional high-pitched laughter of a whore. Toby shouldered his way through the doors. The bright lights hurt his eyes and the stench compounded of raw whiskey, cheap perfume, stale tobacco, and unbathed bodies choked him for a moment. But the color and movement in the place were exciting. He watched the couples dancing on the sawdust-covered floor, swaying sensuously to the music, and hot, compelling desire overwhelmed him. He did not know whether what he felt was sex, the simple desire for a woman's body, or some more complicated prompting toward pure evil, some plumbing of the depths of his spirit that touched a poisonous wellspring in his nature. He only knew that he burned with the desire for a drink, several drinks, and a totally wanton, totally degraded woman. He made his way through the noisy crowd and ordered a drink at the bar, then another. The strong liquor inflamed his blood, and his throat tightened as he watched the pliant, bold movements of the dancers. He had a third drink, put his money on the bar, and went quickly out into the dark street, hurrying toward the house where he had stayed with the bright-eyed little whore.

The same crafty landlady greeted him at the door and showed him into the parlor done in plum-colored plush and gilt-framed mirrors. A heavy scent pervaded the room, a scent that was attractive, but a bit too strong, a bit too obvious, the old, old smell of the brothel. The landlady offered Toby a seat. "Take the load off your feet, neighbor, and I'll show you the finest collection of whores on the river."

"Just a minute," Toby said.

The landlady turned inquiringly. "What's the matter, neighbor? Don't you want to see the girls? If you don't, you sure come to the wrong place."

"You don't remember me," Toby said.

"Can't say's I do."

"A year ago, you threw me out into the gutter to sleep, when I was broke. I spent my money here, and you threw me out."

"Well now, neighbor," the landlady said, "I don't remember you, but you're prob'ly right. Tell you what, though, I'll promise you something, an' you can depend on it."

"What's that?" asked Toby.

"If you're broke tomorrow, I'll see that you get throwed out into the same gutter. That way you'll keep your gutter business in the same place."

Toby laughed; the landlady had a candor that he admired and understood. He took five hard dollars from his pocket and gave them to her, saying, "I want the best thing in the house. And I want a girl that nobody's had tonight. I like to be first in everything I do."

86

The landlady stowed the money into her bosom. "Neighbor, follow me," she said. "I got just what you want. For five dollars you get the girl, the room, *and* a bottle of corn liquor."

"Make it rye," Toby said.

"All right, neighbor, rye it is."

The room was large, with a shuttered window, dominated by an enormous bed of polished brass. This was the best house in The Gut, the right place for an aristocrat, mused Toby, as he sat in a horsehair armchair waiting for the girl, wondering what she would be like. When she came, he was not disappointed. She was young, not more than seventeen, and through the filmy garment that she wore, the soft, still-firm outline of her body showed. Her long black hair was down and her painted mouth was moist and soft looking. She smiled at Toby, closing the door behind her.

"Ain't you goin' to get undressed, honey?" she said, in a warm, tantalizing voice.

Toby's voice caught in his throat as he answered. "Sure. Sure I am."

He got to his feet and pulled off his coat, undressing in front of the girl, deriving a strange, oblique pleasure from the act, as if it demonstrated, in some way, the fact that she was his property for the night, bought and paid for like a black slave. He stood in the half-light with her, naked, then suddenly, with a vicious movement, ripped the thin nightgown from her body, tearing the cloth and leaving her nude. She stepped back, frightened. He took a five-dollar piece from his trousers and handed it to her. "This is for you," he said. "I paid the landlady, but this is for you."

She smiled. "Thank you, honey." She kicked off her satin slipper and tucked the gold piece into the toe, then stretched herself out on the bed. Toby stood over her, looking at her full body, then uncorked the bottle of rye and poured two drinks, handing one to the girl. They touched glasses **and** drank.

"My name's Nina," the girl said. "What's yours?"

"Josh," Toby answered. "Josh Beck." He had heard, somewhere, that aristocrats used pseudonyms in establishments of this character, so he concocted a name combining that of his slave with that of one of Washington's most respected farmers.

They drank from the bottle until it was half gone, then Toby, sitting on the bed, bent down and kissed Nina on the mouth. He made love to her for a little, dizzy and heated by the whiskey and the hot nakedness of her skin. Then he sat up straight on the edge of the bed, staring down at her, and, without thinking, struck her sharply on the breast so that she cried out in pain, and the bright red outline of his fingers showed like fire on the soft skin of her bosom. He struck her again, and she whimpered, but Toby knew she was not forgetting the five dollars stuffed into her slipper. He took her breasts in his hands and twisted them, and this time she cried out again. Then he bent and kissed her passionately, on the mouth, and on the breasts, where the red marks of his hands still showed.

"Why'd you do like that, honey?" she whispered. "Why'd you hit me?"

"I don't know," said Toby. "I don't know."

The whore smiled. "I know," she said. "I know. You want to make like you own me. But you don't own me, except just for tonight."

Toby kissed her hungrily. "I own you," he said. "God damn it, I *own* you. I paid. I paid you. I paid the landlady. I own you."

"Nobody owns anybody, really," she said. "You don't even own niggers, really."

He blew out the light and got into the bed with her, drawing her to him. "I own you, you hear," he said savagely. "I own you."

In the darkness, with the body of the whore against his own, a vision of Agatha suddenly crossed his brain, and a wave of anguished shame consumed him, but it faded in the darkness and the heat and the sweet heavy odor of the whiskey and Nina's perfume.

The next day he bought his wagons and windows, giving orders that they be loaded aboard the packet boat for Arkansas Post. Then he purchased a good supply of staple items for the store, and quantities of catchpenny articles that would appeal to the Indians. Memphis, the great river trading port, offered more goods than Toby had ever seen assembled in one place before, and he was impressed, but he kept his head and dealt shrewdly, gaining a copper's advantage here and there, making the sharpers in the warehouses know that they were doing business with a man who, for all his frontiersman's manner, was as canny a trader as you could find on the river.

Among the new things he saw was a great red iron machine built in two sections, rather like an oversize coffee grinder, but much heavier. It was a hand-operated corn mill, and despite its cost, Toby bought it the moment its use was explained to him. Corn, and the meal ground from it, was the staff of life west of the river, for the frontiersmen as it had been for the Indians. Ownership of the corn mill would bring power and trade to Toby in Washington.

That night he went back to The Gut, to the same brothel, but the intensity of his passion was gone and he passed most of the time in boasting of his prowess as a businessman, describing the ease with which he distributed counterfeit money among the Indians. The shrewd, hard-faced landlady listened to his stories with a cruel smile. She went to the marble-topped sideboard and took what looked like a five-dollar bill from the drawer, handing it to Toby. Toby examined it carefully; it was the best counterfeit he had ever seen, unusually expert, good enough to fool the average white man, let alone an Indian.

"Would you like to buy some of that queer, neighbor?" the landlady asked.

"If the price was right," Toby replied. "It's pretty poor stuff."

The landlady laughed. "It's the best queer in Memphis," she said. "And you know it."

After some haggling, Toby bought two thousand dollars worth of counterfeit for fifty dollars in gold coin. He concealed the stuff with some excitement; if he succeeded in passing even half of it, his profit would be staggering. His conscience bothered him not at all in the matter, and he bought the queer money as merchandise, stock for the store, just as he had purchased the gimcracks with which to attract the Indians.

The next day he went shopping for himself, ordering two suits of glossy black velvet, similar to those that Colonel Withers wore, and providing himself with a tall beaver hat and two pairs of hand-stitched shoes. These he took to a cobbler, ordering extra thicknesses of leather fixed to the soles and heels; when he put them on, the shoes added almost an inch to his height.

He bought an overstuffed walnut rocker and some new silk curtains for Agatha, then took a final walk about the city. He was satisfied; he felt that he had dealt shrewdly and advanced himself, and in some way the dark, passionate interlude in The Gut, while making him tingle with shame when he thought of it, had purged him of a savage undercurrent, so that when he embarked on the packet boat for the Post, he felt calmer, more sure of himself, than ever before in his life. Standing at the rail of the side-wheeler, dressed in one of his new velvet suits, the built-up shoes contributing an exhilarating trifle to his height, he watched a faraway brilliant star rise in the heavens, in the pale evening sky, and at that instant he apprehended his destiny, gaining stature, so that when he reached home, days later, it seemed fitting and natural for Agatha to whisper her great news, a pink flush on her cheeks. This news perfected the picture; his wife was with child. He was to have a son and heir, the product of his own loins, to give shape and meaning to his struggle for money and power. Surely it would be a son. He kissed Agatha, holding her in his arms, and the frantic memory of Memphis was washed away by his happiness.

"A son!" he exclaimed, half to his wife and half to himself and heaven. "My own son!"

14.

Stoge was delighted with Toby's purchases and pleased with his son-in-law's prompt accounting. He was warm and friendly toward Toby, and if he suspected that Toby had indulged himself in Memphis, Stoge gave no sign of it. But he was skeptical about the new corn mill. "Folks in these parts grind their own corn," he argued. "Why should they use this newfangled machine?"

Toby laughed. "Wait and see. Inside of three months there won't be a settler grinding his own. For one thing, this machine does it better. For another, they'll come just to see the danged thing run."

Of course, Toby was right. The new machine quickly became a magnet for townsmen and settlers alike, and there were always several people waiting their turn. The machine put money in Toby's pockets and brought business into Stoge's store, for people coming to have corn ground usually discovered something they needed on the shelves Toby seductively arranged. In less than the three months Toby had allowed, the gristmill was an institution, and Toby built a small log shed behind the store to accommodate it. Stoge chuckled and shook his head. He was particularly fond of his son-in-law these days, and grateful to Toby for making him a prospective grandfather. "You're a sharp one, son," he would say. "Sharp like a briar."

Toby was busy, with his mill and the work at the store, and the task of completing Colonel Withers' house. Josh labored for him with devotion, and the powerful Negro was cheerful, singing at his work. But one day Josh approached his master with a doleful countenance. "We got trouble, Marse Toby," he announced. "Powerful trouble."

"Minnie?" Toby asked.

"Tha's right, Marse Toby. The ole chief done trailed Minnie an' her young 'uns back to Marse Rowden's farm. He don't aim to leave these parts till he find Minnie."

Toby gave Josh his pistol. "That Indian may try to make trouble for you, Josh," he said. "I want you to be able to protect yourself."

Josh nodded. It was not necessary for Toby to say more, and the next morning, when the slave returned the pistol to his master, the weapon had been fired. Toby took the gun, cleaned it, and put it away, asking no questions, but he was not surprised when Josh said, offhandedly, "Minnie say she want you to fix up some papers on her, like you did on me."

Toby looked Josh straight in the eye. "We ought to have the old Indian fix them up," he said.

"He's done gone west," Josh explained. "He tole me Minnie an' the pickaninnies could stay here with you."

Toby nodded. "Tell Minnie and the girls to move into the corncrib," he said.

The Negro grinned, saying, "Thanks, Marse Toby."

A few days later, when Toby rode over the farm, he saw

the buzzards circling the trees and rode into the woods to investigate. He found a savage old razorback sow with her piglets, fighting the winged scavengers away from a long-darkened carcass. Toby surveyed the grim scene without emotion. Evidence of what Josh had done would be destroyed, and Toby would be richer by three female slaves. He was satisfied with the incident. It would not have occurred to him that his attitude was callous or in any way cruel. Life was cheap on the frontier, particularly Indian life, and the redskin had been an old man, ready for the grave. He rode back to the farmhouse for his dinner. He had news for Agatha and Stoge, and when they were seated at table he announced it.

"I bought a thousand acres of land today," he said, with an effort to keep his tone casual.

Stoge dropped his fork. "How'd you pay for it?" he demanded.

"Well, I had what Colonel Withers paid me for the house," Toby explained. "I used that, and some of Agatha's money, and some of my own." Toby, in fact, had had plenty of cash with which to swing the deal, but he wasn't eager to let Stoge know how he had accumulated his reserve and he knew that it would please Agatha to believe that she had helped him.

But Stoge didn't like it. "I'll loan you what you need," he said. "You can return Agatha's money."

"I don't need the money, father," his daughter protested. "I'm glad to have Toby use it."

Toby smiled. "I didn't do so bad on that house," he reminded Stoge. "Clear profit of three hundred and twenty dollars."

Stoge snorted. "If those settlers ever find out how you tricked them into helping build a house you made money out of, you won't feel so swelled up about it. Profit or no profit."

"The colonel wanted his house built in a hurry and I figured out a way to do it. I needed money in a hurry. He got his house and I got my money."

"How about the settlers?" asked Stoge.

"They got a snootful of O-be-joyful and the fun of doing the colonel a favor."

Stoge stood up. "I have never wanted profits that came crooked or by misusing my friends," he said. He left the room. Toby smiled at his departing back. He knew Stoge was angry now, but he also knew that the storekeeper was too fond of his daughter to stay angry at her husband long, and that when he cooled down, Stoge would be pleased by the fact that Toby was now a landholder.

Toby taught Josh to operate the mill, and this gave him more time to wait on trade in the store and to pass his queer money to the Indians and settlers bound for Texas. Between caravans, when business was slack at the store, Toby superintended the clearing of his land. He completed the first unit of his slave quarters and moved Josh and Minnie and the two children onto his own land. And one night, when Squire Tatum was in the right mood, Toby oiled him with Stoge's best brandy. He passed several hours with the squire, listening to the old fellow's stories, pretending to drink along with him. When he left the squire, however, Toby was sober, and in his pocket was a forged bill of sale for Minnie and her children, all properly notarized by the justice of the peace. He rode back to the Rowden farm by starlight, the stiff legal paper in his pocket. He had been in Washington less than eighteen months, and already he had a mill of his own, a thousand acres of land, a family of slaves, a devoted wife, and the prospect of a son.

15.

Thomas Jefferson Giles was born May 5, 1826, a chunky, scarlet baby whose redness and lusty bawling discouraged Toby, who had never before seen a newborn infant. But he kept his apprehension to himself and bent to kiss Agatha. The glow in her eyes betrayed her joy in her son, and the sight of her happiness caused Toby's own eyes to mist with tears. He knelt beside his wife, and his voice trembled with emotion when he spoke.

"Honey, he'll never want for anything. Not for anything."

Agatha touched Toby's hair and stroked it. She smiled benignly, seeming somehow at that moment to be mother to both of them, to her young ambitious husband, and the babe nestled at her breast.

"I know, Toby," she said. "I know."

He rose to his feet and stood for several minutes looking down at his wife and son, seeking words to express the thoughts in his heart, but finding none. At last he turned and went from the room, making his way out of the house and across the town to his own land. He stood with his feet on his own soil, his head uncovered, and came as close to praying as he had ever come. What goodness and nobility remained in Toby, after his brutal childhood and hard youth, were touched by his fatherhood, and he remembered the evil he had done with regret, making high resolve for the future.

A week after Tommy Jeff's birth, the mail rider plastered the town with circulars:

TO BE SOLD AT MEMPHIS

PRIME NEGRO SLAVE MEN—$800 to $1000, *according to age and condition.*

PRIME NEGRO SLAVE WOMEN—$500 to $800, *according to age and looks.*

PRIME NEGRO SLAVE BOYS—$300 to $500, *according to age and size.*

PRIME NEGRO SLAVE GIRLS—$150 to $600, *according to age and looks.*

Terms: Cash. No Complaints; No Returns.
All Sales Final.

Toby was interested in buying slaves. Clearing a thousand acres of wilderness with only Josh and Minnie to help him was proving a hard task. He could use Stoge's slaves infrequently, for Stoge needed them on his own farm. Toby wanted a couple of husky men slaves, young ones with broad backs, to help him turn his wilderness land into a profitable farm. He read the circular with intense interest, then arranged to borrow two thousand dollars from Stoge, planning to be in Memphis when the boat that was to bring the slaves arrived there.

There were others in Washington interested in buying slaves, and a meeting was held in Stoge's store to discuss the matter. Toby was quick to see a profit for himself if he could be commissioned to do the buying for the group, and his plans were made, though he kept silent during the early part of the meeting.

James Beck was the first speaker. He was a South Carolinian, one of the most respected farmers in the district, and though his old frock coat was frayed, he had the bearing of a gentleman. The two dozen farmers in Stoge's store listened to him attentively.

"I propose that we delegate one man to go to Memphis and do the buying," Beck said. "That way we'll save money. No sense in everybody going."

There was general agreement from the men, then someone said, "Before we talk about who's to do the buying, let's find out who wants slaves and how many."

"I'm putting myself down for one man and one woman," Beck said. "I always try to buy my slaves in pairs. I don't like to break up families."

"Now, Beckie," one of the men laughed, "let's not start no argument about slave families. I know you think niggers have hearts and souls like white folk, but that's poppycock. Niggers is just niggers."

"I figure niggers is just like horses and cows," observed a long-faced Mississippian. "Mares gets tired of colts pulling at their teats, and cows gets tired of calves nudging 'em. After they wean their young, they forget them. They can't tell which calf or colt was theirs by the time they're a year old."

"Oh, niggers may remember their young'uns," the first man said. "But that don't prove they got souls."

"Maybe so, boys, maybe so," Beck said. "Let's stop arguin'. How many slaves do you fellows want to buy?"

"I need two, but I can't buy but one, less'n I can borrow five hundred dollars from Stoge," the Mississippian said.

"I've already touched Stoge," Toby remarked, "so put me down for two men. If the price ain't too high, I might take three." He was glad of the chance to explain where the money came from, in Stoge's presence, for some of these men, he knew, resented his good fortune and had been speculating about his source of funds. He paused, then said, "I'm going to Memphis on some other business, and I'd be glad to do the buyin' for all, if that's agreeable."

There was an uneasy silence after Toby sat down, then one of the men said, "Shucks, let's decide who's to buy after we're finished here."

In the end it was James Beck who was designated buyer. Beck seemed to sense Toby's chagrin, and as they filed out of the store he said, "If you're going to Memphis anyway, Toby, I'd be mighty glad of your company."

"Sure, Beck," Toby said. "We can buy together." He was disappointed, but not really surprised. To these men Beck was a solid citizen, a proved farmer, while he, Toby, was a newcomer, an outsider, who had been moving a little too fast for comfort. It would take years, Toby knew, to make himself the town's first citizen, but that was his goal, and he meant to achieve it. The recent trial of a horsethief in town, and the sight of the angry crowds at the lockup, eager to hang the unfortunate man, had reminded Toby of his own acquisition of one of the Maison horses, and the real purpose of his journey to Memphis, though not even Agatha knew it, was to send a letter to Captain Maison, enclosing money in payment for the animal. He was afraid to write from Washington, but he reasoned that a letter mailed from Memphis would be difficult to trace.

Early next morning Beck dispatched a light wagon pulled by a pair of fast-stepping young mules with a trusted slave at the reins, and the following day Beck and Toby departed for Memphis on horseback. It was Toby's first chance to talk with the prosperous farmer at any length, and he was eager to make a good impression, for Beck's judgment carried weight among the settlers. There was a light frost on their second morning out, and this intimation of oncoming winter disturbed Beck, who had just completed a new storage cellar and was anxious to fill it with a good supply of onions, potatoes, turnips, and squash, as well as fruit from the two of his apple trees that were old enough to bear.

"Yes, sir, Toby," Beck counseled, "a full cellar is the settler's fortress against hunger and the cruel might of a long winter. I hope that slave boat arrives on time. I want to get home to see my cellar full."

"I've never had much experience buying slaves," Toby said. "I'm glad you're going to be along to help me pick them."

Beck looked at Toby with the hint of a smile on his lips. "You've done pretty well," he said casually. "You seem to have acquired slaves without much trouble."

Toby frowned; there had been talk among the settlers, he knew, at the time he got Minnie and the girls. The two men rode in silence for a while, then Toby said, "Agatha bought the woman and her young'uns, Beck, with her own money."

"You don't say!" Beck said. "You're a lucky man to have a wife with a stake of her own."

The talk passed to pleasanter things; at last they arrived at Arkansas Post and caught the morning boat for Memphis, only to learn, upon their arrival, that the slave boat would be two days late. Toby was depressed and nervous, but he denied himself a visit to The Gut, for he didn't intend to give Beck anything to gossip about when they got home. He passed a day in his room, composing a letter to Captain Maison. He apologized for taking the horse, saying that he had intended merely to ride over the mountain to see a girl, but that the animal had broken a leg, forcing Toby to shoot it, and that in his panic he had run away, fearful of returning without the horse. He enclosed a hundred dollars, explaining that to get it together he had stinted and saved, and said that he hoped the sum would be enough to cover the horse with its saddle and bridle. The letter, as Toby composed it, was heartbreaking, calculated to soften the hardest man, let alone Captain Maison, who was generous and kind. Toby mailed it in Beck's presence, then made an excuse to go off by himself. His supply of counterfeit was running low and he replenished it, buying a thousand dollars in fives, tens, and twenties for forty dollars in gold. He arranged with the landlady to inquire for mail in his name, and to forward any letters to Washington, cautioning her not to reveal his address to anyone. He took his leave without visiting one of the whores upstairs, though he was tempted, and the landlady cajoled him.

The next morning the slave boat arrived and the city of Memphis took on almost a carnival aspect. The first auction began at ten, but long before that James Beck and Toby were in the milling crowd on the wharf, hundreds of men, craning their necks, trying to get a look at the slaves to be offered. Toby bought a bag of gingerbread, and while Beck was talking with the auctioneer, he visited among the slaves. He picked three of the healthiest, most intelligent-looking men, and gave them each some of the gingerbread, telling them about his thousand-acre place in the Territory and explaining how well he treated his slaves. When he saw that they were eager to become his property, he cautioned them to act as badly as possible on the block, to be surly and unruly.

Beck had no luck with private negotiations. The auctioneer was firm in his prices and hard in his trading. Toby wanted to wait for the auction, for he had learned that a number of prospective buyers, discouraged by the boat's failure to arrive on time, had returned home, thus narrowing the field, so that, with competition not so keen, the slaves might go cheaper on the block than at private sale.

Toby had figured right. The slaves brought fifty to a hundred dollars less at auction than the dealer had been asking of private buyers. Toby's three hand-picked men were so surly that many buyers refused even to bid on them, and Toby got them at a hundred dollars each below the price they would otherwise have brought. He and Beck had no trouble buying the eight men and two women needed to fill their orders, and at very reasonable prices. When this buying was done, Toby had some business of his own. Colonel Withers had asked him to buy a prime young maiden slave, and Toby was determined to get the right kind of girl for the lawyer. He had seen two girls on the boat and inquired about them, persuading the dealer to have them stand for his inspection.

Both young slave women were unusually well built, high-breasted, with a challenging nobility of carriage and light, graceful movements. Toby had them raise their skirts high above their knees, inspecting their legs and feet, then asked the auctioneer to make them bare their bodies. The two young women obediently stripped off their one-piece garments, standing nude before him, and he walked around them, patting their buttocks, running his hand over their firm, round breasts. One of the girls was vibrant with a defiant sexuality, meeting Toby's inspecting eyes with a bold, promising leer, standing firm without flinching when his fingers pinched the flesh of her rump and his hand passed roughly over the nipple of her breast. She was what the colonel wanted, Toby knew, and he picked her for the lawyer's maidservant.

A wet norther blew in before they got their slaves off the boat. The blacks were wearing only the cotton singlets provided by the slaver, so Toby bought warm clothing and heavy shoes for his three men and the colonel's girl. The slaves were valuable property, and, on the frontier, difficult to obtain at any price. Toby had learned that good food, warm clothing, and kind treatment prompted serfs to work harder and more efficiently.

The rains followed them across the river, and the second day on the trail found the roads almost bottomless. Time after time the wagon bogged down. One of Toby's new slaves was always the first man at a wheel and directed the other blacks in the work of getting the wagon out of the mire. Toby was pleased with his purchase. "Beck, that nigger knows how to do things."

"Yep, you got a pert nigger."

"What's your name, black boy?" inquired Toby.

"Boss man back in Mississippi called me Whittler."

"Whittler," said Toby with suspicion. "Did you get that handle because you are handy with a razor in a fight?"

"Naw sir. I doan' do no fightin'. I likes to whittle and make things out of wood."

After five days of trudging travel, Toby and Beck reached home, just before sundown.

Josh took charge of the new slaves, and Toby hastened to reach the warmth and comfort of his fireside. Tommy Jeff was asleep in his crib, but Toby awakened the boy, making the baby smile and chuckle as he held him high in the air, then rocking him to sleep and joining Stoge and Agatha for supper. After he had eaten, sitting in his stocking feet before the cheerful fire, Toby looked across the room at his wife with happiness and affection. Here, in the warmth and security of home, he was contented and happy, and he was glad that he had resisted the temptation to sleep with a whore in Memphis.

16.

Toby believed in keeping himself and his slaves busy regardless of the weather. His land was on the edge of the town, and the main road, north and south, ran through it, the newly blazed trail into Indian Territory branching off it on his property. On this fork Toby decided to build a permanent gristmill, and his slaves were erecting a stout log house for the purpose. In another place, on a bit of high land, a building site was being cleared. Here Toby planned to locate his house.

The days were never long enough for Toby to finish all the work he planned, though he drove himself and his Negroes, but he enjoyed his evenings, and his nightly romp with Tommy

Jeff became more and more important to him, as did the peaceful interlude after Tommy Jeff was in bed and Toby sat before the fire with his wife. The tavern had lost its appeal for Toby, and the rewards of a home, the security of the hearthside, the companionship of his wife, instead of growing dull with habit, became more cherished as he learned to enjoy them.

Stoge had always loved his home, but now, with his grandson there, it meant more than ever to him. Stoge and Toby got on well. Occasionally Stoge was puzzled by some sharp deal of Toby's, but never did he regret his daughter's marriage to the young man from Virginia. They were a happy household, and Stoge wished that the arrangement could be permanent, but he knew that Toby wanted a house of his own, and dreaded the time when it would be completed.

Although the ground was cold and wet, Toby was determined to keep working on the house. He borrowed four of Stoge's best axemen and put them, with his own slaves, to cutting timbers for his home. He built a smokehouse and filled it with wild boar meat, smoked and cured as he had been taught to do it, Virginia style, on the Maison Plantation. And in hunting the wild, savage razorbacks he learned to be a crack shot, for a single encounter with an angry, wounded hog taught him the need to kill with the first bullet.

One Saturday in midwinter a traveler drifted into the store and asked for a gallon of liquor. "Cheapest you've got," he said. "My money's short. I've got a string of horses I'm aimin' to sell or trade."

"Where are your horses?" asked Toby.

" 'Cross the river. At Fulton."

"Bring them up," Toby said. "I might buy a team. Might buy the whole lot, if the price was right."

"Bring 'em up? Hell, man! I can't get 'em across the river."

"Ferry 'em over, if you can't ford 'em."

The horse trader laughed. "I tried that. Got eighteen of the critters on the ferry and every half-wild mustang rushed to

103

one end of the boat an' it capsized. Two got drowned an' I had to pay the ferryman fifteen dollars to put his boat back in shape."

"You got a drove of outlaws," Toby laughed. "What'll you take for 'em?"

"A ten-spot apiece," the trader said. "An' you get 'em across the river."

"Ten dollars!" Toby protested. "Hell, man! You don't want to sell no horses. Why, I'd be crazy to pay that price an' lose half of 'em getting them over the river."

"They'll bring forty, fifty dollars a head, come spring."

"Fine," said Toby. "You wait till spring then." He figured that the man wasn't the type to wait until spring, and he scented a bargain. The horse trader took a pull from his gallon of raw firewater and pondered the matter.

"What'll you give for 'em? Right where they are."

"Five dollars a head," said Toby firmly.

The mustanger took another draught of corn, then said, "Young fellow, you've bought yourself a mess of horses. By cracky, you're in the horse business. Give me a hundred and twenty-five iron men, and give 'em to me quick, 'fore I have enough sense to back out of the deal."

"Not so fast, mister. I've got to count them horses before I part with my cash." As he talked, Toby unwound enough rope for half a dozen lassos; Josh was mighty handy with a lariat and he was depending on the slave's help.

The horses counted out as the dealer said and Toby paid over his money. Then he and Josh cut a dead cottonwood tree, making a buoyant ten-foot log which they rolled into the river. They roped two mustangs and tethered them to the log, then fastened the log with a chain to the ferryman's boat. In pairs, they towed the reluctant, half-wild horses to the opposite shore, and by nightfall the entire herd was across. The total expense to Toby was thirteen dollars. By the light of a bright moon he drove them into his own corral that night, a one-hundred-and-thirty-eight dollar investment that would pay Toby tenfold in the spring.

Sunday afternoon Stoge drove over to Toby's farm, bringing Agatha and the baby with him. Sunday or no Sunday, Toby was working, bossing his slave crew as they snaked heavy house timbers into place.

"What in Sam Hill are you going to do with all that timber?" Stoge wanted to know.

"Build me a house," answered Toby simply.

"Good Godfrey! How big a house?"

"Nine rooms."

"You intend to keep Agatha busy birthing children? Or do you figure on takin' in boarders?"

Agatha looked at Toby and they both laughed.

"One room's going to be my office," Toby explained.

"Goin' to read law, are you?"

"Nope, law don't interest me," answered Toby, " 'cept to steer clear of it. Just an office, that's all." He stood erect, looking at Stoge a little defiantly. "Come on," he said, "I want you to see my horses." Proudly he displayed the drove of wild, unbroken animals, champing and stamping in the corral.

"Mess of danged broncos," Stoge observed. "Ain't one in the lot that would pull a loose tooth out of your head. What in Sam Hill you goin' to do with 'em?"

"This spring, when the Indians start moving west again," Toby said, "I'll sell every last one of 'em. And for good money, too."

"Nobody but an Indian would have 'em," said Stoge caustically. But he saw the shrewdness in Toby's purchase. The horses would bring good prices in the spring. Once Stoge had credited Toby's flash successes to luck, but by this time he knew better. His son-in-law had a flair for business, for any venture with a dollar in it. He was a born trader, as other men are born artists, or farmers, or preachers, or thieves. There was in Toby an ingredient of daring where business was concerned, a sixth sense that offered him intuitive flashes in money matters. And there was the drive in Toby that pressed him forward, the drive for more than money, more than power, the drive to be an aristocrat.

"You're making this wilderness look like a farm," Stoge commented approvingly after a tour of Toby's place. By this time there was quite a group of buildings—the millhouse, slave quarters, food storage cellar, barn, and corral. All that was lacking was the main house, and Toby became impatient at the delay imposed by winter, kicking angrily at the clean snow blanket. However, he had anticipated the hard winter days, when no outdoor work could be done and the grinding gears of the gristmill would be silent. He bought a beautiful handmade bedstead and had it taken apart, so that his slaves could use the pieces as models, carving and whittling others to match. Whittler, one of the new slaves, was an artist with the knife, and during one four-day blizzard he made Toby a bed more beautiful than the model—bright cedar rubbed with sandstone, then buffed with beeswax and bear grease until it took on a sheen like that of new gold.

Toby passed most of his working time at his own place that winter, rather than at Stoge's store in town, so that half of Washington probably knew that a letter for him had arrived from Virginia that day before the news reached Toby himself. The letter had been forwarded from Memphis. Stoge carried the letter home and Toby found it beside his plate that evening when he sat down to dinner. The large cream-colored envelope of stiff expensive paper, with its engraving of the Maison coat of arms, made him tremble with apprehension, then he turned it over and observed with satisfaction that the heavy blob of scarlet sealing wax, embossed with the Maison arms, was still intact, assuring him that no curious hands had tampered with the letter en route. He put the envelope in his pocket indifferently.

"Aren't you going to open it?" Agatha asked. Letters were rarities in Washington, and she was curious.

"Oh, all right," Toby said. He took the letter from his pocket and broke the seal with his thumb. He glanced at the page, his eyes a blur, pretending to read. "It just says that my folks are all right and that my father is sending some money to me, as he promised." He folded the crisp sheet and its envelope and stuck both back into his pocket. Stoge looked levelly across the table at him.

"That letter from your folks, Toby?" he asked.

"That's right."

"How come it's from Maison then? Your name's Giles."

"Maison is an old family name. My mother was a Maison, who married a Giles. Dad looks after the plantation, but my mother's brother handles all the money." Stoge seemed satisfied with this explanation.

After dinner Toby made an excuse to get away, saying that he wanted to see Colonel Withers, but once out of the house he walked quickly to town and went to his old room, behind Stoge's store. There, by candlelight, with the cowhide curtain drawn across the window, he read Captain Maison's letter, or, rather, receipted bill, for that was what the envelope contained. The bill valued the horse at a hundred and fifty dollars, the saddle and bridle at fifty. Under the balance of one hundred dollars, Captain Maison had written, "Balance paid in full by good intentions, honesty, and integrity." These words were underscored and a note below read, "Toby, I must confess I misjudged you. I thought you stole my horse. Sorry."

Toby smiled. He put the receipted bill in his moneybag. The engraved envelope he put in his pocket. Then he took a gallon of Stoge's best brandy and walked downstreet to the tavern, where he knew he would find a sizeable group of settlers, driven to seek diversion by their winter-enforced idleness. He placed the jug of brandy on the table and said to the group, "Boys, the drinks are on me." He uncorked the jug, then carelessly dropped the Maison envelope on the table. He had a few drinks with his neighbors, suddenly recalling, in the close, smoke-filled tavern, the short, violent episode with Ira Walker that had started in this room and resulted in his staying on in Washington instead of going to Texas, and a momentary rush of fear at the narrowness of his escape choked him. Soon after, he picked up the captain's envelope and made his good nights, walking home in the cutting, icy wind. He found Agatha still awake.

"What did your folks say about your being married?" she asked.

"They're pleased," Toby answered curtly. He was anxious to have the letter forgotten, now that it had served his purpose. He knew that he had planted the idea with the settlers in the tavern that he had contact with wealthy relatives in Virginia; that would explain his prosperity and allay their curiosity. The letter seemed to have reassured Stoge regarding his antecedents. But now Toby wanted to forget it, for he hated to get his lies mixed up. He crossed the room and kissed his wife. "Come along to bed, honey," he said. "Stop thinking about Virginia. Our life's here, in Arkansas Territory. I wouldn't trade you and Tommy Jeff for all the slaves and bottom land in the Tidewater, or for all the ships in Norfolk."

"Let me read the letter, Toby," she asked.

He laughed, kissing her again. "You wouldn't be interested in that old letter," he said. "Besides, I threw it away."

"Toby, you didn't!"

"Sure I did," he insisted. "I read it. What's the use of keeping it?"

"Toby Giles!" she said impatiently. "Sometimes I can't under*stand* you!" She paused, smiling at him a little. "Aren't you going to answer the letter?" she asked.

"I guess so," Toby said.

Agatha smiled again, coyly. "There's some news you might tell them," she teased.

"What?" he said.

"Tommy Jeff's going to have a sister," she said.

"No!"

"Well, or a brother."

He was elated, throwing his arms around Agatha, wanting to waken Stoge to tell him the news. That night, in bed beside Agatha, he swelled with pride. Another son! Or a daughter, perhaps. A real family! He was more determined than ever now to finish his house and move into it, as an advertisement to the world that Toby Giles was a man of parts, with a growing family and a stake in the world.

The news of Agatha's pregnancy got around quickly among the womenfolk of the town, and one morning when he rode out to his place to work on his house, Toby was astonished to find fifty frontiersmen already on hand, armed with axes, cant hooks, snaking tongs, and gin poles, all in high good humor, eager to help him raise the walls of his dwelling. A momentary wave of shame crossed Toby's heart as he remembered his trickery of these good people when he built the Withers' house, but this was erased in the excitement of seeing the heavy timbers raised in the air, watching the walls of his house rise as if by magic with the help of so many willing hands. By nightfall, the house stood solid, and the next day a few of the neighbors returned to help Toby and his slaves finish the job. He could not help wondering whether news of the letter from Virginia had not helped establish him with his neighbors, putting off their suspicions of his shadiness in business. He felt now that he was accepted as the son of a man of wealth, a Virginia aristocrat. All that remained was to make an aristocrat of himself, a frontier aristocrat, perhaps, but a blue blood nonetheless.

Stoge came to the housewarming, dressed in his best brown suit and a stiff-bosomed shirt. He watched the guests enjoying themselves, and noted that even Colonel Withers and the preacher were there. He was glad that his son-in-law was so well established and that he was making a home for his daughter, but his heart was heavy at losing Agatha and Tommy Jeff, and he said good night early, plodding home slowly to his empty house, understanding that his daughter, in physical presence, was lost to him forever, and understanding too that the advancing years were crowding him. He stood in the quiet sitting room, suddenly feeling old and alone, and in his solitude he fell to his knees, calling on his Maker for solace, asking divine guidance for his child and the man she had married.

17.

Washington was growing, and this growth was hastened by the fact that there was trouble across the border in Texas. The Mexican government revoked Haden Edwards' colonization grants, and almost daily there were reports of trouble from Nacogdoches, even rumors that only war between Mexico and the United States could settle the bitter differences between the settlers and the Mexican government. Hundreds of settlers bound for Texas, lured by Austin's promises, changed their minds as they neared the border and learned that taking up land in Texas meant fighting the Mexican army as well as the Indians. Arkansas Territory was safe. There was plenty of good fertile land, and the Arkansas Indians, weary of the white man, were moving out, so that even the lands with questionable titles were opened to colonization.

Toby watched the arrival of the new settlers with interest. Some were homesteaders, come to claim land grants and clear their farms. Others were professional men who liked the looks of the growing settlement and banked on its possibilities. Colonel Withers, who had been practicing law in addition to his government duties, now had real competition in young Timothy Hibbard, but that did not interrupt the fashionable gatherings held in the house that Toby had built for the colonel.

Mrs. Withers and her two daughters had arrived. Christine, the elder, was very much a lady, a younger and sharper replica of her highly bred, rather aloof mother. The young men clustered about her, but Toby was quick to see that she held them at arm's length, and that her pointed chin was always a little high, as though the sights and sounds of this raw frontier world were not altogether pleasing to her. He was reluctant to risk his uncertain self-confidence before her haughty gaze.

It was the younger girl, Josephine, whom he found himself watching. Not old enough for beaux, she clearly chafed at the restrictions placed upon her by her mother and sister. The defiance in her walk, the restless, often sulky looks she cast about her in church, where the Withers family now regularly adorned a front pew, drew Toby's eyes. Josephine, walking into the store with her mother, set up in him a disturbance which he dismissed impatiently, reminding himself that she was hardly more than a child.

Colonel Withers had not been near the church until his family arrived, but now he proudly followed his wife and daughters to their pew each Sunday. Toby was surprised to find the colonel well versed in the Scriptures, often engaging the minister in conversation on doctrinal matters, and taking an active part in the organization and management of the congregation.

Another newcomer was Doctor Abram Hooker, frontier physician. Toby and his slaves built a two-room structure for him, the only doctor in that part of Arkansas Territory. The front room was Hooker's office, the back room his bachelor living quarters. The shelves in the front room were lined with books and dozens of bottles of pharmaceuticals. The doctor was a great reader, and his habit of sitting in his rocking chair with a book on his lap whenever he had a free half hour led the village wags to instigate the rumor that he had not finished his schooling. Graduate or not, he looked like a doctor, with his black frock coat, Vandyke beard, eyeglasses, and generally knowing appearance.

The town was proud of its new doctor, and proud of the fact that there were two lawyers with their shingles out. The coming of new blood stimulated activity in the town, and there was always some new project to engage the attention and energies of the church members. The most ambitious of these projects was the new school building. The one-room school was much too small, now that the population had increased, and the good women of the town took it upon themselves to build a new one, calling on leading citizens for donations of money or work or material.

Toby was in Stoge's store when Mrs. Hibbard approached him for his donation. Stoge gave twenty dollars, asking that his name be left off the list and the contribution attributed to "A Friend." But Toby wrote his name down proudly, agreeing to give the shingles for the roof.

"Thank you, Mr. Giles," the lawyer's wife said. "That's the best donation yet."

"You are welcome," Toby chuckled. "I want my contribution to top all the others." He laughed aloud at his own wit, and Mrs. Hibbard joined him. He knew that she would repeat his quip, thus advertising both his generosity and his sense of humor.

Spring came, bringing the robins back, adorning the trees with fresh leaves and bright new buds. Fields were being plowed and made ready for planting—the time for farming was at hand, and further land clearing would have to wait until the crops were in the ground. With a lifting heart Toby watched the bull-tongue plow bite furrows into his land, and with excitement he witnessed his slaves, singing as they sowed the corn in the furrows and firmed the rich earth over the seed. His first crop! The first of many. He smiled with satisfaction, taking up a handful of black loam and rubbing it between his fingers.

His slaves were never idle. When the land was too wet to work, Toby's blacks were felling trees. And the gristmill worked at grinding corn, bringing Toby a fourth of the bright gold meal that streamed from it. It was a happy, prosperous community and Toby was one of the most prosperous.

Every home in the town had its garden, every farm its span of woodland rich with game. The wilderness abounded with deer, wild boar, and various small game. Ducks and geese inhabited the marshes along the river bank and wild turkeys were as plentiful as quail. It was the unspoiled wilderness, with all its abundance, to which had been added the convenience of civilization, and the civilization had not as yet consumed or polluted the wilderness, but permitted it to flourish as God had designed it.

When the warm days of summer came, the hapless Indians appeared again in Washington, breaking their endless journey westward. Toby was busy at the store, and at his corral, trading the horses he had acquired the winter before. Before the summer was fairly over he had disposed of his mustangs, except for a matched pair that he decided to keep. His supply of counterfeit was gone, and he passed the last queer bill with relief, deciding to give up that source of revenue now that he had become a respected citizen. From the twenty-three half-wild horses he had bought for five dollars a head, he realized nine hundred dollars in cash, four sturdy oxen, a batch of valuable Indian blankets, and a new long rifle.

He was proudest of the new rifle, even more delighted with it than the money. The smoothbore musket was being abandoned by the best marksmen on the frontier in favor of the lighter, groove-barreled weapon that offered greater accuracy. Toby discovered to his delight that with the new rifle he could outshoot Agatha; the fact that his wife was a better shot than he had long nettled him, and he spent hours and half a keg of powder improving his marksmanship before challenging her to a friendly match at which he displayed his superiority, or, rather, the superiority of the rifle over the old-fashioned musket.

By this time Agatha was big with child, and Toby was pleased by the knowledge that their second youngster would be born in his own home. He was delighted with himself and his world, and with good reason. That fall the harvest was bountiful. The season had been favorable and the rich virgin loam had responded to husbandry with lush growth and a heavy yield. Toby had to build a second log barn to house his grain, and the kitchen garden nurtured by Agatha and Minnie had enabled them to fill the shelves in the pantry with preserved fruits and vegetables. The rafters were lined with Virginia cured hams and strips of jerked meat.

One night, before the fragrant log fire, Agatha sat in her rocker unbraiding her long hair. The firelight playing on her face reflected the soft glow of her skin. Her pregnancy emphasized rather than detracted from her peculiar beauty, causing her to bloom in a compelling, womanly fashion. She smiled at Toby gently, a smile filled with pride and love.

"It did me good to see that you were willing to share our good fortune with the church," she said.

"I was glad to do it," Toby said.

Agatha laughed pleasantly. "I'm glad you're still Toby, in spite of your success."

"Couldn't change if I wanted to," Toby commented. He sat with his stockinged feet on the hob, toasting his toes.

"I'm not so sure you can't change, Toby," Agatha said. She handed Toby a piece of paper. As he took it, he realized that it was Captain Maison's letter, the receipted bill for the stolen horse. He remembered carrying it home one day after taking it from his moneybag, and realized that he must have left it where Agatha chanced to find it.

"I found it when I gathered up your clothes to be washed," she said. She hung her head, avoiding his eyes, not eager to witness the confusion and embarrassment of the man she loved.

"Did you read it?" Toby asked, not looking at her.

"I'm afraid I did, Toby," she answered. "I couldn't resist just glancing at it, I was so curious to see what your folks thought of me."

Toby was silent for what seemed an hour. The steady ticking of the wooden clock over the hearth counted off the seconds with an inexorable, maddening steadiness. Man and wife sat without moving, until finally Toby looked up and met Agatha's eyes. "Now you know I'm no kin to the Maisons," he said dully. "I lied to you, Agatha. I'm from Virginia, all right, but I'm no aristocrat."

"I didn't marry you because you were an aristocrat, Toby," she said quietly, with great confidence. "I married you because of what you are, in yourself. And because I love you."

Toby leaned forward in his chair. He was filled with tenderness toward this gentle woman he had married, filled with love for her, and eager to make her understand the kind of man he was, and the kind of man he wanted to be, with her help. "My family's common as pig tracks," he said. "My father was a drunken wharf rat in Norfolk. My mother—" he paused and broke off, musing for a moment, "—she did what she had to, I reckon. When I was Tommy Jeff's age, or not much more, I knew that you had to steal if you wanted to eat. Until I was bound out to Captain Maison, I never knew what a meal was. I ate when I found food, usually scraps of garbage from the ships tied up at the Norfolk piers. I had a drink of whiskey when I was four. A drunken English sailor from a Liverpool packet gave it to me. 'Look at the blinkin' little Yank tyke swill it,' he said." Toby broke off again, looking questioningly at his wife, trying to discover from her expression what was her reaction to his revelations.

She leaned toward him, her face intent. "Go on, Toby," she said. "Please——"

"Until I went to the Maison Plantation, I never knew anything but blows. I learned to fight like a wharf rat. And why not? I was a wharf rat. I guess I am a wharf rat."

"You are not," said Agatha. "You're Toby Giles, of Arkansas Territory. Norfolk is behind you."

"I'll blot it out," he said almost savagely, hammering the arm of the chair with his fist. "I'm as good as Maison, as good as any aristocrat in Virginia. I'm as good as Withers, good as anybody. By God, I'll be an aristocrat!"

Agatha rose from her chair and crossed the room to Toby, kissing him on the forehead. "Just be Toby. That's all you have to be."

He looked up. "Don't tell Stoge," he pleaded.

"I'll not tell anyone," she promised. "We'll never mention it again." She took the letter, still held in Toby's hand, tore it twice across and dropped it into the fire. Toby sat in his chair, watching the hungry flames lick at the heavy paper until nothing was left but a blackened crisp.

"I'm glad you know about it," he said. "I'm glad you read the letter."

"So am I, Toby," his wife answered. "It makes me love you more than ever."

18.

Agatha's child was expected in October, but October passed and there were no signs, and November now was half gone, and still the baby had not been born. Stoge was nervous and called daily to see his daughter. The waiting grated on Toby's nerves, making him irritable and causing him to drive his blacks with a fury not usual with him. Minnie, Josh's woman and Agatha's personal servant, coddled her mistress and wouldn't let her carry so much as a cup of tea. But Agatha was light-hearted and unafraid. "I've just misfigured, that's all," she insisted. "I've made a mistake in the date." She smiled at her husband and father, and chided Minnie for the way in which the loyal Negress babied her, saying, "I'm not made of glass, Minnie, you know, and neither is the baby. We won't break like a china dish."

But once Toby saw her when she thought she was unobserved, noting the look of pain on her face and the whiteness of her knuckles as she grasped a table edge for support, steadying herself with an effort of will that seemed to draw on her final resources. And twice, in the night, in the pitch-black dark of the bedroom, he heard her cry out in pain as she turned. He called on Doctor Hooker and arranged for the physician to examine Agatha.

"No cause for alarm," the doctor decided. "Just late, that's all."

Toby wiped the cold sweat from his forehead; he had waited in the hall while Hooker examined his wife. "Whew, doctor! That's a relief," he said, "What's causing the delay?"

Hooker stroked his Vandyke beard and fingered his heavy gold watch chain, speaking very precisely, with an eastern accent. "I find the infant unnaturally placed," he explained. "But I am certain that that will be corrected in labor and that we shall encounter no difficulty with the delivery. Your wife is a fine healthy woman, Mr. Giles. She should have this child and many others without trouble."

But the days that followed were filled with dull, aching dread. Even Agatha's high spirits were no longer sufficient to conceal the fact that she was in pain and afraid. Hour after hour, day after day she waited, hoping for some movement within her body that would indicate that the unborn child was changing its position, but the signal did not come. Then one morning, as a pink, cold dawn rose in the east, painting the windows rose colored, Agatha screamed as the first nerve-racking, soul-shattering pain shot through her body. Toby was up with a jump and off on his horse for the doctor, pulling on his coat in the saddle as he urged the animal with his heels. Some premonition of danger had roused Josh; he was already in the kitchen, stoking the fire under a huge cauldron of clean water when Toby rushed out. The big Negro, deeply superstitious, seemed filled by a vast, formless unease, and his broad black brow was wrinkled with apprehension. "I'se got a awful feelin' somethin' bad is going to happen," he said solemnly. "Somethin' powerful bad. I feels it."

"Shut you black mouf', nigger," his consort said. Minnie was bustling about the kitchen, getting things ready. "Don't start none of that talk. Now is the time for you an' me to pray."

Together the two faithful slaves knelt on the scrubbed boards of the kitchen floor and asked divine providence, the God who had condemned them and their children to slavery, to intercede on behalf of their mistress. When Minnie rose, Josh remained on his knees for a moment, his eyes fixed on the wide puncheon boards of the floor. "Good Lawd," he said softly, "Help Mister Toby, too. He sho' needs it, Lord, anything happen to Miss Agatha."

Agatha Giles' cries of anguish filled the room of the new house as the waves of pain came and came again, each spasm leaving the woman a little closer to exhaustion. Doctor Hooker worked doggedly, but he seemed unable to produce true labor and there was nothing he could do for Agatha's pain. Toby stayed out of the room as long as he could, then went to his wife's bedside, holding her hand, feeling the life ebbing from her body as he held the moist, hot hand in his own. She looked up at Toby, pleading for help, so cruelly racked with pain that her lips were unable to form the words that raced in her brain. The appeal in her eyes was pathetic, and Toby stood at the bedside with her hand in his, unable to help her. At last he could endure her suffering no longer. He bent and kissed her forehead, then walked out into the cheerless fall sunlight. He stood in front of his new house, in the center of the frontier kingdom he had built, and cursed a God who permitted his hopes to be raised so high, then struck down the one thing that gave meaning to those hopes and their fulfillment. The vast, chill landscape was unimpressed, and beyond the ridge the Red River gave its cold answer. Toby stood in lonely silhouette against the low horizon, still hearing through the closed window the protestations of his stricken wife. His fists were clenched until the nails bit into the palms of his hands, and each cry of Agatha's was like a lash across his back, but he did not move, standing there immobile as bronze, his feet firm on his meaningless soil. It was Minnie who broke this trancelike attitude. "Marse Toby! Marse Toby!" the faithful black called, running toward him, "Come quick, Marse Toby. Come quick!"

Hooker met Toby at the sickroom door. No words were needed to express the defeat that the doctor felt. "Giles, it is now a question of saving your wife," he said desperately. "I am certain that the child is dead."

Toby gripped the doctor's forearm, his fingers closing round the flesh in a grip like steel. There was anguish in his voice as he pleaded, "Save Agatha, doctor. Please save her. Don't let her die!"

Hooker shook his head and gently released his arm from Toby's grasp. "You know I'll do everything I can, Toby." He paused, looking Toby straight in the eye. "But there's not much hope. She's too far gone."

They brought his dead son to Toby, and Toby cried, not ashamed of the fact that the slave women saw his tears. He looked at the minuscule, marble-still body, and reached out to touch the silent lips with his fingers. "Bathe and dress my child," he said.

They carried the stillborn child away. Toby sat without moving, while Agatha's cries faded to a whimper. At the end he knelt by her bedside, holding her hand as the life slipped from her body, while Stoge stood at the foot of the bed, one hand on the post, unable to control the tears that streamed down his cheeks. At last Hooker gently closed her eyes. "She is gone," he said. "Her last moments were without suffering."

A cry escaped Stoge. Then he said, bowing his head, "It is God's will. We must try to understand."

But Toby cried, "No! I prayed to God, and my prayers were not heeded. The first time I called on the Lord, he failed me."

"Son, son," said Stoge, "we must try to understand."

Toby stood, looking down at the figure of his dead wife, the wife who had given purpose to his life. "There is no God," he said. "I know that now. There is no God. There is only a Devil."

He threw off the hand that Stoge put on his arm and strode from the room. He wanted to walk, to exhaust his body, and he cut out straight across the brush, heedless of the saplings that struck his face and body, digging his heels into the earth as if he hated it. Finally, unable to continue, he came to a place deep in the woods where there was a natural clearing and threw himself prostrate upon the ground, his face digging into the soft earth, his body writhing in furious passion, the nails of his fingers clawing at the forest floor. "Agatha!" he cried aloud to the faceless wilderness. "Agatha!"

At last he slept, unmindful of the chill fall wind, heedless of prowling animals, the dead sleep of a desperate man for whom the terrors of reality are too great to be borne in consciousness. Stoge found him thus, just before nightfall, and the older man half carried his son-in-law home, kneeling beside him in front of the fire and pulling off his boots, then massaging the blood back into Toby's feet. Toby said nothing for a long time, then he looked at Stoge and said, "Do you reckon Agatha'd mind my taking a drink?"

Stoge shook his head. "I think she'd approve, son," he said.

Toby poured himself a stiff drink of brandy and tossed it off at a gulp. He poured another. In a few minutes the fiery stuff restored the warmth to his veins.

Stoge put a hand on Toby's shoulder. "Son," he said, "maybe it would be best if you and Tommy Jeff moved in with me for a while. Might not be so lonely for you."

Toby answered slowly, and very softly, "No thanks, Stoge." He paused, meeting Stoge's eyes. "I'll fight it out in my own house, under my own roof."

And so it was. They buried Agatha next day, in a pine coffin, with her stillborn son beside her. Toby stood tearless at the muddy graveside, unmoved by the preacher's words, or by the tears of the women who followed the coffin to the cemetery. His grief was marked in his heart and it was bitter. Each clod of earth that fell upon the coffin seemed to punctuate his doubt, his rejection of God. Agatha, who loved him, was the one person who might have softened Toby's heart and turned his soul toward God. But Agatha was dead.

Book Two

Josephine

1.

The weeks that followed Agatha's death were the hardest in Toby's life. Brandy dulled the edge of his grief, and he found that poker, played for substantial stakes in the tavern, blurred for a few hours the harsh fact of his wife's absence. But these diversions were a trap, for the false euphoria the brandy granted gave way in the morning to depression tinged with despair, and the sight of his money melting away on the gaming table depressed him further. Yet he continued to drink too much, and the tense excitement of the poker game exerted a strange fascination. Though he lost more often than he won, the game itself, the rippling cards and clicking chips, the drawn, intent faces of the players, attracted him and he recognized in this contest, so typically American, the world's struggle in microcosm, the whole parade of ruthlessness, bluff, nerve, and the shrewd employment of power he had learned to master in business.

Stoge came to Toby's house nearly every night to play with Tommy Jeff for an hour during the interval between the child's supper and bedtime. Minnie had quietly taken over Agatha's duties, and the house was well run, almost as spotless as when Agatha lived. But it was empty. Not even the sound of Tommy Jeff at play or the busy noises of the slaves in the kitchen helped fill the void that was made by Agatha's going. Stoge Rowden and his son-in-law would sit in the new front room of the house that Toby had made for his wife, both men silent and aware of their loss, finding no words, but taking comfort, even in silence, from one another.

Stoge said nothing to Toby about either the drinking or the gaming, for he knew that Toby was at heart no drunkard and he was certain the passion for gambling would wane. When Tommy Jeff was in bed, Stoge would stay until Toby left the house, often walking with him as far as the tavern, always there if Toby needed him, yet never intruding, never attempting to force his advice on the younger man. On one occasion he asked Toby to forsake the tavern. "My sister's coming up from Memphis," he said. "I'd like for the three of us to have dinner at my house, Toby."

Toby frowned. He remembered Stoge's stern-faced sister, who had been so distant when he met her at the wedding, and he wasn't eager to see her again. He was afraid she might in some way blame him for her niece's death.

But he was mistaken. Agatha Rowden was a woman of character, and she had been skeptical about her namesake's marriage to a foot-loose stranger from Virginia, but she was also capable of great kindness. After dinner, in the living room, she sat alone with Toby. Stoge had gone down to the slave quarters to see to something. Toby fidgeted in his chair. The handsome, gray-haired woman opposite him smiled gently. "You think I blame you for Agatha's death, Toby, don't you?"

Toby avoided her eyes. "I thought you might," he said.

She crossed the room to him and put her hand on his head in a tender, motherly gesture. "I don't, Toby," she said quietly. "It was God's will, and we must try to understand it."

"I will never understand it!" Toby cried. "Why should she have died? Why did God make her die? If there *is* a God."

"Toby, Toby," said Stoge's sister patiently. "You must try to understand."

"No!" said Toby.

Agatha Rowden smiled. "Some day, Toby, you *will* understand. You will learn not to hate." She paused. "I want you to know," she went on, "that if you ever need me, I will be eager to help you. You have only to send for me, and I will come."

Some impulse prompted her to bend and kiss Toby on the forehead. He was touched, completely moved by this stern-faced woman who treated him as a mother might treat a son.

"Thank you," he said, his eyes misting with tears. "I will not forget."

Stoge's sister left the next day, and as he said good-by, Toby understood that in her he had a friend whose loyalty was absolute, and this knowledge comforted him. He drank less, and the long nights became more bearable, though even now he often tossed in his bed until nearly dawn, seeking sleep that would not come, anguishing over his dead wife.

The gambling passed too, but not until Toby had permitted it to draw him almost to ruin. A stranger from Nacogdoches, Señor Felipe Ortega, was a nightly participant in the tavern game, and Toby lost to him steadily, until the Mexican had won over five hundred dollars. But Toby would not quit. People began to talk about his reckless plunging, and one night Stoge cornered him. "Toby," he said quietly, "I understand that greaser Ortega's into you for five hundred dollars."

"That's right," admitted Toby.

"He'll have your farm if you don't watch out," warned Stoge.

Toby's mouth tightened and his eyes became hard. "I'm going to get that money back," he said flatly. "Every last penny of it."

Stoge shook his head. "Forget it, Toby. Charge it up to experience. That Spaniard's no one to play tricks with. They say he's the best rifle shot in this part of the country."

A shrewd smile played at the corners of Toby's mouth. "I've heard that too," he said. "Maybe it'll cost him money."

"What?" asked Stoge.

"I said maybe his shooting will cost him money."

That night Toby stayed home. He busied himself with a chunk of beeswax and some pine soot, working the soot into the wax until he had a black, pliable mixture. He packed the black mass into the bullet mold and allowed it to harden, but upon removal it crumbled. Toby reworked the mass, adding pine pitch until he had the mixture to suit him. He packed the new mixture into the bullet mold, and when it hardened it was surprisingly like a lead bullet, smooth, compact, and almost as heavy. He rolled several of these bullets on the table with a group of real ones and tried them out on Josh. The slave could not detect the difference except by their weight.

The next evening, at the tavern, Ortega taunted him. "Better join us, señor," he said. "I am playing with your money. Do you not want some of it back?"

"Another time, Ortega," answered Toby.

"Better make it soon," the Mexican warned. "It will not be many days before I am gone, poof! With your money."

Toby smiled. He knew that the Mexican was greedy, eager to get the rest of his cash so that he would be driven to put up his farm as a stake. "I don't feel like playing poker with you, Ortega," he said casually. "I might shoot with you, though, for stakes."

The Spaniard laughed. "That, señor, would be a joke. I am the finest rifle shot in Arkansas Territory."

"So you say," Toby observed. "But I think I can beat you shooting."

There was a murmur from the frontiersmen gathered round the tavern table, and someone gave a long, low whistle. No one spoke. Then the Mexican said, "I would be pleased to shoot with you, Señor Giles. But I have not my rifle with me."

Toby snorted in disgust. "Ain't that just like a fourflusher?" he said. "Always bragging, till you call his bluff. Then he crawfishes."

"Plenty of rifles you can borrow, Ortega," one of the men at the table chided. "You can have mine, matter of fact."

The gambler's mouth showed an unpleasant smile. "That being the case, I am at your service, Señor Giles. What are the stakes?"

"The five hundred in your pocket," Toby said.

News of the shooting match spread rapidly through the community. It was to be held on Sunday morning, and by Saturday the news had reached the most outlying settlements. Almost to a man, the residents of Washington planned to be on hand, and there was eager interest even among the women. Everyone felt that Toby would lose, but most of the settlers were cheering for him, as an American against a Mexican. Toby himself was serene, but there was one question yet to be solved, and he visited Stoge at the store. Stoge was busy with Saturday afternoon trade, and Toby waited until the store was empty.

"What kind of fool bet have you made with this crooked Mexican gambler?" his father-in-law wanted to know.

"I'm going to get my money back," Toby said matter-of-factly.

"You're going to throw five hundred good dollars after five hundred bad," Stoge warned.

"If I do, they'll be yours," Toby said, with a smile. "I've got to borrow my stake from you."

Stoge's palms hit the counter top with a noise like the crack of a gun. "Of all the unadulterated gall! That greaser's supposed to be a dead shot with a rifle. You can't hit a barn door."

"I've been doing a little practicing," Toby said. "Besides, I challenged Ortega in front of a dozen men. I can't back out now."

Stoge stared reflectively at the sugar barrel, then turned to Toby. "Tell you what, son," he said finally. "I'll let you have the money on one condition."

"What's that?"

"That you'll stop playing poker and lapping up brandy and start tending to business, so's you can be a decent father to my grandson. That's what." Stoge finished his statement with a friendly smile, but Toby saw that he was in earnest.

"If everybody quit drinkin', you wouldn't have any whiskey business," he commented drily.

"I handle whiskey for the other fellow," Stoge said. "Not for myself and my own family." He paused. "What do you say? Want the five hundred on my terms?"

"You win," Toby said. "But I'd already quit poker, and I'm not really a drinkin' man."

"I know you're not, son," Stoge said seriously. "I know you're not. And I don't blame you for hittin' it a little hard for a while. But now's the time to stop."

After Stoge had gone home, Toby took a gallon of the best Monongahela from the back room and went downstreet to see Squire Tatum. He drank none of the whiskey himself, pleading his need for steady nerves at the rifle match in the morning. But the squire drank liberally, and Toby was able to plant an idea in his head.

Sunday morning was clear. By the time Toby arrived at the shooting ground, Ortega was already there, and several hundred settlers and their families were on hand to watch the fun. There were a few encouraging comments from the crowd as Toby shouldered his way to the center of the ring, but he knew that to a man the Washingtonians expected him to lose.

Ortega swung his bullet pouch and powder horn around his neck, drew the stopper from the horn with his teeth, then loaded his piece, ramming the charge carefully into the barrel. Toby followed suit, taking as much care with his loading, making it a special point to display publicly the black, round beeswax bullet before he dropped it into the muzzle.

"Who's going to hold the stakes?" asked Toby.

"I'll hold the stakes," announced Squire Tatum. "I'm law and order in these parts, and it's part of my duty to see things done proper."

Toby counted out five hundred dollars and watched Ortega peel a like amount from the thick roll he took from his pocket. He glanced at the crowd and saw that everyone was there.

Colonel Withers held court among a group of men at the front of the gathering, and beside him was his daughter Josephine. Toby experienced a jolt as he saw her, and realized all at once that whatever her age—sixteen, some said—Josephine was a woman, more of a woman than many would ever be. The boldness with which she met and held his look made Toby's blood run hot and his heart pound. With an effort he pulled his eyes away from hers and his thoughts back to the business at hand. He turned to Ortega.

"You may shoot first, señor," said Ortega politely. The stranger had the choice, and Ortega was trying to please the crowd. Toby stepped forward and raised his rifle, sighting carefully down the long barrel. He lowered the gun and wet the tip of his finger, brightening the sight, then raised the weapon again to firing position.

"Hold your horses!" Squire Tatum shouted. "Our Mexican friend here is shooting with a strange rifle. That gives Giles an unfair advantage. I suggest they swap guns. Then they'll be even."

"That's fair play," said someone in the crowd.

"Sure it is," said another frontiersman. "Go on, swap."

The Mexican shrugged his shoulders, his gesture indicating his conviction that he could outshoot Toby with either weapon, but he took Toby's gun and handed him the borrowed firearm. Toby wet the sight of the borrowed rifle, took careful aim, and fired, squeezing the trigger precisely. He missed the center of the bullseye by two inches, and Ortega's face loosened into a smile. The Mexican stepped to the firing line, took what appeared to be casual aim, and shot. He lowered his rifle, staring at the target, and an expression of disbelief crossed his face. He had missed the target entirely.

"Madre de Dios!" he swore in his own language. "It is impossible!" He walked up to the target and examined its surface, shaking his head. Only one bullet had pierced the wood, and that one, as everyone in the crowd knew, was Toby's.

131

"The shooting's over, folks!" Squire Tatum announced. "Mr. Giles, here's your money." The squire, who loved ceremony, counted over the thousand dollars slowly while the crowd yelled its praise to Toby. Ortega was examining Toby's rifle, with which he had shot, looking for some defect which might explain his failure, but he could find none. It was an excellent rifle, in perfect condition. Shaking his head, the gambler handed Toby's gun to Josh, who stood waiting for it, a smile on his face.

Settlers came forward to shake Toby's hand, and even Stoge had a grin on his face as he clapped his son-in-law on the shoulder. Then Colonel Withers and Josephine came up.

"Remarkable marksmanship, sir. Truly remarkable. Worthy of a Virginia gentleman."

"Thank you, colonel."

"You know my daughter Josephine?" said Withers.

"I have seen her often," Toby said. "And always admired her."

Josephine extended her hand as a queen to a subject who had won her favor, and her eyes met Toby's with the same bold invitation he had seen in them earlier as she stood in the crowd.

"You were wonderful, Mr. Giles," she murmured, her voice as intimate as her look, and as her warm fingers which lingered in his clasp. Free of the surveillance of her mother and sister, alone with her indulgent father, surrounded by men in a high state of excitement over a masculine triumph, she too was excited. Her lushly red lips were moist and parted, her high bosom lifted with her quick breathing, and she flaunted her womanhood at the hero of the occasion in a way Toby could not miss. The restless, sulky child had become a handsome young woman, with a sheen of animal vitality which Toby found irresistibly attractive. There flowed from her a current of enormous power for passion, perhaps for play, but without softness. Into Toby's mind leaped the memory of his first

132

whore, the sixteen-year-old prostitute in Memphis who had taught him the intricacies of passion for a price and had turned him into the street when his money was gone.

Colonel Withers coughed, and Toby reddened, aghast at his own thoughts as he stared at Josephine.

"You must come and dine with us, young man," the colonel said. "You must be lonely now, after your bereavement. Of course, you may not care to go out. But I think it would do you good."

"Do come, Mr. Giles!" Josephine echoed eagerly.

"I'd be proud to," said Toby.

"Good! Good!" the colonel said. "A week from today, then?"

Toby bowed. The colonel and Josephine departed, and the crowd began to disperse. Toby found Stoge and gave him his five hundred dollars.

"What'd you do to that gambler, Toby?"

"Maybe the crowd made him nervous," said Toby.

"Nervous, hell! He was cool as a clam when he took aim. And they tell me he can drive nails with rifle bullets."

"Oh, hell, Stoge!" said Toby irritably. "He just missed, that's all."

Stoge considered his son-in-law. "You're too sharp for me, Toby. I can't figure if you're just plain lucky, or what."

"Maybe it's 'or what,'" Toby said, laughing. The two men walked back to the store together, Toby falling into step with Stoge, talking pleasantly with his father-in-law, but not concentrating on the conversation. He was counting the months since his wife had died, and there was a certain measure of guilt in his heart. Since Agatha's death he had been celibate; indeed, the thought of a woman had not entered his consciousness, and even during his brandy bouts he had not been moved to visit Memphis or to explore the meager local possibilities. But Colonel Withers' daughter had touched what had been dormant in him, and the memory of her moist, parted lips and the hint of perfume exuded by her hair made the blood tingle in his veins and pound at his temples.

The week that followed seemed interminable, but when Sunday came Toby was due for a disappointment. He dressed for the Withers' dinner carefully, putting on his wedding suit, and wearing a white shirt front covered with tiny hand-stitched ruffles, a garment made by his dead wife. He buffed his shoes with bear grease, wearing the pair from Memphis with built-up heels and soles. As a present he carried one of his home-smoked hams, which his host accepted graciously, asking in detail how it was dressed, cured, and seasoned. Toby explained that he had learned the art of smoking meat from his father in Virginia.

Dinner was formal, and Toby, watchful of the unfamiliar ritual of service, talked little. Colonel Withers maintained a monologue filled with charming anecdote, his wife and his daughter Christine making appropriate responses. But Josephine, seated across the table from Toby, kept her eyes on her plate and had nothing whatever to say. She was plainly in a bad mood, and the reason appeared presently when, as dinner ended, Christine rose and excused herself, saying she must pack. She was going to Arkansas Post in the morning to stay with friends from Paducah who had settled there.

Josephine lifted her eyes at last, turning on her mother a face full of angry resentment. "I don't know why you won't let me go!" she blurted.

"I've told you, my dear," Mrs. Withers said gently and, Toby thought, with a trace of nervousness. Her younger daughter was obviously a little difficult to control.

"Because I'm too young! That's what you always say!"

"Josephine!" her mother warned, with a strained smile. "Curb your temper, my dear. Mr. Giles will think you're a naughty girl."

"I'm not a little girl any more—I'm sixteen!" Josephine ran on headlong. "Why don't you tell the truth, that you won't let me go because I'll take Christine's beaux away from her!"

"Josephine!" Mrs. Withers exclaimed, rising.

"Go to your room, child!" the colonel ordered. Josephine raked Toby with a furious look and fled from the room. Mrs. Withers, a spot of red on each cheek, murmured an inaudible apology and followed her.

The colonel shook his head, chuckling, as he poured brandy into Toby's glass. "A high-spirited filly, my little girl," he said. "Always has been. She has the Withers' hot Kentucky blood, I fear. It will take a man who is really a man to hold a rein on her. Try this brandy now. It's from our cellar at home in Paducah. Our family always had a nice taste."

Toby sipped the brandy, hardly hearing the colonel's gracefully turned phrases. He ignored the slave girl he had bought for Withers in Memphis, who glided swiftly in and out, her lithe body moving with animal grace under her uniform, her eyes challenging when they caught his. Josephine had wiped from his mind all memory of how this girl had impressed him on the day he had inspected her for the colonel. Josephine, provocative, rebellious, filled his thoughts. Her uncontrolled temper, her undisciplined manners before a guest, gave him no uneasiness. On the contrary, he was inclined to sympathize with the wild spirit Mrs. Withers was trying, with such poor success, to fit into the pattern of a lady. His own stubborn will would have made him, in any case, Josephine's ally against the priggish Christine. He sat, while the colonel droned on over his brandy, and longed for the return of Josephine's exciting presence to the room, waiting tensely in the hope that she might rejoin them. It was only when his host became drowsy with his own pompous paragraphs on politics and local affairs that Toby admitted he would not see Josephine again that evening, and took his leave.

Walking home in the darkness, he felt frustrated and dissatisfied with himself. All week he had looked forward to this evening, remembering Josephine's bold glances at the shooting match and feeling again his sudden hot awareness of her as a

135

woman. She had made no secret of her admiration for him that day, when he stood a hero, the victor over the infallible Mexican marksman. Her eyes, her parted lips had been an unspoken invitation. Yet tonight she had ignored him, as though he were no more than one of the Negro servants hovering around the dinner table. His presence had failed to divert her from her chagrin at being kept from a visit to another town. What was there about Arkansas Post, he wondered resentfully. It was only another frontier town of shacks and a few fine houses, like Washington. Had she a beau there? Wasn't he, Toby, interesting enough to her to put thoughts of Arkansas Post out of her head? He could not mean anything to her. He must have imagined it all. Otherwise she would never have given way to petulance and left him to spend a long, boring evening with her father.

Toby tossed in his bed for hours, jealous, angry with himself for being jealous, angry with Josephine for causing it; and meanwhile his mind raced, imagining ways by which he might some day have the passionate girl for his own.

2.

The spring rains of 1828 swelled the creeks and rivers of southwest Arkansas Territory, flooding much of the area. Toby's lands in the creek bottoms were under water, and planting would be seriously delayed. Red River was on one of its rampages, and the water was high enough so that the big boats were able to navigate as far as Fulton. One Sunday morning the river boat *Mabel Belle* tied up at Fulton, with a cargo of windows, doors, and other housebuilding supplies. When Toby learned of the boat's arrival, he went straight to his father-in-law. "Stoge," he announced, "the *Mabel Belle* pulled into Fulton this morning with a cargo of doors and windows."

Stoge's eyebrows lifted. "So?"

Toby paused, looking Stoge straight in the eye. "I'd like to buy the whole cargo," he said. "I owe you a thousand of what you lent me to buy my slaves, but I want more."

Stoge sat without moving, staring at a flyspeck on the wall, then nodded. "Go down there and buy what you want," he said. "I'll stake you." Stoge had learned to trust Toby's business instinct; he did not always approve of his son-in-law's methods, finding them sometimes too sharp, too close to the line, but he did appreciate Toby's intuitive grasp of money matters, and he reasoned that what profited Toby would also profit his grandson, Agatha's child.

"Thanks, Stoge," Toby said. "I'll go down there now."

The *Mabel Belle*'s captain was ashore and the vessel was in charge of a young man who introduced himself as James Black. Black was not empowered to sell the cargo, but he was delighted to show Toby what there was aboard, and the arrangement pleased Toby, for it gave him a chance to look the merchandise over carefully before deciding what to purchase. There were glass-paned windows, wrought-iron door hinges, cut nails, and other fittings.

"Are you a builder?" Black inquired, when they emerged from the *Mabel Belle*'s hold.

"In a manner of speaking," Toby confessed. "I'm a farmer and a storekeeper, but I like to build things."

"So do I," said Black. "This boat bores me."

"What's your regular trade?" asked Toby.

"I'm a silversmith," Black said. "But I can work in any kind of metal."

"Where do you hail from?"

"Jersey. I came down the Ohio from Pittsburgh, then down the Mississippi to Baton Rouge. Just seeing the world."

Toby considered the young fellow shrewdly. He was a well-knit man of about his own age, with powerful shoulders and forearms. There was a look of competence about him that Toby liked, a directness in his movements that indicated he might have skill as a workman. "We need a good blacksmith in Washington, where I come from," he said. "Place about twenty miles from here. Fastest growing community in southwest Arkansas Territory. Why don't you quit the ship and settle there?"

"Think I'd make a go of it?" Black asked.

"There's plenty of work," said Toby. "We can use a man like you."

"I think I'll do it," Black said. He paused. "Why don't you spend the night here on the boat? I'd be glad to have you, and you can see the captain first thing in the morning, before anyone else gets to him."

"Thanks, I'd like to," Toby said.

The next morning, when the captain came aboard, he was still somewhat the worse for wear. His breath reeked of cheap whiskey, and his mean, porcine eyes were bloodshot. Toby was prepared for such an emergency. He had brought a gallon of Stoge's Monongahela with him, and he uncorked the jug, saying, "How about a little of the hair of the dog that bit you, captain, before we get to business?"

The captain grunted. "Dog that bit me's too mean to grow any hair," he said. "But I'll sample your whiskey just the same."

A few drinks of Monongahela improved the captain's temper. He was delighted with the idea of getting rid of his entire cargo to one buyer, and he and Toby came to terms quickly. "Saves me hagglin' with these damn settlers," he said. "Sure, you can have it all."

When the money had changed hands and Toby's slaves were drawing the cargo from the ship's hold, loading it into Toby's wagons, the captain took a little more whiskey. "Giles, I've got some blooded New Orleans hogs aboard. Breeding stock. Think I can sell 'em?"

Toby laughed. "Captain, you can sell most anything around here, except hogs. I don't think you could give 'em away."

"Why not?"

"The woods are full of razorbacks," Toby explained. "All the pork you want for nothing."

"Now, Giles, you know there's no comparison between a blooded hog and a wild boar."

"Try and tell these settlers that," Toby said. "You won't sell any hogs hereabouts. Not if they were gold plated."

When he departed from the *Mabel Belle*, Toby carried with him as a gift from the captain a pair of prize New Orleans hogs. His hams were already becoming famous in Washington, and with the stock these two would breed he would be able to produce sugar-cured pork that would rival the proudest product of Virginia.

Josh climbed up to the wagon seat beside his master, saying to Toby in a low voice, "Marse Toby, when dat boat leave, some of them niggers won't be on it."

"How come?" asked Toby.

"Dat captain, Marse Toby, he don't deserve to own a dog. He's mean. I done talked to them boat niggers an' tole them how you got me away from the Indians."

Toby nodded. "Why don't you stay behind, Josh? Maybe you can help them niggers."

"Yes sah, Marse Toby," agreed the slave. He slipped from the box and disappeared into the brush. Toby began the long drive home, the heavily laden wagons protesting behind him. When the building supplies were stored in his barn, he was pleased with himself, for he knew that he had a monopoly on all such equipment likely to be had in Washington for some time.

The next day he started his axemen clearing land and cutting timbers, then went to see Squire Tatum. He wanted to make arrangements with the town officials to buy land on which to erect houses that he would then put up for sale, but he was astonished to learn that the town had never been properly plotted. The government had donated land a mile square—six hundred and forty acres—for the townsite, and streets had been laid out, but each settler had surveyed his own property. A survey would cost the town two hundred and fifty dollars, and the officials balked at that expenditure.

"Hell, squire," Toby said. "I'll make the survey for them."

The squire's eyes twinkled with amusement. "What would you be wanting in return for your trouble, Toby?" he asked gently.

"Forty acres of land. And it's cheap at that. Land's plentiful and money's scarce."

"I don't know, Toby," the squire said. "I don't know. I'll put it up to 'em."

In the end they accepted Toby's offer. Toby hired a surveyor at his own figure, and when the job was completed the town possessed an accurate plot of all property within the township lines and Toby possessed forty acres of valuable land, sufficient space for eight or ten houses, each with its small pasture and kitchen garden. It was not by accident that the land Toby acquired adjoined the Withers' property. The squadron of slaves employed in digging the foundation of the first house worked with such speed and precision that the project attracted the interest of everyone in Washington, and Josephine was unable to resist her curiosity. Before the main stringers were in place, she had become a regular visitor to the building site, listening with pretty attentiveness while Toby explained the principles of construction. Her interest became less pretty and more nakedly avid as Toby hinted at his plans for the future, plans which aimed at an accumulation of wealth beyond the dreams of anyone in Arkansas Territory.

Seeing this avidity, Toby became clever, not pressing his

point, merely conveying, with the odd word let slip, that he was at present a man of means and that in the future he would be both wealthy and powerful. Josephine's bold looks and provocative manner became more and more subdued as the days went by, and she took on a maidenly propriety worthy of her sister Christine, her full red lips uttering all the admiring little gasps of womanly helplessness before Toby's competence in men's affairs. Toby was not fooled. He recognized this pretty pretense as a sign that Josephine was beginning to take him seriously. Meanwhile, beneath the surface, no matter what they talked about, ran the strong current of sexual attraction. It was implicit in Josephine's manner, though now she held him at a distance and never overstepped the bounds of formal decorum. Toby knew what she was doing, drawing him on and holding him off, and yet he was caught as surely as a mouse being toyed with by a cat. Josephine was an intuitive coquette. Young as she was, she knew how a girl of good family can use her sex by inference even more effectively than by blatant display. Toby was more aroused by one of her fleeting, significant glances than by all the lewd parading of the prostitutes in the Memphis Gut. She worried him, sentencing him to sleepless nights and moments of mortifying embarrassment when, at some instant in a public place, the most tantalizing projections would overtake him, making the blood boil in his veins and pound at his temples, causing him to blush as hotly as a schoolboy.

He must have Josephine, that he knew. He must have her as he had possessed the prostitute in Memphis, as chattel, as a slave. Yet, by her new mask of decorum, Josephine was indicating to him that marriage was the only way, and marriage to one of Colonel Withers' daughters would not be a simple matter. The colonel and Mrs. Withers made it clear that they were an outpost of Kentucky aristocracy here on the frontier. Toby was a nobody, even today, so far as people like the Withers were concerned. Stoge's objection to his marrying

Agatha would be nothing compared to the objection he would meet if he even hinted to Colonel Withers that he hoped to marry his daughter.

Love, in the sense in which he had loved, and still loved, Agatha, had no part in his desire for Josephine. There was no tenderness in his heart when he thought of her, no inspiration to higher moral values. There was only desire, burning, intolerable, maddening desire. And there was the cold hunger for what marriage to her would represent as a symbol of social advancement.

He had learned to understand one thing about Josephine during these days on the building site. While her coquetry tormented him, he had clearly seen her covetousness: she loved money. Why this was so he could not know. He could not guess how, as a child growing into girlhood, she had seen her father squander first his own fortune and then his wife's, losing slave after slave, his stable of thoroughbred horses, finally his ancestral acres and the porticoed mansion itself. She had known, when he had managed by using friends in high places to secure his appointment as land agent in Washington, that he was moving his family to the wilderness because he had lost everything at home. Neither her father nor her mother breathed a word of this to Josephine or Christine, but with the awareness of children they knew. Christine, pliant and dutiful, accepted the change, becoming only a little sharper, a little more rigid in her insecurity. But Josephine's ardent spirit had turned bitter as she saw her little mare sold, her Negro nurse sold, her wardrobe shrinking, her childish world ever more and more constricted, and she knew money, or the lack of it, was to blame. Money was power, money was pleasure, money was the way to everything. As trust in her father dwindled, trust in money took its place.

This Toby grasped; it was the one trait in Josephine of which he could be sure. She loved money, and she could be bought, as the whore in Memphis had been bought, but the price would be higher, enormously higher, and the business negotiations would be no simple matter of handing hard cash to a tough-voiced madam who called you neighbor and sold counterfeit money. The price, Toby quite understood, would be his life, or that part of his life with which he acquired wealth, and since Agatha's death, after his brief, orgiastic interlude with chance and the bottle, that sector of his being, the acquisitive sector, was devouring the rest of him, so that the strong instinct for love which was in him, and which Agatha had drawn forth and nurtured, was pressed to one side. He became almost a monomaniac, seeking wealth for its own sake, though persuading himself that he wanted it so that he could become an aristocrat. He was driven to seek money as an end in itself, as others seek warmth, or refreshment, or oblivion, but his reason demanded tangible purpose as a symbol for his struggle to acquire a fortune. To be an aristocrat—that had been his goal, and since the pale, cool morning in Virginia when he saddled the stolen Maison horse and rode over the mountains to Pittsburgh, the flavor of that goal had sustained him, and the story-book picture of Captain Maison which he carried in his dreams loomed before him in the distance like the Grail. To be like Captain Maison, tall, handsome, scarlet-clad, to sit on a horse with the grace of a guardsman, so that thoroughbred animal and thoroughbred man became by some miracle a single living thing, to walk with the kind of assurance that contained the elan of a dancer and the power of an athlete, to speak in accents almost soft as a woman's, yet strengthened underneath by the iron of authority, to be lord of all that he surveyed, with the wealth of the world his at a handclap—that was Toby's ambition, the ambition he treasured in his secret dreams. To this image and this ambition he now added Josephine, the second symbol, the handle to the Grail. Had Toby understood that what he wanted, in the true, murky depths of his mind, was money itself, he might have turned from it as hard, useless stuff. He thought he wanted Josephine and a scarlet coat, and the way to get those was by getting money enough to buy them.

Colonel Withers, one day, had said to him, "Toby, my boy, that ham of yours was a masterpiece. No Virginia sugar-cured was ever more smooth to the taste. You could make a fortune selling such hams in Paducah or Louisville or Richmond, where people enjoy real quality in food."

The blooded swine he had got from the captain of the *Mabel Belle* were in Toby's pens, and he was struck with the idea of breeding them with the wild razorbacks that roamed in the hills, hoping thus to produce pork superior to any in the area. This meant trapping a number of brood sows, so one morning when work in the fields had been stopped, he followed the hog trails deep into the bottoms, forcing his way through tangled vines and heavy undergrowth that switched his face, until he suddenly stopped like a dog on point, hearing the grunting and squealing of a band of wild swine. He climbed a tree, watching his prey from above, sitting in the crotch of a gnarled old hickory for an hour, his rifle across his lap.

An old boar broke through the underbrush into the clearing, a heavy, powerful animal, with the scars of many combats on his flanks. A younger, lighter boar turned from the sows, the short hairs on his neck and back bristling like a porcupine. The two boars faced each other, and the grunting and squealing of the other hogs ceased, giving way to a silence fraught with tension. Then the younger boar charged and the fight was on. Toby watched it from above, fascinated and terrified, sickened by the spectacle, yet unable to turn away from it. When the heavy tusks struck flesh, deep gashes were torn, yet neither animal flinched or wavered. The old saw-back was a patient fighter, his eyes glaring with bitter rage. It was not blind rage, because he measured his enemy carefully, never charging until in a position to sidestep a counter charge. The old veteran had difficulty breaking through the young boar's guard. Once, as

144

the older animal charged, the younger ducked and with a quick slashing movement ripped a six-inch cut in his opponent's groin. After a half dozen rounds both hogs still stood their ground, their heads gashed and torn, their flanks cut and bleeding. The two boars stood for a moment motionless, their eyes blazing with hatred. Mercy was an unknown thing; this was a fight to the death. Suddenly the young boar charged, then halted his lunge before reaching his target, forcing the old hog off balance and catching his leg in a strong grip, twisting with a vicious pull, so that the sound of the breaking bone made a noise in the wilderness like a rifle shot. Before the old boar could rip his enemy, his foe leaped aside, leaving the crushed leg dragging. The young boar pressed his advantage, relentlessly tearing the old champion to pieces. He made a wild lunge, with his razor-sharp hoofs landing in the side of the crippled boar. Two huge holes ripped through this flesh and with repeated attacks the old boar was nearly torn to pieces, his entrails dragging the ground, but still the fight went on. A drove of sows and half-grown shoats soberly waited for the kill; a silent circle of hungry hogs, with lolling eyes and tongues dripping with expectant saliva. The old boar fought by instinct alone, his snapping jaws and terrifying groans made Toby's blood run cold. When the savage old brute dropped in his tracks the hogs moved in for the aftermath. Toby sat in his tree, watching the animals devour the old boar's carcass. When they had stripped the flesh from the bones, he fired a shot from his pistol, and was relieved when they all lunged into the thicket. But it was several moments before he was able to descend from his perch in the tree and make his way homeward. What he had seen shocked and frightened him, but it fascinated him too, for somehow the entire idea of life in the raw had been exemplified in that struggle between the young tusker and the old, the fight to the death, with no holds barred, and the final indignity of defeat and oblivion when the shoats and the sows moved in to feast on the vanquished warrior's corpse. The murderous savagery of the boars in their struggle exceeded anything he had seen among men, though on the waterfront in Norfolk he had witnessed death battles between drink-crazed seamen and water rats, and knife fights on the frontier where death was the only reward for the loser. He went slowly back to the village, stopping at the tavern for a few stiff drinks. He was still determined to trap a few sows, but he had decided to let Josh get them for him.

And get them Josh did. How the black man managed it, Toby never knew, but at nightfall, three days later, the faithful slave had ten wild sows in a strong pen behind Toby's large barn. In the meantime Toby passed day after day in the wilderness, slaughtering razorbacks, so that, when the cold weather set in, he had more than three hundred hams and shoulders in his smokehouse, and a hundred slabs of side meat salted down to provide food for the slaves.

Toby cured his hams Virginia fashion, in the way he had learned on the Maison Plantation. Cords of hickory were cut for meat smoking, and the slaves were instructed to save oak ash from the clearing fires. Only oak was used in the process. As soon as the hogs were cleaned and dressed, they were hung to bleed and cool. Next came the mixture of salt and oak ash, rubbed into the uncured meat, which was then set aside for more chilling. After a few days hanging in the cold, the hams were steeped in an iron washpot filled with a mixture of milk and wild honey, this soaking helping to remove the strong wild taste and at the same time contributing tenderness and a more uniform texture. Toby had his own secret recipe for the next step, a mixture of sugar, pepper, mustard, vinegar, and spices dampened with sorghum molasses. This was smeared over the meat, and it was then hung to ripen, soaking up the aroma and flavor of the various ingredients. Then the hams and shoulders were sewn in clean white muslin cases, dampened from time to time with a mixture of brandy, wild honey, and spices, until, at last, they were ready for the smokehouse and the slow, steady smoking that cured the meat and blended the flavors. It was a lengthy, laborious process, but it produced hams that were totally unlike the strong, acrid chunks of meat the settlers hastily smoked for themselves, and the colonel's prediction had been correct, for Toby was able to sell his smoked meat at high prices, as a delicacy. The labor involved was slave labor, he reasoned, and cost him little. And the meat brought in cash. Toby had learnt that most farmers were content to feed themselves and their families, and not too concerned with hard money, so that when misfortune overtook them during the bad year that was bound to follow a series of good ones, they were often penniless. Toby wanted cash, and to get it he would have embarked on a hundred sidelines such as meat-curing, had they presented themselves. Already he was merchant, farmer, builder, miller, meat-curer, slaveholder, and man of general affairs. Had there been profit on the Arkansas frontier in the marketing of human dung, then Toby would have traded in that, for he had learned that the value of a dollar is not altered by the humbleness of its source. His stock of dollars rose steadily, and with it his sense of achievement. His mill was busy grinding corn for the settlers, and the tithe from that overflowed his granaries. His hams brought money, and his men were building a second house not far from the first. The first house had been sold at a profit of several hundred dollars, and Toby knew that he would be able to sell as many houses as he could build. He was driving, driving always, toward wealth and the symbol of the scarlet coat, and he knew that he would get them both.

But he made no progress with Josephine. He saw her now at least once each week, and on occasion dined with the colonel and his family, but the girl's armor was not dented. She continued to taunt him with her eyes and mock him with the curve of her moist, sensuous lips, but it was still "Mr. Giles, sir," and "Miss Josephine," and the stiff formalities were preserved between them. One evening, assisting her as she descended the steps, he held her hand a moment too long and her eyes flashed angrily. On another occasion, at a church sociable, he sat beside her so close that their thighs touched. This physical contact heated his blood and made his breath catch in his throat, and he knew that Josephine was aware of this, and that she gloated over his combined discomfort and desire, yet when he moved still closer, pretending to be looking at her hymnbook, she gave him a glance that sent ice through his veins and drew stiffly away as from one with the plague. She was toying with him, he understood, teasing him as a certain kind of woman delights to tease a man. But in the end, he was determined, it was he who would do the teasing, he who would call the tune according to the old prerogative granted to the man who pays the fiddler.

Only once did Josephine's façade of gentility show the slightest crack. One evening, when Toby was escorting her home from the church, she said idly, "What is your ambition in life, Mr. Giles, sir? Your greatest ambition."

He looked at her meaningfully, pausing before he answered, then saying, "If I told you my greatest ambition, Miss Josephine, you'd be amused. You might even be angry. You would think me presumptuous." He paused again, to let his meaning become clear, then went on, "But I'll tell you one of my ambitions."

"What is that, sir?"

He stopped, standing still in the moonlight, and she stopped with him, an amused, half-scornful smile on her lips.

"I want to be the richest man in Arkansas Territory," he said. "I want to make money. Lots of money."

An extraordinary, almost erotic expression appeared on her face, and her eyes narrowed as she said, clutching his arm tightly, "You will, Toby! I know you will. Make lots of money! Lots of it!"

"Do you *want* me too?" he said candidly.

But her mood was gone. She laughed lightly and released

his arm. "Of course I do, Mr. Giles," she said. "You are my father's friend. I wish you well."

"Am I only your father's friend, then?" he asked.

"Oh, and mother's too," she laughed. "Come, Mr. Giles, take me home."

That night, tossing in the darkness, he muttered in his sleep, "Money, money." And he dreamt of Josephine standing nude on the slave block, the block from which he had bought the bold young Negress for Colonel Withers. The arrogant, aristocratic girl stood naked, with her long golden hair hanging loose, while drunken farmers encircled her, making crude remarks above the slave merchant's hawking, reaching out to pinch her buttocks or run their hands across her smooth, firm breasts. Then, in his dream, Toby stepped forward and showered hard gold pieces at her feet, waiting until the slave merchant gathered them from the floor, then seized the dream Josephine by the hair and dragged her naked, but unprotesting, through the streets of Memphis to his waiting wagon train. At the wagon train, when she turned, she had been transformed from the golden-haired aristocrat into the colonel's serving maid, the lewd young Negress who had challenged him and stood without flinching on the day he bought her, when his rough hands explored her body. He woke rudely, with a cry of anguish, shocked by the bold, outrageous channels sought by his mind under cover of sleep. He was damp with sweat, and the night air chilled him, making him huddle in his quilt for warmth, but he slept no more that night, for the secrets that his dreams revealed frightened him and in a strange way warned him of shapeless terror somewhere along the dark road of the future. Toby Giles, not yet twenty-five, was already the prisoner of his own desires, and the prisoner, too, of a mind distorted early in childhood by hardship and fear. He was a driven man, blindly going forward, like a coalpit mule whose eyes are darkened so that he will be content below and never yearn for the sunlight and air to be discovered above ground.

3.

The long summer drought had left its mark on the country. The fields and woods were bare of forage, and that winter it was not possible for the finest woodsman to find sustenance in the wilderness. Migrant Indians, on the long trek west, despaired of completing the trip until spring, and several hundred broke the journey at Washington, camping just outside the town. A little city of tepees and wigwams rose on the outskirts of Washington as the tribesmen holed in for the winter, and though at first the townsmen welcomed the dollars the braves spent in the village stores, the Indian encampment soon became a nuisance, for young braves, bored by inaction, turned to thievery and worse for distraction, and people took to barring their doors and keeping their women off the streets after dark. There was a series of petty thefts, and for several days the town was tense after one of the redskins, primed with firewater, had attempted to rape a young woman. There had been incidents between red men and white, occasional scuffles, and one brawl that ended in a knifing. Everyone was on edge, and some of the hotter heads proposed that vigilance committees be formed. The settlers were worried about the danger to their women, and also afraid that the lawlessness of the braves might spread to the slaves and inspire trouble in the quarters. Settlers watched their blacks carefully, quickly suppressing the slightest disturbance, tightening the reins, and denying liberties even to favored Negroes. It was a time of tension for a community based on slavery, for the roistering Indians, by their presence, disturbed even though slightly the delicate balance in the relationship between whites and blacks upon which the whole social structure of Arkansas Territory and the American South was based.

It was in the midst of this potential crisis that Josh reported to Toby the news that four Negroes, two men and two women, had escaped from the *Mabel Belle* and were now hidden on the Giles farm. Toby hated to pass up the chance to acquire three thousand dollars' worth of slaves for nothing, though he knew that the risk was especially great at this time. He thought it over, then told Josh to put the blacks to work to earn their board and keep.

The next day Toby carried a batch of dull plows to James Black's shop. The young emigrant from New Jersey had done well in Washington. He was an expert at shoeing horses, sharpening plows, making hinges, mending locks, and making knives. His hunting and butchering knives were becoming known as the finest on the frontier. So expert had the young man become at working in iron that he seemed to have no regrets about his lost trade of silversmith. He took Toby's plows, promising to return them within the week, and the two men stood at the door of the shop, chatting idly. Suddenly they heard the baying of a pack of hounds, and a few minutes later the lead dog came into sight, followed by the eager pack, which was herded by several men on horseback. Toby's heart missed a beat when he recognized the captain of the *Mabel Belle*. He greeted the captain, then made an excuse and rode quickly back to his farm, giving three short blasts on his hunting horn, a signal that brought Josh to him on the run.

"Get them boat niggers off the place, and fast," Toby ordered.

"What I gonna do wiv 'em, Marse Toby?" the black man asked.

"Shoot them, if necessary," Toby said angrily. "Get them off my land. Show them the blind trail leading to the river and that cave. Tell them to hide."

"Yessah, Marse Toby. I gets rid of 'em."

Toby rode slowly back to town. To cast suspicion away from himself, he joined the posse that was being formed to hunt down the runaway Negroes. Settlers were gathering to organize the chase—James Beck, the Carolinian, Scott Johnson, Bill Bowes, and even Squire Tatum. Personal differences were put aside when runaway slaves were involved, for the settlers understood that if one Negro was permitted to escape, others would be encouraged to follow. Though no love was lost on the *Mabel Belle*'s captain, every white man in town, with two exceptions, was prepared to leave his work in order to help hunt down the captain's runaways. The exceptions were Toby, who merely went through the motions of the hunt to divert suspicion from himself, and James Black, the smith from New Jersey, who did not join in the chase at all. There were rumors that Black had queer ideas, that he did not believe in slavery, and would like to see the Negroes set free, though Toby had never heard him utter an opinion one way or the other. It was true that Black was uncommonly kind to Negroes, and that, though his blacksmith shop produced considerable revenue, he had never shown any desire to own slaves himself.

Black stood in the doorway of his shop, watching the posse form up, and Toby waved to him as he rode past. The hounds streaked out before the mounted men, taking the scent from an old rag the captain said was torn from one of the slave women's dresses.

"No-good black bitch," he said. "When I catch her I'll fix her so's she won't be able to wear a dress for a month, her rump'll be so sore."

The dogs followed the creek downstream, and Toby had a bad moment when the infallible animal who led the pack picked up the scent and turned from the water, straight toward his farm. His one hope was that Josh had had time to get the slaves off his place and to get back to his work, so that everything on Toby's farm would appear to be normal.

He had underestimated Josh. Near Toby's slave quarters the leading hound suddenly stopped and began to sneeze pathetically. James Beck dismounted and himself sniffed at the ground. "Someone's sprinkled pepper on the track," he said. "We'll have to pick up a new scent."

"Who'd've done a thing like that?" asked Toby.

"Bet it was that Yankee blacksmith," someone guessed. "They say he don't hold with slavery none. Thinks niggers ought to be free."

Josh left his work in the fields and approached his master, hat in hand, looking curiously at the mounted posse, especially at the captain of the *Mabel Belle*, who glowered suspiciously at him. "Somep'n wrong, Marse Toby?" the slave asked.

"Josh," Toby said, "we've traced some runaway niggers as far as right here. You seen anything of 'em?"

"I see four niggers go through heah fast," Josh said. "Two mens and two womans. One of them niggers was ugly. He had a big gun, a big pistol."

"Where would that black bastard get a gun?" the captain wanted to know.

"I doan' know wheah he gets it, white boss, but he sho' got it, an' he'll use it, too," Josh said. "He jam dat gun in mah ribs and make me git him some black pepper from de kitchen."

"Which way did they go, Josh?" asked Toby.

"Toward de river, Marse Toby. Said dey was goin' to Loosi-ana, wheah dey got frien's."

The posse made for the river bottoms, and the hounds sniffed up and down the bank, but they did not pick up the scent again, though long after nightfall, with torches blazing in the darkness, the tired settlers continued the hunt. At last, near morning, the captain agreed that further search was use-less and the tired men rode slowly home. Toby threw himself into a chair, totally exhausted, physically and nervously, filthy with river mud. He took the drink that Josh brought, drank it at a gulp, and handed the glass back to the slave. "Another one, Josh. I'm beat out."

"Yes, Marse Toby." Josh poured a second drink. As he handed it to his master, he smiled. "You owns you'self four new niggers, Marse Toby," he said. "An' dey glad to belong to you, 'stead of dat cap'n."

"You did a good job, Josh," said Toby. He seldom complimented a slave, believing that praise would spoil a Negro, but he couldn't refrain from telling Josh that he had done well. He dismissed the slave and sat, holding the second whiskey in his hand, wondering how he was going to fit the four new blacks into his organization without bringing condemnation on himself. But he was too tired to wrestle with the problem. He had Minnie draw him a tub full of water and scrubbed the river filth from his body, then turned in, so tired that he fell at once into a deep, blank, dreamless sleep.

Tommy Jeff was growing like a weed. Stoge would have spoiled the lad with his gifts and attention had not Minnie's care and devotion prevented it. She was kind to him, but firm, and he was developing into a fine, well-mannered child, a little on the solemn side, but with more than a hint of his mother's quiet humor lurking in his eyes and at the corners of his mouth. Toby was devoted to the boy, and never missed his hour with him, just before Tommy Jeff's bedtime. But he left the rearing of him to Minnie. Tommy Jeff loved his father and Stoge, and he adored Minnie, but the person he seemed fondest of, next to his father, was a woman he had seen only four times in his life. That was Stoge's sister, Agatha, who endured the exhausting journey from Natchez twice during the year to visit her nephew. Tommy Jeff, perhaps with some childish intuition, recognized in his aunt a projection of his dead mother and talked of the kindly spinster for months after each visit. "Where Agatha?" he would say in his sweet, childish voice. "Where Aunt Agatha?" And Toby would smile and stroke the boy's hair, though mention of the beloved name sent a cruel, knifelike pain through his heart.

When she was leaving at the end of her second visit, Agatha stood holding Tommy Jeff's hand. "Toby Giles, if you ever want to get rid of this boy, you send him to me," she said. "I'm tempted to kidnap him anyway, and take him back to Natchez with me."

Toby laughed. "Guess we'll keep him a while, Miss Agatha," he said. "Anyway, he's too young for Natchez."

Agatha blushed, understanding Toby's meaning. "Toby Giles!" she said. "The idea!" But she wasn't a prude, in spite of her strait-laced appearance and schoolmarm's voice. She smiled and said, "Seriously, Toby, if there's ever anything I can do for you or Tommy Jeff, you let me know."

"I sure will, Miss Agatha." Toby felt curiously warm toward the gray-haired woman. Her kindness and sincerity touched him, and somehow he felt toward her as he would have wanted to feel toward his mother, who had offered usually neither affection nor blows, but merely a dull, stuporous indifference, submitting to his father's curses and beatings with the same listlessness with which she accepted his brutal, alcoholic lust, there in the dark, slab-boarded shanty on the Norfolk waterfront. Toby remembered some of it vividly, and the memory made him burn with shame and embarrassment. He remembered his father, stumbling into the shanty, pulling his mother's slatternly dress from her body, then throwing her roughly to the straw pallet on the floor. He remembered the sound of his mother's body as she fell and the sound of his father's hulk as he dropped beside her. He could not remember, in all his childhood, ever being kissed by his mother, or ever seeing any show of affection between his parents. The picture that he retained most vividly was his father, in drunken lust, taking his mother's body without regard for the sleepy children in the darkened room who huddled in terror through the whole proceeding. When Miss Agatha leaned forward and kissed him on the forehead, as a mother might kiss a grown son, the gesture brought tears to his eyes, tears of love for this simple, good woman who was his wife's aunt, and tears of self-pity for his own lost childhood. When Agatha had gone, he took Tommy Jeff on his lap and sat with the child for a long time, saying nothing, brooding over the past, and the thoughts that ran through his troubled mind were thoughts that have captured fathers like Toby since the dawn of time. "My son, my son!" he might well have cried. In that moment, with the boy on his lap, the memory of Miss Agatha's lavender in his nostrils, the dark, shameful recollection of Norfolk like a scar on his brain, in that moment he forgot his ambition, and forgot Josephine, thinking only of his son and his son's future, and the fact that he intended the lad to enjoy everything he had been deprived of in childhood—kindness, attention, love, security.

He sat this way for perhaps an hour, then realized that Tommy Jeff was asleep in his arms. He carried the boy to his room and undressed him carefully, trying not to awaken him, but as he tucked him into his bed, Tommy Jeff came half awake and his arms encircled his father's neck. "Good night, daddy," he said, his voice heavy with sleep.

"Good night, Tommy Jeff," said Toby. "Sleep well. Don't be afraid."

"What should I be 'fraid of, daddy?"

"Nothing, son. Nothing." The tears welled up in his eyes again; he bent and kissed his son, then hurried from the room, sitting alone before the fire with a forgotten glass of whiskey in his hand, staring at the brilliant message of the flames, confused and oddly bedeviled, like a traveler told at a fork in the road to go in both new directions at once. Josh found him asleep in the chair, the untouched whiskey in a pool beside his chair.

"Marse Toby," the slave said. "You doan' want to be sittin' here asleep with the door not barred. No tellin' who might slip in."

Toby laughed, rubbing his eyes. "Guess you're right, Josh. I just dropped off."

He got into bed and soon fell into a troubled sleep. An hour later, perhaps more, he awoke with a start. Outside in the darkness he heard the pounding hoofs of a horse, and a second later a hail of pebbles hit the window of his bedroom. "Hello! Hello!" called a voice. "Hello, hello! Toby! Toby Giles!"

He went to the window and called, "Who's there?" dimly seeing a rider in the starlight.

"It's me, James Beck. Get your horse and come quick. A drunk Indian just shot Stoge."

For a moment Toby could not find speech. Then he said, with a tremor in his voice, "Is he bad hurt?"

"Plenty bad," Beck said curtly. "Doc Hooker's on his way."

Toby dressed quickly and buckled on his pistol, then took his rifle from its rack on the wall. "How did it happen, Jim?" he asked, turning to Beck, who stood waiting for him.

"The Indian was plumb crazy drunk. He wanted liquor and Stoge wouldn't give it to him."

"Where's the Indian now?" asked Toby.

"Stoge thinks he winged him. But the skunk got away."

"If Stoge dies," Toby said slowly, "I've lost the best friend I ever had. He's been like a father to me, Jim."

"I know it," said Beck. "And this town will lose its best citizen. They don't make 'em better than Stoge Rowden."

"Stoge just can't die, Jim," said Toby. "He just can't."

"I hope not, Toby," Beck said, shaking his head. "But he's powerful bad. Powerful bad."

Beck had not exaggerated. Stoge was stretched out on the floor of the store with a bolt of muslin under his head, and Doctor Hooker was working on him, trying to stop the bleeding, but it wasn't necessary to be a doctor to understand that

157

the life was leaving Stoge's rugged body. Toby knelt beside him, and Stoge smiled up at him.

"Guess my time's come, son," he said.

"Don't say that, pa," Toby said, involuntarily calling Stoge by the nickname Agatha had always used.

Stoge touched his hand. "Ain't no use, Toby. I've got to cross the Jordan. But I'm not afraid."

Toby cried then, in front of everyone, not ashamed of his tears, and his eyes were not the only moist ones in the gathering. Few men in the town of Washington were as respected and loved as was Stoge Rowden. There was hardly a soul in all of the district who could not remember some favor or kindness the big storekeeper had done him.

"My lungs are full of grass spurs," Stoge said. "I better talk while I can. Squire!"

"Yes, Stoge?" Squire Tatum said.

"Write down what I say," said Stoge. He waited until Tatum had pen and ink ready, then went on, "I, Stoge Rowden, do hereby will my store, my lands, my slaves, and everything else I own to Thomas Jefferson Giles."

"Is that all, Stoge?" asked the squire.

"Yes," said Stoge. "I'll sign it."

Tatum held his hand while Stoge wrote his name at the bottom of the will. Then Stoge's head sank back to the pillow. "Make a good man out of Tommy Jeff, Toby," he said.

"I will, Stoge. I promise."

"If you ever need help, get in touch with my sister. She's all wool, Toby."

"I know it, Stoge. I know it."

A few moments later Stoge Rowden died, his hand in Toby's, a kind of smile on his face as he began the journey that all men make. Doctor Hooker bent forward and closed the lifeless eyes. "He's gone, boys," the doctor said. "He never had a chance. The Indian got him in the chest and the bullet went right through his lungs."

Toby rose. Someone in the crowd let out a roar of rage, shouting, "Boys, we're going to kill every God-damned Indian in the country. Get your horses!"

It was Toby who stopped them. "Boys," he said, "Stoge wouldn't want us to kill a lot of innocent people. Most of the Indians are peaceful enough. It's just a few that go bad. Let's get the Indian that killed Stoge, and hang him."

"Let's burn 'em all out," one hothead insisted.

"No, no," said Toby. "What good would it do?"

"Toby's right," Doctor Hooker said. "Stoge wouldn't want us to kill a lot of people that didn't have anything to do with it."

"Well, then, what's our next move?" asked James Beck, addressing Toby. "We'll follow you through hell, Giles, to find the drunken bastard."

Toby put a hand on Beck's shoulder. "Thanks, Jim," he said. "I know you will. All of you. But I think I can find him."

"How?" Beck asked.

"Yeah, Toby, how you gonna git the skunk?"

"I know the old chief pretty well," Toby said. "I think he'll find the man that shot Stoge." Toby cast an eye over the crowd, then went on. "Squire, I want you and Jim Beck and me to ride out to see the old chief, and I want the rest of you to promise not to do anything till we get back."

"All right," someone agreed. "Go see the old son-of-a-bitch. If he don't give you the man that did it, we'll string him up to the highest tree in the country."

Toby and his friends approached the Indian encampment with their rifles at the ready, prepared for trouble. But the old chief emerged from his tepee and greeted them peacefully, giving them the sign of friendship, the raised hand, palm outward. "I hear that a dark shadow has crossed the white man's path," he said.

"You have heard correctly," Toby said.

"My wigwam is open. You are welcome. We will talk."

The three white men were offered seats near the fire and the chief squatted on the floor, facing them, his fierce old warrior's features accented by the firelight so that his face appeared to have been fashioned out of immobile, hammered copper.

"We have come for the man who killed Stoge Rowden," Toby said. "You have said that a dark cloud has crossed the white man's path. We want the man who made that cloud."

"You'd better find him for us," James Beck said. "Or we'll kill every Indian in your camp."

The old chief nodded soberly. "I myself have cried to the Great White Father when the outlaw white man has killed my people. He sent me paper from far away, saying he cannot help what outlaw white man do. I, like him, cannot help what outlaw red man do."

"We must have the murderer," Toby said relentlessly. "Or all of you, men, women, and children alike, will pay for his crime."

"My best scouts are in the woods. They search for the one made crazy by the white man's firewater. They will find him."

"They better find him," Beck said.

"They will find him," the chief promised.

"Words will not satisfy the white man's anger," said Toby. "We must have the murderer."

As the chief was about to reply, two young braves approached the wigwam, holding between them a whimpering woman with long stringy arms and a face like a walnut, fear showing plainly in her black eyes. In her bony hands she held a soggy, bloodstained rag. The old chief addressed her in native dialect.

"Talk English," James Beck commanded. "We can't understand that lingo."

"This woman, she does not understand English," the chief said calmly. He resumed his questioning, and when he had finished he translated the interchange. "Her man was home with a bloody shoulder. Then he ran to woods."

"Find this man, and bring him in for trial," said Toby.

"He will be found and brought to you," the old chief promised. "My scouts will search the hills and river bottoms, marsh by marsh, swamp by swamp, bush by bush, tree by tree."

The next day the sky lightened and a bright sun rose to warm the earth. The settlers had been waiting for this break in the weather, for they were eager to get to their fields, but instead of plowing they took down the long rifles from their walls and did sentry duty at the red men's encampment, keeping the Indians hemmed in, permitting none to enter or leave the camp save the scouts dispatched by the old chief in search of the wounded murderer. Stoge's body rested in state, in a cypress coffin on two trestles, his burial delayed until the killer could be found. In death the big storekeeper looked like a man peacefully resting, waiting for a friendly hand to awaken him, and Toby understood, gazing at Stoge's peaceful countenance, that his father-in-law had gone to his Maker without fear, and that in whatever world was beyond the grave Stoge would take his place in happiness, rewarded for a life on earth devoted to decency and kindness.

The day passed, and another, then a third, and still the killer was not brought in, though Indian scouts, exhausted and covered with river mud, returned to camp with the report that they were on his trail. It was impossible to delay Stoge's funeral longer, so at ten o'clock on the morning of the third day the people of the town and the surrounding country gathered to pay final tribute to the man who had been their first citizen. They marched, about a hundred of them, with bowed heads, to the burying ground on the hillside. Toby remembered that it had been almost a year since he and Stoge had followed Agatha's coffin to the same resting ground. He stood with his head bared, his pistol strapped around his waist, thinking of his dead wife, hearing scarcely any of the words of the preacher.

Suddenly, as if by magic, the old chief appeared and approached the gathering. His body erect, his step firm, he walked quietly through the crowd to the grave, placing a long-stemmed pipe of peace on the raw, spaded earth. "This man Stoge red man's friend. He die because he refuse to do evil."

"It'll take more than a clay pipe to satisfy us," James Black said grimly. "We want that killer."

The old chief rose and faced the tense crowd. "Before tomorrow's sun has set, the one made mad by firewater will be in your stockade," he promised. He made the sign of friendship, then turned and walked slowly away. There was muttering in the crowd, and one or two hotheads moved forward suggestively, but they were restrained.

"Let him go, boys," Toby said. "Give him a chance."

The old chief's promise was kept. The next morning he led his braves into town and at the courthouse door they surrendered the killer. The trial was short, the verdict guilty, and the sentence hanging. The unfortunate wretch, nearly naked, his body scarred by his struggle with the wilderness and covered with the filth of the marshes, was led to the foot of the towering pine behind Stoge's store. Squire Tatum put the noose around his neck, and the other end, tossed over a bough of the tree, was tied to the horn of Bill Bowes' saddle. Bowes touched the horse's flanks with his spurs and the animal drove forward quickly. The condemned Indian was jerked into the air, his body twitching spasmodically as he slowly strangled to death, while the grim, silent settlers looked on.

At sunup next morning the old chief appeared at Toby's door. "My people are moving westward," he said. "You will be glad to see us gone. Yet we are a peaceful people. Our shoulders are bowed by the white man's greed. Our whole lives are like this forced journey, ever westward, filled with pain and strife. We look upon the earth, its streams and its trees, its hunting grounds, with eyes that long for a home. It is the dream of our hearts. And yet there is no home."

"You will find it," Toby said. "You will find it in the West."

"Our Great White Father says that the land he has given us is a land where the water is cool to the lips, where the summer grass is green, where the winter is mild and the game plentiful." The old Indian's lips were firm. "We go now, my friend, to search for this promised land."

Toby shook the old man's hand, then stood in his dooryard, watching the straight old figure depart. He had always felt a strange kinship with the Indians; somehow, in their search for a home, the red men resembled himself in his search for a passage to riches and power, and somehow, too, their less admirable qualities reminded him of his own social inadequacy. A sense of sadness overtook him as he watched the old chief pass from view, a keen awareness of the breath of time, the tumbling years ahead, the wasteland of his future. Two people who had loved him were gone; there remained on this earth only two others who cared, really, whether he lived or died, prospered or starved, was happy or driven to fathomless grief. Those two were Tommy Jeff, now off with Minnie, protected from knowledge of the tragedy, and Stoge's sister Agatha in Natchez, to whom he now must write. He sat down with paper and pen, almost afraid to begin the letter, but discovered to his amazement that once he had written Agatha's name at the top of the page, the words came to him without thought, and though he was not used to writing, he covered several pages, pouring out to Stoge's sister the grief that was in his heart and that he could not have revealed to another living soul, or, to his sorrow, to God Almighty. He had tried to pray the night Stoge died, and tried to communicate with God during the preacher's oration at the funeral, but his heart had turned to stone both times. When Agatha died, he had turned from God, cursing His very name, and a share of the loneliness and fear he felt stemmed from this defection. But he found in Stoge's sister a surrogate for God, and for the mother he had never really known. He wrote to her as a stricken son might write to a mother who loved and understood him, and when the letter was finished and on its way to Natchez, a kind of peace overtook Toby.

4.

Stoge's death, of course, made Tommy Jeff one of the richest people in Arkansas Territory. The farm and store, by themselves, were enough to do that. But Toby knew that Stoge had, hidden somewhere on the farm, a cache of gold, and he surmised that it ran to thousands of dollars. He wanted a chance to search for the money without arousing suspicion, so he decided to move into Stoge's house.

The Rowden slaves had been assembled by Cato, and Toby addressed them from the saddle, believing that a man on horseback gained authority over those on foot. "Cato, now that Marse Stoge is gone," he said, "I'm taking over. Stoge always told me you could be depended upon. Now, some planters hire overseers to drive their slaves, but I don't hold with that, any more than Marse Stoge did. Cato, I want you to carry on, just like when Marse Stoge was alive. And all you slaves, I want you to do just what Cato tells you to do, or what my man Josh tells you. You do what they tell you, 'less you want a slave driver punching you."

A tall young black in the front row said soberly, "We ain't never had no trouble 'mongst ourselves, Marse Toby."

"See that you don't have," Toby said.

"All us niggers likes it where we is," Cato said. "Ain't no niggers got a better home than us, Marse Toby."

"I'm glad you appreciate it," Toby said. "I want all my slaves to be contented, but I want them to stay in the collar. We got lots of work to do, and every day we can spare from the crops I want land cleared. Josh is way ahead of you on that, Cato," he said. "You don't want to let another nigger beat you, do you?" Toby knew that if he could rouse these slaves by competition with Josh's blacks, both groups would work twice as hard as they would under a hired slave driver. He understood Negroes, and other owners who drove their slaves and believed in the whip were often surprised to find that Toby got more from his blacks than they. Satisfied that the slaves understood what was wanted, Toby rode back to town. He removed the funeral wreath from the door of Stoge's store and opened the place for business. Two settlers were sitting on the porch, waiting. One of them, a six-footer with a full beard, got to his feet. "When it's fitting and proper, Toby," he said gently, "I'd like to git me some supplies."

"Have to start with somebody, Jake," said Toby, "and it might as well be you." The man was Jake Muldrow, one of the most prosperous settlers in the area. He handed Toby a list of supplies, and said, "I'll stop by in an hour, Toby. No hurry." Then, acting on some impulse, Muldrow extended his big hand and Toby took it. The two men stood for a moment, their eyes meeting, then Muldrow said, "All of us is gonna miss Stoge mighty bad, Toby. But we know you're gonna carry on just like he did. We're all behind you, boy." He released Toby's hand, and there was a moment's silence. Then Toby said, "Thanks, Jake. I can't take Stoge's place. I know that. But I'll do the best I know how."

"That'll be good enough for us," said Muldrow.

When Muldrow returned for his supplies, Toby handed him the bill, which came to seventeen dollars.

"Put that on the book till fall, Toby, will you? I always paid Stoge at harvesttime."

"That's fine with me, Jake," said Toby. "I aim to run the store just the way Stoge did."

When Muldrow was gone and the other customers had been taken care of, Toby got out Stoge's ledger, poring over the closely written pages. The book was practically a directory of the town. Almost every family in and around Washington was in debt to Rowden's store. Some owed small current bills. Others seemed to have yearly accounts that ran to large sums. A number of accounts were long past due. Toby took pencil and paper and made a list of those that were sizable, going down the alphabet. It was then he discovered that Colonel Withers owed the store nearly five hundred dollars and had made no payment in four months. There were rumors that the colonel was losing steadily to the gamblers in the tavern, and the overdue account seemed to bear out the gossip. More than half of the colonel's bill was for cigars and liquor. The colonel liked to live well, and apparently lived beyond his income.

As he studied Stoge's ledger, the realization slowly dawned on Toby that he had acquired more than simply money when Stoge's store passed into his hands. He had acquired power, for there is no better way to keep a man in your control than to have him owe you money. Toby realized that Colonel Withers' bill was as good as a knife at the colonel's throat, and he was clever enough not to press for payment, but rather to encourage the colonel's use of credit. He had, as yet, no formulated plan, but he wanted Colonel Withers' daughter Josephine, and his instinct told him that in some way this bill of the colonel's would help him get her.

Each night, when his work was finished, Toby continued his systematic search of Stoge's house. Room after room was searched. Beds were ripped apart so that feathers floated in the air like snowflakes. Furniture was examined for secret hiding places. Walls were tapped and the floors were checked, but at the end of a week the hiding place was still undiscovered. Toby found Stoge's purse, containing five hundred dollars in cash and a batch of promissory notes, but the big cache defied him. He had not been able to conceal his search from Cato and Linda, and the two old slaves annoyed him with their questions and suggestions.

Then, one Sunday morning, after a night of searching, Toby noticed that one of the wide doorjambs showed signs of handling. He sent Cato away and bolted the door. As he worked at the jamb, the large wrought-iron nails slipped from their holes and he pried the plank loose. Inside the log partition was the gold he sought. Stoge had hollowed out the log, making a shelf eight inches wide and more than a foot deep, and on this shelf the fortune was stacked, bills and gold pieces, in neat piles. Toby counted the money quickly. There were ten thousand seven hundred and forty-six dollars. Added to the money and notes he had already found, it made a total of thirteen thousand dollars—more than he had dreamed of, the foundation stone of a great fortune. He knelt for a long time, handling the money, hardly able to believe that it was real. Then he put it back on the shelf and carefully replaced the doorjamb. He went to the door and called to Linda.

"Linda, I can't find a damned cent," he said. "If Marse Stoge hid any money, he didn't hide it in the house. He must have buried it somewhere out in the fields."

Linda considered this for a moment, then said, "Yessah, Marse Toby. He might have did that."

"You tell Cato to keep his eyes open when he's working in the fields. Maybe he'll find it."

"I tell him, Marse Toby."

Toby was satisfied that word would be passed to the quarters and would somehow make its way to the town, to the effect that he had not found Stoge's hidden fortune. He was not eager to have the settlers know that such a huge sum was in his possession. Besides, according to Stoge's will, the money legally belonged to Tommy Jeff, and difficulties might be made if it were generally known that Toby had it.

By this time the furor over the runaway slaves from the *Mabel Belle* had died down, and Toby decided that he must get papers on the four blacks, who had been hidden on his place under Josh's care. In a disguised handwriting he drew up the forms, then signed them with the name "Ike Wharton." This done he sent Josh to fetch Squire Tatum. The squire arrived, puffing a little, and somewhat nettled. "Sort of puttin' on the dog, ain't you, Toby?" he asked. "You used to come to the barbershop to see *me*."

"Just resting, squire," said Toby with a smile; he was tasting his new authority and enjoying the flavor. Toby Giles might go to Tatum's barbershop to see the squire, but the squire came to see Stoge Rowden's heir when he was sent for.

"Gettin' awful high-toned, sendin' a nigger for me," Tatum said. "You figurin' on turnin' out Colonel Withers and becomin' our leadin' 'ristocrat?"

"I might do that," answered Toby coolly. "I sent for you because I thought it would be more comfortable here on the porch. I've got some business to talk over. I bought some slaves from Ike Wharton last night and he left this morning before we could get you to witness the sale." Toby poured a stiff drink of brandy and handed it to Tatum. "I figured we'd get the papers signed up now, squire."

Squire Tatum considered the clear amber fluid in his glass, then said suggestively, "Sounds to me like an upside-down trade, Toby."

"I bought these niggers and paid for 'em," Toby said angrily. "Thirty-one hundred dollars in gold."

"Whew!" the squire whistled. "Toby, I ain't sayin' I won't witness your paper. But I feel this is a job callin' for a fee."

Toby nodded. "I agree with you, squire. I always pay for

168

services rendered. You owe a thirty-one-dollar account at the store. I'll cancel that."

The squire's face fell. He had hoped for some cash, but he agreed to Toby's terms, saying only, "Throw in a gallon of brandy, son, and it's done."

Toby handed him the papers, and the squire scanned them, reading aloud. "Here ye. All men who have ears to listen. This is to proclaim to the world that I, Ike Wharton, have this day sold four slaves to Toby Giles, Esq., for the sum of thirty-one hundred dollars in GOLD. The coin of the realm being good United States money. Now, one nigger I call Polkie—being about thirty-five years old, weighing about a hundred and ninety pounds, five foot eleven inches tall, black kinky hair, black watery eyes, coal-black skinned. The little finger missing from his right hand, the letter 'X' seared on his right rump. Now this other nigger I call Tap, being about twenty-five years old, weighing about one hundred and fifty pounds, five foot eight inches tall, bright black eyes, bushy black hair, chocolate-colored skin. No marks except for a hole in the lobe of his right ear. Both men healthy, with all their organs. Now the first she nigger I call Plumpy, being about thirty-five or forty years old, five feet seven inches tall, a hundred and eight pounds, kinky black hair with a sprinkle of gray. Low-hanging sucked teats, good worker, good brood woman. Two scars on left forearm, third finger of left hand broken. Now the second she nigger I call Orleans. Twenty years old, bright eyed and smart. A hundred and thirty pounds, soft round breasts with unsucked paps sticking out straight. Good disposition, good worker. All four niggers free of disease and able to do a full day's work. Two of these niggers bought by me in Nashville, Tennessee, and two of them raised by my father's slaves. I will defend the right and title to these niggers to the death. Signed, Ike Wharton."

The squire paused when he had finished reading, looking at

Toby from the corner of his eye. "That feller Wharton must be a lawyer, way he gets up these papers."

But he witnessed the documents, signing them with a flourish, and carried away a gallon of brandy, together with a receipted bill for his debt at the store. Toby watched him go; he knew that the squire had been impressed with his new authority, nettled a trifle, perhaps, at being topped by a younger man, but nevertheless impressed. Toby meant to take his place as the town's leading citizen, and Squire Tatum could help him. He wanted the squire to be his man, and he wanted no doubt about who was boss. During the weeks since Stoge's death he had gradually assumed most of Stoge's prerogatives. He did not want to offend the settlers by moving too fast, but the moves he made he wanted to be definite. He wanted people to realize that he had power, and knew how to use it.

The added responsibilities of the store and of Stoge's farm kept him so busy that, though Agatha had been dead for more than a year and he could have taken part in the town's frivolity without fear of censure, overt or implied, he found little time for gaiety. He was training Josh to take complete charge of his own farm, and Whittler, one of his best slaves, was entrusted with the operation of the gristmill. Cato ran Stoge's place. But Toby had to supervise all three enterprises, in addition to his duties at the store. Once he hired a drifter going through town, and watched the man during his first days, as Stoge had watched him, and when he caught the fellow pocketing a new ten-dollar bill, he ran him off the place with a pistol. Then he hired Irene Lake, the mail rider's wife, to relieve him at dinnertime and to come in on Saturdays to help out. But he needed dependable full-time help, and let that be known around town, so he was not surprised one day when a man who introduced himself as Jett Morrison came into the store to talk with him about a job. Morrison looked like a gentleman. He was well dressed, mild-mannered, and courteous, with a pleasant, straightforward manner. Toby was amused to find himself cross-questioning Morrison in much the way Stoge had talked with him when he left Ira Walker's Texas caravan.

"How long'd you live in Missouri?" he asked Morrison.

"Twelve years," the prospective employee answered. "I lost my wife there, or I guess I'd have stayed."

"What do you plan to do in Washington?" asked Toby.

"What I want to do is to go into business," answered Morrison. "I have a little capital."

"So?" said Toby.

"Are you interested in selling the store, Mr. Giles?"

"The store is not for sale," Toby answered flatly. Even had he wanted to, Toby could not have sold Stoge's store. The store belonged to Tommy Jeff, and selling it would mean getting special orders from the courts.

"How about selling me a half interest?" Morrison asked.

"Might work that out later," Toby said. "If we found out we could get along together."

"All right, Mr. Giles. I don't blame you for being careful. What about my working for you for, say, six months? That way you can learn more about me and I can learn more about you."

"I'm ready to hire you today, on that agreement," Toby said.

So Jett Morrison came to work in the store, leaving Toby free for his other affairs. Toby put Whittler into the store, to help Morrison and to look after his master's interests, but as the weeks passed and Morrison became more and more efficient, Toby gradually permitted the newcomer to take full charge, and to a limited degree he trusted him, though he followed the practice he had learned from Stoge of personally checking the ledger each day and counting the cash in the till.

With his new leisure, Toby was able to take part in some of the town's festivities. He went to dances occasionally with Irene Lake, the mail rider's wife, attracted a little by her frank, candid stare and well-rounded body, and he passed a certain amount of time in the tavern, but he kept away from the gaming table and was careful about his drinking. His real reason for frequenting the tavern was to watch Colonel Withers at the card table. The gossips had been right, he discovered. Withers was losing steadily and heavily, playing with a kind of reckless indifference, a filled brandy glass always at his elbow, a beautifully wrapped, costly cigar held lightly between his long, aristocratic fingers.

"Let Colonel Withers have anything he wants," Toby told Jett Morrison. "He's a kind of special customer." And the colonel's bill mounted until he owed more than a thousand dollars. His relations with Toby, when the colonel was sober, were still of the formal Kentucky nature. When the colonel was fogged a bit with drink, he became more friendly. Once each month Toby dined at the Withers', and as his embarrassment passed and he became accustomed to the decorum of Mrs. Withers' table, the meals became a source of real amusement, for beneath the façade of elegant manners, he and Josephine carried on a taunting, dangerous flirtation, a flirtation accomplished entirely by inference, by the sly glance, the meaningful curve of the lips. In her attitude toward Toby, Josephine was almost scornful, and she delighted in letting him know how the young bucks of the town swarmed around her like flies. Whenever he asked her for the honor of accompanying her to a taffy pull or church festival, she feigned surprise at his boldness and always pleaded another engagement. Yet on the few occasions when he danced with her, she conveyed more than a little of her smoldering passion to him in the way she permitted her body to touch his, and the coquettish way she smiled when he whispered into her ear. She was playing with him, Toby knew, teasing him, trying to drive him to distraction by leading him on, arousing desire in him, then thrusting him away. But he was not as taken in as Josephine imagined, and in fact was somewhat amused. He held the cards in his own hand, all of them aces, and when the time was right he would play them. In the meantime, let Miss Josephine play the aristocrat. One day he would own her. She would be his property, to do with as he liked. He saw her when the chance afforded, pressed his advantage occasionally, and permitted matters to slide. He flirted with Irene Lake, and once, in the dark of the night, sought brief, animal release, in the accustomed aristocratic manner, with a tawny young girl from the quarters. But his sights were set high, and he was sure of himself. It was Josephine he wanted, and Josephine he would get. Meanwhile, he prospered. The store was doing well under Morrison's supervision, and both farms were producing, though the drought had affected the yield. The gristmill added to his revenue, and his slaves were building another house, for which he knew he would find a ready buyer. He planned to dispose of his surplus hams and shoulders in Memphis, bringing in additional cash. Toby figured that good, sugar-cured, smoked hams should bring a dollar and a quarter apiece.

Life in Washington droned on; the town became a settled, almost sedate community rather than a rough frontier outpost, though the winds from the west brought rumors of trouble in Texas, and the settlers were seldom permitted to forget the near-by presence of the inexorable wilderness. One hot afternoon, riding into town from his farm, Toby overtook a saddle-weary traveler. As Toby rode abreast, the horseman greeted him, then asked, "Is there a barbershop in this town? I need some prettying up." The voice was soft, with a slow southern drawl, and the rider was a tall, competent-looking woodsman who needed, as he said, the attentions of a barber. Both he and his kit bore the stains of the trail.

"I get my barbering done at Squire Tatum's," Toby said, looking the stranger over. "He's a fair barber and a juicy talker, if you like conversation."

"I don't care much for juicy talk, but I do need a shave." The stranger prodded his horse to a trot and rode into town beside Toby.

"Where you hail from, stranger?" Toby asked.

"Born in Georgia. But I came up from Louisiana, this trip."

"We got a good farming country here," said Toby. "Lots of good land you can buy from the government, cheap." Toby was always interested in new blood. Each new settler meant a new customer for the store, a new customer for the gristmill, a prospect for a glass-windowed house. New people brought new money, and Toby got his share of whatever money found its way to Washington. But this stranger was no farmer.

"Don't care for dirt grubbin' much," he said.

"Your face looks familiar," said Toby. "Seems like I've seen you somewhere."

The stranger smiled, then replied, "Could be, pardner. I've been there." Something in the stranger's assurance and bearing impressed Toby, and he soon discovered why. By the time Toby reached the tavern a little later the town was already buzzing with the news that the famous frontiersman, James Bowie, was in town.

"James Bowie?" Toby asked.

"Yes," Colonel Withers said. "James Bowie. They say he's fought more duels and killed more Indians than any other man in the country."

"Where is he now?" someone asked.

"Down to Black's, ordering some kind of special knife made," James Beck volunteered.

Toby sauntered downstreet to Black's smithy. The blacksmith was engaged in conversation with Bowie, but both men greeted him when Toby approached. Black held in his hand the model for a knife, carefully whittled from white pine, a beautiful tool, with a fine, tapered blade.

"This is an excellent pattern," Black said, "but I believe I can make a suggestion for improvement."

"Let's have it. My brother Rezin helped me make this pattern, but I want the best possible knife."

"If you make it of solid steel, like this wood pattern, the

knife will be off balance," Black explained. "The handle should be ground down and inlaid with wood, or horn, so's to give the right balance."

"I used to fight with swords," said Bowie reminiscently, "but one day I broke my sword and had only fifteen inches of blade left. I found I could handle that better than a saber, and I've fought with knives ever since."

"I've heard about your duel on the sand bar," said Black. "They say you killed your man, even though he had his sword."

"That was back in '27," Bowie said. "I was just lucky. That fellow was good with a sword."

"They say you're a better woodsman than Sam Houston," put in Toby.

"You're wrong there, Giles," Bowie protested. "Sam Houston can outhawk the hawk, outfox the fox and even out-Indian the Indians."

"He couldn't outpolitic the politicians in Washington though," mused Black. "That bunch of mudslingers sent him out of Tennessee in disgrace."

"Yes, I saw him in exile," Bowie recalled. "Rode down the Mississippi with him. Old Six Foot Six was on a low limb then."

"Folks say he's got his wigwam on the Arkansas, up near Little Rock," supplied Toby.

"Some folks say the Cherokees are going to join with the Creeks, Osages, and Choctaws, to make war," observed Black. "They say Sam Houston may join with 'em, against his own people."

"Don't you believe it," Bowie replied. "Sam Houston may be the adopted son of Chief Oo-Loo-Te-Ka, and the Cherokees may call him the Raven, but you'll never make me believe that old Six Foot Six will go back on his friend General Jackson and take part in an Indian uprising."

"From what I hear," said Toby, "Houston isn't in shape to

take part in anything right now. He damned near died of malaria fever, and I hear he's at Boiling Springs now, getting it sweated out of him."

Black took up an old rifle barrel. "I think this piece of steel will serve our purpose," he said. "It's an old gun barrel, but it's fine metal."

"I leave that to you," said Bowie. "When can I have the knife?"

Black considered the piece of metal in his hand. "Say a week? Ten days?"

"I'll be back in ten days," said Bowie. "I'm going over to Boiling Springs to see Sam Houston. Sounds like he needs a friend near by."

The frontiersman departed, leaving Toby and Black alone in the shop. Toby picked up the wooden knife model Bowie had left. "Is this design as good as Bowie thinks it is?" he asked.

Black took the model from Toby, holding it balanced in his hand. "Toby, this is the best knife design I've ever seen. I've always wanted to work on something like this, and I'm glad to have the chance to do it for Bowie."

The unsharpened plows of the settlers piled up outside the smithy door while Black devoted the next ten days to the making of James Bowie's knife. Toby dropped by the shop daily. He was fascinated by the knife and the man it was being made for, and he passed an hour or so every afternoon, watching Black shape the recalcitrant steel until the unyielding metal took on the exact shape of the beautifully carved wooden model. Then the slow process of tempering began, and the careful grinding of the blade and point. Toby watched James Black place a silver dollar on a stump, then drive the point of the knife through it, smiling with satisfaction when he examined the point and found it unblunted. The smith gave the knife a few strokes with his hone, then shaved some black hairs from his arm.

The blade finished to his satisfaction, Black stopped work on the knife long enough to sharpen the plows of his neighbors. Then he ground down the handle, inlaying it with seasoned walnut fastened with six brass rivets. He sanded and ground the handle until it matched Bowie's model, then secured the wood inlay further with a binding of solid coin silver.

"Jim, that's a work of art," said Toby. "I want one just like it."

"Cost you a gold eagle, Toby," said Black.

"Don't care about the price," said Toby. "I want a knife just like Bowie's." Somehow, Toby felt that possession of a knife exactly like Bowie's would give him a kinship with the glamorous frontiersman, though neither he nor Bowie knew that the first knife Black made would be associated in the future with dark and bloody legend.

Toby carried his knife to Memphis when he went to the city to sell his hams and shoulders. He had planned to visit The Gut, but when he walked down through the narrow, stinking alleys, he found himself disgusted, and the whores held no attraction for him. He bought clothes, striped material for a suit, ruffled shirts, lace collars, fringed vests. He bought a pair of soft morocco boots, and had them built up, so that they would add to his height. And he bought, or rather ordered, one of the new wood-cutting mills—a mule- or horse-powered outfit that ripped boards from logs, making the tedious hand adzing unnecessary. There would always be a market for smooth boards in Washington, he knew.

Toby rode back to town from Arkansas Post with Cleve Lake, the mail rider, and though he had been a little embarrassed at meeting Lake, worried for fear Lake might be touchy about his attention to his wife, Irene, he found to his surprise that the mail rider was grateful for it. "Irene gets mighty lonesome, being left to herself the way she is," Lake said.

"Womenfolk like their men around, Cleve," Toby said. "Especially when they want to go somewhere."

"That's what Irene's jawin' about. Says she never gets a chance to go to the sociables."

"Look here, Cleve," Toby said, "if Irene wants to go to a shindig, and you ain't there to take her, all she has to do is let me know. I'll see she gets there and back."

"That's powerful nice of you, Toby. It'd mean a lot to me to know there was somebody to take her that I could trust. Course, there's lots of wild fellers that'd like to fool with Irene, but they ain't like you. I can trust you."

As he rode along beside the mail rider, Toby thought of Irene Lake and the warm, exciting way in which she had responded when he danced with her. He had not tried to make further advances, for he didn't want trouble with Cleve, or gossip from the settlers, but here was Cleve begging him to take Irene out. It was almost too good to be true.

He had his chance at the Thanksgiving dance. That year the harvest was good and the settlers were jubilant. The puncheon floor shook with the weight of the merrymakers and the rafters echoed to the noise of the dance. Even the hard-shell Baptists and the straitlaced Methodists turned out—sitting on the sidelines, to be sure, and there to pick their neighbors to pieces. Cleve Lake was somewhere west of Arkansas Post, fighting the vicious November weather on the trail, and his high-breasted, moist-lipped wife, in a dress that revealed a good portion of the creamy skin of her bosom, was escorted to the dance by Toby Giles.

Toby had a jug of brandy hidden outside the hall, and he found to his satisfaction that Irene became more hilarious after each swig she took, clinging closely to him as they danced, her bared bosom heaving with excitement, her soft flesh hot to the touch, her breath coming sharply. She giggled engagingly when Toby whispered risqué stories into her ear as they wheeled and dipped about the floor, and once in the dark outside the hall, when they visited the brandy jug, she kissed him passionately and meaningfully. His words became bolder and her re-

178

sponses became more definite as they danced away the evening, and when the fiddlers finally played "Home, Sweet Home," her attitudes were as lewd as those of any prostitute in Memphis. The liquor had destroyed her façade of respectability, and she gave way frankly to lust. That night Toby found her tigerish in her passion, and her plump, smooth body was aflame with desire for him. She was insatiable, and all of the tricks he had learned in Memphis from the fancy girls in the depths of The Gut would not satisfy her.

When she awoke, at daylight, she knew she was in bed, but not her own. Toby lay beside her, still sound asleep, his naked body touching hers. Their clothes were heaped in an untidy pile on the floor, where they had been dropped after the pair hastily undressed in the dark. Irene dozed off again, but when she heard Linda in the kitchen, shaking up the breakfast fire, the reality of the situation struck her and she leaped naked from the bed with a scream. She staggered into the kitchen, still befuddled by the brandy, her hair in disarray, her body showing the marks of Toby's passion. The old slave Linda was master of the situation. She looked at Mrs. Lake with a smile and said, "Why, Miz Lake, you ain' got nuffin' on. Lemme he'p you dress yo'se'f." She soon had Irene clothed and on her way home in the dawnlight, early enough so the neighbors wouldn't see her. Then she busied herself with the breakfast, jabbering with Minnie. Resting in bed, Toby could not help overhearing the two slaves talk.

"Miz Lake say Marse Toby plain took advantage of her," Linda said.

"How that?" asked Minnie.

"She say he done raped her whilst she was sleepin'."

"Sound fishy to me," Minnie observed. "Lessin' she rapes awful easy."

"She sho' mus'," ruminated Linda. "Dat's jes' about the most wakenin' thing I knows."

"For a fac'," asserted Minnie.

179

Toby cleared his throat.

Minnie took the hint, and said, "Linda, I ain' seed nothin', an' I doan' know nothin', an' I wouldn' know nothin' even if I had seed somethin'—which I ain't."

"Me neither!"

Irene got home without being seen and there was no more talk of her being raped. Indeed, Toby found her pliant and willing during the intervals Cleve was on the road, though she never again stayed the night, and did insist on more precautions than they had observed on the evening of the dance. It was partly because of Irene that he decided to move back into his own house. Cleve's place was nearer to his house than to Stoge's, and there was a side entrance to his office through which Irene could slip after dark, unnoticed by the neighbors or Toby's slaves. Irene seemed to require sex as she needed food and drink and air to breathe. She frankly disliked Toby, and Toby disliked her, but they suited each other in bed, and the arrangement was useful to both of them. Toby formed the habit of giving her small gifts of items from the store, and occasionally he gave her a gift of money. He liked to feel that he was paying for his pleasure, and he wanted no claims to be made on him later. He kept his ear to the ground for gossip, but he heard none. Apparently the settlers thought Toby was too busy with his various interests to have time for tomcatting, with Irene Lake or anyone else.

He found himself using his office now, conducting his business from a central point, receiving visitors there. The large square room was forbidding. It was twenty feet each way, with a ceiling eighteen feet high. In the center of the room Toby had had built a raised platform, or dais, two feet high. In the center of the dais he had placed an enormous walnut desk and a comfortable chair. His visitors sat on a bench on the floor itself, so that no matter how tall they were, they had to "look up to Mr. Giles."

Both the settlers' unpaid annual accounts and their notes for borrowed money accumulated interest to Toby's credit at the rate of ten per cent. Toby was firm on this point. If the credit or the money wasn't worth ten per cent to a man, then let him pay cash! This practice gave Toby a nickname that stuck. He had hated the nicknames hung on him earlier—"Chubby" and "Rosy" and the like—all references to his youthful appearance, but he liked this one. "Ten Per Cent Toby" the settlers called him. *Good old Ten Per Cent.*

Toby used to repeat the nickname to himself with a chuckle. He blessed the man who had invented interest, and he had never heard of usury. He was Ten Per Cent Toby, the most important man in town.

5.

Toby received Colonel Withers in his office. The Kentuckian's face was drawn and lined. All of his debonair manner was gone, and his proud bearing had vanished. The colonel was a man in desperate trouble, and Toby knew it. This was the moment he had been waiting for, the moment he had planned. He listened to the colonel's plea with a certain cruel pleasure. "I've got to have money, Toby," the harassed man declared. "I've got to have it."

"Have your gambling friends demanded payment?" Toby asked.

"I owe no gambling debts. They're paid. I need the money to cover a shortage in my land accounts."

"A shortage in your accounts with the government?" If

Withers had been trifling with government funds, then he was in more serious trouble than Toby had imagined. The unfortunate man faced disgrace and prison.

"Forty-two hundred dollars, Toby. I've got to have the money."

"Who knows about it?" Toby asked.

"The auditor just finished checking the books. He's given me a week to raise the money."

"Why come to me?" Toby asked.

"Where else can I go?" Withers said. "You are the only man in town who can put his hands on that much cash."

"What kind of security do you intend to offer?" Toby asked.

"My home and furniture. And my word of honor, sir." The colonel resumed a trace of his accustomed stiff dignity. Toby laughed, and observed that his laugh affected Withers like a whiplash across the face.

"Colonel, I built your house. You know that the house won't cover a fraction of the sum you want."

"My word, sir?"

"The government took your word, didn't it? Didn't you swear some kind of oath when the president commissioned you?"

Withers' head dropped. He made no attempt to answer Toby.

"Colonel," Toby said quietly, "if I were a member of your family, I might take a different view of the matter."

"What do you mean by that, Giles?" The colonel's head shot up.

"Well, say I was engaged to be married to one of your daughters. I wouldn't be anxious to see my future father-in-law go to prison, would I?"

"Are you trying to buy one of my daughters with your filthy gold?" Withers leapt to his feet. "Sir, I should horsewhip you!"

"Sit down, colonel. Right now, you couldn't afford to buy the whip." Toby was enjoying himself. He was sure of his ground, and it gave him an almost sexual pleasure to humiliate this Kentucky blue blood, to see the man grovel. "I'm not proposing to buy anything. I'm asking to marry one of your daughters."

"You are not fit to marry my daughter!"

"Then I'm afraid my money won't be good enough for you either," Toby declared quietly. He rose to his feet, towering over the colonel from the height of the dais. "Good day, Colonel Withers. I am a busy man, and there are other matters that want my attention." He ruffled the papers on his desk suggestively. "I have a number of requests for loans here, loans that I shall be able to make, because they will be secured by proper collateral." Withers turned stiffly, seemed to hesitate for a moment, then stalked from the room without a further word. He must have heard the sound of Toby's low chuckle as he closed the door behind him. The chuckle gave way to a laugh as Toby thought of the colonel's righteous rage. The auditor had given him a week, mused Toby, in which to produce forty-two hundred dollars. There was only one place in Arkansas Territory that Withers could hope to get that much money, and that place was right here, in Toby's office. The colonel would be back, Toby knew, with his hat in his hand.

A day passed, another, and a third. Toby passed Withers on the street and the Kentuckian greeted him with chilly formality. At the tavern, Toby watched Withers squander the last few dollars he owned in a desperate effort to run up a stake. The colonel was not gambling for pleasure now, or for the effect of grandeur. The casual manner with which for years he had tossed a handful of gold pieces into the pot was gone. He peered at the cards with passionate intentness, playing safe, too safe, dropping out when he should have stayed, then risking everything on one hand, naked fear unconcealed on his face as he watched the winner scoop up his money.

"That's it, gentlemen," Withers announced, getting to his feet. "I'm finished for the night." He went through the tavern door into the darkness. Toby knew that two courses presented themselves to the colonel. Withers could take his pearl-handled pistol and put a bullet through his brain, in the accepted fashion of ruined Kentucky gentlemen, thus escaping from the wreck he had created, leaving his family penniless and in disgrace. Or he could swallow his pride and call on Toby again, this time prepared to meet the terms that Ten Per Cent had stated.

Of course he called on Toby again, after dark on the evening of his fifth day of grace. Toby admitted him through the private entrance leading directly into the office. The colonel came straight to the point. "Toby, I was hasty. I'm prepared to discuss a loan now, on whatever terms you suggest."

When the two men were seated, the colonel crossed his legs and asked for permission to smoke, lighting a long, tapered cigar when it was granted. "I'll say very frankly, Toby, that I'd rather have Christine marry you than to marry that blue-bellied Yankee she's in love with."

"It's Josephine I want to marry, colonel," said Toby.

"She's too young, Toby. In a year, perhaps, it would be all right. In a year, yes."

"Can you wait that long for your money, colonel?"

The two men faced each other, their eyes locked, and in the end it was the colonel who broke. "Very well, Toby. I will agree to your marriage to Josephine. When can I have the money?"

"I can give you the cash this moment," said Toby. "But before I do, I must be certain you can make good your end of the bargain."

"My word of honor, Toby."

"Colonel, I told you once that the government had your word of honor. That didn't prevent your being four thousand short of government money. I want you to take me to your wife, now, so that she understands our deal and agrees to do her part."

"My God, man! Leave my wife out of this!"

"Me leave her out! Hell, I'm not dragging your wife into this mess, Withers. You dragged her and your whole family into it when you used money that didn't belong to you."

"My wife is a good woman, Toby."

"I know that." Next to Agatha and Stoge's sister, Toby considered Mrs. Withers the finest woman he had ever known. "She'll have to know of your shortage and why I am making this loan."

"I am in your power, sir."

"I'll try to help you soften the blow. Tell Mrs. Withers my reason for making the loan is because I want—that is—I love your daughter. Tell her I couldn't stand by and see the woman I love disgraced."

"I'll tell her everything."

Toby rose. "Of course, colonel, I shall expect you to sign a note, bearing ten per cent interest, for the money. If the marriage takes place, the indebtedness will be canceled. If not, I must have some means of collecting my money."

"Draw up the note and have it ready. I'll go see my wife."

"Would it be better to bring the money to your house?"

"No. Mrs. Withers would prefer to come here. This is a confidential matter among the three of us."

The note that Toby drew up was carefully worded. It contained not only a promise of Josephine's hand, but also amounted to a full confession of guilt regarding the misuse of government funds. Toby counted out the money. He took it into the parlor and stacked the gold coins on the table. He knew that Withers could not resist hard money and would sign over his soul to the Devil to get it.

An hour later, Toby saw the couple driving toward his house. He met them at the door and invited them into the parlor. Mrs. Withers' dignity astonished Toby. Her fine head inclined a little as she said, "The colonel has told me everything, Mr. Giles. I want you to know that we are grateful to you for saving us from this disgrace."

"I could not stand by and see the father of the woman I love go to jail, ma'am," said Toby. He had delighted in humiliating the colonel but he had no desire to injure his wife.

"I should have agreed to your marriage to Josephine without the loan, Mr. Giles," she said. "Her future will be secure with you. Josephine is self-willed, she needs a strong hand. You, Mr. Giles, have a strong hand." As she said this she glanced meaningly at her husband, who sat, eyes downcast, ashamed of himself.

The colonel's eyes brightened when he looked at the gold. "Do you have the note ready for signature?"

"Yes, I have it ready."

"Do you want me to sign it, Mr. Giles?" Mrs. Withers asked.

"That is entirely up to you, Mrs. Withers."

"Your signature isn't necessary, mother." The colonel signed without looking up.

"I think I want to sign it." She rose, walked erect and resolute to the table, and signed the paper. "This should bring you to your senses."

The colonel raked the gold into his leather bag. "I'll handle Josephine. This will be a wise marriage for our daughter." The colonel seemed like a new man as he walked to his surrey with the gold.

As soon as they reached home, the colonel put his flow of flowery words to work. "This gorgeous spring weather gives me a yearning for a boat trip. The first boat of the season will soon be sailing down the river."

"Where would you go?" asked Mrs. Withers, playing her part.

"Why, New Orleans, of course. Ah, there, my dear, is a city! The Crescent City—a city of untold beauty, of dreams come true, a city of unlimited delights! Half Spanish, half

French; a place to live and love in. The most romantic city on earth." He hummed an old Creole lullaby.

"I've heard you hum that tune before; what is it?" asked Josephine, looking dreamily out the window.

"It's a Creole lullaby, daughter. A romantic people, the Creoles! Like their native New Orleans. A city of palms and palmettos, tall as the masts of great ships, and the papaw trees with the sky above them as blue as sapphires, surrounding waters sparkling in the sun or glowing with the light of the stars."

Josephine had caught her father's enthusiasm, her imagination was stimulated. "You always make New Orleans sound so exciting and wonderful. I'd love to go there."

"You'd be a queen there, Josephine. A beauty among beauties. I can picture you strolling down Canal Street—under its ancient oaks, huge and silent like stately soldiers standing in their cloaks of Spanish moss, guarding lovers while they ride in swanlike gondolas along the canal in the moonlight. New Orleans is a perfect honeymoon city."

Josephine closed her eyes and leaned back in her chair. She imagined herself in one of the fragile little boats floating under the moon, the fragrance of the orange blossoms drifting by.

"Oh, if I could only go there!" she murmured, and added with sudden savageness, "or anywhere away from this prison of a house!"

Mrs. Withers' face looked pinched. The colonel cut short his rhapsody on the charms of the Delta City and came to the point.

"Josephine, Mr. Giles has asked for your hand."

Josephine sprang from her chair. "He has? Oh, at last, at last! Oh, I knew he would!" She began to waltz around the room.

Both her parents stared at her, shocked at her unabashed eagerness. Seeing their tight faces, she stopped before them, her wild delight gone as suddenly as it had come.

187

"You aren't going to let me!" she accused, full of hatred and suspicion. "You won't let me marry before Christine!"

The colonel coughed. "On the contrary, my dear. Your mother and I feared you would not consent to marry a—er—a man of business."

"Whom should I marry, a gentleman like my father, who can't keep two silver dollars together in his pocket?" She uttered a hard, contemptuous laugh. "Who else is there to marry in this God-forsaken wilderness you've brought us to? Who but Toby Giles?"

Mrs. Withers said in a stifled voice, "I think you are lucky to get Mr. Giles, Josephine."

Josephine laughed again. "Do you think I trusted to luck? I worked for this, mother! I want Toby Giles! He'll take me away from this, away from your nagging, and Christine's—he'll set me free! I'll be a married woman! I can do as I please, buy what I please! Toby will give me anything! And besides—" her eyes narrowed to slits and she smiled secretively, "besides, I like him!"

It was true. Toby's strong, virile figure, his energy, above all his driving ambition struck fire in her as her leashed animalism did in him. She responded to the violence under his mask of reserve, and to the knowledge that he was a man who would stop at nothing to get what he wanted. He had a fierceness to match her own, but she did not doubt for a moment that she could manage him. He would be her slave, her genie. Through him she would satisfy at last all her gnawing hungers for possessions, for gaiety, for freedom and power to indulge her wildest whims.

Mid-afternoon found Josephine in her prettiest frock, walking into the store. Toby was alone.

"Father tells me you have asked to marry me," she said at once. "Why didn't you ask me?"

Toby smiled. "I'll ask you now. Miss Josephine, will you marry me?"

188

She leaned across the counter toward him. "Take me away from here, Toby!" she cried, a wild appeal in her eyes. "Take me to New Orleans! I want to be gay, I want excitement. Toby, I want to live!"

"You shall," Toby promised. He came out from behind the counter and she flung herself into his arms, pressing hard against him. "There's a steamer due at Fulton this week," he said, half choked with excitement at her closeness so that his voice was hoarse and strange. "Some people call New Orleans the city of sin."

"All the better," Josephine said tauntingly, and pulled away from him. "We'll have the wedding right away. I want to take that boat!" She whirled out of the store.

Toby rode home that evening in deep meditation. Tommy Jeff was asleep when he arrived, but he woke the boy gently, seating himself on the edge of the bed. "Son," he said quietly, "do you remember your mother?"

"No, daddy," Tommy Jeff answered sleepily. "But Aunt Agatha told me she is an angel in heaven."

"She was an angel on earth, son," said Toby. "There will never be anyone like her. But she's gone." He hesitated, holding his son's hand. "Tommy Jeff," he said, uttering the words with some difficulty, "how would you like a new mother?"

"Fine, daddy," the boy answered. "I'd like that fine."

Toby nodded. A wave of chill fear crossed his heart for an instant, a grim foreboding, but he put it aside. "Well, son, you're going to have one. A brand new mother."

Toby covered the boy and remained at his bedside until Tommy Jeff was asleep again. Then he went into the sitting room. It was late and the house was as still as death, with only the night cries of woods creatures far away to break the dense silence of the night. Toby sat down before the dying fire, paper on his lap, quill in his hand, to compose a letter to Stoge Rowden's sister. For some reason he was afraid; he had been ruthless with the colonel, courteous but firm with Mrs. Withers. He had managed to break the news to Tommy Jeff. But this task, the task of telling Agatha's aunt that he intended to marry again, did not come easily. At last, some time in the morning, he finished the letter. He sent it off, and waited for the answer with a schoolboy's anxiousness. When it came, he had to laugh at himself. For Agatha, Aunt Agatha, said: "Toby, I'm glad! If I were thirty years younger, your Kentucky belle wouldn't have a chance! I would have scratched her eyes out. Congratulations. And all my love to Tommy Jeff." As he read the letter, he could almost hear the singing in his heart. She was pleased! The letter wiped out the fear that had accused him, sitting on the edge of Tommy Jeff's bed, and wiped out too the shame he had felt when confronted by Mrs. Withers' dignity and poise. He was like a man charged with new life, flinging himself into his business, driving his slaves, bursting with new plans. Suddenly, riding into town one day, he found himself singing. He stopped the horse and sat for a few minutes, amazed, then slapped his thigh and said aloud, "By God! I'm happy!"

6.

In the pale morning light the hull of the steamer showed black against the graying, pink-streaked sky. "The *Dawn!*" said Josephine eagerly, reading the name on the vessel's stern. "The *Dawn!*"

It was, indeed, the river steamer *Dawn*, a flat, bargelike craft with a paddle wheel astern. Toby had paid fifty dollars for passage to New Orleans, and this included use of one of three passenger cabins situated just forward of the steam boiler, on deck. The room was fetid and tiny, with a narrow, unmade bunk, and when Josephine saw it she burst into tears. "Toby Giles!" she cried. "I will not stay in this awful hole."

A second fifty dollars secured the use of the captain's cabin, three times the size of the one assigned them, and containing a double bed made up with sheets that were passably clean. With a little feminine imagination, Josephine was able to transform it into her version of a glamorous liner's accommodations. "There!" she cried gaily, tripping about the cabin in a pert dance step. "You see! I knew you could get something better than that awful hole. For our wedding night, Toby!"

That night, actually, was their wedding night. They had been married the day before, but the previous night had been passed on the wagon trail to Fulton, in a jogging buggy that swayed and bumped over the rutted ox track, making either sleep or love-making impossible. So it was that at dawn on the second day of his marriage, Toby had yet to possess his bride. Had he been given his choice, though the day had just begun, he would have drawn the curtains, ordered a jug of brandy, and taken Josephine to bed then and there.

But he held his passion in check. After breakfast the newly married couple sat on deck during the first perilous stage of the journey downriver. The stream was choked with half-submerged logs, and snags and cypress knees stuck out of the water on both sides. The river described a thousand curves, making navigation difficult and progress slow. It was far from exciting, and as darkness fell Josephine was yawning daintily behind a whisp of lace handkerchief. Her face was prettily flushed. "Toby, I think I'll go to our cabin," she said casually. "Will you join me later?"

"I'll come with you now," said Toby.

"No, Toby. Please wait."

But he was at the door behind her and followed her into the

191

cabin. She turned, her eyes flashing with anger. "Toby Giles! I want to get undressed. You might have the decency—"

He shoved her roughly into the stateroom and closed the door behind him, turning the key in the lock. "I want to watch you," he said.

"Watch me undress! The very idea! I never heard of such a thing in all my born days."

"You're hearing of it now," said Toby. There was a jug of brandy on the washstand. Toby poured two stiff drinks and handed one glass to his wife. "Drink this, honey," he said. She took the liquor, holding it in her hand as though for a moment she contemplated dashing the contents of the glass in his face, then sipped a little of it and sat on the edge of the bed. The cabin was lighted by the yellow glow of an oil lamp, making a pool of light near the place where Josephine sat, leaving dark, mysterious shadows in the corner of the room. There was no sound outside except the gentle swishing of the mighty river in its passage to New Orleans. Their breathing was audible. They sat without speaking, looking at one another, taking an occasional sip of the brandy. Finally Toby said, his voice hoarse, "Honey, take off your clothes. Take them off. All of them."

The brandy had made Josephine lightheaded. She giggled. "Why Toby, I never heard of such a thing." But she obeyed him, removing her garments one by one, taking her time, until she stood in nothing but her stays. She turned her back impudently and said, "Help me, Toby. Unlace me." He unlaced the confining garment and it fell to the deck. She stood revealed, the ribbed marks made by the corset showing clearly on her skin. He stood back and looked at her, walking around her as he had walked around the mulatto girl in Memphis, running his hands over her breasts and thighs. Her ripe, beautiful body was firm and alluring. As he walked around her, touching her, he saw first fear in her eyes, then a kind of defiance, related to the challenge of the slave girl on the block, and finally unconcealed, raw passion. He blew out the light and tore the clothes from his body, then drew her to him, pressing her body against his own as they stood in the dense darkness, broken only by a thin shaft of silver moonlight that slipped through a space between the curtains. He kissed her, and found her mouth slack and eager, then gently pressed her back on the bed. She was unbelievably responsive, eager for him, and afterward, as he lay on his back, exhausted, spent, the insinuating suggestion presented itself to him that his wife might not have been a virgin. There was physical evidence of virginity, yes, and a fear that might have been feigned, but in bed with him, in the throes of their passion, Josephine had betrayed an almost lewd abandon that he thought could have come only from experience. There had been dozens of young bucks squiring Josephine at dances and parties. He wondered. He finally dropped off to sleep wondering, and all of his life, after that night, he was never to stop wondering.

Toby's first act in New Orleans was to take Josephine to call on his broker. Charles Lefevre was the only gentleman Toby knew in the fabulous Delta City, and he had a powerful compulsion to show off his beautiful bride, a Kentucky gentleman's daughter.

Josephine demurred. "I can't go like this, Toby! I must go to the hairdresser. I must have some new clothes. I look like a country girl!"

Toby surveyed her with proud possessiveness. "You look just fine to me. We'll go as you are," he told her firmly, enjoying the sensation of mastery.

"I won't be laughed at by these fashionable ladies!" she cried, and though she stamped her foot he saw that she was near to tears. He put his arms around her.

"No one will laugh at you, honey. None of these New

Orleans belles can hold a candle to you. Of course you want some pretty frocks. Mr. Lefevre will tell us the shops his wife goes to."

Thus soothed, Josephine put on her bonnet and mitts and took her parasol. Riding in an open carriage from the hotel, she could not sit still. Her head turned constantly, her eyes darting from the shops and the leisurely crowd strolling in the sunshine to the ladies in carriages passing by. She was enchanted with the promise of gaiety and luxury beyond her most fanciful dreams. The Delta City was, with Marseilles, Shanghai, San Francisco, and Paris, one of the few great, truly cosmopolitan cities on earth. White, yellow, brown, and black mingled indiscriminately, and the Creole flavor of the town was everywhere, the dash and élan of the French, crossed with the courtliness and romance of the Spanish. The keynote of the city was movement. It was a gay town, a town devoted to the pleasures of the flesh, to frank, unembarrassed enjoyment of what life offered in the here and now, and such a city, abounding in dancing places, gaming halls, tippling shops, fashionable couturiers, artful hairdressers, shrewd jewelers, flashing, glamorous crowds, wide streets that offered a perpetual pageant, intimate, secretive sectors in the Vieux Carré, the touch of naughtiness in every gesture, the hint of sex in the very air itself—such a city seemed to have been born for the delectation of Josephine Giles, nee Josephine Withers, sometime budding belle of the Bluegrass, presently wife of Ten Per Cent Toby.

As Toby had anticipated, Mr. Lefevre was charmed by Josephine. He suggested a fashionable hairdresser, promised that his wife would give her a list of dressmakers, bootmakers, and milliners, and invited them to a supper party at his home that evening.

The evening at the Lefevres' was the first of a continuous round of dinners, supper parties, and balls. The broker's friends, like the broker himself, were far from reluctant to entertain the rising young businessman from Arkansas Territory and make his honeymoon a happy one. Sometimes they dined in state in one of the fine houses, sometimes in the dining rooms for which New Orleans was already famous, and where Josephine gorged herself on the exotic foods like a greedy child.

By day she led him on a tireless exploration of the shops. Toby found that he had underestimated the cost of an aristocratic wife, and though he had known that gaiety came high in New Orleans, he had not reckoned with Josephine's extravagance. Whatever she saw, she must have, and their room became crowded with boxes from jewelers, dressmakers, bottiers. She loved fine fabrics and flashy raiment. Sometimes she went too far. Once, in a fashionable Canal Street shop, she demanded a pair of hose that were made of black silk mesh interwoven with gold. The saleslady demurred. "Those hose are for a different class of customer, madam," she said. They were, indeed, the stockings worn by the high-priced harlots who frequented the crystal gambling hells off Canal Street, almost a part of the uniform of the gilded New Orleans whore. "Ladies of quality wear this type of hose, madam," the saleslady said, displaying a pair of somber black silk. Josephine's gold head rose sharply, and when she spoke her words were like lashes of a whip. "Ladies of quality wear what they like!"

But wherever they went, Josephine had only to enter a room with her proud high-bosomed walk and survey the field with her insolent glance, and the young gallants could not hurry toward her fast enough. They shouldered each other aside to bend over her hand, begged for dances, and competed in the extravagance of the compliments they showered on her. Toby, sitting soberly with the older men, listening to talk of matters which held the greatest interest for him, would look up to see Josephine whirling by in the arms of one dashing partner after another, her laughing face bolder and bolder with champagne and with the headier wine of masculine attentions. Sometimes, indeed, his eyes searched the ballroom for her in vain. The lush, walled gardens with their whispering secrecy were all too tempting to Josephine.

Later, when they had returned to the hotel, he spoke to her about her lack of discretion. He was sure that Mrs. Lefevre and some of the other ladies had noticed it. "You're young, but you're old enough to know how a lady behaves, Josephine. Your mother—"

She slammed her hair brush on the dressing table and turned on him, her temper ablaze. "Are you going to hold me down too, Toby Giles? Are you going to nag me about how a lady behaves, like my mother and my prissy old-maid sister? What do you think I married you for?"

"I know what I married *you* for!" he shouted, his rage rising. "You're my wife and I'll see that you behave accordingly!" In his anger he had picked up a beribboned hatbox and was about to dash it to the floor.

"My new bonnet, Toby!" she cried in alarm, leaping up and snatching it from him. "Why, I do believe you're jealous," she said in a coaxing voice, leaning against his shoulder.

"Why shouldn't I be?" he fumed, but his anger was already melting at her nearness, and he took her in his arms.

She wanted to see everything. Toby indulged her insatiable curiosity by visiting the Levee with her, driving past the grog shops inhabited by flashy Creole Negroes and laughing mulattoes. She was peculiarly attracted by the provocatively dressed white harlots, and Toby was again struck by the notion that his wife, for all her youth and her genteel upbringing, was a whore at heart. She was angry when she learned there were streets in New Orleans where he would not take her, even by daylight.

There came a day when Toby had had enough of the city. His money was dwindling. He was eager to get back to Washington and the absorbing business of making money. Most of all, he was sick of sitting by, watching Josephine flirt unashamedly with the gilded youths of the city's best families.

196

Before their elegance and grace, the glib flattery which poured from their lips into Josephine's ears, their unwearied dance of attendance on her slightest whim, he felt himself clumsy and tongue-tied, a crude oaf from the backwoods. Hardest of all to endure was Josephine's prodigal response to it all. She was careless to the point of alarming him, and the fierce pleasure of possessing her when they were alone at night no longer compensated for the jealous agonies he suffered during the evening, and even the daylight, hours. Josephine's frilled and ruffled gallants pursued her to the milliner's, to the jeweler's, treating Toby with veiled contempt, while to Josephine, Toby was no more than a piece of convenient furniture the moment another man appeared. Toby's jealous rage mounted with each day, until he could take no more. He wanted her to himself, at home in Washington, where no man could place him at a disadvantage, where he was strong and important and able to face down any rival.

One morning he left Josephine asleep and sought out the office of a cotton broker he had met at the Lefevres'. That was the one really happy day Toby spent in New Orleans—a morning in the broker's office, discussing cotton, lunch at a businessmen's establishment on the river front, and an afternoon examining one of the new cotton gins.

"Greatest cash crop in the world, Mr. Giles. It's the hope of the South." The broker watched the ingenious machine strip the seeds from the cotton bolls. "White gold, Mr. Giles. White gold."

Toby agreed. When he left New Orleans, he meant to carry with him enough top-grade cottonseed to start a crop in Arkansas. What could be done in Louisiana, in Carolina, in Georgia, could be done in the rich black bottom lands on the Red River. The broker was right. Cotton, to the South, was white gold, and a man like Toby was all that was needed to turn it into hard, yellow gold.

When he returned he found Josephine in a storm of tears.

"On our wedding trip!" she wept. "How could you leave me alone all day!"

Contrite, he drew her into his arms, but she pushed him away. "We're going home," he said then bluntly, though he had meant to break the news to her more tactfully.

She stared at him, incredulous, and then, in a sudden burst of violence, she slapped his face. He caught and held her hands, and she fought him. In the end the struggle aroused him and he took her by force, brutally, caring nothing for her feelings, and somehow the act of violence satisfied him more than if she had responded with passion. She lay on the bed, her clothing torn and disorganized, sobbing into the pillow. "Toby Giles, I hate you. Hate you! Hate you! Hate you!" He turned and walked from the room. But he had not gone far before he realized that Josephine might be angry enough to go out into the city alone, and he was struck by the sudden understanding that if she did that, the marriage vows would have little meaning to her. He was determined that regardless of how she felt toward him, no other man should have her. She was his property, bought and paid for, and he meant to protect his property as he would protect his gold or his slaves or his farm animals. He turned and retraced his steps. He was amazed to find Josephine dry-eyed, fixing her coiffure for the evening. As though nothing had happened, she came to him to hook her into her newest gown. "Well, Toby honey, aren't you going to take me to the Duplessis' ball?" she asked sweetly. Then he understood that no indignity, no outrage would deflect Josephine from her pursuit of pleasure.

The next day he borrowed a thousand dollars from Lefevre, paid the last of Josephine's bills, and booked passage on the packet boat. Josephine made one last protest against going home. "You promised me I could enjoy myself to my heart's content. Now when I'm having such a good time, you want to drag me back to that dismal Washington!"

"Never mind, honey," he petted her, and added astutely,

"think what fun you'll have, showing off your new pretties to all the ladies at home."

"Especially to Christine," she murmured with malicious anticipation. But she was sulky and unresponsive for most of the journey northward to Arkansas Post.

Toby did not mind. He diverted himself in the smoking room, telling the assemblage of hard-drinking planters about his Negroes, his corn mill, his farms, and his store, letting them know that Toby Giles was the first citizen of the town of Washington, Territory of Arkansas. If he boasted a little more than necessary, it was perhaps to salve the wounds dealt to his self-esteem by Josephine and her fine gentlemen in New Orleans.

By day he hung over the rail, impatient with the packet boat's sluggish progress up the river. He was eager to get back into harness, for his thoughts were on money, chiefly on the white gold he had seen bring fantastic prices on the Delta. Like many another southern plantation owner, Toby Giles had caught the cotton fever. In his mind's eye, as he rested with his forearms on the packet boat's rail, watching the shoreline drift slowly by, he could see limitless acres in cotton, miles of black bottom land white as snow with the soft round bolls that spelled money in the bank. The mills of the Black Country in the North of England devoured cotton insatiably, as the broad firebox of this packet boat devoured the fat logs shoved into its maw by stripped-down, sweating ebony slaves. There would always be buyers with ready cash, in New England and Old England, eager to bid for every bale of cotton the South could produce. In Carolina, Georgia, Alabama, men of wealth hired other men, with hard faces and long whips, to drive the blacks in the cotton fields to greater efforts. Grow! Grow! Grow! was the cry. Bleed the land for cotton! Eli Whitney's marvelous machine made it possible to process every boll of cotton grown, and buyers waited in the great ports, with gold in their hands, pleading for cotton, and more cotton. In these daydreams, going home, Toby saw himself fantastically rich, richer than Captain Maison ever dared hope to be. And though his wife's extravagance and penchant for flaunting her physical charms disturbed him, her love of display, in a real sense, catered to his vanity. He had little time for display himself. He was too busy, too preoccupied with his grandiose dreams for the future. Josephine and Tommy Jeff were the instruments by means of which he could advertise his wealth and power to the world. Josephine, garbed in her flamboyant New Orleans clothes, with jewels in her hair and French perfume at the lobes of her ears, in silks and satins and lace and finery, was a living, inescapable, overwhelming demonstration of her husband's wealth and generosity. Tommy Jeff, reared as an aristocrat, given the finest education, would be living proof of the blue blood coursing through his father's veins. Toby wanted to spend a portion of his wealth as conspicuously as possible, and he had never learned, really, to spend it on himself. So his high-bred harlot of a wife, though she might goad him by flirting with other men, and stab him with the agonies of frustration by withholding what was his right by marriage, still served a purpose, filled a role in his scheme. Yet he was deeply troubled by Josephine. Her insatiable appetite for pleasure, her undisciplined temper, the same candid sexuality which had drawn him to her so irresistibly now gave him pause. Every encounter with her was a struggle for mastery, and she was capable of the coldest and cruelest taunts in her need to humiliate him and prove her superiority. She was not only beautiful, but also an amoral young animal, and he was beginning to doubt whether morality would ever become part of her character as she matured. She would grow, he surmised, not in goodness but in cunning, and the power she knew she possessed to arouse him to wild desire would become an ever sharper weapon in her hand. These unarticulated thoughts, the unhappy wisdom gained on his honeymoon, sometimes evoked chill fear of the future, a shapeless dread of some disaster to come.

When the packet boat tied up at Natchez to discharge and take on mail and freight, Toby announced his intention of going ashore to visit Stoge's sister. He did not ask Josephine to accompany him. Indeed, he shrank from the thought of presenting her to Miss Rowden. Either the omission, or the mere announcement of his plan inspired Josephine, who had hardly spoken to him during the trip, to the blackest of her tantrums so far.

"You will not get off this boat to see that woman!" she raged. "You are married to me! Forget about Agatha and all her relations!"

Agatha's name, flung at him out of lips curling in contemptuous fury, touched him on the raw. "Leave Agatha out of this!" he said warningly.

"Exactly what I mean, Mr. Giles! Keep her out of my life! She's dead, you hear me? Dead!"

Toby's fist clenched involuntarily with the impulse to smash Josephine's pretty face. Then it came over him that she, too, might be jealous. Josephine's quick intuition must have told her that he had loved his first wife as he could never love his second, that the memory of Agatha held a place in his heart which Josephine could not invade. The jealous torments he himself had suffered stayed his hand. "Don't be upset, honey. I won't go if you don't want me to," he told her, in a surge of warm sympathy as close to tenderness as he had yet felt for her. But he got no thanks from Josephine for his considerateness. The cold-hearted girl was too single-mindedly bent on her own satisfactions to recognize understanding or acknowledge gratitude.

So Toby stayed aboard at Natchez, watching the Negroes handle the cargo, staring morosely at the rooftops of the city. Somewhere, out there in Natchez, was Stoge's sister, Agatha's aunt, and he felt a deep sense of betrayal, not of Stoge, or of Agatha, but, somehow, of Agatha's son, Tommy Jeff. When they reached the mouth of the Arkansas River, nineteen days after leaving New Orleans, Toby was a troubled, unhappy man, displeased with himself and the way in which he had shaped his life. But he knew the therapy needed to cure this black fit of depression. The answer was work, and more work. Get the cotton in, get the sawmill driving, get the store going, get the farms working harder. Work, drive, plan—make money. It was better than liquor, better than women, better than all the esoteric diversions available on the New Orleans Levee. It was better than food and drink to Toby; it was his lifeblood.

7.

Josephine Giles, in her new finery, stepped daintily to the pier at Arkansas Post and was delighted to see that Cleve Lake, the mail rider, was on hand to meet the boat. Cleve's jaw dropped when he saw Josephine, and it took him a minute to catch his breath, so impressed was he by her New Orleans clothes. "My God, Miz Giles," he finally said, "you look jes' like a queen."

Josephine did not protest the comparison. She smiled benignly on Cleve. "Thank you, Mr. Lake. And how is Irene?"

"Right fine," said the mail rider. "She's goin' to have a baby."

It developed that Cleve and Irene now lived at the Post, for Cleve had taken over the management of the stagecoach line to Washington, as well as the mail route. Nothing would do but they must all stop by and see Irene. After her clothes had been properly admired and she had gone into an ecstatic account of her revel in New Orleans, Josephine said candidly to Irene,

"Cleve says you're going to have a baby. You've been married so long without children, I didn't think you could have any."

"Yes, I'm going to have a baby," said Irene. She looked straight across the room at Toby, and Toby felt a tiny thrill of fear mixed with pride course up and down his spine. In that look, his onetime paramour told him her secret. There was a challenging moment of silence, then Josephine giggled. "Well, if *I* don't have a baby, it won't be Toby's fault," she said. Even Irene was shocked by her boldness. Toby was furious, but unwilling to show his displeasure in front of the Lakes. He simply got to his feet, his face scarlet, and said curtly, "It's time for us to start, honey."

Cleve Lake looked at Josephine admiringly. "Miz Giles, you're gonna knock their eyes out in Washington. They won't stop lookin' for a month."

The mail rider was right. Josephine was a sensation in town, and if some of the comment was less than admiring, and some of the whispers downright critical, neither she nor Toby minded. She was attracting attention, from both men and women, and she was making the town understand that Toby Giles had sufficient means to enable his wife to do as she pleased. "Ladies of quality wear what they like," she had told the stuffy sales lady in New Orleans. Here in Washington, on the frontier, she would set the pace, decide fashion and decorum. She would make the style, and the others could fail to follow at their peril. Her natural arrogance went well with her clothes, and she looked, passing through the rude town, if not like a queen, at least like a king's friend. She had sex, raw, undiluted sex, and she knew how to make it manifest. Colonel Withers, watching his daughter, shook his head with both pride and dismay. Somehow he felt that Josephine's success reflected credit on himself, and he was pleased, yet he understood that the taste of New Orleans had irrevocably touched off a fire in the girl and he knew that Washington would never contain her in the role of a dutiful businessman's wife. Something, somewhere, sometime, would explode, for there was wild blood in Josephine, his own wild blood, the headstrong, willful blood that coursed through his own veins, the dark, mad spirit that flares up in Kentuckians on occasion and makes for duels and murders, adulteries and feuds.

For a month, Josephine exulted in her triumph, playing the queen at the local dances, dressing every day as though for a promenade on Canal Street, rather than for a walk to the Rowden store, through the muddy wagon tracks of Washington. The name of New Orleans was constantly on her lips, and she never tired of describing her adventures on the Delta, skirting dangerous ground as she hinted at amorous opportunities, at dashing strangers enraptured by her charms, at her own success with the *beau monde*, and the fact that the lace-fronted bucks of St. Charles had strewn rose petals at her feet and all but dragged her carriage through the streets. Josephine's greatest triumph was at the expense of Christine, who had no husband, no honeymoon in New Orleans, and who, in the dazzling aura of her younger sister's presence, seemed to grow more pinched and faded each day. Josephine patronized her mercilessly, until Christine fled Washington altogether, to take refuge with Mrs. Withers' relations in Kentucky, where eventually she found a husband to match her own uncompromising gentility.

Curiously enough, the women of Washington seemed never to tire of hearing the tales of Josephine's adventures. Privately, they cluck-clucked their disapproval, and whispered into each other's ears: "The very i–dEEah!" but they were fascinated, and they were envious.

Then Josephine's bubble collapsed. Toby returned from the sawmill one evening to find his wife convulsed with sobbing.

"Why, honey, what's the matter?" he asked.

"I'm going to have a baby," she cried. "That's what's the matter. I'm going to have a baby."

"Why, honey, that's the best news I've heard in years. That's wonderful!"

She sat up in the bed, her eyes flashing with anger. "You may think it's wonderful, but I don't. I hate it! I'll get fat and ugly. I won't be able to dance. I won't be able to wear my new clothes." She burst into uncontrolled sobbing again, and Toby tried to comfort her, but she would not be consoled. After a time he left her; when he returned the door to the room was barred and no amount of pleading would persuade her to admit him. He stood outside the room, contemplating the plain board face of the door, understanding dully that he had ceased to be master in his own house.

But he was master elsewhere. The store, under Jett Morrison's stewardship, was piling up cash reserves. The mill was making money. And there was the prospect of cotton in the future. It was too late to plant that year on most of the acreage, but Toby turned his slaves into the fields to harvest a patch of early oats and break the land for late cotton. His gin would not arrive until next year, but he planned to store the fleecy bolls and have them ready for delinting when the machine had been set up. He wanted money to buy and clear more land, and the quickest way to get ready cash was to build more houses, so he put all available slaves to work hewing and skinning logs for new structures. He was busy with his own affairs and the affairs of the town, for no one in Washington seemed able to undertake a project without first consulting Ten Per Cent Toby, either for a loan, or credit, or just plain advice. They might sneer at his ambition, and his wife's ostentation, and mock the fact that he was not a woodsman, but they feared and respected him, and, most important, almost to a man, they were in debt to him. As the months passed, it became apparent that though Squire Tatum was the law in Washington, Squire Tatum was Toby's man and that legal matters in the town were apt to be settled to Toby's liking. Toby began his eighth year in Arkansas Territory firmly intrenched as Washington's most powerful citizen. He was the man who always knew the way the wind was blowing. He seemed always to know what to plant, and when. He was always just a little ahead of the others, and many a townsman and settler gave him grudgingly his ten per cent, half hating him and half admitting to himself that he envied him.

There was, however, little to envy about Toby's home life. He slept alone, while his wife rested behind a barred oak door. She used her pregnancy as an excuse for forbidding the most trifling intimacy, and he had not so much as kissed her cheek since the night he found her in tears, bemoaning the fact that she was with child. Toby turned for companionship to his son, and this roused Josephine's anger, so that she found fault with the boy no matter what he did.

"Giles," she said haughtily, "I want to speak to you about your son," she declared one evening. "The slaves are spoiling him. He gets too much attention from them and takes up too much of their time."

"A growing boy needs a lot of attention," Toby said.

"I require attention too!" she exclaimed. "I will not have that miserable boy infringing on my rights."

Toby's eyes hardened. "Josephine, I want you to understand that Tommy Jeff is to have all the love and care the servants can give him. I won't have him abused."

She met his sudden hardness with defiance. "I am mistress of this house. My wishes must have first consideration." She turned and swept from the room. A moment later Toby heard the heavy bar of her door slip into place. He wondered idly how she passed the time during all the hours she now spent in her room behind a barred door. He knew she was selfish and ambitious, and that she saw in Tommy Jeff the one obstacle to her future. Under the law, she knew that Tommy Jeff shared Toby's property. The entire fortune, growing as it was, could never be hers alone, or her children's. And she put a high price on her body, a high price on the few spasmodic moments of physical gratification she had offered Toby. In return for her marriage to Toby, she wanted every acre of land, every house, every slave, every dollar Toby owned or would own in the future. Toby understood now that she hated him, despised him, in fact, but he also knew that she recognized in him the Midas touch, the driving energy combined with business acumen that had made him prosperous and would one day make him rich. And while she detested Toby, she did not detest his wealth. That she wanted for herself and for the child in her womb, so she declared war on Tommy Jeff, harrying the child during the early months of her pregnancy until Toby, one night discovering the boy in near hysterics, decided to move him, with Minnie, to Stoge's house. Then he sat down to write to Miss Agatha, in Natchez, a pleading letter, setting forth his troubles, and finally asking her to abandon her' own work and come to Washington to rear Tommy Jeff, giving him the care lost to him when Agatha died, the care he had hoped he would get from Josephine.

Of course, she came. Soon Agatha was settled in Stoge's house, with Tommy Jeff and Minnie, and Toby found that he had two homes, one the stormy establishment over which Josephine presided, the other the peaceful, well-run house directed by Stoge's plain-faced, good-hearted sister. He found that he passed more of his time with Tommy Jeff and Agatha than in his own house, and this, naturally, roused Josephine to jealous anger. Though she disliked Toby and would not permit him to touch her, indeed, hardly spoke to him, she resented any other interest he developed, flying into rages when he returned after spending the evening hours at Stoge's house, playing with his son. Toby accepted her tirades in silence, feeling it useless to contest with her, and hoping that she would become more tractable after the birth of her child.

During the last month of her confinement, Josephine moved into her mother's house and announced that she was too ill, under too much strain, to entertain visitors, including her husband. During that month Toby enjoyed the first peace he had encountered since his marriage. He spent each evening with

Tommy Jeff and Agatha, usually having his evening meal with them. He came to know his son well, for the first time, and he came to know and love Agatha. Tommy Jeff was now four, a solemn, intelligent child with his mother's fine eyes and a good deal of his mother's gentle gravity. He was blooming under his aunt's care, gaining weight, and he had lost the look of fear that haunted his face during the months he had been persecuted by Josephine. Agatha was teaching him to read, and Toby would often sit in his stocking feet before the fire, watching the boy trace large letters on the school slate Agatha had brought with her from Natchez, his heart filled with affection for the youngster and for the good woman who was giving him the love and care he needed.

Herbert Withers Giles was born on a sparkling November morning in 1830, in his grandfather's house, and several hours after the event Toby learned that he had a second son. He hurried to the Withers' place and found Josephine propped up in bed, a dozen pillows behind her, declaring to an assemblage of Washington wives that never again would she be persuaded to go through the agonies of childbirth merely to provide Toby Giles with an heir. She greeted Toby coolly when he entered the room, then turned back to her friends and the history of her accouchement. Mrs. Withers led him to the next room, where his son lay huddled in his swaddling clothes, a tiny, lobster-red bundle of humanity. As they stood looking at the child, Mrs. Withers impulsively put her hand on Tobys' arm. "Mr. Giles, try to understand my daughter. She is willful and stubborn, wild, perhaps, but you wanted her. Try to understand her."

Toby tried. He called each day to see his wife and child, bringing presents for Josephine, trying to express his willingness to forget the ordeal of the last months, her rejection of him, her cruelty to Tommy Jeff, her insufferable arrogance. But he met a chill, accusative silence, a haughty contempt against which he was powerless. When, after a month more of rest in her mother's house, Josephine returned home with Herbert, Toby's heart was heavy. He knew that he should have been joyous at the thought of having his son and his wife under his own roof again, but he was not. He saw only turmoil in the future. His marriage had been a mistake, a grievous mistake, and one that could never be remedied.

There was always work. The fresh, lush bottom lands had produced a bumper crop. Barns and cribs overflowed with grain and forage. Cellars were crammed with vegetables, dried and preserved. The settlers were prosperous and a mood of optimism swept through the community, so that men whose faces had been dark with worry that spring as they remembered the relentless drought of the year before, smiled at each other when they met in the street. Toby's patch of late cotton had done better than he expected, and though some of the settlers scoffed at the new crop, Toby smiled shrewdly behind their backs and stowed away the bursting bolls, waiting for the arrival of his gin. That fall, the fall of 1830, marked his best year to date. The prosperous farmers crowded the store, making purchases long deferred, and the volume of business far exceeded that done under Stoge's regime. Also, the settlers had cash, and Toby knew that it was time to press for payment of long-overdue accounts, each bill with its ten per cent per annum added. The farmers grumbled, but they paid, for they knew that in the spring they would want credit again, and Toby was a hard man, a harder man that Stoge Rowden, who would never have refused credit to a hungry family no matter what the amount of the bill. Credit, in Toby's mind, had nothing to do with kindness. Credit was a commodity like any other, to be paid for at the going rate—ten per cent.

Meanwhile, Toby made the best of a bad arrangement. His working day was divided between the store, the sawmill, the cornmill, his farms, and the two houses his slaves were putting up, plus an hour, sometimes two, in his office, going over his accounts and receiving visitors who had business with him. The noon hour he passed at Stoge's house, having dinner with Agatha and Tommy Jeff. Evenings he spent at home, with his stone-faced wife, who sat across from him at the evening meal, her countenance impassive as that of a Roman emperor's consort, her words addressed more often to the slaves than to her husband. Since the night she learned that she was pregnant, there had been no physical contact between them, and when Toby attempted the slightest intimacy, he was rebuffed. But he knew that he would be offered the chance to take Josephine to bed—when Josephine wanted something badly. Actually, again it was Colonel Withers who was in need. Toby's loan had saved him from disgrace and prison, but it had not altered his extravagant habits. He was in desperate need of cash again, and this time, instead of turning to Toby directly, turned to Josephine. "You must help me, daughter," he said.

Together they worked out a plan. "Toby will never give you the money," Josephine said. "He's married me now, and that's that."

"But you can get the money from him," said the colonel.

"Perhaps," said Josephine. "But you will have to sell Memphis." Memphis was the servant girl Toby had bought for Colonel Withers. "You will have to sell Memphis and her daughter, Tensie."

That evening, at table, Josephine took a softer tack. She smiled at Toby. "Toby," she said, "Herbert takes a great deal of care. I got along very well before he was born, but now I simply don't have time for anything. If I had a maid like Memphis—"

"Memphis is a fine maid," agreed Toby.

"She's been trained by mother. She knows just how to serve aristocratic people." Josephine was shrewd. She knew that one of the desires closest to Toby's heart was the desire to live like an aristocrat, to be an aristocrat. "And Memphis's girl Tensie would be just right for Herbert. She's just perfect for an aristocratic child's nurse."

"But Memphis is your mother's maid. She belongs to your father."

"I do believe father would sell us Memphis, Toby," Josephine said sweetly.

Toby saw the light. "Do you mean to tell me that your father's in trouble again? He can whistle somewhere else for the money this time. We have slave women of our own you can train."

"Our slave women! Field hands! Kitchen help!"

"You can teach them," Toby insisted.

Josephine wept and stormed. Finally Toby said, his mouth set in a cruel line, his words carrying a knife-edge, "Very well, Josephine. I'll buy Memphis and her daughter."

"You will!"

"On one condition."

"What is that?"

"Unbar your door tonight."

Josephine's face turned scarlet and her breath caught in a gasp. For a moment, Toby thought she was going to explode. Then she said, her voice level, "Very well, Toby."

That night she kept her word. Her door was unbarred and she rested nude on the big bed, and when Toby advanced upon her she made no move to resist him. But sleeping with her was about as gratifying as going to bed with a statue, and when, late that night, Toby crept back to his own bed, he felt thwarted, and somehow humiliated, and he marveled at the fact that this woman was able to mortify him by submitting to his will. The next day he called on the colonel, and was not surprised when the colonel pretended to be loath to part with Memphis and Tensie, finally agreeing to sell the slave and her daughter for a price absurdly high—twelve hundred dollars for Memphis, three hundred for Tensie.

"I hate to see that nigger leave my house, Toby," Withers said, "I don't believe anything could have persuaded me to sell Memphis, except to a member of my own family."

"You sure wouldn't have sold her for anything like that price except to your own family, colonel."

The colonel flushed and coughed embarrassedly. "Well, my boy, business is business. I don't have to tell you that. Memphis is a valuable nigger."

"I know that, colonel. I bought her for you. But she's not twelve hundred dollars valuable, except to you. And me. For reasons of my own."

Toby had purchased Tensie sight unseen. When he saw her, a bright-skinned, pretty little girl, something familiar about her features made him gasp; then a slow smile crossed his face, and he understood why Colonel Withers had not been happy to part with Memphis. The high-breasted, strident slave girl had gone outside her race to father her child, but she had not gone outside the Withers' residence. In a way, Toby was amused. It was a good joke on Josephine.

Spring came early in 1831, bringing flooding rains and exceptionally high water. The steamers were up the Red River sooner than usual, and one of them carried a one-stand cotton gin and screw press consigned to Toby Giles. With the gin and press the New Orleans broker had shipped fifty sacks of cottonseed. A letter urged Toby to plant every seed, and assured him that there was a ready market for every scrap of cotton he could urge from the earth.

Long before planting time, while other farmers shunned the outdoors, Toby was in the open with his slaves, pushing back the wilderness. They did not bother to fell every tree. The large trees were killed by cutting a ring around the trunk through the outer bark and cortex. The trees soon died, and when the underbrush around them had been cleared, sufficient sunshine reached the ground. Toby was a good rule-of-thumb agronomist; he understood that planting corn year after year wasted the land to ruin, so he practiced a common-sense method of crop rotation that was scorned by some of his neighbors, but that kept his fields the most productive in the community. His best land, of course, went into cotton, king crop of the South. He was stingy with his seed, but allowed a few neighbors a bushel or two for planting, figuring that he would buy the product at a price that would assure him a profit. Possession of the only gin in the area gave him a commanding position among potential cotton growers, and from the beginning he was "Cotton King" of Washington and of all that section of Arkansas Territory.

As summer and fall passed, Toby found that the Arkansas bottom lands were ideal for cotton. The heavy gumbo and marl soils produced the finest crops of all. When the broad fields whitened as the bolls of cotton opened under the merciless sun, Toby smiled with satisfaction. He knew that he had found a job for every black boy and girl being reared on his place at his expense. Even a toddler could follow his mother in the cotton field, picking the fleecy white puffs the gin was waiting for. Toby, on horseback, surveyed his domain, the expanse of brilliant whiteness gleaming in the sun, the bent slaves picking with deliberate efficiency, their long bags trailing behind them, and he felt proud of his own foresight. Even Josephine was impressed; cotton, to any native-born Southerner, spelt wealth and prestige. It was, in a sense, a gentleman's crop, an aristocrat's crop.

The ginning and baling proved slower than the picking, but when the last white bit of fleece had been packed, Toby was satisfied with his production—eighty-one bales of prime staple. And twenty bales were bought from the men to whom he had sold the seed, making a hundred and one bales of cotton that Toby would ship downriver. He was tempted to follow the cotton bales to New Orleans, and Josephine pleaded with him for a holiday, but he remembered the expense of his wedding trip and his wife's reckless behavior in the dives along the Levee, and decided against the journey. When the *Mabel Belle* steamed out of Fulton, she carried Toby's cotton, but Toby remained on the dock. Seventy-four days later he had a letter from his broker, a matter-of-fact communication that informed Toby that the cotton had brought a gross of twelve thousand five hundred and ninety dollars. Deducted from the gross was freight downriver at ten dollars a bale, wharfage and storage, and the broker's commission, at a figure familiar to Toby—ten per cent. The net credited to Toby's account was over ten thousand dollars. From this sum the New Orleans broker had deducted money advanced to Toby and a thousand dollars paid out for machinery. The rest, more than seven thousand dollars, was in a bank in Memphis, waiting for him whenever he wanted it. Toby was more excited by this money he had earned himself than he had been when a chance discovery of a loose doorjamb disclosed Stoge's hidden treasure. He was a planter, a cotton planter, and the fact delighted him.

That night across the dinner table he addressed his wife. "Would you like to visit Memphis?" he asked.

Her face glowed with excitement. "Oh, Toby! If we only could. I am dying of boredom here."

"Very well. But if you come with me, you come as my wife. In every sense. Do you still want to come?"

She agreed. If it reflected upon Toby's manhood that in order to sleep with his wife he had to buy her, this fact did not trouble him. He had, long since, accepted Josephine for what she was, and, in a sense, she kept her share of the bargain, serving as hostess when they entertained and contributing to Toby's prestige in the community by maintaining her position as the most fashionable woman in Washington. If she had changed from an ardent girl into a shrewd, scheming woman with her eye on the main chance, then, too, so had Toby changed from a somewhat reckless, adventuring youth into a money man, an alchemist of business. Once, in the fury of an argument, his wife had charged him with having a dollar sign where his heart should be, intending this reference as an insult. Actually, he had been pleased. He began to delight in his own shrewdness and in his own ruthlessness where money was concerned. He had found a kind of romance in the money itself, and, in money's manipulation, the greatest excitement he had ever known.

But not the greatest peace. That he discovered in Stoge's old house with his son and Aunt Agatha. The noon hour became the most treasured hour of the day for him, and he was sustained by his daily visit with Agatha and the boy. Toby, in truth, was a man whose life was lived on three levels. In business he was all action, all drive, every inch of him living up to his nickname—Ten Per Cent Toby. In his own house, with Josephine, he engaged in warfare, in a constant battle involving his will against hers. In Stoge's house, he relaxed. The goodness in his nature, the generosity, the spark of idealism that had been dulled by the hardness of his life, all emerged, and in the truest sense he was most a man during these daily noontime visits with his son and his dead wife's aunt. But for Agatha and the boy, Toby Giles might have become a monster, truly having a dollar sign in the place where his heart belonged. As it was, his ruthlessness was tempered by his son's unspoiled goodness and by the simplicity and purity, the self-sacrifice of Agatha's deeply Christian life.

If there were men in Washington who pitied Toby, suspecting that life with Josephine was not what every man would pick, there were more who envied him his wealth and power. There were those who admired him and those who hated him, those who toadied to him, hoping for a loan, or a hint that would help them catch the crumbs from Toby's table. There were women who compared their own husbands unfavorably with Toby, as a money-maker, a provider, and there were a few who frankly saw in him a profound physical appeal that transcended mere appearance—a fundamental, driving energy that was irresistible. There were, in all the broad world, only four people who had ever understood him, and two of these rested in everlasting peace beneath the green sod of the burying ground on the hill. With Tommy Jeff he could be himself; with Agatha, he could be honest, a luxury denied him in his relationship with Josephine, and ruled out naturally in his business affairs.

Toby, of course, reflected his times. This was the era of the Common Man, a time when the frontier itself had been endowed with a kind of glamour and moral virtue all its own. The muddy boots of trailsmen from the hills of Tennessee soiled the damask of the frail French chairs in the White House itself, and a tough frontiersman with the manners of a mule-skinner sat in the president's chair. Andrew Jackson was vibrant proof of the frontier virtues, the superiority of the tough-handed men who were opening up the country, over the pallid, bookish Adams tribe who hailed from Boston, the Athens of America. Toby's morality was very much the morality of the country itself—a harsh, cruel, growing country, often crude in its drawing-room habits, often ruthless as a bull-tongue plow toward obstacles that stood in its way. The beaten Indians, driven westward, soured by one broken promise after another, were a case in point. An expanding nation, wanting land, had no time to consider the niceties of justice, or lose sleep over the sanctity of agreements, when the agreements had been made with a powerless group. Who can blame Toby Giles for being the product of his times? Who can blame Toby Giles for following the dollar at the cost of his soul, when the forward groups of a whole nation sanctioned the power and prestige of wealth, no matter how acquired?

8.

Josephine wanted to go to Memphis for more finery and factory-made furniture for the house, but Toby's thoughts were far from furniture and clothes. He wanted slaves. He knew that with a cotton crop, the man with the most slaves would do best. And whole families were important, for chopping cotton was a job slave children could do, and they did not have to be hardened to field labor in order to pick the bolls. Toby gave his wife five hundred dollars and told her to spend it as she pleased. He went to see his new banker, at the institution where his cotton money had been deposited, and he was surprised to find himself treated with great deference, as an important planter. And the banker was helpful. "If you're interested in buying niggers, Mr. Giles, I might be able to put you on to a good thing. We have a number of planters in debt to the bank, in default on their notes, and their slaves have been put up as lien. I think you can save some money by looking them over."

Toby took the banker's hint. The first lot of slaves was sickly, suffering from tuberculosis, and Toby passed them up. No matter how cheaply they could be bought, he was too shrewd to have them on his place, where they would infect his own healthy blacks. The next lot were more to his liking. They were a strong, well-fed crew, but their master was a drunkard whose business had gone to pot while his slaves loafed in the quarters. They were indolent and dirty, scarcely civil when he saw them. But they were tough—good field stock, and he didn't doubt his own ability to bring them into line. The price he finally got them for was ten thousand dollars, for sixteen blacks: eight men, five women, and three children. He had only five thousand to spare for slaves, for he had no intention of touching the reserves in his cache. These were cotton niggers, and Toby believed in having each venture carry itself. If they were cotton niggers, then cotton should pay for them. He had no difficulty in getting the money from the banker, nor had he anticipated any. In fact, the banker seemed to approve of Toby's method. "Debt doesn't worry me," Toby told the banker. "And I need black men in my fields more than I need iron men in the bank."

Josephine spent the five hundred dollars and four hundred more besides. This time it was lingerie that caught her imagination. She bought the best French silks, decorated with Belgian lace, the finest the stores of Memphis had to offer. Toby got value received. On the first night in Memphis, in the hotel bedroom, he possessed her with the same contempt he might have displayed toward a prostitute he had bought in The Gut. But he was pleased by the impression she made when he accompanied her about the streets of Memphis. She was a striking figure, a woman who prompted men, and other women too, to stare. Her fine, golden hair and imperious carriage stamped her as someone out of the ordinary. She created an impression of power, luxury, and arrogance. To Toby's mind, she was the picture of what a high-born aristocrat's wife should look like, and on these occasions, when he felt himself the envy of the young bucks of Memphis, he almost believed that his strange marriage had certain merits.

Toby made a point of seeing that his wife was never alone in the evening. If she flirted when he was there to watch, that was one thing; but he would not take a chance on her recklessness or her liking for low entertainment, which could have been satisfied almost as well in Memphis as in the larger city down the river. Memphis was a cynical, wide-open town, riverwise and sophisticated, a magnet for every gambler, fancy woman, and cutthroat in the district. And it was a refuge for fugitives. There were men in Memphis, flourishing, who would not have dared to walk the streets in daylight in Boston, New York, or Philadelphia. There were rogues aplenty, many of them with the vagrant charm and gallantry with women that rogues often possess, and Josephine liked rogues. He saw to it that she had no opportunity to humiliate him, and he was not sorry when the time came for them to leave Memphis.

Washington was filling with new people, many of them folks of quality who brought money with them and who knew how to build fine houses, based on stylish eastern models. The craftsmen who followed these people were building structures that relegated Toby's home to the background, so that the Giles house, once the most imposing residence in town, was now rather crude and old fashioned. This filled Josephine with resentment. She could not bear to be second to anyone in Washington, and she harried Toby with complaints. But he was adamant. He too wanted a new house, but at that time he was thinking of cotton, and every cent he spent went into land and slaves.

"Next year," he told his wife. "When I've made another cotton crop."

During the mild winter, many new acres were cleared for spring planting, and in his eagerness to get the crop in the ground, Toby rushed the season. An Easter cold snap, bringing a killing frost, wiped out a hundred acres, leaving the tiny green sprouts withered as though touched by fire. The next day found Toby's slaves replanting, and this time the cotton got a good start. Toby smiled with satisfaction as the blossoms appeared, first white, then yellow and blue. He watched even more eagerly as the blossoms dropped and the squares formed, then grew into firm bolls that had only to bulge open to push forth the fleecy staple that could be turned into yellow gold.

Josephine was pregnant, as a result of the expedition to

Memphis, and when she discovered her condition she was furious with herself, for she had resolved that never again would she bear a child of Toby's. She knew that her pregnancy would make Toby happy and be visible evidence of his triumph over her, so she resolved to conceal the fact from him for as long as possible. She laced her stomach tightly, drawing the corset strings so close that she could hardly breathe. Her door, of course, was barred at night, and had been since their return from Memphis. Toby, busy with his new slaves and with other business affairs, did not observe the change in his wife's appearance.

And he found it necessary, because of his business, to dabble a little in politics. Arkopolis, now renamed Little Rock, had been no bigger than Washington in 1820, when it was designated capital of Arkansas Territory, but it was located on the high bank of the Arkansas River, at the intersection of several important roads, and twelve years had turned it into a thriving city, while Washington, county seat of Hempstead County, remained a town, though a lusty, booming, and ambitious town. Hempstead was the oldest and most densely populated county in the territory, and with statehood looming in the near future, the citizens fought to retain their power.

During Stoge's lifetime, things had been more informal. Government agents charged with feeding migrating Indians and authorizing supplies for Texas-bound settlers had made their arrangements directly with the merchants along the frontier trails. Now a storekeeper who wished to have a share of this government business had to go to Little Rock with his hat in his hand. Before Toby knew what had happened, so busy was he with his mills and his farms and the new excitement of cotton-growing, a rival merchant in Washington had the government contract, and this valuable business was lost to Rowden's store. It taught Toby a lesson. From that time on he devoted a share of his interest to local politics, making friends with Elias Rector, who was said to be close to James Conway, Hempstead County's favorite son for governor.

New settlements were springing up around Washington, so that the town no longer stood isolated in the wilderness. Ten miles west of town the Maurin brothers, with the Clark and Stuart families, had founded a colony. Fulton was a booming river town, with an almost maritime flavor. Washington kept pace with the progress of the area; a new opera house was built near the courthouse, and dozens of new business ventures were launched. Block Brothers, Britton and Cheatam, and other firms in the mercantile line gave Jett Morrison stiff competition, but he managed to hold his own, despite the loss of the government business. Times were good and the town was booming, and there was plenty of business for all.

The tavern had become a hotel. A new owner added a second story, with a dozen sleeping rooms, and the place became headquarters for travelers passing through the area, with the downstairs common room regularly crowded with strangers and local residents, so that a man could always find companionship for a friendly glass, conversation if he wanted it, or a game going whose players would welcome him. The tavern, of course, became the focal point of the town's politics, and Toby made it his business to drop in to the taproom several times a week for a glass of whiskey and a visit with the boys. In this way he kept himself posted about political affairs.

One evening in the tavern he was having a drink with Elias Rector, mending fences over the matter of the government contracts he had lost to a newcomer. "You're bucking hard competition, Toby," Rector advised him. "The other fellow has drag with Little Rock."

"I drag as much weight as anybody in Washington, Elias, you know that," Toby said. "With my money and your brains, we shouldn't have any trouble."

Rector looked at Toby quizzically. "Where would you figure on spending your money, Toby?" he asked quietly.

"Wherever it would do the most good," Toby said candidly. He knew that it would be unwise to make his offer of a bribe more specific, and he knew that Rector understood that he, Toby, stood prepared to pay for favors received. At this moment a rider pulled up outside the door and dismounted. When he entered the tavern, Toby saw that the newcomer wore buckskins, and thought for a moment that he was an Indian. But as the man stood in the doorway, Rector suddenly let out a whoop. "As I live and breathe! Sam Houston."

It was, indeed, Sam Houston, former governor of Tennessee, now in the limelight all over the country because of his assault against William Stanbery, a congressman from Ohio. The tall frontiersman in his buckskin breeches put on no airs. "Hi, there, Sam," Rector shouted. "How come you're ridin' that stump-tailed pony?"

"There's nothin' wrong with Jack, Elias. He takes me where I'm goin'."

"And where would that be, Sam?"

The tall woodsman hesitated. Every man in the tavern was watching him, hanging on his words. Houston glanced around the taproom, then back at Elias Rector. "Texas," he said simply.

Rector called for drinks. "Sam," he said, "I'd like you to meet Toby Giles. Smartest businessman in this part of the territory."

Toby shook hands with the legendary figure. "Are you a friend of Mr. Rector's?" Houston asked. "If you are, you're a friend of mine."

"I hope I'm one of Elias' friends," Toby said.

Rector laughed. "You're my friend, Toby," he said. Then he turned to Houston. "Sam, I couldn't let you ride to Texas on old Jack. As a matter of fact, I want old Jack for myself, so you an' me're tradin' horses." Rector jerked his head, indicating a fine young saddle horse tethered outside the tavern. "That's mine, out there."

222

Houston nodded. "Thank you, Elias. I can use a good horse. I've got a job to do that's going to take a heap of riding."

"If you run into James Bowie on your trip, say hello from Toby Giles," Toby put in.

Houston's face lit up. "You know Jim Bowie? Jim rode down the Mississippi with me when I was down and out. He was my friend when I needed a friend."

A vague surge of jealousy swept through Toby. Though he hated the wilderness and had been only too glad to quit the trail when the chance to leave Ira Walker's wagon train presented itself, he yet felt a pang of envy at the camaraderie of the frontiersmen, the freemasonry of the wilderness. These men who had traveled up and down the country, fought duels, opened up the wilderness, conquered a new empire, were in themselves a kind of aristocracy.

"What you gonna do down Texas way, Sam?" Rector wanted to know.

The tall frontiersman took a pull at his drink. "Going to try to get those hotheads to pull together. Then with God and Andy Jackson on my side, I hope to help 'em get out from under the Mexicans. Texas is white man's country. Or ought to be."

Toby had a hunch that there was plenty of federal money behind Houston's venture. "If I can do anything to help, Mr. Houston, please let me know. I've always furnished Austin's settlers with supplies, and I'd like to do the same for your people."

Houston estimated Toby shrewdly and when he spoke his words had a sting. "Helping a country gain its freedom means sacrifices, not profits, Mr. Giles. However—"

Rector laughed, breaking the slight tension. "That's always the way with you, Sam. You think everything can be done by a few good men with long rifles. Takes money too. Takes people with business sense to open up a country."

223

Houston smiled. "Guess you're right, Elias. I never have been much of a money man." He extended his hand. "Glad to have seen you, Mr. Giles. We'll meet again."

"I hope so, Mr. Houston."

Toby stood in the tavern doorway, watching Houston ride away on Rector's horse, Rector riding beside his friend on Houston's old pony. He had a feeling, somehow, that his meeting with Houston had been fortunate. At any rate, it had served to emphasize his importance in the eyes of the other Washingtonians. The tavern hangers-on crowded around him. "What'd he say?" "What'd Houston say, Toby?" "Where's he goin'? Texas?" "Bet he makes them greasers run!"

Toby smiled knowingly. "You heard as much as I did," he said, with a look in his eye that indicated they hadn't.

By January, Toby's cotton stood on the dockside at Fulton, waiting for a steamer to carry it to New Orleans . . . one hundred and seventy-four bales produced on his own land, plus fifty-four bales bought from other settlers. The price of cotton had never been higher, and the chunky, tightly packed bales represented a small fortune. Toby had a sudden idea. The breath of excitement brought into town by Houston, the whiff of the outside world, made him eager for a trip. That night at dinner he said to his wife, "How about a trip to New Orleans? My cotton's on the dock at Fulton. We could go by the next boat."

Josephine's head came up sharply. She looked as though she had been struck across the face with a whip. "I can't go," she said. "And you will not go either, without me."

"Why can't you go? You been talking for a year now about going to New Orleans."

Josephine stared sullenly into her plate, then raised her head and said, hatred and loathing in every word, "I can't go because I'm going to have another baby."

"What!"

"You heard me," she said bitterly. "I'm going to have another baby."

He rose and went around the table, attempting to kiss her, but she leapt to her feet and brushed past him. A moment later he heard the heavy bolt of her door shoot home. The faint sound of her sobbing reached his ears as he sat dumfounded, unable to finish his dinner. Another child, he mused. But when? It must have been on that trip to Memphis, but in that case it should have shown long ago. He called Memphis, and the slim slave girl entered the dining room.

"Memphis, I want you to tell me the truth now. Is Miss Josephine going to have a baby?"

The sultry slave girl hung her head. "Yessah, Marse Toby. She sho' is. She bin lacin' herse'f in dem coh'sets fit to kill her *an'* de baby. I done tole her she goin' to hu'ut he'sef, but she doan' pay no 'tention to me, Marse Toby."

He dismissed the slave. The intensity with which his wife hated him was made alarmingly real by her action in concealing her pregnancy, even though such concealment must have meant anguish and acute physical danger. He could not understand it. He had never been cruel to her, never denied her the slightest luxury. Why should she hate him with such passion? He wished that he could dismiss her from his mind, but he could not. He was still impressed with her cold beauty, and by the fact that she was an aristocrat, an authentic example of Kentucky blue blood. No matter what tortures she inflicted upon him, she was still his triumph, still the living, breathing proof of the fact that he, a dock rat from the water front in Norfolk, had married into the highest class.

She went, of course, to her mother's house to await her confinement, protesting that the duties of running her home and superintending the care of her son were too much for her, though in fact she had slaves at her beck and call, and had no need actually to lift a finger. During her absence, Toby sent

Herbert to stay with Miss Agatha and Tommy Jeff. Herbert was a spoiled, headstrong boy, indulged by his mother and coddled by the slaves. Toby felt that contact with a well-mannered child like Tommy Jeff would be good for the lad, and he was right. Under Agatha's care, Herbert's behavior improved, and somehow he seemed actually happier than he had been when he was permitted to do exactly as he pleased.

Toby decided to surprise Josephine by having the house remodeled during the period she was staying with her mother. He called in Whittler, the gangling, lackadaisical slave with the slow chuckle, who was an artist at woodworking, and gave Whittler general directions, leaving the working out of the details to the black man.

Whittler went into the canebrakes, selecting thousands of trim, straight canes about an inch in diameter. Each cane was painstakingly polished with bear's grease, then worked into an attractive design for the parlor ceiling. The outer rim of the pattern was made with green canes, later, when they had turned to yellow-gold, to be polished with beeswax.

An adzer worked on the parlor walls, smoothing out every uneven spot until the walls were slick as paper. Then limewash was prepared, dyed blue-purple with huckleberry juice. Josephine's room was redone with a rattan ceiling and purple walls, the color squeezed from beetroot. Toby wrote to his New Orleans cotton broker, enclosing a drawing of the room, showing its height and size, and asking the man to buy the finest carpet and appropriate furnishings. Miss Agatha joined Toby in the task of remodeling his home, sewing curtains of blue and gold cloth, making cushions and seat covers. One evening, after Herbert and Tommy Jeff had heard their bedtime story and had been put to bed, Toby sat up, before the fire, talking with Agatha.

"You know, Toby," she said quietly, "Brother Stoge once wrote to me, telling me he wanted me to have half of everything he owned."

Toby's jaw fell. It was beyond his comprehension that anyone could forgo a fortune. "I didn't know that," he said.

"I destroyed the letter after you married Agatha," she said. "I trusted you, Toby. I still trust you. And you have given me more than wealth. You have given me Tommy Jeff, and I love the boy more than I love life itself."

"Miss Agatha," Toby said with a catch in his voice. "You're a good woman."

"I am one of the common herd," Miss Agatha said. "Just one of the sheep in His fold." Her eyes brightened and her voice softened. She was a deeply religious woman. "I am glad to be humble. I would far rather be a child of God than the greatest aristocrat in the land."

"What do you mean?" asked Toby.

"A good man and a Christian gentleman cannot be counterfeited," Miss Agatha said. "But I have found sham aristocrats as well as genuine ones. Aristocrats are like bread, Toby. Some are fine, like cake. Others are coarse, like corn pone, though both are bread." She seemed to be speaking partly in riddles, with some special meaning she wanted to convey to Toby.

But Toby was nettled. "If a fellow has money, he can buy the cake," he declared. "I want my sons to have the best. You will raise Tommy Jeff to be a true aristocrat. I only wish I could put both my sons in your hands." Never before had he been so frank about his unhappy marriage, and as he spoke he lowered his eyes, avoiding Agatha's gaze. The good woman shook her head.

"No, Toby," she said. "A child should never be taken away from his mother."

"A fine mother—" Toby said.

"She is Herbert's mother, and your wife," Miss Agatha declared firmly. "You married her for better or worse."

"It's been all worse," Toby said, frowning.

"We must take what God sends," Agatha said. "And try to understand His meaning."

Toby cared less for God's will than for the opinion of the settlers in Washington. Divorce was unheard of, a disgraceful thing. If he attempted to divorce Josephine, he would be shunned on the street like a man with the plague. His business would melt away, and all the power and prestige he had built through the years would vanish like dust. In New Orleans, perhaps, they might wink at divorce, or even in Richmond, or Norfolk. But not on the frontier. Marriages had often been made without benefit of parson, but they were permanent. A man didn't change his mind.

As he rode home in the pale moonlight, his thoughts turned to his first wife, and he jerked the reins of his horse, guiding the animal away from the familiar track toward home. He rode to the burying ground and dismounted, standing before Agatha's stone, reading the lettering by the light of the moon, feeling, under the winter stars, that strange emotion of contact with infinity that sometimes overtakes us when we are alone at night in an open place. The great dark vault of the heavens was marked by the stars wheeling in their courses, and Toby felt, in a sad, true way, that he actually spoke to his dead wife when words burst involuntarily from his lips: "Agatha, Agatha! I'm so lonely! I need you. I'm so alone." He knelt by the grave, praying, in a way, though not to the God whom he had cursed, but to his first wife, who had loved him.

9.

Violet Giles was a round-faced, rosy-cheeked baby with eyes, nose, and hair like her father's. Josephine instantly disliked the child, refusing to nurse it, so that Violet took the breast of a young slave woman. Josephine had experienced a difficult time. The tightly laced corsets had taken their toll, so that this confinement, which should have been easier, was much harder than the first, and her consequent bitterness toward Toby was greater. All of her suffering, and the fact that her pregnancy and the illness that followed deprived her of social pleasures, she blamed on Toby, seeming to feel that he had in some way conspired to get her with child in order to humiliate her. Not until she had returned home and discovered the newly decorated rooms did her mood lighten. She could find no fault with the new decor, moreover, and was momentarily cheered by her new surroundings. But she hated her life, and hated Toby. In a way, she hated her children, being indifferent to Violet, and overindulgent of Herbert. Even when an epidemic of mumps swept through the area, striking both her children, and Tommy Jeff, she seemed unconcerned.

Herbert and Violet recovered quickly, but Tommy Jeff could not shake off the illness, and the merciless summer heat seemed to aggravate his condition. At first Toby thought he had merely contracted an especially severe case of mumps, but when the boy failed to respond to treatment, he became worried. Tommy Jeff wavered near death, suffering severe intestinal disturbance, then great difficulty in breathing. Some three weeks later, the lad was gripped by neuralgic pains and severe headaches. His body seemed touched by a kind of paralysis, and at the end of the most severe bout his legs were useless, lifeless things. The boy took his illness bravely, a hesitant smile on his wan, wasted face, but the sight of his son's suffering reduced Toby to tears, and he pleaded with Doctor Hooker as he had pleaded when Agatha lay on her deathbed. "Do something, doctor. Anything."

"It takes time, Mr. Giles. We've never seen anything exactly like it before."

Miss Agatha devoted herself completely to the boy, giving

him gentle massages that seemed to relieve him, but nothing that was done seemed to halt or even slow up the creeping paralysis that gripped Tommy Jeff. Strong doses of ergot were administered, and Tommy Jeff's legs and feet were blistered by repeated applications of mustard plaster. Hundreds of steaming baths were given, and the withered legs were steeped in strange brews of wild herbs.

But nothing helped. Tommy Jeff was now completely helpless, unable to raise his legs from the bed.

"Let me take him to Natchez," Miss Agatha pleaded. "He can be seen by the finest doctors in the South."

Toby stood at the side of the sickbed, looking down at the damaged body of his son, seeing his dreams for the future shattered. He loved Herbert, but the boy was ruined by Josephine. Toby's hopes had rested with Tommy Jeff. The boy was to have been a projection of himself, an extension of his own drive toward power. Through Tommy Jeff, Toby had planned to realize ambitions he could never hope to achieve himself. These ambitions dissolved to ashes as he looked at the wasted body on the bed.

"Very well, Miss Agatha," he said sadly. "It's best that he go."

With Tommy Jeff, Miss Agatha took Whittler, Whittler's woman, Orleans, and Minnie's daughter Moonbeam, three of Toby's best slaves. He wanted them to have every comfort money could buy.

He sat on his horse, watching the coach roll out of sight, and rebellion surged through him. Why should God deprive him of his wife, then of his son? What had he done? What crime had he committed? He had merely tried to make his way in the world. Why was he being punished so severely? What was Providence trying to teach him?

He turned his horse and rode back toward his house, but the thought of seeing Josephine sickened him, so he rode into town to the tavern, sitting at a table by himself, drinking raw brandy, trying to blur the sharp edges of his despair. But the brandy didn't help. In the end, he went back to his house, entering through the private door that led to his office, losing himself in his account books, dulling his sadness with the columns of figures, the record of hard cash earned—proof positive of his success, of his hard core of triumph, no matter what disaster overtook him.

10.

Now that his first son was gone, Toby turned to Herbert, fixing on the younger boy the ambitions he had had for Tommy Jeff. He made it a point to pass an hour with the boy before supper in the evening, and to bring him gifts. But Josephine had already distorted the youngster's mind, so that Herbert had learned to play one parent against the other, and Toby worried because the lad was spoiled, so headstrong that when he was crossed there was no way of reasoning with him. Violet was the opposite, a tractable, gentle child, always smiling, adoring her father.

Toby wanted another son, but he found his wife determined on that score. "I do not expect to ruin my figure and make myself an old woman just to give you children," she declared. Her door remained bolted at night, and she refused the slightest caress, making it clear that physical contact with her husband disgusted her.

And so, when Toby went to Memphis to claim a cotton remittance of fourteen thousand dollars and to pay off the money he had borrowed to buy slaves with, he visited The Gut for the first time in years. But the experience did not satisfy him. The garish, overfurnished room in the brothel offended his taste, and the false, enacted amorousness of the whore failed to excite him. He was too old, too experienced for prostitutes. In another country, or another era, he would have taken a mistress, but men did not take mistresses on the frontier in the eighteen thirties. Toby lived in celibacy, and the energies he might have expended on his wife, had she been willing, were poured into his business affairs.

Meanwhile, there were ominous rumblings from over the border. American settlers were pouring into Texas, bringing money with them, and the Mexican government permitted them to enter, but conditions there grew steadily worse. The Texans were more oppressed than had been their ancestors by the British Crown before the Revolution. Mexican soldiers policed Texas, it was reported, attempting to force the Protestant settlers to make their confessions to Catholic priests. Worse still, they commandeered firearms from the American settlers, a fatal move, for on the frontier a man's shooting iron ranked in his affections just below his wife and children. When the Mexican government ordered all slaves freed, even though the order later was modified to except Texas, the people of Arkansas lined up solidly behind the Texans. Feeling against the Mexicans ran high, and already there were hints of war. Toby listened to the rumors that he heard in the tavern, and to the more sober, more accurate information that he got from Elias Rector and his other political connections. War, he knew, would mean a flow of money from the East toward the frontier, and if money came into Arkansas Territory, he intended to have his share of it. Meanwhile, he was growing rich.

Others were not. One evening, while Toby was enjoying his romp with Herbert, his father-in-law called. It was an unusual hour for the colonel to appear, and when he refused the drink Toby offered, Toby knew that something was wrong.

"Can I see you in your office, Toby?" the colonel asked, after greeting his daughter and his grandson.

"Certainly, colonel," said Toby. He led the way. Inside the office Toby closed the door and took his seat on the raised chair. A thin, unpleasant smile played upon his lips as he said, "How much is it this time, colonel?"

The colonel's face betrayed his anxiety. "Toby, I've got to have sixteen hundred dollars."

Toby riffled the papers on his desk, taking his time before he finally said, "You've come to the wrong place, colonel."

Withers winced as though Toby had struck him. "You loan money to others, Toby. Why not to me?"

"I loan money on good security. Your word of honor doesn't come under that classification."

"I must raise the money, Toby."

"You haven't any more daughters to sell, colonel," Toby said. "And I wouldn't be interested if you did have."

The colonel's desperation was such that his pride and arrogance had melted. He pleaded with Toby. "Son, I've got to have the money. I'll be ruined. Disgraced." His words were those of a man in panic, but they had no effect on Toby.

"I have helped you twice, colonel. The second sum was my last donation."

The colonel departed, after a short talk with his daughter. That night Josephine's door was open, and when Toby possessed her she gave herself freely, with a great display of passion, and even as he was making love to her Toby marveled at the woman's ability to act. He could not help comparing her manufactured ardor with that of the prostitute in Memphis. But, he smiled to himself, lying on his back in the darkness after their love-making was over, this prostitute was not going to be paid. He had no intention of giving Withers money, though, as the weeks passed, he found his wife's door still opened to him.

At last Colonel Withers appealed to him again, this time in

Josephine's presence, but Toby refused. "I will be ruined," the colonel said to her. "I will be disgraced. Think of what it will mean to you. Your sister. Your mother." He staggered from the room, leaving his daughter alone with her husband. Josephine faced Toby, her eyes ablaze, her breath short. "Toby, you must give him the money."

"No. He will learn to run his affairs without gouging me for money every time he's in a jam."

Josephine's breasts heaved and her lips were drawn with anger. "For weeks I have submitted to your filthy lust, and still you refuse to help my father. If my love isn't worth more than that to you, you will never touch me again."

Toby smiled. "A husband doesn't have to buy what he's already paid for. I bought you once."

Josephine turned and swept from the room, the sound of Toby's low, mocking laughter in her ears. He heard the door of her room slam and a moment later the sound of the bolt being drawn. He didn't care. He was chuckling to himself as he mounted his horse and rode into town to the tavern. It catered to his pride to humble these two, to make them crawl.

The next morning Toby was in the store, checking over Morrison's books, when Josh found him. "Marse Toby! Marse Toby! Come quick! Colonel Withers done die in his sleep and Miz Josephine mos' crazy."

When Toby reached the Withers' home he found his wife and her mother in the parlor, attended by the slave women, Memphis and Minnie. Mrs. Withers' face betrayed her anguish, but she bore herself with dignity. Josephine was near prostration, and it occurred to Toby that this grief was the first honest emotion he had ever seen exhibited by his wife. So far as her selfishness permitted her to love anyone, she had loved her father, perhaps because of the very worthlessness that made her resemble him.

Toby addressed Mrs. Withers. "I came as soon as I heard," he said. "Tell me about his death."

"He went in his sleep," Mrs. Withers answered. "I found him dead in his bed." As she spoke Mrs. Withers raised her kerchief to her eyes and gave way to tears. Josephine was consumed with sobbing. Toby moved quietly into the colonel's room. The Kentucky aristocrat, or what remained of him on this earth, looked peaceful enough, and though Toby experienced a certain measure of guilt in the knowledge that sixteen hundred of his dollars might have postponed the event, nevertheless, he realized, as he looked at the colonel's untroubled countenance, that perhaps it was for the best.

Toby went back to the parlor. Mrs. Withers had been helped to her room, and Josephine was alone. She was no longer huddled with grief in a chair, but standing in the center of the room.

"I'll go for the doctor," Toby said.

"Wait," she commanded ominously. "Look at this." She opened her hand and showed him what she held, a vial labeled "Strychnine." Toby realized with a start that it had come from Rowden's store. "I found it on the rug beside the bed, where he dropped it," Josephine added.

Toby stared at the bottle. Then Colonel Withers was a suicide! He looked up to find Josephine's eyes fixed on him in cold hatred. "You killed him, Toby Giles. You could have saved him, but you chose to let him die. I'm going to tell them all, I'm going to tell the whole world that my husband killed my father!"

Toby met her searing gaze with a meaningful look. "I don't think you'll tell anybody, Josephine. Give me the bottle."

She glared at him for a long bitter moment, and then with something like a snarl she put the bottle in the bosom of her gown and turned away from him.

Toby had no trouble persuading Doctor Hooker that the colonel had suffered a heart attack. Withers had been a heavy, steady drinker, and his wife knew that he had been in financial difficulties. Mrs. Withers heard Doctor Hooker's diagnosis with sad resignation.

Josephine was silent. She had had time to think about the consequence of her threatened revelation, and her silence now was a tacit admission that she would not destroy her marriage. Hateful though it might be, it gave her the power, the luxury, the opportunity for display which were more to her than love, and which she could have only as the wife of the town's richest man. As for Toby, he felt little grief or guilt for his father-in-law's death, but he realized that it provided Josephine with one more pretext, however unjust, for her hostility toward him.

The day after the funeral Toby rode out to meet the stage from Little Rock. He buttonholed the auditor before the man saw anyone else and informed him of the colonel's death, then offered cash payment in settlement of the shortage. Had Toby been asked, he could not have explained why he was willing to spend sixteen hundred dollars in this way to prevent the colonel from being disgraced after death, when nothing on earth, no pleading, no begging, even the offer of his wife's body, could have persuaded him to have given one penny to Withers while the man lived. Perhaps it was a vagrant, quite genuine sympathy for Mrs. Withers, who had always been kind to him, perhaps a desire to avoid scandal that might touch him. Certainly he did not make the gesture out of love for his wife or respect for the colonel's memory. He had no love for his wife, only the desire and the determination to break her to his own will, and he had long lost all respect for the colonel's birth and breeding.

Withers, of course, left his wife penniless and heavily laden with debt. Toby tried to persuade the government auditor to appoint her land agent in the colonel's place, but such positions were at that time not open to women. In the end, Toby paid her debts and got her a job as teacher in the Washington school.

Miss Agatha wrote from Natchez that Tommy Jeff was now able to get about with the aid of crutches and wooden braces fashioned by Whittler. He was happy in spite of his affliction, and displayed a brilliant talent for books. Toby wrote to his banker in Memphis, transferring five hundred dollars to Miss Agatha's account. Money was the only way he could display his gratitude for the way in which she was caring for his crippled son. When he tried to write a letter expressing his gratitude, his phrases were stilted.

His sense of guilt and incompleteness gnawed at him, however. One day he did a curious thing. Riding home from town he passed the new church. The pastor was unloading firewood when Toby pulled up his horse and sat in the saddle, gazing upward at the tall, empty steeple. "Preacher," he said finally, "when are you going to get a bell for that belfry?"

The pastor smiled, holding a split chunk in his arms as a woman might hold a child. He was a gentle man, in spite of his broad shoulders and heavy, strong hands. "Well, Mr. Giles, with crops as good as they've been this year, people ought to be especially thankful. I expect we'll raise the money for a bell this fall."

"Preacher, I'll buy you a bell myself," Toby said.

The pastor frowned. "One should not make jokes about the house of the Lord, Mr. Giles."

"I'm not joking," Toby said. "The first boat up the Red River next spring will have your bell on it. The finest bell money can buy in New Orleans."

That night Toby wrote to his broker in New Orleans, asking the man to have a bronze bell cast. Again, had Toby been asked why he made this spontaneous, generous gesture, he could not have answered. Since the day he cursed his Maker, after Agatha's death, he had never conceded that he had anyone to thank for his good fortune except himself, his own shrewdness. He certainly had not got religion. He certainly felt no kinship with God. Yet buying the bell in some way gave him pleasure, and not merely because it gave him status in the eyes of the congregation.

A few days later a Negro slave rode out from town to Toby's farm. "Marse Rector say Mr. Sam Houston done come to town, suh. He be mos' pleasured effen you'd join him and Mr. Houston at de tavern."

Toby lost no time in getting into town. He found Elias Rector with Sam Houston and Albert Pike, having a private talk in the corner room. "You remember Toby Giles, Sam," Rector said. "He's our leading merchant here. Leading cotton grower, too."

Houston shook hands with Toby. "Of course I remember Mr. Giles," Houston said. Two years earlier, when Toby had seen him on his way to Texas, Houston had not looked well. Today he seemed ten years younger. His shoulders were square, his friendly blue eyes were bright, his fair skin had been tanned by the Texas sun.

"Governor," Toby said, "you look like a new man."

Houston laughed. "I've been a new man ever since my acquittal," he said. "If they had taken me before a justice of the peace and fined me ten dollars for assaulting Stanbery, it would have killed me. I would have died in obscurity. As it was, they gave me a national tribunal."

The three friends talked, admitting Toby as one of their number, though he felt like a pygmy in the presence of giants. At length Houston said, "What are you doing now, Albert?"

Pike smiled. "I'm trying to write a history of Freemasonry," Pike replied. "It's a long hard job. Sometimes I wonder if I can do it."

"You will write it, and it will be good," Houston predicted. "When it's done, I want to read it."

Elias Rector laughed, a warm, politician's laugh. "Sam, if you try to read what Albert writes, you'll need one of Noah Webster's new American dictionaries to help you over the rough spots. Albert knows some powerful long words."

Houston joined in the laughter, then said, rather soberly, "I could use one of Webster's dictionaries, all right, but what I need right now is some help in delivering Texas to my old boss." The famous frontiersman paused, considering a spot on the wall opposite him. "It's going to be a difficult job, but with Andrew Jackson and God both on my side, I think I can do it."

"We need God's help," Houston agreed. "And we need the help of Arkansas too. Folks thought that when Santa Anna overthrew President Bustamente, things would improve for the Texans, but Santa Anna's worse than Bustamente ever was. I've been down there the last two years, trying to get the leaders together. Some of them were hard to convince. Stephen Austin had to be thrown into prison by the Mexicans before he saw the light."

"You know we'll help, governor," Toby said.

"You bet, Sam," Rector put in. "The heart of every Arkansas settler is with the Texans."

"I am to meet with men from all over the nation," Houston said. "And my mission must be kept secret. Mexico has many spies in our midst." Houston turned to Toby. "Mr. Giles, do you remember a Mexican named Ortega? Thin fellow with a little dark moustache?"

Toby reddened. "Sure do, governor. That greaser took five hundred dollars off me at poker." He paused, then added, "But I got it back."

"Well, he's in Washington again," Houston said. "And I don't think he's here to play cards."

"I'll take care of him with pleasure," Toby promised. He suspected that Ortega was the reason he had been invited to the conference, and this suspicion was confirmed when Houston rose.

"We must all be careful," the governor said. "It is vital that Texas be set free, not only to Texas, but to Arkansas too. And secrecy is important. The time to strike has not arrived. We must accumulate supplies and train our men. You can help us with supplies, Mr. Giles."

"That's right, Toby," Elias Rector said. There was more meaning in Rector's remark than the words themselves conveyed. Toby understood his friend to mean that the lost government contracts might soon be returned to Rowden's store.

In the main taproom Toby found Squire Tatum. He drew the squire aside and explained the situation, indicating Ortega, who sat at a table across the room, a glass at his elbow, a deck of cards in his thin, well-manicured hands. "Sam Houston says he's a Mexican spy," Toby whispered. "We ought to run him out of town."

The squire nodded. "Sam Houston's word's good enough for me. I never did like the greaser nohow. Or any greaser. Where do you want us to bring the bastard?"

"Out to my place," Toby said. Riding home, he made his plans. He wanted to scare the Mexican in such a way that all other Mexican spies would take warning from Ortega's fate and keep out of Washington. When he passed his slave quarters, he pulled up his horse and called Josh from his bed. "Ain't we got some pine pitch on the place somewhere, Josh?" he asked.

"Yessah, Marse Toby. We keeps some fo' to mend de house gutters when dey leaks."

"Build a fire under one of the iron washpots and fill it about half full of pitch. Get it good and hot."

The slave soon had a good fire going. The blaze lighted up the night, which was bitter cold, with a norther blowing in. Toby turned his horse and rode back a way to join the night riders. A dozen settlers surrounded the unfortunate Mexican, Ortega, who sat on his horse with his hands tied behind his back. "Which tree we gonna hang him to?" one of the riders asked.

"Let's don't hang him, fellows," Toby said. "We'd just have to cut him down and bury him. Besides, we want this greaser to live to tell the tale. Then the other greaser spies'll think twice before they pay us a visit."

The Mexican protested vehemently. "I am not a spy, señors. I am a gambler. I gamble for a living."

A settler guffawed. "Toby knows you're a gambler, Ortega. But you got a little side line too, 'cordin' to Toby."

"Let's strip him naked," Toby said. "Then we can give him a coat of tar and some goose feathers."

"Good idea!" someone roared.

"Tar an' feathers! Good idea!"

The Mexican was quickly stripped of his clothes. He stood naked in the raw, biting wind. "Where's a mop?" someone called. "Here's the nigger with the tar, but where's the mop?" Josh came struggling up with a heavy bucket of molten tar.

"Never mind a mop," Squire Tatum shouted, pulling off his coonskin cap. "I'll use this."

The screams of the tortured Mexican rent the frozen air as the hot tar was applied to his body, followed by goose feathers from an old pillow Josh carried from the house. When the settlers were finished with him, Ortega looked like a ghost. "Get going," Toby ordered. "And tell all your kith and kin just what happened to you. This is just a sample of what will happen to the next greaser that spies on us."

"Keep goin' till you cross the Rio Grande!" Squire Tatum shouted. "Don't even let us hear of your stoppin' in Texas."

In the Mexican's money belt they found three hundred dollars. Toby handed the cash to the squire. "Take this money to Sam Houston, squire, and tell him it comes from Ortega."

News of Ortega's treatment spread quickly, and for weeks the streets of Washington were clear of Mexicans. Many departed, leaving the territory; others kept away from the town.

During his stay in Washington, Houston led a guarded, mysterious life, keeping close to his room in the hotel. Occasionally the general appeared in full Indian regalia, riding off to a secret powwow with his redskinned brothers. He was one of the few white men on the frontier who enjoyed the complete confidence of the tribesmen. Men from all parts of the country traveled to Washington to see Houston, and the lights in his room burned far into the night, causing gossip to insist that a monstrous, continuous poker game was in progress. But Toby knew that poker played with cards was far from the minds of the close-lipped men who called on Sam Houston. The poker being played in Houston's room was another kind of game and the stakes were high. The stakes were an empire—the vast lands of Texas, across the river. Shortly after Christmas, as mysteriously as he came, Houston departed, riding back to Nacogdoches astride Elias Rector's mare. Only a few citizens knew that he proposed to deliver Texas to Andrew Jackson; not more than a handful of men in the country knew how he intended to do it. But a man with eyes understood that something unusual was afoot. Wagon travel over the Southwest Trail normally fell off to a trickle during the tough winter months. Even the stage and the mail had difficulty getting through the boglands. But this winter, horseback travel increased, and Toby observed that most of the riders were seasoned frontiersmen, lean, iron-jawed, untalkative men, hardened to the outdoors, at home in the wilderness. All of them were riding south, toward Texas, and most of them paused in Washington to replenish their supply of powder and lead. A few bought extra rifles, and before the spring thaws permitted the first boat to nose up the Red River, the supply of rifles was about exhausted.

News from Texas was scanty and often unreliable, but enough of the truth seeped through to keep the people of Washington on edge. Then, too, Arkansas was clamoring for statehood, and this gave the people an unusual interest in national affairs. They were conscious of the fact that what happened in Texas had a bearing on their own future, and they consequently watched developments over the border closely. Many Arkansans caught the Texas fever again, joining the southbound riders. One of those who talked of going south was James Beck, the Carolinian. Toby hoped that Beck would join the Texas-bound settlers. Though he had nothing specific against Beck, he had always felt uneasy with the man. Beck, in some way, managed to convey the idea that he knew more than he said, and he was one person Toby feared, so far as the story of Toby's birth was concerned. One day Beck stopped in at the store and after making his purchases said casually to Toby, "Met a fellow from your home place the other day. Name of Swanson. Said he knew Captain Maison well."

Toby frowned, pretending to be trying to remember. "I don't recall any Swansons," he said.

"He didn't know you either," Beck said. "But he seemed to know every other prominent family in Virginia."

"He can't know William Maison well," Toby insisted, "or he'd know me." Toby had told his story and he intended to stick to it, though often he felt that the structure of lies he had erected concerning his past was a danger to him. And things seemed to run in a chain. That night at supper Josephine said, "Judge Garfield and his wife are going to Washington, D.C."

"So?" said Toby. "What's that got to do with us?"

"They've asked us to join them," Josephine said.

"I have no business in Washington, D.C.," Toby said. "My business is here in Washington, Arkansas. And so is yours. Looking after your children."

Josephine smiled. "I thought we could visit your folks in Virginia on the way," she said. "I'd like to meet your family."

Toby's hand hit the table with some force, so the dishes and cutlery rattled. "We are not going to Virginia!" he declared.

"Why not?" asked his wife.

"Because I say so!"

"Are you ashamed of your family?" asked Josephine. "You talked big enough about them before we were married." She got up from the table and swirled from the room, leaving Toby confused. He would have been more confused had he known that the next day she rifled his papers, finding the old envelope from Captain Maison, then sat down and composed a letter to the Virginian.

A few days later, when Toby tried the door of Josephine's room, he found it locked. He returned to his own room without comment, but the next morning at breakfast he said, his voice level, with a lot of anger beneath the words, "I've told you not to lock your door. Don't do it again."

Josephine laughed. "When you let me go to Virginia, you will find my door unlocked. Not before."

That night Toby dined in town, sitting in the tavern until quite late. When he returned home he was flushed with brandy. He went straight to the door of his wife's room, tried it roughly and found it locked, then heard the sarcastic tinkle of her laughter as she realized his anger. He went to the tool shed and returned with a hatchet, chisel, and screw driver. Without a word he started to remove the hinges. When he had unscrewed them from the post, he called for Josh and had the slave lift the heavy door, prying it free on one side, then sliding it clear of the lock. A shaft of light fell across the darkened room and Josephine leapt from her bed with a scream. "What is the meaning of this outrage, Toby Giles?"

"When you come to your senses, I'll rehang the door," said Toby.

For several weeks the door remained off its hinges, the empty frame a silent symbol of the division between Toby and his wife. Memphis, Josephine's personal slave, on several occasions made drapery curtains to cover the door space, but each time Toby ripped them down. When guests in the house, and there were many, for Josephine nowadays liked to give parties, asked why the door had been removed, Toby would smile and refer the question to his wife. Then, one night, after a large party, Josephine confronted her husband. "Toby, I want that door put back."

Memphis said, "Marse Toby, sah, it ain't fitten fo' a lady to dress with no door on her room."

Toby smiled at the slave. "Your mistress knows how she can get the door put back," he said. He was looking at Memphis and did not see his wife's hand shoot out. Her palm struck his cheek with some force, making a sound like a pistol shot. The smarting blow enraged Toby and he stepped toward his wife, slapping first one side of her face, then the other, so that she reeled backward under the blows. Memphis screamed and Toby turned on her, ordering her back to her quarters. Josephine clung to the bedpost, terrified. Toby advanced toward her. She wore a low-necked gown, cut so that the cleft of her bosom showed, and Toby, still in a rage, seized the top of the gown and ripped downward, revealing her body. "You can give me what I want, or I'll take it," he said savagely. "If I take it, I'll take it when it damn well suits me."

Josephine watched him, reading the purpose in his eyes, dreading the physical violence promised by the tense, grim set of his mouth. She stepped backward, faltering. "No!" she cried. "No, Toby! Please don't!" He caught her wrist, and felt her body quiver.

"Well, lady?" he asked.

She was beaten, for the time being. Her eyes dropped and she said, her voice little more than a whisper, "Please rehang the door, Toby."

"Under my conditions?"

She nodded, then suddenly dropped to the floor in a dead faint. Arrogant though she was, Josephine had little ability to withstand physical fear. Toby's blows, and the dread fear that he intended to take her by force, had been too much of a shock for her nervous system. Toby picked her up and placed her on the bed, then turned and walked from the room. The next morning he had the door rehung. He had won a victory, but the victory was sour. Though Josephine, through fear, left her door unlocked, in the months that followed Toby seldom asserted his connubial rights. When he did, he found her cold, submitting to him with unconcealed loathing, responding not at all to his passion, so that in the end it was really she who won, for he felt himself ridiculous.

11.

The news of the fall of the Alamo and the report of Houston's victory at San Jacinto reached Washington at about the same time. Now that actual warfare between the Texans and the Mexican soldiery had started, officialdom saw the advisability of granting statehood to Arkansas, and on July 4, 1836, the territory became the twenty-fifth state of the Union. To Toby and the other businessmen of Washington, statehood was important. It meant a chance to get their own man, James Sevier Conway, into the governor's chair at Little Rock. It meant patronage for those in political favor. It meant equality of status with the rest of the country. To Josephine Giles, statehood for Arkansas meant just one thing—a chance to attend the inaugural ball. She knew that Toby had contributed generously to Conway's campaign, and she was determined to take full advantage of her husband's influence with the new chief executive.

The ball was the most formal and most colorful affair ever held in Arkansas, and people from all over the state sought invitations. Only the most important citizens were favored, and the ballroom was crowded with beautiful women and handsome men. A sprinkling of army officers in full-dress uniform added glamour to the scene.

Josephine was the center of all eyes. Her gown was daring, in black and gold, the low bodice showing the upper curve of her rounded breasts, the back revealing the delicate slope of her beautiful shoulders. It was a gown craftily designed to suggest even more than it revealed, for something in the way it was cut and fitted, a closeness at the hips and under the breasts, suggested that the woman who wore it was bold. Every woman in the room envied her beauty, corrupt though it may have been. In the startling gown, her golden hair piled high on her head like a crown, her breasts displayed in a challenging manner, the curves of her body accented by the skillfully designed garment, Josephine caused heads to turn and tongues to wag. She seemed to combine all of the frank vulgarity of The Gut, or the Levee, with a grand arrogance. A young army officer, resplendent in his full-dress regimentals, bowed low as he asked her to dance, and a moment later they swept across the floor, making a colorful, almost continental picture. Artfully, Josephine flirted with the slim young soldier, and the tongues of the matrons along the wall cluck-clucked their disapproval. Toby stood near the arched entrance to the ballroom, watching his wife and her partner, a thin wave of contempt sweeping through him. He saw Mrs. Withers on a gold-backed chair, conversing with half a dozen elderly ladies, and decided it would be safe to leave the room. Governor Conway, not unaware of Toby's financial help in the campaign just concluded, had said, "Join us, Mr. Giles. We are going to withdraw for a little talk." A chance to talk with the governor of Arkansas and his closest associates was the real reason Toby had consented to attend the inaugural ball. With a glance at Josephine and the young lieutenant, and a meaningful nod and smile at Mrs. Withers, he turned and went down the long corridor, finding the governor and his party seated in comfortable chairs in a small, book-lined study, enjoying excellent cigars and superlative whiskey. Toby was pleased when the governor called him by name. "Come in, Toby. Join the party." And he soon found that he was in his element with

247

these men. He was astonished and gratified to discover that they deferred to him when questions of business arose, asking his opinion respectfully. "What do you think, Giles?" Governor Conway would ask. Or "As a businessman, Toby, what's your opinion?" He warmed to the governor immediately, and to the governors' friends, saying later that James Sevier Conway was as easy to talk to, when you got to know him, as Squire Tatum, back home. An hour passed, and another, before the group began to disperse. Toby rose, shaking hands with the governor, thanking him for the privilege of being invited. Conway smiled, a hand on Toby's shoulder. "I should thank you, Toby. It's men like you that make Arkansas. Please feel free to come to Little Rock any time you have something to talk over. You'll always find the door open."

Toby found his way back to the ballroom, exhilarated by the smooth, powerful bourbon and the governor's kind words. He saw Mrs. Withers, sitting alone, and scanned the undulating sea of dancers, looking for his wife, but failing to find her. He approached his mother-in-law. "Where's Josephine?" he asked.

"I think on the veranda," Mrs. Withers replied, inclining her head toward a pair of French doors. Toby turned and walked toward the doorway, pausing for a moment behind a large potted palm, arrested by the conversation of three ladies who sat on the other side of the palm, so engrossed in their conversation that they failed to observe him.

"You'd think the woman would have better breeding," one woman said. "I'm told she comes from one of the finest families in Kentucky."

"She is so beautiful," a second said, "that she claims the privilege of doing as she pleases."

"Her dress is bad enough, but her behavior is scandalous. And I should think the governor would be displeased by the behavior of that young lieutenant."

"Her husband must be blind, or a fool," the first woman said.

"Although Mr. Teague tells me he is a very important man in Washington."

"I doubt if she is invited to another ball like this one, no matter how important Mr. Giles may be. I would hesitate to ask her to my home. After all, I have two young sons, about that lieutenant's age."

The other two women tittered gaily at this and Toby drove blindly through the French doors onto the veranda. He stood for a moment in the darkness, his head whirling. Then, when his eyes became accustomed to the darkness, he saw Josephine and the young soldier, leaning against the stone railing, each holding a glass. He approached them with as much dignity as he could muster, and the young man was intelligent enough to make a quick, though polite, withdrawal. Toby stood close to his wife, his words coming through thin, angry lips. "You're being talked about," he said. "I won't stand for it."

The high note of Josephine's laughter rang in the darkness, making others turn. "You're being talked about yourself, Mr. Giles," she said sarcastically. "A dozen people have told me how important you are, how rich you are, how close to the governor."

"This is a stink you can't put perfume on, Josephine," Toby said, keeping his voice low. "You're making a spectacle of yourself. That dress is bad enough, but the way you've been behaving—"

Josephine's head rose sharply in the air. "I have done nothing to be ashamed of!"

"You will not dance with that barracks rat again!" Toby announced.

"I will do exactly as I please!" Josephine said. She gathered her skirts and walked quickly into the ballroom. Toby stood in the darkness, watching her go, then followed her. He found Mrs. Withers where he had left her, and said, making no effort to conceal his anger, "Get your daughter out of here, madam, before she disgraces both of us."

Mrs. Withers rose. "Very well, Toby."

Back in the bedroom, at the hotel, Josephine faced him, her eyes flashing with rage. "You behaved like a fool, Toby," she said.

"And you, Josephine, behaved like a slut."

"Do you expect me to sit on the sidelines, like an old woman, while you swill whiskey with the men? I'm young. I want to enjoy myself."

"I warn you, Josephine. You will behave as a wife should, or you will regret it."

Josephine turned, preparing for bed. A quarrel would only cement the affair in Toby's memory, and she wanted him to forget it, for she planned to see the young army officer again. She recalled with excitement his gallantry, the delicate, inferential way in which he had flirted with her, his slim, strong body, the tapering waist and broad shoulders exaggerated by the cut of his uniform. He was young, even younger than she, and she wanted youth. In her eyes, Toby was already growing old. There was a touch of gray in his hair, and he had taken on weight, a certain thickening at the hips and around the waist that betrayed the advancing years. And for her he had none of the romance of the young officer. Toby had become a man of affairs, a businessman. When he turned away from Texas, years ago, and took a job in Stoge Rowden's store, he had committed himself to business, to money.

In his own bed, while Josephine's thoughts turned to the lieutenant, Toby felt his rage subside and give way to a kind of sullen hopelessness so far as his marriage was concerned. He saw no common ground on which he and Josephine could meet to build even a surface happiness. Physically, his wife detested him; socially, she held him in contempt. There was only one way in which he could hold her even partially in line, and that was by his control of the purse. She loved money and the things

money could buy, and she reveled in the prestige of being wife
to the town's richest man.

Back in Washington, Josephine wistfully yearned for the
young lieutenant and resumed her mundane life with regret.
But Toby was glad to be back to his business and to his children. More and more he turned to the children for whatever
happiness he found. Every spare evening was devoted to Herbert and Violet. He found his daughter responsive, a sage, well-
mannered child who adored him. Herbert was another matter.
Since he had been old enough to crawl, Josephine had kept
Tensie, Memphis's mulatto daughter, constantly with him to
satsify his every wish. In consequence, the lad was arrogant and
spoiled, unable to do the simplest thing for himself, a petty
tyrant in the household whose every whim must be granted if
a tantrum was to be avoided. He was a bright youngster, with a
keen, shrewd mind, and he did well in school, though he found
it difficult to get on with the other six-year-olds, most of whom
had been reared in good frontier fashion with the aid of a thin
birch rod. Toby tried not to add to the difficulties created by
Josephine, but he loved Herbert, and the boy had a way of
getting around his father. Toby found himself granting Herbert's wishes, though often he knew the indulgence was bad for
his son, because he could not resist seeing the pleased expression
on Herbert's face when some favor was granted. He bought
Herbert a calico Shetland pony and taught him to ride. Whenever schoolwork permitted, Toby took his son with him on his
rides around the farms. He was trying to instill in the youngster
some respect for business, some appreciation of how the money
was made. He found Herbert responsive and even respectful
where money matters were concerned, but in other areas he encountered only Herbert's condescension and contempt. Josephine had planted well the seeds of arrogance in her son, who
regarded his father as a good enough fellow in business, but so-

cially inferior and culturally indifferent. Josephine had created for Herbert an image of his grandfather, Colonel Withers, that was so exaggerated as to resemble only slightly the real Withers, as he had lived, and it was on this myth that Herbert was going to pattern himself, so impressed was he by the constant assurance of his mother that blue blood flowed in his veins, the blue blood of Kentucky. He was proud of his Withers ancestry, and of the Withers part of his name, and Toby, had he not been frightened for the boy's future, would have been amused at the proud way the youngster sat his little pony, as sure of himself as if a blooded Arabian were between his legs.

Naturally, Violet suffered because she loved her father, and Josephine lost no opportunity to remark that while the handsome Herbert was unquestionably a chip off the Withers block, the rather plain Violet took her looks from Toby's family. If, indeed, she would sometimes add, Toby had any family to take after. Toby and Josephine were constantly at war over the children, and the two youngsters became symbols of the strife that existed between their parents. If Toby bought a gift for Herbert, Josephine felt that she must top it with a more lavish present. If he bought a dress for Violet, she would ridicule it. Despite her mother's antagonism, Violet remained a sweet, self-effacing child, dutiful and well-mannered, hiding her grief and seldom giving way to tears until she was alone in her bed. It was not a happy household, for husband and wife or for their children, and it was sustained merely by Josephine's love of money and Toby's reluctance to disgrace himself and make the children miserable by precipitating an open break. Often, in the dead of night, riding home from the tavern, where he had gone for a few hours surcease from the constant bickering at home, Toby would be tempted to turn his horse west, away from town, simply to ride on into the night, to disappear, leaving everything behind him, his pockets as empty as they had been when he arrived in Washington as a youth. But now he was too old, too set in his ways, too attached to the power he had seized for himself. He was simply not that kind of man; he was a townsman, not a frontiersman. He was related, in kind, to the eastern men in stovepipe hats, in New York, Boston, and Philadelphia, rather than to the buckskin-clad long riflemen who had torn the wilderness from the Indians and Texas from the Mexicans. Money was Toby's business, not romance or adventure. He wanted money because he wanted status. Now he had both money and status, and it bewildered him that the sense of wellbeing he had expected to accompany both did not appear. He was more unhappy, more unsure of himself today than he had been when, as a boy, he had crawled to bed under Stoge's store the night after his fight with Ira Walker. There, under the floor boards, the rain dripping a tattoo outside, he had thought of Captain Maison's plantation and promised himself that here in this town he would find a fortune and become an aristocrat. He had the fortune and he supposed that he lived as elegantly as any man in town. But he was not happy. He recalled, often, a remark Agatha had made just before she carried Tommy Jeff off to Natchez. There were two kinds of aristocrats, she had said. Some were fine, like cake, while others were coarse, like cornbread. He wondered which his sons would be: fine cake or cornbread?

With statehood the affairs of the residents of Arkansas Territory, now the sovereign state of Arkansas, became more formalized. In the past, self-government had been the rule, and self-protection. If the tribes were rising and readying for the warpath, the men of each community took down their rifles from the pegs on the wall and mounted guard. Things were arranged informally, and leadership was arrived at more or less naturally, the stronger, richer, more prominent men automatically taking the lead in community affairs. Now, things were different. The settlements were towns and cities, governed from Little Rock, and the state militia was formed to deal with disturbances in an organized fashion. The recent war between

Texas and Mexico had made Arkansans conscious of the military, and of the need for protection from Indians, renegade whites, and, perhaps, from the republic to the south.

Captain Harlow Robertson, from the Carolinas, a young, experienced soldier, was assigned to command the militia detachment in Washington. He was a tall, elegant Southerner, dressed in a new, becoming, tight-fitting uniform and possessed of that cavalier charm so often conferred on those born in Charleston. He frankly admitted being a man subject to all the failings of the flesh. He liked his glass, he liked a well-turned pheasant, he was fond of a fine handmade cigar, and he had a discerning eye for the ladies. Soon after his arrival in town he was established in the social whirl, sought after for every party, subject to admiring feminine glances wherever he went, recipient of grudging admiration from the males. He could ride and shoot with the best of them, and on the frontier, even in a settlement as established as Washington, these abilities made up for the fact that he put oil on his hair and worried too much about the polish on his boots.

Of course, Captain Robertson was made to order for Josephine Giles. The young bloods of the town, even the most reckless, gave Josephine a wide berth. Not that they didn't admire her beauty, or that they were undisturbed by her frank sexuality and provocative manner. They were afraid of her husband, for every resident of Washington was aware of Toby's power and unwilling to cross him. This fear escaped Robertson. He was a government official, a career officer, and so not concerned with business affairs. He and Josephine both felt a mutual attraction when they first met at a reception tendered the captain by the town. They danced, they flirted, they permitted themselves considerable boldness under the cover of innuendo. To Josephine it was tonic. The gay, handsome stranger touched a spark, and she became more reckless than she had ever been at home before.

Josephine's Thanksgiving dance that year was one of the high spots of Washington's social season, an expensive and elaborate affair, carefully planned, commanding the attention of Josephine and all the house servants for weeks before the holiday. All of the better families of the town appeared, but Toby observed that many of them paid merely courtesy calls and that few remained after sampling his special New Orleans food and his Havana cigars. By the time the dance got under way, those who were left were Josephine's regular hangers-on—and Captain Robertson, easily the most glamorous figure in Arkansas that night, in his full-dress uniform, his natural charm pointed up by the numerous drinks he had consumed during the meal. With Josephine in his arms, he whirled about the floor, teaching her intricate little steps he said were the rage in Charleston. He whispered boldly in her ear, and she smiled back, once tapping him gently on the cheek with her fan when his remarks became a bit too suggestive.

Usually, Josephine ignored her husband when she gave a large party, but tonight she found time, between dances with Robertson, to see that his glass was filled, that he was getting plenty to drink. "Enjoy yourself, Toby. Relax! You work so hard, you deserve a little relaxation." Toby drank more than usual, and by the time the guests departed he appeared to be sodden with whiskey, slumped in an arm chair, unable even to rise and bid a host's good night. His mouth hung open and one arm dangled limply, the fingers of his hand trailing on the floor.

"Josh!" called Josephine. "Your master's drunk again. Put him to bed."

"Yes ma'am, Miz Josephine." The faithful servant gathered Toby in his arms and half dragged, half carried him to his room. Josephine waited until she heard the sound of Toby's boots dropping to the floor, first one, then a long interval, then the other. A slow smile crossed her face as she blew out the lights and went to her room. It was in darkness, but the pale liquid sheen of the moon, pouring through the window, showed the silhouette of her visitor. She moved swiftly across the room to him. "Darling," she whispered. He took her in his arms and pressed a kiss on her lips, a moist, passionate kiss that sent tingling desire burning through her veins, so that all caution left her and she bared her breast to Robertson, kissing him again, pulling his lips toward hers. "There's nothing to be afraid of, darling," she whispered hoarsely. "Toby's dead drunk. His slave has put him to bed."

They moved toward the bed, still locked in passionate embrace. Robertson fumbled with the fastenings of Josephine's dress, and she helped him, then pleaded, "Tear it! Tear it off me!" And the sound of rending silk made an ominous noise in the darkness. Josephine's body stood revealed in the moonlight, like sculpture, and a low cry escaped the captain's lips as his eager hands ran over her flesh. "Darling," he whispered, pressing her back toward her bed. "Darling." Josephine was on fire with lust; never before had any man so roused her to passion. She clawed at Robertson's uniform, her hands seeking his flesh. A racing sensation of triumph filled her, and in her ecstasy she almost swooned. Then came a loud, imperative knocking at the door.

The lovers sprang apart, Josephine standing in disarray, the captain quickly buttoning his tunic. The knocking came again, and like a flash Robertson disappeared through the window. "Who is knocking?" Josephine called, her voice trembling with fear and frustrated desire.

"It's me, Miz Josephine. You better bolt your window. I see somebody in de yard, prowlin' 'round."

She stood for a moment, trying to regain her composure, then said, her voice muffled, "Thank you, Josh." She waited until the sound of Josh's footsteps died away, then went to the window, calling softly, "It's all right, come back. It's all right." She stood in the window, her naked body mocking her, and called again, "Come back! Come back!" But there was no answer. Far off in the distance, through the silent night, came the sound of Robertson's horse, riding off. She turned, lighting her lamp, and the ruined dress on the floor seemed to leer at her in mockery. She kicked it savagely under the bed, then covered herself with a wrapper and sat by the window, staring out at the darkness, rage and frustration welling up in her breast.

A knocking sounded at her door again, and someone shook the handle furiously. "Open up, God damn it. Open up! I've told you to keep this door unlocked."

She unlatched the door and Toby stood before her, disheveled, swaying slightly. His drink-inflamed eyes surveyed the room. By this time he had sobered considerably and was about to accept his wife's explanation, that Josh had warned her, when his eye fell on a lace collar. He pretended to stagger to a chair, closing his eyes and seeming to doze. He understood now why Josephine had been so eager to have him drink. With burning, half-closed eyes he watched his wife pick up the lace collar and use it for a handkerchief, trusting to luck that he was still too drunk to understand the truth.

He remained in the chair for the rest of the night, brooding, fighting down the rage that swelled in his breast, fighting the urge to take a pistol and shoot the captain dead that morning. A duel? That would be foolish, reckless, certainly, against a man known to be an expert shot with a pistol. Outright murder would mean that the story would have to be told in court.

But there were other ways.

The next day he had a talk with Elias Rector, and soon after that the belles of Washington were heartbroken to learn that Captain Harlow Robertson, U.S. Army, had been relieved of his command and ordered to Little Rock. There were rumors. Some shortage of funds, perhaps? Mismanagement? Dereliction of duty?

Whatever the charge, Robertson's career as a soldier was finished and there was no future in the career he selected after that —the career of drunkard. News drifted back to Washington, reports of his scandalous conduct in Little Rock, his constant drinking, and, finally, of his departure for Texas. One day, this year or next, Toby knew, news of his death would reach the town, and on that day he would realize the revenge that other men might have attempted with a pistol on the instant.

The Robertson incident worked a curious, though temporary, change in Josephine. It frightened her. She knew that Toby was aware of everything that happened, for he had found the torn dress, ordered one of the slaves to mend it, and, one morning at breakfast, presented it to her without a word. Had Toby challenged her with infidelity, had he shot Robertson, or ordered the man from his house, Josephine would have been more than mistress of the situation. She would have delighted in Toby's rage. His cold-blooded, methodical ruin of Robertson frightened her. She seemed to be dealing not with a man, who reacted as other men did, but with a kind of monster.

Then, too, her flirtation with Robertson left her burning with physical desire, unallayed passion, and even Toby's love seemed to her, in that state, more desirable than none at all. Her door was often left ajar at night, and she went out of her way to provoke Toby sexually, but she might as well have been dealing with a man carved from wood. He was finished with her in that way; he wanted no man's leavings.

For nearly a year things went on in this way. Josephine still went to parties, but her behavior was beyond reproach. She kept away from dark corners and firmly turned away the admirers she once had encouraged. She joined the sewing circle at the church, and even, on occasion, took Herbert to Sunday School. She kept a respectable, quiet household. Toby's love for her was dead, if, indeed, he had ever loved her, but he was pleased by her behavior, for it contributed to his peace of mind.

Then came another change. One evening, he returned home to find the house filled with people, many of them half drunk, the noise of their raucous laughter making the roof shake. They were not the better people of the town, but the rougher element, the hard-drinking kind. He got them out of the house as quickly as possible, without actually ordering them to leave, and said nothing about the incident. He became more seriously alarmed when, a few weeks later, Josephine began to attend public affairs without him, having Memphis drive for her. Toby dropped in at some of these gatherings, and each time he observed that his wife seemed bolder and more flirtatious than ever before. She delighted in having swarms of attentive men around her, and deliberately ignored or snubbed Toby when he attempted to join her group. One night he found her on the porch at the town hall, in the dark with one of the town's notorious gay blades. Both had been drinking, and Toby observed that Josephine's dress had been unbuttoned in front, so that the firm white flesh of her bosom showed. He held a riding whip in his hand and he struck the man across the face with it, ordering his wife inside. The man stood for a moment, as if trying to find courage to draw his pistol, then mumbled an apology and disappeared into the darkness. Toby smiled grimly at his back; there would be no duel with that one, he knew. Few men in Washington cared to take a chance on Toby's displeasure. He turned and went into the building, where he found his wife, her clothing in order, smiling serenely at an admiring group of young men. He was blunt. "Get your things," he said. "We're going home."

"I came with Memphis, and I'll return with her!" she answered.

"I sent Memphis home. Get your things."

Furiously, she followed him, getting into the carriage. "How dare you send my servant home without my permission?" she asked.

"Memphis is not yours," said Toby. "She's mine. I paid for her."

"You paid for her! That's all you understand! Money. You bought her and paid for her. Well, you don't own me, Mr. Toby Giles. I intend to do as I please."

"When did you come to that conclusion?" he asked.

She laughed. "It took two letters to Captain Maison, the man you called your father, to get the truth, but I got it," she gloated. "He said that you were not his son."

Toby made no attempt to answer her. He drove home while she poured out her hatred, ridiculing him and his pretensions to aristocracy. But when they entered the house, he turned to her and said quietly, "Josephine, before you go to bed, I have something I want to read to you."

"You have nothing that would interest me," she answered.

"On the contrary. The document I have will interest you greatly. It has a bearing on *your* family."

She followed him into his office. From the strongbox he took the confession that Colonel and Mrs. Withers had signed when he loaned the colonel the money to meet his obligations to the government.

"This, in effect, is a bill of sale for you, Josephine. I'll read it to you." He read the paper slowly, putting emphasis where he wanted to. Josephine heard him in silence, her face turning white with rage and fear. When he finished, she sprang from her chair.

"It's a lie!" she cried. "It's a forgery!"

He shook his head. "Oh, no, Josephine. I think you will recognize your parents' signatures. Come closer. See for yourself."

When she saw the two names, she screamed with rage, grabbing at the paper like a mad animal, then raking Toby's cheek with her sharp nails. Toby held the paper firmly, but when she clawed at him again, he slapped her with his open hand and she fell fainting to the floor. Toby stood looking down at the limp form of his wife, and for the first time felt pity for this woman, so torn by pride and greed that she could be neither wife nor mother. She was giving nothing to life and receiving nothing from it. Stooping, he picked her up and carried her to her room, where Memphis waited. As he stood at her bedside, she opened her eyes and saw his face. Then she screamed, "Get out of my sight! Get out!"

Toby went to his room and washed the blood from his face.

Josephine's nails had gouged deeply, and the marks would show for days, but Toby hardly noticed. The anguish in his heart transcended any pain of the flesh. He took off his clothes and got into bed, moving slowly, like a man half drugged, and finally succumbed to an uneasy, dream-ridden sleep. For the first time in his life, Toby felt true emptiness and despair. For the first time, he dreaded the morrow.

Of his whole life, only one bright, redeeming feature remained—Tommy Jeff. Agatha's letters kept him informed of the boy's progress. He was brilliant in his studies, she wrote, amiable and filled with kindness. Though his legs had mended to the point where Tommy Jeff could move around with the aid of braces and crutches, there was no hope that he would ever be completely cured, and Toby marveled at the boy's faith and persistence, the strength that enabled him to face life bravely, cheerfully, despite his handicap. He must get that strength, Toby decided, from love, the love that he felt for others and the love bestowed on him by Miss Agatha. And, with all his riches and all his power, Toby felt suddenly poor and bereft, without love, and in his sorrow he cried out in the night like a trapped, wounded animal. Josh came running, tapping at the door. "Is they anything wrong, Marse Toby? Anything I can do?"

"No, Josh. Nothing. I had a dream."

He had had a dream, years before, in the snug bunk place under Stoge's store, while the rain dripped rhythmically to the ground. It was the old dream, the familiar one, of success and power, the bright future, the fairy princess and the gallant prince, the old dream that has driven men since the dawn of time. And the dream had, in a way, come true, but in the coming true it had curdled, for destiny gave to him with one hand while it took with the other. It gave him money and power, and it struck down love. The best of him was buried on the hillside, part in Agatha's weathered grave, part in Stoge's. He was a bitter, unhappy man, and he understood that from now on he and his wife had, in fact, to live in a state of armed truce, she girded with the letter from Maison, power to make him absurd in the town, he protected by the paper her father and mother had signed. And he was trapped, by the very wealth he had fought so hard to acquire. He could not clear out—the time for that was past. He could only go on, blindly, moving forward, piling up more money, piling up more power, slowly counting out, like coins, the remaining days of his life.

Book Three

Cornbread Aristocrat

1.

Herbert Giles, at sixteen, had all the flair that had marked his grandfather, Colonel Withers. He was a straight, tall, handsome lad, with an arrogant way of carrying his head, and always dressed in the height of fashion. He seemed not in the least contrite, though the letter on Toby's desk, from the principal of the Kentucky academy, was hardly a document to rouse Herbert's pride. The latter flatly stated that the institution did not care to have Herbert Giles return to school that fall.

"What is the meaning of this letter, Herbert?" Toby asked.

Herbert laughed. "It seems to me the meaning's clear enough, father. They don't want me back."

"What's the trouble?"

"Well, father, you know we Giles like to kick up our heels. Perhaps I *was* a bit wild."

"What do you propose to do?"

"Look what you've done," Herbert said. "You never went to an academy or a college, and you're one of the richest men in the state."

Toby flushed. Herbert knew how to appeal to Toby's pride, and Toby was proud of the fact that he was self-made. Nevertheless, he coughed and said, "Education helps a fellow, Herbert. I don't hold with a lot of hifalutin stuff, but a man does need writing and figuring."

Herbert smiled pleasantly. The boy had a good deal of charm, and he was already adroit at handling people. "Grandfather Withers went to the academy, and I wouldn't say he had done *quite* as well as you have, father."

265

Comparison with Withers, in Toby's favor, turned the trick. "If you want to make money, son, more power to you. I'll teach you all I know," he said, beaming at the boy.

"Money's all you need, father," Herbert said. "I've heard you say that a thousand times."

Toby nodded. "I'll find a better school. One where they'll teach you to write and figure and not bother you with a lot of folderol."

He was delighted with Herbert's man-to-man attitude and with the boy's frank admiration for his success. He would have been less pleased had he heard Herbert talking with his mother, later on. The two made a handsome picture. Herbert, the slim young aristocrat, and his mother, now, in her early thirties, coming into the full flower of her beauty, her figure rounded but still firm, her hair still glorious, the somewhat more mature line of her chin giving her an appearance of dignity that she did not actually possess.

"And what did your father say about the letter from Kentucky, Herbert?" Josephine asked.

"He said that if I wanted to make money he would show me how."

"Really!"

"Yes, mother. Isn't it amusing? I refrained from telling him that *making* money suited his station in life. *Spending* it suits mine."

Josephine laughed, stroking her son's hair.

"It's all a matter of function, mother," said Herbert. "Father makes the money, but he hasn't the faintest idea of how to enjoy it. You and I have."

These two understood one another. For years they had joined forces against Toby, with poor Violet lost in the middle. There was an unusual familiarity between them, and Josephine took no offense when Herbert said, with a knowing smile, "Has father decided to rent the old Rowden house to Captain Mimms? I think it would be pleasant if he did."

Josephine flushed slightly and avoided Herbert's eyes. "Yes, I think he's going to rent it to the captain. It belongs to that brat of his in Natchez, really, so he can't sell it."

"Ah, my half brother, Thomas Jefferson Giles? Half brother in more ways than one, I gather." Herbert surveyed his long, straight legs and seemed satisfied. "I think I should shoot myself if I were a cripple," he said. "At any rate, it's nice that Captain Mimms has found a home."

After the departure of Captain Robertson, the Washington unit of the state militia had fallen apart. A series of desultory young officers had served their terms, but there had been little public interest in the force. Now, eager for a show of strength against the northern politicians, the officials at Little Rock had ordered that the militia be brought up to strength, and Captain Olin Mimms had been ordered to Washington to command the unit. Mimms was simply a somewhat older, somewhat more experienced Robertson. He had a wife and several children, but these did not trouble Josephine, for Mrs. Mimms was a mouselike little woman who never went out in society, keeping close to her home and children. The captain, however, seldom stayed home. He drove a well-matched pair of diminutive ponies, hitched to a small, smart spring wagon, and this rig was usually to be seen hitched in front of the house in which the most exclusive party of the evening was taking place. The captain's uniforms had been made in Richmond, cut in the most extreme, fashionable manner, emphasizing his figure. He danced well, and liquor made him gay and even more than naturally gallant. He was sought after by the most exclusive people in town, and it was his social prestige as much as his attractiveness that caused Josephine to set her cap for him. Down the years, her prestige had fallen. While her father lived, she had enjoyed respect. Her mother, too, had bolstered her position. But now her mother was gone from Washington for good, gone to Ohio to Josephine's sister. The glamorous lineage of the Withers family was forgotten. What remained was Josephine's daring and impetuous conduct. She had, for years, shocked the churchgoing element with her costumes, her rough parties, her shameless man-chasing. She had become the subject of shocked gossip among the matrons of the town and of crude gossip among the young bucks. Only Toby's power and prestige sustained her, and it was with great bitterness that she realized that Toby's standing in the community was superior to hers. She determined to ensnare the captain. He was still young, desirable, the kind of man that made her heart pound a little and her blood run faster. And he was her passkey through locked doors, back to a preeminent position in Washington society. Josephine had charms; she was shrewd and beautiful, and she understood the use of her powers. Before very long she had the captain infatuated.

As Captain Mimms was being drawn into his wife's spider web, Toby watched with a kind of sardonic amusement, giving her grudging admiration as he saw the young soldier succumb to her designs. But Toby had the grim knowledge that in the end it was he who would win. When he learned that Josephine was paying regular visits to the old Withers home, which she steadfastly refused to sell, though her mother announced that she never would return to Washington, Toby saw his own program taking shape. One afternoon, when Josephine was safely occupied, Toby paid the old Withers place a visit. He knew the house better, perhaps, than anyone else, for it was the first house he had built. Inside he looked around, and gave a long, low whistle. The place was neat and clean, and new curtains of heavy material hung from the windows. It was apparent that his wife intended to use the house, and there was only one purpose to which she could put it.

Toby went outside and selected a crack in the log siding that would give him a clear view of the large bedroom. He dug out a portion of the mud packing, making a peephole, disguising it carefully and returning to the inside of the house to clean up the floor. When he had finished, he tried the hole from outside and a grim smile crossed his face. He could see the large bed with ease.

Toby's lodge met on the first Friday of each month, and Toby seldom missed a meeting. The meetings always lasted until late, and when they were over there was usually an informal gathering at which the whiskey freely flowed; on that night Toby rarely appeared home until dawn was breaking, and sometimes did not return at all, passing the night in a room at the tavern. He knew that Josephine would bank on his absence, so the following Friday, on lodge night, he made quite a point of his going. He let Captain Mimms see him enter the lodge building, and watched while the captain turned quickly away. Inside the lodge room, Toby pleaded urgent business and excused himself.

He walked quickly through the darkened streets toward the old Withers place, a pistol buckled around his waist. As he approached, a noise warned him and he drew back into the shadow of the trees. Then a rig drew up, and he watched Josephine step down and glide noiselessly into the house. A few moments later, Captain Mimms arrived. Toby's fingers were on the butt of his pistol and he was tempted to kill the captain then and there, but some wild, depraved impulse restrained him; he wanted to see his wife in Mimms' arms; he wanted to witness her infidelity with his own eyes. He crept slowly along the wall and took up his place at the peephole he had made. The curtains were so tightly drawn that not even a crack of light showed at the windows, but when he put his eye to the chink in the wall, he looked into a well-lighted room. He watched Josephine and her lover melt into a passionate embrace. The captain's hands passed over Josephine's body, exploring her breasts, her waist, her hips, her thighs. And he saw a Josephine who had become a stranger to him, a wild, adventurous woman, completely abandoned to her passion. She relaxed in her lover's arms, and with her free hand boldly unfastened her dress, disclosing the fact that she wore nothing beneath it, and when the rich satin fabric fell away, she stood in bold nakedness. So close was Toby that he heard the captain's ecstatic gasp as he beheld Josephine's loveliness. He watched Mimms fondle Josephine's breasts and saw her moist lips turn upward. Finally, after the captain had torn the clothes from his body, Toby stood in a kind of fascinated agony, watching them consummate their passion, the lights still burning. He drew his pistol, prepared to fire through the crack in the wall. The narrow chink between the thick logs was too small to allow aim. His shot would miss its target. Then, gradually, his reason overtook him, and the frantic jealousy, near madness, turned to cold, calculating rage. He lowered the pistol and turned away, going quickly and silently from the house. He would have his revenge, a complete revenge. But he would take it in his own way.

For days he brooded over his problem, not permitting his wife to know that he was aware of her infidelity. He noticed a new excitement in her, and despite his rage and determination to seek revenge, he admitted to himself that Mimms, and probably Robertson, had touched a chord in Josephine that he had failed to find. These men had done what he had not been able to do—they had released the floodgates of his wife's passion. He wondered how many others besides Mimms and Robertson had enjoyed the full power of Josephine's ardor, remembering trifling incidents from the past, meaningful glances that had passed between his wife and this young man or that one, and it occurred to him that almost from the first the woman he had married had been unfaithful to him, in spirit if not in actual fact. He recalled the night in New Orleans, on their wedding trip, and the young mate of the river steamer that carried them north. He recalled the lieutenant at the governor's ball, and a hundred others. He had seen nothing, through the chink in the wall, that should have surprised him, for his whole marriage had been preparation for what he had witnessed. He should not, in justice, blame Mimms for taking what was flagrantly offered him. Nevertheless, something in him dictated revenge, as much against a man who had taken his property, property that had been bought and paid for, as a man who had violated his home. The horns that Toby felt on his forehead were only partly the horns of a jealous husband, for in truth Josephine had rendered him almost incapable of honest jealousy where she was concerned.

Toby knew how to wait, and how to keep his own counsel. Only Josh knew that trouble was brewing. One evening he discovered his master alone in his office, mixing soot with pitch and beeswax. The slave remembered the bogus bullets with which Toby had defeated the Mexican, Ortega, and he frowned. But Josh said nothing. The faithful black man would have resisted the fiercest torture before he would have betrayed his master. In Josh's eyes, Toby had quite literally saved his life when he traded for him with the old chief. Josh was more than a chattel slave; he was as completely Toby's property as Toby's own right hand.

In the tavern, Toby encountered Mimms, apparently by accident. The officer seemed slightly embarrassed, but his embarrassment faded when Toby greeted him in friendly fashion and insisted on buying him a drink. Toby knew that the other man was laughing at him, gloating over him, behind the smooth façade of his elegant manners, and this knowledge only strengthened Toby's determination to destroy him.

"Captain," he said casually, "I understand you are trying to recruit more men for your militia."

"Yes, Mr. Giles, I have been instructed to bring the regiment up to full strength."

"Well, captain, I've spent most of my life in Arkansas, and the best way to get recruits for anything is to have a big blowout. Plenty of barbecued pig and lots of corn liquor."

Bill Bowes was standing at the bar and he laughed, agreeing with Toby. "Toby's right, captain. With a barrel of corn, you'll get plenty of joiners. I might even join myself, if I got likkered up enough."

"I need your help, gentlemen," Mimms said. "Few of the citizens seem to realize the need for a strong militia. There's been lots of talk about abolition in the North. Those Yankees may try to free our niggers before we know it."

Toby shook his head. "We'll never have a war about slavery," he said. "The Yankees are too smart. They know a war would ruin both the North and South. They may try to *buy* our niggers. That's another matter."

"Them Yankees don't give a damn about ruining the country," Bowes said.

"Hell they don't," Toby objected. "I never saw a Yankee yet that wasn't crazy about a dollar."

Bowes laughed. "What part of the North are you from, Toby?" he asked. "Anyway, we're gettin' off the subject. We were talking about the captain's militia."

Toby nodded. "Why not plan the shindig for the fifteenth of August? That's a Saturday, and everybody'll be in town. With enough corn liquor, you should get a hundred recruits. And don't worry about meat for the barbecue. I'll see we have plenty of fresh-killed hogs for that."

Thursday afternoon, before the day of the barbecue, Toby looked up Captain Mimms again. "Captain, I thought you might enjoy going with me tomorrow to kill a few razorbacks for the barbecue," he said.

"Gladly," answered Mimms. "I've always wanted to kill a wild boar."

"You mean you've never hunted razorbacks?" Toby asked.

"No, but there's always a first time," Mimms smiled.

They met early the next morning and set out for the river bottoms. When they reached the ridge land, covered with oaks, they spotted a drove of razorbacks eating acorns. "You take the young boar to the right and I'll take that fat sow to his left," whispered Toby.

Both rifles went off at the same instant and two hogs fell mortally wounded. Toby gave his horn three sharp blasts, signaling Josh to bring the mule sled for the game. Toby had made it a point to give Captain Mimms a rifle identical to the one he was using. Waiting for Josh to arrive, both men carefully reloaded their rifles, Toby using the beeswax bullet. They helped Josh load the two razorbacks and resumed their hunt, Captain Mimms never knowing the rifles had been switched.

Toby led the way, deeper into the bottoms, picking his route carefully so that Josh would have trouble following with the mule and heading straight for the feeding grounds of the larger, more ferocious boars. Neither man spoke, their silence complete and apprehensive, each man a little awed by the wilderness, and, in a way, afraid to speak for fear the thoughts in his mind would spring out. They slogged through the deep mire, slipping and sliding in the mud, fighting their way through the dense undergrowth. Suddenly Toby stopped, halting the captain with his hand. There was a noise from the thicket, and a moment later a large tusker appeared, not more than twenty paces from them. He was the largest, most savage-looking razorback Toby had ever seen. The short hairs on his back bristled with rage. Toby sprang toward a low-limbed tree and quickly hoisted himself and his gun out of danger. Mimms dropped to one knee and raised his rifle to his shoulder, firing as the boar charged. The wax pellet struck the animal between the eyes, heightening his rage, and in a split second he was on the captain in all his fury. Mimms fought, clubbing with his rifle, but the boar's first charge slashed his leg badly and made it difficult for him to fight the animal off.

From his perch in the tree, Toby watched Mimms turn and try to run, then fall headlong as the boar's tusks bit into his buttocks. The captain writhed on the ground as the boar methodically cut him to ribbons. Finally, his eyes filled with the fear of death, he looked upward and saw Toby. "Kill him, Giles," he managed to cry. "Kill him!"

But Toby laughed. "How'd you like a woman now, captain? One like my wife, Josephine? Think she'd call you darling now?"

Toby watched the boar finish its work. When Mimms was done for, he sighted carefully and fired, killing the bloodthirsty razorback with an expert shot. He reloaded the gun and climbed down from the tree. He stood over the captain for a moment. Mimms was dead, his body slashed to ribbons, his face a pulp. Toby looked at him for a long minute, then drew back his foot and kicked the dead body savagely. Satisfied at last, he raised his horn and blew it, signaling Josh to come up.

The slave arrived quickly, out of breath and panting. He had left his mule behind and arrived too soon to suit Toby. He wondered if Josh had witnessed the murder.

" 'Fore God, Marse Toby, what happened?" the Negro asked.

"A tragic accident, Josh. Captain Mimms missed the boar and the beast killed him. Throw him over your shoulder and take him back to the sled."

When they reached the mule, Josh put the body down and started to remove the two razorbacks from the sled. "Pitch him in between the two hogs," said Toby, leading the way back home. Josh and the mule followed.

It was dark when Toby and Josh arrived at the house. A full, red moon threw an eerie light on the landscape. Toby stopped. "Pick him up and put him in my arms," he commanded. "And open the door into the parlor."

Josh obeyed his master, a look of horror on his face. Toby's footsteps were deadened by the thick carpet, and Josephine did not hear him approach until he was almost beside her. She stood near the table, arranging roses in a bowl. As she turned, sensing Toby's presence, Toby dropped the mutilated body at her feet. "There is your lover, Josephine," he said. "Not as handsome as he was this morning, or as healthy, but your lover, just the same."

Josephine uttered a low, piercing scream and sank back into a chair. She covered her face with her hands and shook with sobs. Toby stood watching her. Then, without a word, he turned.

"Where are you going?" she cried.

"To town to report the accident to the sheriff," he said pleasantly.

"Don't leave him here! For God's sake, take him with you!"

"Oh, no, darling," Toby said. "He's yours. Look after him."

She rose from her chair, rage and terror on her face. "You murderer!" she said. "You murderer!"

Toby stepped toward her and she backed away. "Captain Mimms met with an accident, Josephine," he explained patiently. "I had no reason to kill him, had I?"

"Murderer!"

"Now, now. You know I had nothing against the captain. If you were to accuse me of murder, what motive would you give? What reason have I to wish him dead? Is there any?"

He stood, smiling at her. He knew that Josephine would never accuse herself, and to accuse him, she must denounce herself as an adulteress. She was powerless. He smiled again, looking at the mutilated body on the floor, then turned and walked from the room.

2.

Summer passed into fall, and when school time approached, Herbert announced flatly that he did not intend to continue his education. Toby agreed reluctantly, feeling that there was no use forcing the boy to go to school merely to suffer the humiliation of seeing him expelled. He put Herbert in charge of Stoge Rowden's farm, giving him a liberal salary. During the pleasant fall months Herbert did not mind riding about the farm, bossing the Negroes, cutting a figure on his blooded mount. But when the harsh November days arrived, he was less attracted by outdoor work. He found a thousand excuses to neglect the farm, and could always depend on Josephine's support.

Herbert had developed into a handsome young man, and with plenty of money to spend he had no difficulty finding female companionship of any sort he desired. It was said in the tavern that if a girl had been out three times with the Giles boy, it was a cinch she had had to fight for her virtue. If she went out a fourth time, you could bet on the fact that she had lost it. And he had already begun to drink.

Toby's reaction to Herbert's harum-scarum ways was mixed. When the boy was sober, he made a fine appearance, and Toby was proud of him. He had a kind of sneaking half pride, too, in the tales they told of his son's prowess with the ladies. And the lad was smart; he had a shrewd, clever mind and a ready tongue. But he was a liar, a cheat, and a snob, and Toby knew that in the future he would become more, not less, of a problem.

Violet was seventeen, not pretty, but with the ripe, wholesome kind of good looks that pleased her father. She had a beau, young Jack Jenkins, whose family had left the hills of Tennessee for Texas, wintered at Washington on the way south, and left Jack behind so that he could finish his education. Toby disapproved of Jack, for he had bigger plans for Violet. He hoped to send the girl to Natchez, where Miss Agatha would send her to the seminary. But these hopes faded a little as he watched the friendship between Violet and Jack ripen into something deeper.

Josephine, since Mimms' death, maintained only the most formal relationship with Toby. Though she was well into her thirties, she still attracted men like flies. Her current flame was the young son of the town's leading preacher. She was more discreet than she had been with either Robertson or Mimms, and if she went beyond a frank flirtation with the boy, she concealed it well.

The one bright spot in Toby's Christmas holiday was a gift from Tommy Jeff—a massive, hand-carved desk. A letter that came with the gift asked Toby to stop sending money to Tommy Jeff. It announced that his son now owned a factory for building hand-carved furniture. He could earn his own living and support Miss Agatha as well. The letter ended with protestations of love that brought tears to Toby's eyes. His first-born, reared by someone else, handicapped by the dreadful disease that had left him crippled, had done what Herbert could never do. He had made a man of himself. Through the years, Agatha had written that Tommy Jeff, under Whittler's guidance, had become an expert furniture carver and designer, but Toby had always thought it was merely something to help the boy pass the time and forget the fact that his crippling illness prevented him from running and playing like other youngsters. Now his son was proprietor of a factory, self-supporting, a man of substance. Toby became aware of a great failure somewhere in himself; he sat, looking at Tommy Jeff's gift, and it dawned on him that he was, in the truest sense, a failure, in spite of all his success.

The New Year's ball in Little Rock was now the outstanding event of the season. Toby had no interest in such affairs; balls and parties bored him. He agreed that Herbert escort his mother, and Sunshine, Minnie's half-Indian daughter, accompanied them. Instead of staying two weeks, as arranged, they stayed four, and when they returned it was without Sunshine. Josephine curtly announced that she had sold the girl, and Minnie was brokenhearted. Toby was enraged. He had made it a practice never to break up slave families. Two suspicions rose in his mind, one that Herbert's gambling debts were so large that the girl was sold to pay them, the other that Josephine's conduct in Little Rock had been so reckless that she wanted the girl who had witnessed it out of the way. She had abandoned the minister's son by now, and was in hot pursuit of a married man, a man who, to Toby's knowledge, had also attended the ball in Little Rock.

Toby studied Herbert, trying to understand the boy, trying to get closer to his son, but he met with a suave rebuff each time. Toby made it clear that he regarded his father as no gentleman, and though he was always courteous nowadays—overcourteous, in fact—behind the smooth façade of his manners lurked contempt so thorough that Toby was never unaware of it. The boy's behavior was intolerable, yet there seemed to be nothing Toby could do that impressed him enough to make him mend his ways. Hardly a month passed during which Herbert was not the cause of some extra expense or humiliation. It was rumored that he had fought more than one duel.

Violet was Toby's only real support at home, since Josephine and Herbert were united against him, so it was with a good deal of grief that he learned that Violet was leaving him. One night, as he came home, he found his daughter waiting for him in front of the house. "Father," she said, "are you prepared for a shock?"

He smiled at the girl. "Honey, I'm just about shockproof."

"Jack Jenkins and I are married," she announced.

"No!" Toby cried, then checked himself, seeing the hurt expression on his daughter's face. He touched her arm. "I don't mean that, honey, I don't mean that at all. I was just surprised. Where is Jack? I'd like to talk to him."

"He'll be here tonight, father. You can talk to him then."

Giles was pleasant to Jack, though mortally disappointed

that his daughter had been married without letting him know first.

"I wanted to break this news to you, Mr. Giles," the lad insisted, "but Violet said she could tell you better."

Toby's voice softened. "Jack, please don't take my daughter away from me." He sat looking at his child and at the man she had married. What came to his mind was old Stoge Rowden, as Stoge had looked when Toby announced that he wanted to marry Agatha.

"My folks love Violet too," Jack said. "We'll take good care of her."

"Stay here, Jack," Toby pleaded, "and I'll give you the best farm in the county. I'll help you in every way I can."

The young couple exchanged glances, Jack seeming to ask a question with his eyes. But Violet shook her head. "No, father," she said, a good deal of determination in her voice. "Jack and I want peace and contentment, a chance to live our lives without interference."

Toby shook his head sadly. He knew what Violet meant. She was searching for something she had never found in her own home, and he could not deny her the right to search, for he longed for the same thing. "What do you want from me?" he asked quietly. "Whatever you ask for is yours, if I have it."

"We want your approval of our marriage," said Jack. "And your good wishes."

"Is that all?" Toby asked.

Jack nodded. Toby put his arm around the boy. "I'm a poor judge of humanity, Jack," he said. "Horses I can understand, and things that have to do with money, but I guess I just don't understand people. I'm proud to have you for a son-in-law, boy."

Jack was pleased. "Thank you, sir," he said. "I'm going to do my best to make her happy."

"I want you to pick two of my best slaves as your wedding gift," said Toby. "Any two you want."

Jack reddened slightly. "I appreciate your offer, Mr. Giles. But I don't believe in slavery."

"What?" Jack's statement, coming from a Southerner, and a farmer, was as bizarre as though the boy had said he didn't believe in winter, or in the fact that the earth was round. Slavery was a fact; a simple law ordained by nature. "Are you an abolitionist?" Toby asked.

"I don't know anything about abolitionists," Jack said. "I just don't believe that the Lord intended one man to be master over another." The boy spoke fearlessly, with great conviction. Toby was amazed.

"Jack, niggers aren't men, when you come down to it. They're like mules, or cattle."

"They are men, Mr. Giles, men like you and me. Only their skins make them different."

"Well," said Toby blankly, "whatever's right and whatever's wrong, you'll have a hell of a time making money on a farm without slaves."

Jack agreed. "That's why I'm headed for ranching country. I can look after my own herds," he explained.

Toby supervised the loading of the three heavy wagons, heaped high with household goods and provisions. In his pocket was a fat envelope containing five thousand dollars in currency, and this he was determined Violet should accept. In spite of his strange ideas about slavery, Jack impressed Toby as a man worth helping.

During the loading of the wagons, Toby had failed to notice the fact that all of the slaves were lounging around the quarters, sullen and grumbling. It was long past the time when they should have been in the fields, and when Toby saw them he sent for Josh. "Why aren't the niggers working?" he wanted to know.

"Dey waitin' fo' orders from Marse Herbert, suh," the slave explained.

"Tell them to get on with their work," said Toby.

x

An expression of fear crossed Josh's face. "Please, Marse Toby, you tell 'em. Marse Herbert doan' like fo' me to boss his slaves."

Toby walked over to the group of Negroes and told them to get to work. They turned sullenly away and plodded toward the fields. Toby noticed that they seemed lifeless and dispirited.

"What's wrong with those niggers, Josh?" he asked.

Josh turned his head away, hesitant to answer, but when Toby repeated his question sharply, Josh replied, "They ain't happy, Marse Toby. Marse Herbert, he's hard on 'em."

Toby's mouth set in a thin line. He believed in discipline, and would have shot a slave who disobeyed his orders, but he believed that discipline could be achieved without beating the blacks. He left Josh and walked back to the house. Herbert was still in bed, suffering the pangs of a head-splitting hang-over. He rubbed the sleep from his eyes and sat up. "Oh, it's you," he said.

"Herbert, you will have no further authority over my slaves," Toby said. "I allow no one to beat them, and if I ever hear of your laying the lash to them, you'll answer to me. I will put stripe for stripe on your own white back." He went out of Herbert's room, having relieved himself of part of his anger, but knowing full well he had made no impression on Herbert. He found Cato and Linda waiting for him.

"Marse Toby," Linda said, "this old black mammy has raised dat chile from a baby. Miss Violet needs Linda, an' I wants to go with her."

"Linda, do you mean to tell me you'd leave Cato?"

"I wants to go too, Marse Toby," Cato put in.

Toby studied the two old slaves, wondering how much they were prompted by love of Violet and how much by the desire to get away from Herbert. After a moment he said, "If Miss Violet will take you, you may certainly go." He went to his office and wrote out a bill of sale for the two slaves. He found Jack at the wagons and gave him the paper. "This makes it legal, Jack," he said. "If you want to give them their freedom when you all get to Texas, that's up to you."

His son-in-law nodded and thanked him. A few hours later the teams strained under the heavy loads, the harness creaked, and the big wagons began to move away, toward the West. Toby rode beside them as far as Fulton, then kissed his daughter good-by and shook hands with his son-in-law. Riding back to Washington alone, Toby, for the first time in his life, felt old. Suddenly he became aware of the weight of the years—of all his dreams fading long before they reached fulfillment. A real sense of the tragedy of his life possessed him as he sat on the patient horse, slumped in the saddle, his head bowed, returning to a home that held no love now, with Violet gone.

3.

A year passed, and another. Letters came regularly from Violet, with an occasional note from Jack. They were prospering and happy, and though he missed his daughter, Toby realized that going away, away from this house with all its hatreds and jealousies, was the best thing she could have done. Had she and Jack remained in Washington, Josephine would have devoted all her energies to breaking up the marriage, as much for something to do as for any other reason. Four or five times a year, Toby sat down and laboriously composed long letters to Violet and to Tommy Jeff, letters filled with his love for them, but telling nothing of the trouble at home.

And there was trouble. Herbert, with time on his hands, forbidden to rule the slaves, became the town drunk and the town lecher, a dissolute, utterly abandoned human being at twenty-one, a near-degenerate at twenty-two. One afternoon, in the bright sunlight, Toby was leaving the tavern when he saw his son driving recklessly down the main street, lashing the horses in a crazy rhythm, roaring drunk, a shifty-eyed half-breed girl in the seat beside him. She was a notorious prostitute, shunned by even the most depraved men. The sheriff approached and greeted Toby, and the two men watched Herbert as he whirled by. Then the sheriff said, "What do you want me to do, Toby?"

Toby turned, deciding suddenly. "Put 'em both in jail. Lock them up and keep them there until you hear from me."

The sheriff frowned. "You mean you want me to put Herbert in a cell?" he asked.

"That's right. That's where he belongs."

"Just as you say, Toby," the sheriff agreed. He turned and mounted his horse, riding off after Herbert and the girl. Toby rode home.

Herbert's absence caused no comment from Josephine the first night or the second. He often passed the darkness in someone else's bed when he was carousing. But on the morning of the third day Josephine asked, "Do you know where Herbert is?"

"I do," said Toby.

"Where is he?"

"In jail."

Her coffee cup dropped from her hand. "What do you mean by allowing your son to be put in jail?"

Toby chuckled. "I didn't allow it, as you say. Herbert fixed that up for himself. I just told the sheriff to keep him there."

"That is the most contemptible thing I've ever heard of." Josephine swallowed hard, tears coming to her eyes. "If you don't go down and get him out immediately, I'll go myself."

"Go, if you like," Toby said. He called to the slaves. "Minnie! Have Mrs. Giles' horse saddled. She's riding down to the jail."

"Toby!"

"Or would you prefer the buggy?" Toby asked.

"You are coming with me," she said.

Toby smiled, shaking his head. "Not today, Josephine," he said.

"Then I'll go alone. I'll bring him home."

"Do as you like," Toby said casually. "But I don't think you'll bring him home. I told the sheriff to keep him there till he comes to his senses, or to let him work out his fine on the county roads."

She acted as though she had been slapped in the face. "You mean that Herbert—a Withers—is to work on the county roads like a common drunkard?"

"His name's Giles, Josephine," Toby reminded his wife. "And I only got a glimpse of him, the other day, because the buggy was going too fast for a good look, but I'd say he was an *un*common drunkard. I don't know when I've seen a man so drunk."

Josephine turned, hurried to the sideboard, and poured herself a drink of brandy. During these last years she had been drinking steadily, and the effects of alcohol showed on her face, thickly powdered though it was. She drank the brandy at a gulp, then poured another. "Toby, for Herbert's sake, be reasonable. This disgrace will kill the boy."

"Oh, no," said Toby. "The disgrace won't hurt him. I wish it would, but he's beyond that. What'll hurt him is too much of that stuff you've got in your hand. And too much bedding down with half-breed whores."

"Toby Giles, you are the vilest human being on the face of the earth!" she screamed. For a moment, Toby thought she was going to dash the brandy into his face, but she thought better of that and drank it, swaying slightly, clutching at the sideboard to steady herself. Her beauty was finally beginning to go, though her figure was still rounded and provocative, and her hair was still gloriously golden. It was her face that displayed the evil in her heart, and that evil could no longer be concealed.

Toby rose from the table. "Go down and talk to him," he said. "I think the experience will do you both good."

She went, and when she returned, without Herbert, she was in a towering rage. The knowledge that Toby's power and prestige were greater than her own always galled her. She could not accept the fact that being a Withers no longer had meaning in the town, while being Toby Giles, who owned the mill, and the gin, and the best farm land, and a dozen houses meant just about everything.

"Did you see Herbert?" Toby asked. "Does he want me to come and get him out?"

"He will die before he sends for you. He hates you."

Not quite true. A week passed before Herbert's courage wilted and he sent the sheriff to tell Toby that he wanted his father's help. Toby found him in a cell by himself, unshaven, dirty, and nearly contrite.

"You sent for me, Herbert?" he said. "What do you want?"

"Get me out of here!" Herbert pleaded. "I don't deserve this."

"You were drunk and disturbing the peace. That's one of the things they put people in jail for."

"A fellow has a right to rip, snort, and buck a little."

"Sure he does," Toby agreed. "But there's a limit. Flaunting that half-breed whore in people's faces was a little too much."

"I've heard you say a million times that if you have the money you can do as you like."

Toby was silent. Herbert pressed him. "And I'll bet you did things just as bad when you were a young buck."

Toby shook his head. "When I was your age, Herbert, I was working in Stoge Rowden's store, twelve hours a day, trying to get a start."

"Get me out of here!" Herbert shouted.

Toby nodded. "I will," he said, "when you promise me you will behave like a gentleman from now on. Either promise me that—and I'll hold you to it—or you can work out your fine on the roads."

The prospect of the county road was too much for Herbert. He sat, staring at the scabrous wall of his cell, then finally nodded his head in sullen agreement. "All right. I promise."

"No more liquor?" Toby said. "No more whores?"

"All right, father," Herbert agreed.

Toby called the sheriff, and a few minutes later father and son walked out of the jail together. Toby, hoping against hope, tried to persuade himself that this experience might frighten Herbert into settling down. And it did, for a time.

Another year dragged by and Herbert behaved passably well. He drank more moderately, though on the Fourth of July he took too much corn and was badly mauled in a free-for-all fight. If he sought the whores, he did it quietly. He went through the motions of being a dutiful son, though his attitude toward Toby remained unchanged. It was one of hatred, contempt, and fear.

Toby was not inclined to grant Herbert the slightest responsibility, but after twelve months of probation he felt obligated to give the boy a chance to demonstrate his new maturity. Toby's cotton broker in New Orleans had retired, selling out to a rival firm, and Toby had intended to go down the river himself to see the new owners. With certain misgivings, he decided to send his son, and Herbert set off for the Delta, in charge of two hundred and twenty bales of cotton and a bargeload of fine walnut and hickory lumber. Toby rode as far as Fulton with the boy, and stood on the pier, watching the boat steam around the bend, hoping in his heart that he had made no mistake.

He returned from Fulton to see a strange rig in the yard. Josh came out to meet him, taking his horse by the bridle.

"Marse Toby," he said, "Marse Jack Jenkins heah to see you. Cato an' Linda done come with him."

The old slave seemed sad, and he avoided Toby's eyes. Toby dismounted. "Is Miss Violet with them, Josh?" he asked.

"No, suh," Josh replied, shaking his head.

"Where is she?" Toby asked. "Is something wrong?"

Tears came to the black man's eyes. "She done passed away, Marse Toby. Miss Violet done passed away wid de gallopin' consumption."

Toby stood in the dooryard and lifted his eyes to heaven. Then he raised his fist and shook it at the placid vault of the sky. For the third time in his life he cursed God, who had visited him with such misfortunes. First Agatha, then Tommy Jeff, now Violet, his baby. His first thought was to blame Jack Jenkins, but when he talked to the man, he changed his mind. Jenkins showed the effect of his grief. He was like a man half alive. "She didn't want to write to you about her illness, Mr. Giles. She didn't want to worry you." He reached into his pocket and produced a soiled envelope, handing it to Toby. "Here's forty-one hundred and thirty dollars, Mr. Giles. I'll pay you back the rest when I can."

Toby put a hand on Jack's arm. "I want you to keep the money, Jack. It will help you get started."

"No, thank you, sir. I can get along."

"Please keep it, son. I want you to."

"Very well, sir, and thank you." Jack handed him the bill of sale for Cato and Linda.

"Keep the slaves too," said Toby, but Jack refused.

"They belong here, Mr. Giles. They loved Violet, and wanted to be with her, but now that she's gone, they belong here."

Toby nodded. "What are your plans, son?" he asked. He was tempted to ask Jack to stay, to become a third son to him, with a full share in the business, but he checked the impulse, for he knew that the boy would refuse.

"I'm headin' back for Texas in the morning," Jack said. He offered Toby a hard, square hand, callused by toil.

"Good luck to you, son," Toby said. "If you ever need anything, come to me."

"Thank you."

Jack climbed into the seat and rode away. Toby stood listening to the sound of his horse's hooves until they could be heard no more, then turned and went into the house. He found his wife, who had loathed the child while she lived, in a great rage at him. "You murderer! You have killed my child. Permitting her to go to Texas with that common good for nothing!"

Toby crossed the room to Josephine and took her wrist in his hand, holding it so tightly that she feared he intended to break her arm. "I want you to keep your mouth shut," he said. "I don't want you to mention Violet again. It was you she ran away from."

Josephine, for a moment, seemed about to speak, but the pressure of Toby's hand on her wrist increased and she remained silent. He released her and went out of the house, riding into town. For the first time in many years he got conscientiously drunk, but it was no good. No amount of liquor served to blot out the images of Violet that raced through his brain, pictures of her as a tiny baby, as a young girl, starched and fresh in a blue pinafore, as a young lady with tight braids, swinging home from school with her books in a strap, as a young woman, a bride, going off to Texas with the man she loved. He sat alone in the tavern while these pictures seemed to accuse him, and suddenly he brought his fist down on the table with such force that the bottle was thrown to the floor. The landlord appeared quickly. "Mr. Giles! Is anything wrong? You look as if you'd seen a ghost."

Toby shook his head. "No. Nothing wrong. I was dreaming."

The landlord picked up the bottle. "I'll get you another, sir," he said. "This one's empty."

"Sure, another. Another bottle," Toby said. He threw back his head and unfamiliar, hysterical laughter poured from his lips, so loud that the tavern habitués turned to stare. "What's the matter, Toby?" someone called. "Had a drop too much?"

Toby's laughter stopped as abruptly as it had started. He nodded soberly. "That's it," he said. "I've had too much. Too much."

A month passed, and another, then a third. Boats came up-river regularly, but none of them carried Herbert. Finally Toby wrote to his broker, asking for information about his son. He framed the letter discreetly, so that the broker would not suspect that he mistrusted Herbert, but before a reply could arrive, Herbert himself appeared in town. Jett Morrison informed Toby of his arrival.

"Where'd he go?" Toby asked.

"He was headed for the tavern, last I saw of him," Morrison answered. The man paused, not anxious to offend Toby. "He—he looked pretty bad, Toby," he went on.

Toby nodded grimly. He found his son in the tavern, both hands around a glass of whiskey. Herbert showed the effects of the three-month debauch. His clothes were filthy, he had lost weight, his face was pale. He greeted Toby sullenly, then became defiant.

"I was having a good time," he said. "Who can enjoy himself in this hole? Besides, I lived like a monk for a year, and I had a blowout coming to me."

"What about the cotton and timber?"

"Sold." Herbert raised his glass in a mock toast. "Sold by a master salesman."

Toby knocked the glass from his hand. Herbert shook his head. "You shouldn't do that, father," he said, wagging his finger. "Waste not, want not. Whiskey is a positive good."

Toby realized that the boy was drunk as a lord and that there was little use in questioning him. Nevertheless, he could not resist asking, "Do you have the cash with you? Or letters of credit?"

Herbert shook his head. "You see, father, it was this way. You know Canal Street? Beautiful street, Canal Street. Widest street in the world. You know it, father?"

"Yes, yes," said Toby impatiently. "I know Canal Street. What about the money?"

"It's this way, father. It's this way. On Canal Street, in old New Orleans, I met a girl. Beautiful girl. All girls on Canal Street are beautiful girls. Widest street in the world. Widest girls in the world. Wonderful street. Wonderful girls."

"You mean you spent the money? All of it?"

"It was necessary to live like a gentleman, father. New Orleans is a very expensive city. Not like here at all. Wonderful city, New Orleans. Wonderful city. Widest city in the world. Got widest street in the world, too. Widest girls in the world walk on widest street in the world in the widest city in the world."

Toby slapped him across the face. The sting sobered Herbert for a moment, and he shook his head slowly. "But tha's not all. The worst is yet to come."

"Go on," said Toby.

"Well, father, iss this way. You know New Orlean's a French city. Right?"

Toby agreed.

"Well, I got the French disease."

"Syphilis?"

"What else?"

Toby rose from his chair. "Come on, Herbert. Come home."

The boy followed him through the door, stumbling a little. Involuntarily, Toby drew away from him, avoiding physical contact, and Herbert laughed. They went on home in silence, the sun causing the liquor to go to Herbert's head again, so that he was half-stuporous by the time they reached the house.

In the doorway, about to face his mother, Herbert turned, and with a note of sincerity in his voice said, "Father, I tried to lose myself on the water front, to disappear. But I couldn't endure the hunger."

Toby nodded. "That, at least, does you credit. But you're better off at home. Go and scrub yourself with lye soap. Get a change of clothes before you see your mother."

Josephine, at first, refused to believe the truth, but at last Toby convinced her that her son had brought home the disease. "I want you to take care of your son," Toby said. "The aristocratic chip off the old block."

Josephine winced. Toby stepped closer and said, in a low, almost savage voice, "And I want him kept away from Tensie. Strictly away, do you understand?"

His wife's face betrayed horror. "What do you mean?"

"You know very well what I mean. Keep him away from Tensie. I'll not have my slaves infected. Slaves are valuable. They cost money."

"Are you insinuating—?" She was enraged, her cheeks turned scarlet with anger, her voice trembled. Toby smiled.

"I am insinuating nothing. I am simply stating a fact. Keep Herbert away from Tensie, do you understand? If you don't, it will be the worse for both of you."

Her head sank. "Very well," she mumbled, her voice almost inaudible. As he left the room, Toby heard her gasp, then burst into tears. "My son!" she cried. "Herbert, my son!"

Toby had sent Josh for Doctor Hooker, and he talked with him after the physician had examined Herbert. "It's too late, Toby," Hooker explained. "I can do nothing for him. The disease is in his blood stream now. Every drop of blood in his body is infected."

"Is he dangerous to others?"

"That depends," said the doctor. "Naturally, he will infect any woman he is intimate with. He must be kept strictly away

291

from women, for his own sake as well as theirs. As for infecting anyone else—there is danger, yes. But if precautions are taken, cleanliness observed, the danger is not too great."

"Is there no hope of a cure?"

Hooker frowned, pursing his lips. He closed his black bag with a definitive snap, then said, "Privately, I think not. But they say that the waters at Boiling Springs sometimes effect a cure. I suppose it is worth a trial."

"I'll send him tomorrow!" Toby exclaimed. "Perhaps they can cure him. Perhaps this experience will scare him into behaving like a man."

"I hope so," said Hooker. "You have my sympathy, Toby."

After Hooker departed, Toby went to Josephine. She had seen Herbert and the boy had confirmed Toby's report. Josephine was in tears, tears of self-pity. She blamed Toby bitterly. "You sent him to New Orleans. He's only a boy. The temptation was too much for him. Those women—on the Levee."

"They are women, like other women," Toby said. "Like yourself."

"How dare you!"

"Oh, Josephine, don't be dramatic. Get yourself together. Have Linda pack your things and Herbert's. You are taking him to Boiling Springs tomorrow."

"Boiling Springs?"

"Hooker says the waters there may boil the poison out of his system. He hasn't much hope, but it's the only thing to try."

"Very well. I will take Memphis and Tensie."

"No. You will take Linda and Cato. They will look after you, and I don't think that even Herbert will bother a woman as old as Linda."

Josephine looked at him with loathing. Then she rose and went out of the room. In the morning, she and Herbert left for Boiling Springs, taking Linda and Cato. During the weeks that they were gone, in spite of his depression, Toby enjoyed a kind of peace by default. He busied himself, passing all of his waking hours at work, stopping off at the tavern for an hour or so in the evening for a glass and a talk with Elias Rector or one of the other politicians. He tried to put Herbert and Josephine out of his mind, and he contemplated a visit to Natchez to see Tommy Jeff. But before he could put the plan into effect, a letter arrived from Josephine asking him to send Josh to fetch them home from the Springs. From the tone of the letter he understood that Herbert's cure had not gone well, and his suspicion was confirmed when he talked with his wife the evening they arrived.

"The doctor there says he's his own worst enemy. He won't cooperate. He breaks every rule."

"Every rule?"

She nodded, avoiding his eyes.

"Did he molest Linda?"

She burst into tears. "He tried. He tried. He's mad, Toby. Completely mad." For the first time in all the years of their marriage, Josephine seemed to admit defeat. She left Herbert strictly to Toby, realizing that the boy was hopeless. Toby instructed Josh to watch Herbert day and night, and though this meant more work for Toby, since Josh was, in effect, his foreman, he knew that it was the only way he could avoid some horrible outburst on Herbert's part.

It was Tensie, Memphis's daughter, that Herbert really wanted, though none of the slave women were safe from him when he was possessed by one of his wild, maniacal spells. He and Tensie had been childhood companions. She had been first his playmate, then his servant, then his concubine. She was still his personal servant, but Toby had called her aside and told her the truth, ordering her not to permit Herbert to touch her again.

Herbert's illness was, by now, known to all the slaves, and his appearance near the quarters set them all on edge with fear. Each day his eyes became more shifty and hungry looking. The slaves had always feared the violence of his temper, and there was hardly one on Toby's land who had not suffered under the lash in Herbert's hands. Now they found him more cruel than ever, and they feared for their women.

Herbert would creep from his room at night, making his way to Tensie's cabin, but Memphis was always there. Finally Josh summoned sufficient courage to tell Toby about Herbert's nightly prowling. "Don't do nobody no good, Marse Toby," he said. "It scares the niggers. Dey can't sleep. And if dey can't sleep, dey can't work."

"Have bars put on the windows in the quarters," Toby ordered. "And send Tensie to me."

Memphis's daughter appeared a few moments later. She was a slim, golden-skinned girl, with fresh red lips. The attractive curves of her body were revealed by the tight-fitting cotton garment she wore. "Tensie," Toby said, "I don't want you to be Master Herbert's personal servant any more. You can work in the fields and I'll have one of the men look after him."

Relief showed on the black girl's face. "Thank you, Marse Toby. I thank you." She turned to go, but Toby stopped her.

"Don't be alone in your cabin," he said. "Always have Memphis or some other woman with you, understand?"

"Yessuh, Marse Toby." She hesitated, then added, "Yo' mighty kind, Marse Toby."

When a young slave man appeared with Herbert's breakfast, Herbert was enraged. He lashed the poor black across the face with a riding whip and went into a tantrum, giving full vent to his depraved passion, shrieking for Tensie at the top of his lungs, smashing things in his room, until finally Toby was summoned to quiet him. After this outburst he was sullen for several days, refusing food and not moving out of his room.

But when his depressive mood had passed, he was roused again by desire for Tensie. That night he crept down to the slave quarters and hid himself near her cabin. Just then he heard one of the slaves call Memphis, and watched her hurry out into the darkness, leaving the door unbarred. He slipped into the cabin. A shaft of moonlight struck Tensie's figure on the bed, and he saw that she was alone. His body against hers wakened Tensie. She did not scream, but fought like a tigress. She flung herself backward from Herbert's embrace, and they rolled to the floor.

Tensie fought fiercely, prying his fingers loose, then gaining her feet to run for the door. But Herbert, with the superstrength of the depraved, sprang after her like a cat and blocked the way. They crashed from one side of the cabin to the other, smashing crockery, until the sound of the fray roused the other slaves. Josh and Memphis were the first to enter the cabin. The sight that met their eyes sent terror to their hearts. Tensie clawed and scratched, her mouth twitched and her lips moved fearfully, but she made no sound. Her eyes were lighted by fear, glowing like live coals.

Josh held the light high, and when the beam struck Herbert he released the girl and scrambled to his feet. He stood, half naked and exposed, panting like an animal, then suddenly, without warning, wild, maniacal laughter issued from his throat, a strange, inhuman sound that rent the night. Tensie, clad only in the shreds of her nightgown, slipped quickly through the door, and the slaves disappeared. In Minnie's cabin, Memphis dressed the girl. "Effen he try that again, kill him. You ain't got meek blood in your veins. It's the same as his'n. Colonel Withers was yo' pappy."

For the rest of the night, there was little sleep in the slave quarters. News of Herbert's attempt on Tensie spread quickly from cabin to cabin, and by morning Toby's slaves were nervous and unruly. What had been a smooth-running, happy community of blacks had become a dangerous, disorganized group, and there was angry muttering among the younger men, who feared for their women. If Tensie was in danger, then no young woman in the slave quarters was safe. Josh went from one slave hut to the other, talking with the men while the women and children huddled in the corner. Then he determined to speak to Toby, and sought out his master. "Marse Toby, we had trouble in de quarters las' night," he said quietly.

"Tell me about it, Josh," said Toby.

The old Negro related his story falteringly. He was committing the capital sin; he was accusing a white man, but he knew his master, and he permitted Toby to draw him out gently, prying the details from him, until finally his master was possessed of the whole sordid story, even to Memphis's statement regarding Tensie's parentage. When the slave had finished, Toby's face was clouded with anger. He went to Herbert's room, finding his son in a sullen mood, his eyes listless and dull. The hyperactivity of the night before had passed, leaving Herbert depressed and lifeless. Toby spoke without preliminary. "Herbert, I am instructing Memphis, Tensie, Minnie, Linda, and every other slave woman on the place to protect themselves against you, should you make that necessary."

Herbert sneered. "You mean you told a nigger to attack a white man?"

"You are no longer a man, Herbert. You are an animal. A sick and dangerous animal. And I have always protected my slaves."

Herbert laughed. "Not always. I imagine some of your grandchildren are running around the quarters right now."

Toby left him, anger deep in his heart. This was his son—this half-mad degenerate who had turned the house into a stockade, the slave quarters into a fortress. In one wild, impulsive moment, Toby was tempted to shoot the boy dead, as one would shoot a mad dog, but this thought was so monstrous that he put it from his mind.

For months the household lived thus, Herbert keeping to his room, watched day and night, the slaves sleeping behind thick hickory bars, the women going always in pairs. Josephine refused to accept any of the responsibility. She had forced Memphis to tell her the truth about Tensie, and the knowledge that the mulatto girl was her half-sister and Herbert's aunt was almost too much for her to bear. First her father, then her son. But she blamed it on Toby—if she had not married Toby, these things would never have happened.

One morning, when the field hands were chopping cotton, Herbert found himself unguarded. He watched his mother drive off toward town, then crept from his room. He discovered Tensie, going back and forth from the kitchen, and cunningly, without making a sound, he crept up behind her, seizing her with one hand while covering her mouth with the other, preventing outcry. Tensie went limp, pretending to submit, and Herbert's grip relaxed a trifle. Instantly the slave girl snatched a billet of wood from the stove pile and struck fiercely at Herbert's head. It was a well-aimed blow. Herbert fell heavily to the floor, his skull crushed by the heavy piece of wood. For a second, Tensie looked at him while he lay dying there on the kitchen floor. Then she turned and went quietly for her mother.

It was Josh to whom they turned, of course. The old slave knelt beside Herbert, feeling his pulse, then shook his head. He thought carefully for several minutes, then stood up. "Now take that cotton out of your ears and listen to me," he said. Josh addressed the dead man, while the others listened.

"Marse Herbert, us slaves is busy, choppin' cotton."

"I don't give a damn, Josh. You're going to take me hunting."

"Not today, Marse Herbert. We got work to do."

"Get the horses, Josh. We're going boar hunting."

"If them is yo' orders, Marse Herbert, then we is goin' boar huntin'. But Marse Toby ain't gonna like it."

Josh turned to Tensie and Memphis. "Now you know just how I come to leave the fields," he said. "I didn't want to go boar huntin', but Marse Herbert made me."

"I knows exactly how you went," said Memphis. "You, Tensie?"

The girl nodded, her eyes fixed on the dead man.

"Be sho' yo' remembers," Josh warned. "Now git on to work, jus' lak nothin' happen."

"Where yo' goin'?" Memphis asked.

"Boar huntin'," answered Josh.

Late that night Josh returned, bringing home Herbert's body. He stood in Toby's study, explaining the boy's death to his master. "I didn't want to go, Marse Toby. Hones' I didn't, but Marse Herbert made me. They wasn't no way of stoppin' him. An' when he got to huntin', he was awful venturesome."

Toby nodded. "I see." He examined the body by candlelight; it was marked and scarred, deeply gashed as though Herbert had been tossed by an infuriated tusker. Toby swayed, dizzy and a little sick, remembering Captain Mimms' body after the wild boar had finished with it. In a sense he felt that his sins were coming home to roost, though he had no doubt about the way Herbert had died, and he knew that his son had deserved it. "Take the body to his room and wash it," he commanded. "And send Memphis to me."

Josephine questioned Memphis and Tensie at great length, then turned to Josh, but she could make no dent in their version of Herbert's death. She displayed no grief; indeed, when Toby saw her, the expression in her eyes was rather one of relief. But she could not resist saying, "Isn't it curious that Herbert was killed by a wild boar, just as Captain Mimms was killed? I wonder what the sheriff will say."

Toby met her gaze. "The sheriff will say what I want him to say. He will think what I want him to think."

"Who killed Herbert, Toby? Tensie? Memphis?"

"He was killed by a razorback," Toby said bluntly.

"But you told the slaves to defend themselves against him," Josephine persisted.

"Fortunately, that didn't become necessary," Toby said. He fell silent, the image of his dead son invading his mind. He knew that one of the slaves had killed Herbert, but whether it was Tensie, or Memphis, or one of the men protecting his woman, he didn't know. It was dangerous, he understood, to permit a black who had killed a white man to go unpunished, but he meant to stand by Josh and support the old slave's story. For one thing, if he did not, and it became known in the town that a slave had killed Herbert, a maddened mob might raid and burn his quarters, slaughtering every Negro on the place. This would mean the killing of dozens of innocent Negroes, along with the guilty one, and it would not bring Herbert back. Besides, in his heart, Toby knew that Herbert's death was a blessing. He would not have had him returned if he could have done so merely by raising his finger and uttering a word. The boy had been mad, incurable, a threat to every living creature within his range.

The town accepted Toby's story of his son's death without question. The boy was not mourned, though most of the townspeople expressed their sympathy to Toby. Trudging back from the burying ground, Toby felt empty; Herbert's death wrote the end to the longest and most unhappy chapter of his life. With Violet gone, and Herbert gone, and nothing but bitter, guarded hatred between him and Josephine, he felt almost as though the end of his life had come.

But he went on, a dogged, disenchanted man, rejecting friendly, sympathetic overtures on the part of his friends because he thought them pity, keeping to himself, and brooding, endlessly brooding, sifting the sands of his past in an effort to discover where he had failed, trying to find the thing that had caused his dream to fade.

Was it, he might well have wondered, something within the dream itself? But he did not. Toby's dream, or part of it, was the American Dream, and never for a moment did he question it. But it seemed to him that he was in some way the victim of a gigantic hoax, a huge and cosmic joke.

4.

Toby read and reread the letter from Tommy Jeff, hardly able to believe the words, yet more excited by them than he had been in years. His son was to be married. The son he had given up as a hopeless cripple was engaged to be married. In the letter Tommy Jeff described his bride to be, seeming to seek Toby's approval, and something about the way his son wrote of the girl made Toby understand that she was fine and good. The letter freshened Toby's spirits like a brisk summer shower on a field of parched corn, and he could not contain the news, but must share it with someone. He ordered his horse saddled and rode into town, seeking out Doctor Hooker. Hooker was washing his hands, having pulled a tooth for one of Bill Bowes' slaves. Toby handed him the letter. "Read that!"

Hooker read the letter quickly and a smile appeared on his face. He had always been fond of Tommy Jeff, and one of the things he regretted most was the fact that the lad's illness had defeated him. "By God, Toby, that's great news!" he said. "Great news!"

Toby eyed the doctor shyly; since Herbert's death he had avoided his old friends, including Hooker. "Doc," he said tentatively, "do you suppose you'd like to have a drink with me on this?"

"Surest thing you know," said Hooker. He pulled on his coat and the two men walked down the street to the tavern. Hooker watched Toby's face for a moment, then laughed. "I don't know who this is better for, Toby," he said. "You or

Tommy Jeff. I haven't seen you with so much giddap for a year or more."

"I may be a granddad yet," Toby said.

"No reason why you shouldn't be," said Hooker.

In the tavern the talk was of war, as it had been for months past. The subject of slavery, and states' rights, preoccupied both the settlers and the thousands of Texas-bound pioneers who passed through the town. For years Toby had scoffed at the idea of war. He had the money man's notion that powerful men would not do things that were unprofitable, and war would be unprofitable for both sides. But now he had his doubts. The Southerners were hotheaded, seeming almost eager to spring to arms in defense of their own institutions and the sanctity of their own state sovereignty, and the Yankees appeared to be placidly goading the South to a point where warfare in the field would be the only course open to the slave-holding states.

It occurred to Toby that had war come before Herbert's excesses had destroyed him, the boy might either have been redeemed in combat or have gone down in battle as a hero. Herbert had been the type that sometimes is re-created by wars. He wondered how war would have affected him. He himself was too old to go. Tommy Jeff was crippled. None of his family would participate. But war would destroy him, or in any event would destroy the things he had worked for, the fortune he had built. In a quiet, prescient moment, Toby had a vision of the war-ravaged South. Doctor Hooker interrupted his wool-gathering. "Jim Beck's gone to Texas," the doctor said. "Now there's a man few people understand."

"I never understood him," Toby said.

"He was your friend, Toby."

"Mine?"

Hooker nodded. "Jim told me he liked you better than any man in Washington. You know, Toby, Jim is the son of one of the oldest and wealthiest families in Charleston. He and his father had a falling out because Jim married the daughter of a dock hand."

"I never thought of Jim Beck as an aristocrat," mused Toby.

Hooker nodded. "He is, though." The doctor paused. "Speaking of friends, Toby," he said, "you ought to drop by and see Squire Tatum, if you want to see the old boy alive. He's living on borrowed time."

"No!" said Toby.

Hooker smiled. "Toby, we're all getting along, we old-timers. How old are you?"

Toby frowned, the truth of Hooker's remarks striking him sharply. "I'm nearly sixty, doc," he said. "Nearly sixty. But sometimes it seems hardly any time at all since I came into town with Ira Walker's caravan, nearly forty years ago. Seems like a man hardly gets started before he has to think about getting finished."

The two friends drank in silence, looking at one another. Then Hooker said gently, "Supposing you had a chance to do it all over, Toby. What would you change?"

Toby considered the bourbon in the bottom of his glass. Then he smiled ruefully and said, "Myself, doc. I'd be somebody else."

"An aristocrat?"

Toby shook his head. "I don't think so. Somebody more like my son-in-law, Jack Jenkins. Or my son, Tommy Jeff."

"I understand," Hooker said.

"No, doc," Toby said thoughtfully, "no, you don't. In order to understand, you'd have to be me. And you can just get down on your knees and praise Christ Almighty that you aren't me."

The talk with Hooker made Toby restless. He was conscious of his age as he had never been, and aware of death as a reality, something to be met in the almost visible future rather than an event so far off that it needn't be considered seriously. Toby wanted to see his son before he died, and he began to make his plans, saying nothing to Josephine. The cotton yield that year was good, and Toby bought every bale that was offered for sale. All winter his slaves were busy accumulating a bargeload of prime walnut timber. Toby waited only for the spring rains to lift the river level high enough for the first boat to get through.

Josh drove his master to Fulton and helped him supervise the loading of the cotton. Toby stood on deck, his forearms on the rail, watching Fulton drop away in the distance as the boat headed downstream. Again he was headed downriver, to New Orleans, and though he tried to push it from his mind, the memory of his wedding trip with Josephine intruded upon his thoughts, depressing him. He turned from the rail and went into the smoking room; a half dozen planters sat at tables there, drinking and smoking and talking war. Toby joined them, introducing himself. "My name's Giles, from Washington."

"Well, Mr. Giles," said one of the group, a florid, heavy man with a jewel in his shirt front, "pull up a chair and wet your whistle."

"Sure, Giles," said another. "Join the party."

Toby felt a warmth in his heart; these men, men of affairs, recognized him as one of their number, welcomed him as a member of the lodge. He sipped his whiskey, refusing the cigar the red-faced man offered. He looked casually around the room at the group. All of them were successful and prosperous, some as successful as he, others nearly so. He wondered whether any one of them, in all his life, had experienced as much happiness as his daughter and her husband had enjoyed in the brief interlude the Lord gave them. He doubted it. These men were driven men, like himself. Something in their blood lashed them on, urging them to plant more than their neighbors, sell more than their neighbors, own more than their neighbors. Without such men, Toby understood, the frontier would never have been opened. He knew that he and men like him had played a great role in the drama that saw Arkansas won from the wilderness and nurtured to statehood, that saw a rude frontier hamlet like Washington, a collection of log huts nestled among the sand hills, grow into a thriving city. It was trade that did it, for trade brought people, trade meant development. Yet the traders, somehow, seemed to lose themselves in the struggle.

The talk here, again, was of war, and the florid man with the diamond in his shirt turned to Toby, "And how long do *you* think it'll take us to lick the Yankees, Mr. Giles?" he asked, laughing so that the long ash from his fine cigar tumbled onto his sleeve. "We've had all kinds of guesses from a month to a year. What's your opinion? How long before our boys march into Washington and Philadelphia, once the shooting starts?"

Toby hesitated, the whole company watching him. Finally he said, "We will never lick them. They are too strong for us. And they will defeat us. But they will defeat themselves in the process."

A chorus of shouts greeted Toby's statement. "Why, man, we'll wipe them Yankees off the face of the earth inside of six months. Everybody knows one southern boy's worth half a dozen Yanks."

Toby shook his head and smiled. "Where? In a backyard, bare-knuckle fight? At forty paces, with dueling pistols?" He paused. "Maybe. This war's not going to be like that."

"What do you mean?"

"They'll starve us out," said Toby. "They've got the money, and they don't need an army. All they have to do is wait. Just wait, and watch our cotton rot in the fields, and watch us starve."

"Why, man, you talk like a fool!" the red-faced one angrily exclaimed. "Ain't nowhere on earth that you can raise food the way you can in the South. And we got the niggers to do it."

Toby shook his head. "You can't stay home and boss your

niggers and march off to Philadelphia at the same time. If there's war, and it looks like there will be, the South is licked before it starts. They will starve us out, men, women, and children, black and white." He got to his feet, feeling the hostility behind him as he left the smoke-filled room and went out on deck again.

In New Orleans the clouds of war had pushed the price of cotton up. Toby sold his crop at a fabulous profit, and also did well with his walnut. He had planned to pass a week or two in New Orleans, but the war talk got on his nerves and he was too old, too tired for carousing. He wanted to see his son, and he wanted peace and contentment. Peace and contentment he understood he would never have, but see his son he would, and he booked passage on the next boat north, asking the cotton broker to forward his money as a letter of credit to a bank in Natchez.

He kept to his cabin on the trip north, avoiding the smoking room and venturing on deck only in the morning to watch the sun come up and at evening to watch it set. The packet carried a large complement of Yankee travelers and, of course, an even larger number of Southerners, and as the days passed and the arguments grew more violent, the tension increased. Toby avoided the partisans of both sides. He was a Southerner and a slaveholder, and he realized that war with the North would cause his own holdings to melt away. Naturally all his sympathies were with the South and with the southern way of doing things. So far as slavery was concerned, it had never occurred to him that a moral issue was involved, any more than that there was a moral issue involved in overworking a farm animal. Only a foolish man beat his horse and drove the animal beyond the limits of its endurance, for in so doing he was destroying a valuable piece of property.

Toby had always treated his slaves well; far better, in fact, than the average planter, because he had learned that good treatment meant good work. He fed his Negroes well, for example, gave them good clothes, saw that they were not beaten, and that their food was wholesome and palatable. He would not break up a slave family if it could possibly be avoided. But had you called him a humanitarian, he would not have understood you. He could not for the life of him understand the North's agitation over slavery as a moral issue, and the firm suspicion was beginning to form in his mind that the Yankees were less worried about the moral issue involved in slavery than in the fact that slavery meant cheap labor, and cheap labor meant that the South might one day build its own factories, making cotton cloth at prices the North, using wage labor, could not hope to meet. In any case, Toby understood that money was what really won wars, and when it came to money, the North had it. This led him to the conclusion that a war for the southern cause would be lost before it was even started. And such a viewpoint, defeatist to the core, no matter how logically presented, was not a popular one among the hotheaded southern youths who crowded the packet boat's smoking room.

When they docked at Natchez, Toby saw his bags put ashore and hired a high-backed hansom cab. He called to the driver, "Do you know Tommy Jeff Giles?"

"Tommy Jeff Giles?" the man said. "I sure do. Do you know him?"

"Yes," Toby said. "I know him."

"Then you know one of the finest men in Mississippi," the driver said. "You want to go to Mr. Giles' place?"

"That's right," Toby answered. He was astonished that the first cab driver he encountered knew Tommy Jeff and Tommy Jeff's house; in a city the size of Natchez, it indicated that Tommy Jeff was an important citizen.

Moonbeam, Minnie's daughter, dressed in a neat cap and apron, answered Toby's hesitant ring at the front door. For a moment the girl stared at Toby, not recognizing him, but aware of the fact that she knew him. Then her face lighted up, and she cried, "'Fore de Lawd God—Marse Toby!"

"Hello, Moonbeam," Toby said. "So you know this old gentleman, do you?"

"Shucks, Marse Toby, you ain't old. You'se jes' well-seasoned. Now come in this house."

A faint voice called from the parlor, "Who is it, Moonbeam? Who's calling?"

"Come an' see, Miss Agatha, come and see fo' yo'self!"

Agatha Rowden walked slowly, aided by a cane, but her back was still straight and her fine old head was erect. Her face was thin and withered like parchment and her hair was white as paper. She peered at Toby in the dim light of the hall; her old eyes were failing her and she came closer. "For the land's sakes, Toby Giles!" She threw her arms around him and kissed him. For all his sixty odd years, at that moment Toby felt like a boy. "Why didn't you let us know you were coming?" she asked.

"I wanted to surprise you," he said. He followed her into the sitting room and they both took chairs. "I've come from New Orleans."

The old woman peered across the room at him. "It's the best surprise you could give Tommy Jeff," she said. "He'll be overjoyed to see you."

"Where is he?"

"He's at the factory, hard at work. But he'll be home soon."

Toby coughed. He shifted position in his chair, then said, "How does he . . . I mean, how does he manage . . . with his. . . ."

Agatha laughed. "You don't know your son, Toby. You could cut off both arms and both legs, and he still wouldn't give up." She glanced around the room. "You see this furniture?" she asked. The room was lavishly furnished with fine, hand-carved pieces, perfect examples of the best cabinetwork being done in the country.

"It's a fine room," Toby said.

"Come with me," she said. Toby rose and followed her down the hall to a spare room. The fittings and furniture were beautiful; they were what Toby would have selected for himself, granted the imagination and knowledge, and the master craftsman at hand to execute his orders. He stood in the doorway, looking at the room, then exclaimed, "It's beautiful! Beautiful!"

Agatha smiled. "This room has been waiting for you a long time, Toby," she said. "Tommy Jeff made every stick especially for you."

"It's light and beautiful," Toby said, "yet it looks strong and dependable."

"That's the way Tommy Jeff thinks of you, Toby. As strong and dependable. I think he tried to tell you something with this furniture. I think he was trying to put his idea of your character into it."

Toby was silent, then finally said, "I think I understand. I think I know what you mean." For the first time since his daughter's death, he felt the presence of love—pure, unselfish love for him that had nothing to do with his power or money or position. His eyes misted with tears, and he moved away toward the window, afraid that he would betray his emotions. Agatha seemed to understand.

"I'll leave you now, Toby, so you can freshen up. Tommy Jeff will be home soon."

He nodded, still facing the window. The door closed quietly behind Agatha and he turned, looking more closely at the room and its furnishings. He remembered Josephine's efforts at decoration, her extravagance and bad taste. He remembered his own pitiful attempts to make his home luxurious. And he wondered why this room, simple as it was, was the most beautiful and luxurious that he had ever seen. Toby Giles, born on the dockside, engaged from the very moment of his birth in a death struggle with poverty and later in a savage struggle for wealth, had not been trained to give a name to art when he saw it. Yet he recognized something in this room that made it different from other rooms. What he saw, of course, was the artist's hand; for his son was an artist, a master designer, and each piece of furniture—the stately four-poster bed, the chairs, the carved washstand—bore their maker's thumbprint. Toby walked around the bed, caressing the satin finish of the wood, marveling at the perfect, discreet carving. This room had been made for him; something in the design of the furniture and its arrangement was an expression of everything secret and best in Toby's character. He wondered how his son, who hardly knew him, had apprehended so well the hidden side of his nature. It was as though the room spoke to him, giving him reassurance and courage, and making him aware of his son's love.

Toby's revery was interrupted by the sound of a team on the driveway beneath his windows. He looked down and saw a matched pair, drawing a closed carriage, slow at the turning and disappear under the porte-cochere. He heard Agatha call to Tommy Jeff, "Your father is here, son." And he heard Tommy Jeff's delighted response. "Father! Here? Where is he?" He turned, brushing his thinning hair quickly, and hurried to the door to meet his son. As he reached the door, Whittler was lifting Tommy Jeff from the carriage. For a moment, what he saw struck Toby's heart like a blow. He saw the head and shoulders, chest and forearms of a handsome and powerful man, attached to legs withered and helpless, small as those of a child. But a moment later the smile on Tommy Jeff's face made him forget this, and he hurried forward to greet the boy. Then Tommy Jeff took his crutches and stood looking back for a moment, while his wife descended from the carriage. "Here's your new daughter, father. This is Ruth."

In his dreams, Toby had often envisioned his son's wife, but his dreams had never approximated the reality. Ruth was beautiful—not in the way Josephine had been beautiful, with a veneer of sexual attractiveness over a nature filled with greed and evil, but with a beauty that seemed to come from within, from genuine strength of character and nobility. She was tall, exquisitely dressed, with a dignity that made it apparent to all that here was a truly fine woman. They stood, father, son, and daughter-in-law, without speaking for several seconds; then Whittler coughed quietly. "Marse Toby," he said, "doan' you rekernize dis old nigger? You ain't fo'gotten Whittler, sho'ly?" Toby turned, smiling at the old man. The Negro's hair was white, and his shoulders were bent. His apparent age made Toby realize the shortness of the time left to him, and for a moment he was shocked. Whittler had been a young, healthy slave when he gave him to Tommy Jeff. Now he was an old man. "Old nigger," Toby said with a smile, "I could never forget you. But you look about to dry up and blow away. Don't my boy feed you?"

Whittler laughed. "I runs off my fat, Marse Toby, tryin' to keep up with Marse Tommy Jeff. Marse Toby, dat man cover more ground on them crutches than you and me on our good legs."

"He gets around, does he, Whittler?"

"Ain't no stoppin' him, Marse Toby," the old slave said.

At dinner that night they pressed Toby for news of Washington, of his business, of Josephine, but he was reluctant to speak of his own affairs, being content to watch his son at the head of the table, graceful and witty, his daughter-in-law at his side, stately and beautiful, and Agatha beaming on them all with happiness. The food was expertly prepared and perfectly served from polished silver dishes. The table, spread with fine linen and decorated with an artfully contrived centerpiece of flowers, arranged in a gleaming silver dish, was lighted by candles that bathed the company in a soft, pleasant glow. There was a feeling of security in Tommy Jeff's house, a feeling of rightness, and Toby somehow hesitated to be evasive, though he dared not tell the truth. When urged, he talked simply, telling of Violet's death in Texas, and Herbert's fatal accident. Of Josephine he simply announced that she had been too tired to make the trip. "The next time I come, I'll bring her," he promised.

Dinner over, Tommy Jeff tinkled a small silver bell beside his plate and Whittler came quietly into the dining room, pushing a wheel chair. The slave helped his young master into the chair, then Ruth rose from the table and wheeled Tommy Jeff into the parlor. Toby followed, with Agatha on his arm. "Please take that chair over there," she said. "Then you'll be close to Tommy Jeff."

Ruth smiled at her father-in-law. "I know you and Tommy Jeff want to talk. Miss Agatha and I will go busy ourselves with women's affairs."

The old woman and the young one departed, leaving Toby alone with his son for the first time. There was a small silence for a few minutes. Then, hesitantly, Toby began to speak. "Son," he said, "I can't find words to express my admiration for what you've done. I thought I'd accomplished something, but your achievements make me look like a failure."

"Thank you, father," Tommy Jeff said. "You're too generous. I only hope I can do half as much in life as you have." He paused, then said, "Would you mind very much if I had Whittler massage my legs? They get kind of weary."

"Of course not," Toby said. He watched the old slave unstrap the braces from his son's legs, then kneel before his master, rubbing the withered, blighted limbs until the angry red marks disappeared. Toby wished with all his heart, as he sat watching, that he might get down on his knees and do this service for his son. For some reason, though there were many things in his life with which to charge himself, he felt most guilt about something that had been an act of God and no fault of his own—Tommy Jeff's crippling illness. It seemed to Toby sometimes as though Tommy Jeff's affliction and

Agatha's death had been punishments visited upon him by the Lord, punishments aimed at his ruthless ambition and driving, acquisitive course through life. Could he have brought Agatha back to life, or restored the use of his son's legs, Toby promised himself, he would gladly have returned to the depths from which he had raised himself, gladly have slunk back to the Norfolk water front, gladly have relinquished all wealth and power, for now the wealth seemed tainted and the power empty.

"I know now how a horse feels when the head strap is removed," Tommy Jeff smiled. "This feels good."

Finished, Whittler rose and covered his young master's legs with a soft wool blanket. "Ah knows you won't take nuthin', Marse Tommy," he said, "but eff'n I remembers rightly, Marse Toby would suffer a little whiskey right at this time of day."

"Certainly, Whittler," Tommy Jeff said. "Certainly."

When Whittler had brought the whiskey and departed, Toby said, "Son, I sold a cargo of cotton and lumber down-river for fourteen thousand dollars. I have the money with me, and I want to give it to you. I want you and Ruth to have it for a wedding present."

Tommy Jeff smiled. "Thank you, father. I appreciate it. But I don't need it. I am making more money than I need."

"More money than you need?" It had never occurred to Toby that a man ever had more money than he needed. In Toby's experience the acquisition of wealth always urged a man to acquire more. He never had as much as he wanted, and certainly never more than he needed. "How can you have more money than you need?"

"My needs are simple," his son explained.

"I want you to have the money," Toby said doggedly. "I brought it for you, and I want you to have it."

Tommy Jeff smiled. "Why, father? Why do you want me to have this money?"

Toby frowned. He sat staring at the carving of a chair leg,

and for some time neither man spoke. Then Toby said, quite simply and humbly, "It's the only way I can show my love for you, son. I am a money man. I have given my life to making money. Now I am old, an old man, getting ready to die, and the only way I can express my love and admiration for you is to give you money. Please take it."

"Of course, father," Tommy Jeff answered. "Of course we'll take it." Tommy Jeff wheeled himself a little closer to his father. His hand touched Toby's knee. "Father," he said quietly, "I have always thanked God for His goodness to me, and to those I love. In His own way and in His own good time, He has taught me to know that it is better to have withered legs than a withered soul."

Toby's head was bowed. His eyes were on Tommy Jeff's slim, strong hand. The long, tapered fingers were those of an artist, an artist in wood rather than in words or clay or paint, perhaps, but a true artist, nevertheless. The words his son had just uttered had deep meaning, meaning that sifted into Toby's consciousness as he sat staring at his son's hand. His eldest son, his only son now, had found the true key to happiness, the real secret of life, and all of Toby's struggle was suddenly made meaningless, for he understood that his life had been devoted to reaching a false goal, a goal, in fact, that did not exist, on earth or in heaven. His thinking had been wrong, and his understanding. If Captain Maison was a great man and a good one, the greatness and goodness did not derive from the captain's house or horse or scarlet coat. These things were on the surface. The greatness and goodness Toby had sensed and admired when, as a boy, he watched the Tidewater aristocrat ride out in the morning, came from within.

Toby drank his whiskey slowly, permitting its warmth and strength to seep into his body. The talk turned now to the one burning topic of the day—war between the North and South. Toby told his son the things he had seen and heard on his journey downriver and up. "What I thought was an impossibility now seems certain to occur," he said. "We will have a war that will ruin us both, North and South alike."

Tommy Jeff nodded. "I am almost thankful that I am a cripple," he said. "Too crippled to fight. I am a Southerner. I believe in states' rights. But I do not believe in slavery. I could not fight in defense of something I believe is wrong, and I could not fight against my own people, my own southern motherland." Tommy Jeff paused, smiling ruefully. "It hasn't been easy. I have listened to many arguments these last few months, and often I have had to bite my lip to keep from expressing my honest sentiments."

"I know," Toby said. "I found out in the smoking room of the packet boat that you have to run with the crowd or keep your mouth shut."

The next morning Toby accompanied Tommy Jeff to the factory. It was a humming, busy place where thirty Negroes worked at lathes and benches, turning the hardwood into intricate shapes, bringing Tommy Jeff's designs to life. The blacks worked swiftly and efficiently, each man going about his job with a directness and competence that surprised Toby, who had seen Negroes work well only under close supervision by a tough white slave driver or a trusted slave.

"How many slaves do you own?" he asked.

"None," Tommy Jeff answered. "Unless it might be Moonbeam. These people are free."

"Free niggers?"

"Yes," Tommy Jeff said. "Every one of these men has worked out his freedom. You might say, each one of them has bought himself from me."

"I don't understand you," Toby said.

"Well, I pay my workers according to what they do. When they do more than their set task, I credit their earnings to their account for the buying of their freedom. Now all of my Negroes have earned the right to be free men."

"You mean they could quit and walk out on you, just like white labor?"

"Of course."

"Why do they stay?"

"They seem to like it," said Tommy Jeff.

Toby shook his head. "How can you make money and pay niggers for their labor? It's against every principle I ever heard of."

"It works out fine," Tommy Jeff said. "I use only skilled labor, as you can see. Every man in this shop is an expert mechanic. I could enslave their bodies, I suppose, but I can't enslave their minds or their talents."

Toby watched the Negroes at work, realizing that he had never seen happier, better looking, or harder working blacks. Times were changing, he understood that, and somehow he realized that men like Tommy Jeff and Jack Jenkins were the men of the future, the men whose sons would build the new South, while the hotheads who thirsted for war were men of the past, men whose attitudes and ways of life would be consumed in the cauldron of battle. He had been conditioned to think of Negroes as chattels; it was difficult for him to understand his son's belief that they were, by right, free men. But he saw with his own eyes a proof of Tommy Jeff's theory. He was confused, he was a bewildered old man whose world was crumbling and whose standards were being rejected by history, yet he had enough vision to admire his son and to understand that men like Tommy Jeff, given the chance, could build a happier, more prosperous South. That evening he expressed to Agatha his admiration for Tommy Jeff. "You have made a real aristocrat of my son," he said. "A true aristocrat."

"I never thought of making an aristocrat out of Tommy Jeff," she said. "I raised him to be a Christian gentleman."

Toby smiled. "I know now what a real aristocrat is," he said. "All my life I have admired something without understanding what the thing was." He paused. "I have never forgotten what you once said to me about aristocrats."

"What was that, Toby?"

"You said the genuine were like fine cake and the counterfeits like corn pone. That's what I made of myself, I guess. A cornbread aristocrat." He chuckled. "I should have saved myself the trouble."

Agatha reached out and touched his hand. "You have achieved a great deal, Toby," she said gently.

He laughed bitterly. "I've made money. Is that an achievement? I'd throw every penny into the Mississippi if I could have half of Tommy Jeff's dignity and happiness. Half? A tenth! A hundredth!"

Agatha shook her head and smiled. "I don't mean material achievement, Toby."

"What then?"

"You have earned the love of good people." She paused. Toby's head was lowered, and she went on. "Agatha. Stoge Rowden. Tommy Jeff."

He raised his head and his eyes met hers. "And you, Miss Agatha," he asked. "And you?"

She nodded, smiling, "I love you, Toby. And I know the sadness in your heart."

Toby went to bed that night, filled with a peace that he had not known for years. Yet he understood that he must go. A strange and compelling urge had overtaken him these last few days, a warning that not much time remained, and an insistence that there was still much to be done before death or war made it impossible. He said good-by to Tommy Jeff and Ruth, and to Agatha, with tears in his eyes.

"You'll come again, father," said Tommy Jeff. "You'll come soon again."

"Of course, my boy. Of course I will."

But in Agatha's eyes he saw that she knew the truth; that

he would not live to come again, that he was saying his last good-by.

5.

On the packet boat going home from Natchez, Toby had his first real heart attack. His heart had been showing signs of strain for some time, and Hooker had warned him to slow down. Now, caught by a pain in his chest like the stab of a knife, he fell to his knees and clutched the post of the bunk in agony, unable to move for a number of minutes. When, at last, he found strength to pull himself on the bunk, his breath was short and he felt exhausted. During those few minutes, his hands gripping the bedpost as a drowning man might grip a bit of driftwood, he had looked death straight in the face, and he had not been afraid. He had been warned, he had suffered pain, but he had not been afraid. And he had not been surprised. For days, now, something had seemed to tug at his sleeve, an unseen presence seemed to have insinuated itself into his consciousness, telling him to make ready. It was this prompting, coming from he knew not where, that had caused him to leave his son's house, though he would have liked nothing better than to remain there indefinitely, enjoying the peace and contentment he experienced in the presence of Ruth and Tommy Jeff and Agatha.

An hour after the attack had passed, his heart beat more normally again; he felt overtired, as though he had worked too long, driven himself too hard, but otherwise he was perfectly

317

comfortable. He understood, however, that the disease would strike again, soon, and without warning. He went to the smoking room and ordered a glass of port, drinking it slowly as he sat at a small round table in a corner of the room, oblivious of the clamor that surrounded him. He fell to thinking of Josephine, and to wondering how she had behaved during his absence.

Not that it mattered.

Josephine was no longer a young woman, though she still had the power to attract men. Her sexual desires had coarsened as she grew older, and she became more predatory as the time approached, at racing speed, when her body would no longer give her power. She had become almost rapacious in her desire, and as the years passed she sought out younger and younger men, until many of the mothers of boys passing into manhood hated and feared her. Only Toby's wealth protected her; but for money she must long since have slipped into the abyss that awaits such women, for as fading beauties often do, she had turned to alcohol for solace from the shock her mirror's greeting gave her each morning.

To Toby's surprise, when he arrived home a few days later, his wife seemed glad to see him and made a display of affection and regret over his long absence. Shallow-minded as she was, Josephine understood that the country was in danger and that she had need of a protector. But she found Toby indifferent to her concern. He greeted her perfunctorily, then sent for Josh and Cato. The two old slaves waited upon him in his office. He acknowledged their greetings, then plunged straight to business.

"We're not planting much cotton this year, Cato, Josh."

"Not plantin' *cotton*, Marse Toby? Dat's de money crop," Josh exclaimed.

Toby leaned back in his chair and smiled at the anxious black man. "Josh," he said, "have you ever tried to eat a dollar?"

The slave chuckled. "'Fore Gawd, Marse Toby, I ain't hardly ever seed one, let alone eatin' it. But I 'spects it'd make mighty po' chewin'. An' I reckon it wouldn't stand by a man like side meat and grits."

"You're right, Josh. There's no nourishment in it."

With a pencil in his hand, he went over the plans for spring planting with the two trusted Negroes. Every acre he could possibly manage Toby was putting into food—crops that could be dried, or preserved and stored. He meant to grow enough food to last out a long siege.

The next day he went downtown to Rowden's store. Though Morrison had been operating the business for a quarter of a century, Toby still owned the building and half of the stock and good will. He lost no time in selling the building and his interest to Morrison, and this done he sold Stoge's house. For everything he put on the market, Toby demanded gold, even though he might have got somewhat better terms had he been willing to accept paper. He wanted cash, hard money.

The week after his crops were in the ground, Toby had his second attack, this time, fortunately, in his room. It was no worse than the first attack, and he told no one but Doctor Hooker. Hooker advised him to follow a regime that would have ended all his activities; he thanked the doctor, paid him, and went on as before, superintending the cultivation of the crops through the growing season, watching over them at harvesttime. When the crops were gathered, he put the slaves to work cutting every prime walnut tree they could find on his property, then had the logs sawed into furniture widths and carefully stacked to prevent warping and bluing. When he had a bargeload of handsome walnut lumber, he loaded his wagons and hauled it to Fulton to wait for the first boat to Natchez. After the lumber stood on the dock, he sold two wagons and eight oxen, at low prices, and again for gold. He surveyed the pile of lumber with grim satisfaction. There was food for Tommy Jeff's furniture factory, and if he read the signs aright, lumber would be as hard to come by as food when war was an actuality. He took a last look at the walnut, his parting gift to Tommy Jeff, then turned his horse and began the long ride home.

That night he sent for Josh. "Josh," he said, "I want you to take me down to the cave on the river bluff, where you hid those boat niggers that ran away from the captain."

Josh shook his head doubtfully. "I ain't been in them bottoms for a long time, Marse Toby, but I reckons I still knows how to git there."

"I'll have Minnie fix us a lunch and we'll leave first thing in the morning."

"That's a hard trip, Marse Toby. Cain't I do what you want by myself?"

"No," Toby answered curtly. "I'm going."

The next morning Toby made the exhausting journey to the river bottoms, pausing often for breath, brushing off the protestations of his faithful slave. "Marse Toby," Josh complained, as they reached the top of a rise, "yo' gots to take it easy."

"I haven't time, Josh. I haven't time to take it easy."

When they found the cave, Toby nodded with satisfaction. The hideaway was just as inaccessible as it had been years ago, when Josh hid the runaway slaves there while a posse hunted for them all over the country. The forbidding cliff line housed the cave and brought it above the high-water line, but the floor, walls, and ceiling were irregular and Toby knew some sort of wooden floor and siding would be needed to protect the things he intended to store. He climbed back through the narrow entrance and surveyed the place from the outside. On one side the cliff was bordered by a dense canebrake, on the other by boggy marshes and cypress swamps. The entrance, on the ravine side, could easily be concealed.

"Josh," he said, "I want you to fetch six or seven men here and straighten up those walls and level the floor. The dirt you move from the walls will just about fill the holes in the floor.

That way there won't be fresh dirt outside for folks to see."

Josh nodded. "I knows what you means, Marse Toby."

"When you get the walls squared and the floor level, line the whole place with heavy timbers. Make it tight. We're going to store food in there."

"Food, Marse Toby? What food is that?"

"The food that's going to keep you niggers from starving when the war comes," said Toby.

It was pitch dark when they reached home. Toby fell into his bed and Josh pulled the clothes from his body. He was completely exhausted. The next day he awakened late, dressed himself with difficulty, and refused breakfast. He rode down town to see Doctor Hooker. Hooker listened to his heart and shook his head. "I told you months ago that you'd better slow down."

"I haven't got time to slow down, doc. I've got too much to do."

"You'll have time to die if you don't slow down," the doctor said wryly.

Toby buttoned his shirt and grinned at his old friend. "I can't die just yet, doc. I've still got a few things to do. When they're finished, you can bring it on."

"If you're hell-bent on working, quit riding that damned horse and use your buggy," the doctor advised.

Josh was busy with his work at the cave. Taking eight of the best men from the field slowed down Toby's farming, but he did not mind, for the cave was more important than the few acres that had been put into cotton. He paid no attention to Josephine's protests when he took Memphis and Tensie out of the house and sent them to the fields. "Minnie can do the cooking," he told her, "and a little dust on the furniture won't hurt it."

Determined to have the cave prepared before cotton-picking time, Toby made several trips to the river bottoms to inspect the work. Each trip was an assault on his feeble reserve of strength, which was dwindling perceptibly. On one occasion, he and Josh passed the night in the cave because Toby could not muster energy for the return trip.

Never before had the cotton crop been neglected for any other work. Picking, ginning, and baling the fleecy staple had been the prime operation in Toby's activities. But this year the cotton came last. It was food Toby wanted stored, and night after night Josh led caravans of slaves through the cane-brakes and swamps, piling the cave high with shelled corn, dried beans, corn-field peas, jerked beef, potatoes, turnips, side meat, and even nuts gathered from the forest. Salt, sugar, and coffee were taken from the home cellar and moved to the river hiding place.

During all this activity, Josephine watched and waited. She knew that Toby was converting all his property into gold, and one day he showed her his cache of bullion. Her eyes brightened as they feasted on the stacks of bright yellow coins, brightened as they had never gleamed for him. "There it is," he said. "A life's work, frozen in metal."

"How much is there, Toby?" she asked. He told her, and the sum caused the breath to catch in her throat. He knew that she would not trouble him again; with that amount of gold in her possession, the coming war would worry her not at all. As he passed her room, after locking the safe, he heard her singing, and a smile crossed his face.

He did not intend for Josephine to have the gold. While the cotton was being ginned, enough was held back for a last bale, and, making sure that his wife was out of the house, Toby removed the gold from its hiding place. With Josh's help he packed the money—fifteen hundred and four gold eagles carefully concealed in the folds of an innocent-looking bale of cotton. A week later he sold his gin. The store and sawmill were long since gone; this was the last of his major holdings, aside from the house itself. He had, in effect, withdrawn from the economy.

Toby was a Southerner, born and bred, and a southern slave-holder. Had he been told, a year earlier, five years earlier, that this night would see him holding a conference with his slaves, he would have burst into incredulous laughter. Yet that was precisely what he was doing. He had Josh bring every grown slave man and woman to his office. The Negroes lined the walls, crowding the place, their eyes, shot with fear, fixed on their master's face. Toby sat on his dais, glancing around the room before he spoke, then he said, "All you niggers know I'm sick and can't look after myself. Old Cato here and Josh are my headmen, and I want every one of you to listen to what they say and do what they tell you. Old Cato don't have to do hard work any more. That's for you young bucks."

Old Linda glanced at her master. "Marse Toby, is you tellin' me I gots to take orders from Cato?"

Toby laughed, saying, "Linda, I'm talking to these young niggers. Nobody's going to tell you what to do."

The frail old woman smiled at Toby, then stared defiantly at Cato. "I jus' wants to know, Marse Toby."

Toby nodded. "All you niggers except Cato and Josh get back to your quarters now. Keep a tight lip about this meeting. Don't say anything to anybody." Toby sat silently while his sixty-five slaves filed slowly out of the office. Then he turned to Cato and Josh. "Sit down and make yourselves comfortable," he said.

The two black men looked at one another, then at Toby. Neither of them had ever been seated in the presence of a white man before. "Go on," Toby said. "Sit down." Awkwardly, with some embarrassment, the two faithful slaves took chairs.

"I can see trouble coming," Toby said. "Big trouble."

"We feels it too, Marse Toby."

"You niggers are going to be in a hard place," Toby said. "The Yankees are going to set you free, but they won't be here to feed you."

"Us'n ain't messin' with no Yankees, Marse Toby," said Cato.

"We's stayin' with you," echoed Josh.

Tears misted Toby's eyes. He was sincerely touched by the loyalty, the devotion of these old slaves. Then he shook his head. "I'm afraid I won't be here," he said quietly.

"Where you go, we go," said Josh.

Toby smiled. "No, Josh," he said. "Not yet awhile." He got out a large map of the United States and spread it on his desk, calling the slaves to his side. "The Yankees and the Southerners are going to have a war," he explained. He pointed to Washington on the map. "Here we are." He took a pencil and drew a rough mark along the Mason and Dixon line. "Down here are us Southerners. Up there are the Yankees."

"Them Yankees sho' is a fur piece off," said Josh.

"They'll come," said Toby. "Mark my words, they'll come."

"I don't want to get messed up in no shootin'," said Josh.

"You'll get messed up whether you like it or not," said Toby. "When wars come, they hit everybody. Now you, Josh, you won't be here. You and Minnie are going to Natchez, to Mr. Tommy Jeff."

"Is you goin' with us, Marse Toby?"

Toby's heart leaped. The idea of passing his last years with Ruth and Tommy Jeff was tempting. But he shook his head. "No. I'm staying." He turned to Cato. "Cato, the most important thing in war is food. People have starved to death with their pockets full of gold. Dead rats have been sold for food at a hundred dollars a piece. If you have food, you can survive the war. If you haven't got it, you die."

"Yes, Marse Toby."

"You know what's in that cave, Cato. There's plenty there for all of you, if you use it right. It's up to you to see that the food lasts, that none of it is wasted."

"I understands, Marse Toby."

"All right," Toby said. "You can go now, both of you."

The two slaves rose, pausing at the door. Toby stood up, watching them, and then, with a catch in his voice he said, "God bless you. God help you both."

Doctor Hooker warned Toby that the next severe attack would be his last. He took Josephine aside and warned her that the slightest exertion might bring on the fatal assault. Josephine listened with apparent concern and promised that she would hold Toby in check. But he would not be held. He had one more important task to perform, and he meant to live to do it. Cato had been sent to Fulton to guard the cotton. The day word arrived from the old slave that the boat had docked, Toby prepared Josh and Minnie for their trip. He gave Josh the cash he had received for the cotton gin, and told him to have Minnie sew the currency into his clothes. Then he rode with them to Fulton, giving personal instructions to the captain of the boat. Josh carried with him a letter to Tommy Jeff, telling of the gold concealed in the bale of cotton. Toby stood at the gangplank with Josh, and their eyes met. For forty years they had been master and slave, each filling his portion as ably as he knew how. In this moment, their last together, they ceased to be master and slave and became two men, two friends. Both men understood, though neither spoke. Toby swallowed the lump in his throat and said, almost brusquely, "You understand, now, Josh, just what to do?"

"Yes, Marse Toby."

"Good-by, then. Good luck."

"Good luck to you, Marse Toby. God go with you."

Toby stood on the river bank, watching the steamer pass out of sight as it rounded the bend. He was completely spent, let down, but he had the rewarding sense that he had done what had to be done. He turned his horse and rode home, taking to his bed. Old Cato served him, bringing his food, and when Josephine noticed this she came to Toby's room. "Why isn't Josh looking after you?" she asked.

"Josh is in Fulton," Toby replied.

"In Fulton?"

"I sent him with Minnie to guard a cargo of cotton I've got on the dock waiting for the boat."

She accepted this explanation, but asked, "When the cotton is sold and you get your letter of credit from New Orleans, will you have to go to Memphis to get the money?"

"Somebody else will go to Memphis this time," he answered wearily.

She hammered at him, impatience giving an edge to her voice. "Will you have to sign over the letter of credit before they will deliver the money in Memphis?" she asked.

Toby smiled, playing with her. "If a letter of credit comes from New Orleans you will have no trouble getting the money," he said. He did not feel that it was necessary to tell her that there would be no letter of credit from New Orleans. Toby chuckled. Things had been arranged to his liking. Josephine could have the land, and welcome to it, for most of it was worn out. She could have the niggers, too, for soon the Yankee army would come and free them. And when the war came both land and slaves would be a burden.

Day after day, waiting in his bed for a letter from Tommy Jeff, Toby had plenty of time to think. His old heart ticked slowly, like the works of an ancient, wornout clock, and the drive that had possessed him all his life was gone. He turned to the past, instead of the future, for he understood that his future was irrevocably behind him. His life seemed short, now that it was ending. It had been like a storm, like a storm on a sultry, black summer's night. And even though now, at the end, he was winning out against Josephine, it had been a failure.

He realized that there was in his life one great lack that made everything else meaningless. That was the lack of a spiritual prop, lack of love for God. He turned over in his mind the characters of the people he had known and loved. Each of them had loved God. Agatha, his first wife, had been a good Christian woman. Stoge had turned to God for guidance. Miss Agatha had told him she would rather be a child of God than an aristocrat. Tommy Jeff had said that he preferred withered legs to a withered soul. Even old Sam Houston had felt that the Lord was on his side when he rode away to free Texas.

Through the window, from the slave quarters, came the plaintive strains of an old spiritual, the Negro slaves singing sweetly and in unison. "Nobody knows the trouble I've seen. Nobody knows but Jesus." "Nobody knows the trouble I've seen," Toby whispered the words to himself, falling off to sleep.

It was too late now to make amends, too late now to call on the Lord for help, he thought. He had given his life to the works of the Devil, and now he had nothing to offer the Lord.

The weeks passed, and each Sunday found Toby propped up in a chair near the opened window. He listened to the church bell, the bell he had ordered made in New Orleans, ring out its call to the worshipers, and he felt the urge to join them, to enter the house of the Lord with them. The bell seemed to be calling him, summoning him to the side of God, and he knew that soon the selfsame bell would be tolling out a dirge for him as a handful of sorrowing friends followed his body to the burying ground. He wondered what good words the parson would find to offer at the bier of Tobias Giles.

The next time Doctor Hooker called, Toby gave him a bill of sale for his new surrey and fine span of mares. "Take it, doc," he said. "I won't be needing the team. Besides, it's all you're going to get." He smiled at Hooker, and the old friend reached down and patted his shoulder.

"You might pull through this, Toby. You might."

Toby shook his head.

The time was close, too close. The next day Cato brought him the letter he had been waiting for, the letter from Tommy Jeff, telling him that Josh had arrived safely in Natchez. But the closing lines, written by Ruth, were the most important he had ever read in his life, for they told him that Ruth and Tommy Jeff had a son, and that the boy's name was Tobias Giles. "May God bless him," Toby muttered, "and make him a better man than his grandfather." He called old Cato, asking for a candle, and held the flame to the letter until it was burned. Then he smiled at his old slave. "Cato, get me a stiff drink of brandy. I feel like celebrating." The brandy warmed his blood and made him drowsy. Soon he drifted off to sleep, relaxed and happy over the news the letter had brought him.

The next attack came Sunday morning, as Toby tried to walk from his bed to the chair by the window. His body crumpled under its own weight and he crashed forward, falling to the floor. The heavy fall stunned him, and when he called for help his voice was weak. It was several minutes before Cato returned and found him on the floor. The old slave managed somehow to get him on the bed, and this time Toby understood that it was his deathbed. Somehow, he didn't mind. His job was done, and he was ready. He struggled, making an effort to speak, and Cato knelt at his bedside, catching the last, faintly muttered words of his master:

"Cato, when war comes, and my wife Josephine gets hungry, feed her."

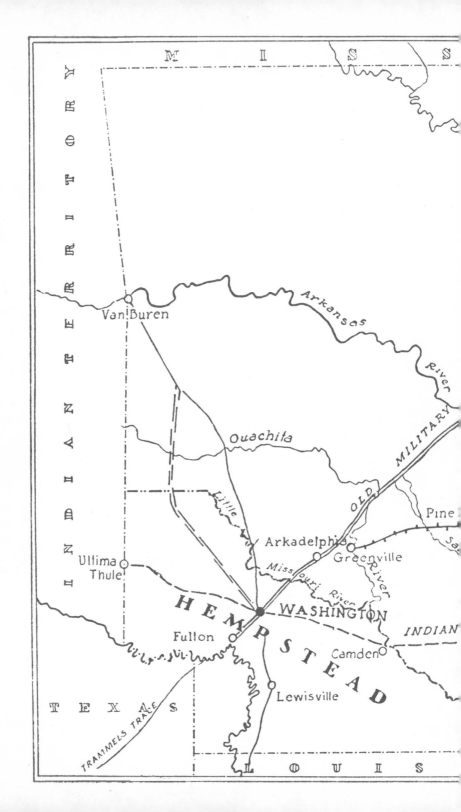